DRAWING DEAD

A Faolan O'Connor Novel

by
Brian McKinley

© Copyright 2016 Brian Patrick McKinley
All events, characters, and locations are products of the author's imagination or are used fictitiously.

PART ONE

THE BRING-IN:
October 1935

They used to tell me I was building a dream
And so I followed the mob
When there was earth to plow or guns to bear
I was always there, right on the job
- Bing Crosby, "Brother, Can You Spare a Dime?"

Chapter One

Faolan O'Connor had business to resolve before he died.

The call he'd been waiting for came around eight. "It's on for tonight. Chophouse in Newark." said Charlie Luciano's rough voice.

"Well hello to you too, dear." Faolan answered.

The chuckle on the other end of the line was as genuine as a three dollar bill. "Glad to see you ain't lost your sense of humor," Charlie said and Faolan heard the tension under the words. "Heard you was under the weather. Sure you feel up to this?"

"I'll climb off my deathbed for this job. I owe Dutch."

"That's what I figured. Ten o'clock." He hung up without saying goodbye. Faolan already knew that was the last conversation they'd ever have.

He dragged himself from his bed, trembling and aching, and dressed in his best olive suit. The tailored pants were baggy on him from all the weight he'd dropped this week and he had to cinch the belt up as tight as it would go. His joints ached like an old man's and the skeleton that greeted him in the mirror was almost a stranger. He slipped on a gray topcoat and an olive fedora to match his suit then took the case he'd already packed downstairs to the front desk of the Waldorf hotel. "Faolan O'Connor, checking out." The irony of the statement made him chuckle.

The desk clerk looked him over with uncertainty bordering on disgust and slid the printed bill across the desk toward him. Faolan pulled a wad of bills from his pocket and paid, having stashed his wallet in his case along with his new Browning. He didn't see why Charlie's vulture should get either.

"Hey sport, can you post this for me?" he asked and pulled a thick manila envelope from the inside pocket of his coat.

"Certainly, sir." The clerk took the envelope, but paused as he noticed the addressee: THOMAS DEWEY, SPECIAL PROSECUTOR'S OFFICE. CITY.

"Early Christmas present," Faolan said with a smile that became a wince. A cramp stabbed his elbow like a knife and twisted in the bone.

"Are you ... feeling poorly ... sir?" The clerk looked around, but there was nobody else in sight at the moment.

Faolan gritted his teeth and willed himself to ignore the pain. He'd be damned if he was gonna fuck up this last job. Just to spite the cramp, he used that arm to lift his small suitcase onto the desktop. "Just an old war wound. I want you to check this bag for me and give it to whoever comes in looking for it."

"I—I'm sure I don't understand, sir."

"I'm leaving it behind for a friend, that's all."

"I see. And your friend's name?"

"Can't remember."

The clerk's eyes narrowed. "I'm sorry, but that would be against the Waldorf's policy."

Faolan laid his remaining five hundred-dollar bills down on the desk. Overkill, for sure, but what the hell?

The clerk's resistance melted like ice in August. He scooped the bills up like a casino dealer and put the bag behind the desk. "Very good, sir."

Faolan started to turn away, but a thought made him turn back. He reached under his shirt collar, there was an inch now between it and his neck, and fished out the St. Patrick's medal Ma had given him years ago. It was silly to even keep it, honestly, but he wasn't quite ready to give it up. "Here," he said, pulling it off and dropping it on the desk, "put this in the bag too."

He walked out of the Waldorf and buttoned his coat, even though it wasn't cold for October. A black Packard sedan sat idling at the curb half a block down. Though Faolan headed right over, the guy in the passenger seat still felt the need to lean across the driver and yell: "Put a little shake on it, would ya?"

This was Bug Workman, a curly-haired fireplug who happened to be one of Lepke Buchalter's top hitters. The older, taller driver was Mendy Weiss, another torpedo. Faolan climbed in the back.

"How you feeling, kid?" Weiss asked, pulling back into the traffic of Fifth Avenue.

"Heard you was in a real bad way, pally," Bug added before Faolan could answer. *Christ, did somebody take out an ad?* "Me, I'd say you look like five pounds of shit in a ten pound bag. Maybe you shoulda stayed home in bed."

Faolan removed his hat to smooth his blond hair back. Fucking fever had it falling out in clumps the past few days. He caught sight of his reflection in Weiss's side mirror and saw a boyish face with the skin drooping like melted wax. He shoved his hat back on. "You bring the drop piece?"

"You don't got one?" Weiss asked.

"Never use your own gun on a hit," Faolan told him.

The Bug pulled a .38 S&W from the glove box and passed it back to him. "Fucking ridiculous, us making a special trip up here just for you. We was all set to do the job just fine, but then you gotta come sticking your snout into the trough like a greedy little piggy."

Faolan checked that the serial number had been filed off and that all the chambers were loaded. The grip was rough, so it wouldn't hold a print, and the action seemed smooth enough. This was the 1905 model with the four-inch barrel: not quite a belly gun, but not as accurate as he preferred.

"Fallon 'The Wolf' O'Connor," Bug continued.

"Fay-lan," he said.

"Whatever. I ain't real impressed so far. What do you say to that, Piggy?"

"I say that mouth of yours is gonna land you in trouble some day." Faolan glanced out the window as they turned onto Canal Street and headed for the tunnel.

"How about right now?"

"How about right now what?"

"My big mouth, Piggy. You planning on giving me some trouble?"

Faolan watched the Midtown lights give way to the darker tenement streets near the tunnel and helped himself to a Camel. "You don't need no help from me finding trouble."

"You got that right, pally," Bug said with no hint of irony whatsoever. "Hey, Mendy, you catch *The Goldbergs* last night?" The Bug blabbed all the way through the Holland Tunnel and on into Jersey City, but Faolan tuned him out. In his considerable experience, any hit was tricky; there were so many details that could fuck you up no matter how much you planned. Tonight's hit had been thrown together in a big hurry and there was a lot riding on it, so the potential for fuck-ups was very high. Bad odds any way you figured it, but this was his only chance.

The Commission had finally ordered a hit on Dutch Schultz.

The official reason had to do with protecting Special Prosecutor Thomas Dewey. Dutch planned to kill Dewey, which would bring down more heat than the select members of Charlie's "board of directors" were comfortable with. In reality, Charlie and his partner Meyer had a good excuse to rid themselves of the troublesome Dutchman and divide up his remains.

Faolan had his own reasons.

The Dutchman would die by his hand tonight if it was his last act in this world. He would need to stay sharp for this one given his current condition.

His gums ached like a sonofabitch.

"Hey Piggy," Bug called back, twenty minutes into their ride. "Just so's you know, I got dibs on rolling the stiffs once the job's done."

They were in Newark now nearing their destination. "You wanna waste time searching the Dutchman's pockets? Knock yourself out."

"Hey, that's one of our perks. Commission okayed it for—"

"Quit beating your gums, we're here," Faolan told him, scanning the front of the Chophouse as they pulled up. His watch read ten thirty. For the last few weeks, Schultz had been holding court in the back room of this place.

The street was deserted: brick-faced shops, cement pavement, and stone tenements glistened in the damp. Through the front windows flanking the door, Faolan couldn't see anyone in the barroom except the bartender. He popped his door and got out as soon as the car came to a stop. Bug did the same, a Winchester pump shotgun in hand. Weiss remained in the idling car by prior agreement.

"Bartender to the left, behind the bar."

"I got him," Bug said, pushing past him to the front door. Faolan noticed how the reflected neon from the sign overhead turned a nearby puddle into a pool of blood. His stomach rumbled.

Opening the door, Bug stepped through with his shotgun leveled. "Don't move. Lay down."

Anticipation and adrenaline combined to make Faolan feel super alive and hyper-aware. He saw the individual threads that made up the weave of Bug's overcoat and heard the tiny squeaks of leather shoes as his so-called partner walked across the linoleum floor of the bar. As Faolan moved to follow, the roar of the car's engine outside and the smell of exhaust and ozone in the air threatened to sweep him away like the finest trumpet solo Satchmo ever played.

His long strides caught up with Bug's as they moved down the narrow aisle between the long bar and the little tables pushed up against the right wall. Faolan heard the bartender—now face-down behind his bar—muttering prayers under his breath. He smelled the bartender's sweat, the fear in it, and the scent excited him.

The place was lit by a row of frosted globes hanging down over the bar and Faolan caught a reflected flash off the farthest table. Bug passed it, oblivious, as he continued into the short corridor that led past the bathrooms to the small dining room in the back.

On a table near the men's room door lay a nickel-finished 1911 model Colt .45 right next to the salt and pepper. Faolan snatched it up and dropped it into his coat pocket without breaking stride. He didn't get why so many hoods favored Colts. Its ejector had a habit of jamming and its accuracy was a joke, but he wanted a back-up gun.

He pulled back the hammer on his revolver as they entered the back room. Ugly green walls, dingy carpets, chipped booths, and scratched tables: this little shit-hole in the wall was the best Dutch could do for a temporary headquarters? Schultz was a cheapskate to the bitter fucking end.

Faolan slides into his killing groove and time seems to slow.

His crystal blue eyes scan the room, empty except for the three men at the far corner table. Before they so much as blink, Bug's shotgun speaks, blowing a hole in the side of fat old Abadabba Berman and setting Faolan's sensitive ears to ringing.

Plug the accountant first. Nice thinking, shithead!

Lulu Rosencrantz—a gorilla wearing a tin Deputy Sheriff badge that allows him to carry—draws his heater as he rises. Faolan fires.

To his grooving eyes, it's as if Lulu's shirt blossoms with a carnation made of blood. He fires again as Abadabba settles onto the table-top, moaning.

Another carnation forms on Lulu's chest.

Bug pumps his shotgun, ejecting the empty shell.

Faolan shifts his barrel an inch and takes aim at—

Tall, skinny, and bald: Abe Landau, another hitter. *Where's Schultz? Where the fuck's the Dutchman?*

Faolan fires anyway, punching a shot through the upper shoulder of Landau's business arm as the hitter reaches for his piece.

Ignoring the cramp building in his shooting arm, Faolan fires again. He watches the bullet pass through Landau's arm and hit Lulu in the right wrist as the gorilla clears his Colt from his shoulder rig.

Ignoring his shattered wrist, Lulu tips the table forward for some cover—spilling poor Abadabba onto the floor—as he and Landau both take aim.

Bug's shotgun roars a second time, buckshot splashing across the tabletop, Lulu's chest, and Abadabba's back.

Forcing himself to remain steady despite the shiver traveling up from his toes, Faolan fires again.

This shot hits Lulu's right elbow, ruining the arm but doing nothing to prevent the lefty from shooting back at them.

The first shot goes wild as Bug ejects his spent round and Faolan lines up his last shot between Lulu's eyes.

Landau's first shot is better, catching Faolan in the shoulder—

There's no pain, but the bullet's impact throws his aim and wastes his last round. Beside him, Bug turns tail and runs. Faolan drops the empty revolver and reaches in his pocket for—

The Colt ... *Laying right near the bathroom!*

Dutch is known to carry a Colt like this one stuffed into his waistband. If he were on his way out and needed to use the john, he might set the gun down first.

Yanking out the .45, Faolan ducks back into the corridor as bullets smash into the paneling around him. As he gets to the bar side, he sees Bug behind the bar trying to open the register. *Schmuck.*

Even though the entire exchange of gunfire only took half a minute at most, Schultz must be on the alert. Readying the Colt, Faolan pushes open the men's room door.

His quarry, one Arthur Flegenheimer, who is better known as Dutch Schultz, does indeed wear his white fedora and gray topcoat as if preparing to go out. A stall door is still swinging closed and he's in the act of rushing toward the door when Faolan enters. He skids to an awkward stop, looking a bit unsteady on his feet.

They lock eyes for just a second.

Stocky and below average height, Dutch has the looks of a bank clerk and the social grace of a racetrack bookie. He's worth millions but wears two dollar shirts and off-the-rack suits. Tonight, he reeks of beer and his fly is still open. Dutch Schultz is a man who will never have class.

A loud *ding!* announces Bug's success in opening the register.

Dutch turns away.

Faolan's finger tightens on the trigger.

A bullet slams into the door just behind his head—his shot goes low, ripping into Dutch's abdomen rather than his heart.

Clenching his teeth against the pain, Faolan sees Landau and Lulu stagger into view like a pair of monsters from a nightmare.

Bug scurries around the bar, stuffing a handful of cash into his coat pocket, and runs flat out for the door. Faolan turns back to Dutch. One shot just isn't enough.

Another bullet strikes the floor by his right foot just as he fires—

The shot goes wide, hitting the tiles of the back wall as Dutch stumbles back into the urinal and drops to the floor. *Goddamn Colts!*

Landau and Lulu stumble into the corridor, raising their guns.

Fuck! Faolan runs for the door. Bug, however, makes the mistake of glancing back as he reaches the end of the bar and puts a foot wrong—

The stocky gunman flies forward, ass over teakettle, and kisses linoleum near the phone booth in the corner. His shotgun skids to the front door.

Up ahead, the cigarette machine takes a few rounds, but Faolan waits until he makes it to the front door to risk a glance.

The wound on Landau's shoulder is worse than Faolan thought: the bullet severed an artery and jets of blood pulse out in a heartbeat rhythm while the thin man continues to stagger toward him. The sight is morbidly engrossing.

Behind Landau limps the bloody monstrosity that is Lulu Rosencrantz, also fighting to lift his gun and fire.

Grabbing the shotgun, Faolan gets the door open and rushes out. He dives into the cover of the idling Packard and throws the shotgun down behind the passenger seat.

"Step on it, they're coming!"

Weiss hits the gas and the Packard speeds off. Faolan looks out the back window and sees Landau stumble out onto the sidewalk after them, still firing. One step: blood still squirting from his neck. Two steps ... Landau collapses into a set of trash cans against the wall of the Chophouse.

The groove ends.

Faolan's senses snapped back to normal. His heartbeat began to slow.

"Shit!" Weiss cried. "We left Workman!"

Faolan saw The Bug run into the street at that very moment, chasing their dust. Still wasn't too late to stop and pick him up.

"Nah," Faolan told Weiss, reaching into his jacket for his Camels. "He went out through the kitchen."

Let the little fucker walk home.

* * * * *

When Weiss didn't turn around and shoot him, Faolan knew his killer would be waiting for him in Manhattan.

They'd swapped the Packard for a Lincoln a few blocks from the Chophouse and left the shotgun to ensure that the trail ended there. Faolan held onto the .45 because he knew he wouldn't be keeping it long.

Canal Street glistened like polished leather under the streetlamps as Weiss pulled the car to the curb. Faolan climbed out, giving Weiss a parting nod. Weiss refused to look at him as he pulled into the light traffic and disappeared.

Faolan glanced at the darkened coffee shop half a block up where an old, red Ford two-seater waited. He walked toward the car and wondered who Charlie sent. When he got within ten feet, the door opened and a broad-shouldered guy in a dark rain coat and gray hat got out. The tall, boxy shape of the car made it difficult to recognize the driver until he stepped into the light.

"Howdy, stranger," said his childhood pal Benny Siegel, flashing the devil's own grin. "Need a lift?"

"Benny," Faolan said, making his surprise sound glad rather than hurt. They met at the curb, shook hands, and embraced like brothers.

When you hit somebody on your own team, you wanted them to let their guard down, so you sent somebody they trusted.

Benny held him at arm's length for examination. "Shit, pal, you look like somebody really gave you the business. You take one in the wing, there?"

"Just grazed me. Looks worse than it feels."

Benny nodded. "Go ahead and get in. I gotta swing by the docks and get a package before we see Charlie."

Faolan's fingers tightened around the Colt in his pocket as Benny turned away. Put one in the back of Benny's head, and he could take the car before anybody saw anything. Wasn't like him to play lamb to the slaughter and his instincts told him to take action to protect himself, but if he killed Benny, they'd never stop looking for him. He climbed into the passenger seat. "Charlie got you picking up his fucking groceries now or what?"

"Benny the errand boy, that's me. You take care of the Dutchman?" Benny tossed his hat up on top of the dashboard and pulled into the street.

Faolan's gums ached again, almost on fire, and his whole body trembled with hunger. He forced it down. He took the Colt out of his pocket and handed it to Benny, knowing he couldn't resist the temptation if the gun was right in his reach.

"The gun that plugged Dutch Schultz. Keep it as a souvenir."

Benny glanced at it, nodded, and slipped it into his pocket. "He's dead? You seen it?"

"I saw him go down. Place was a fucking shooting gallery, but them goons of his weren't no pigeons."

"So, there's no telling whether this guy pulls a Jack of Diamonds is what you're saying."

Jack of Diamonds, that was cute. Jack Diamond, Faolan's mentor and best friend, had a little extra juice in him that had allowed him to survive five attempts on his life. Faolan used to have that little extra juice, too, but he'd traded up and now he had more than a little. For the first time, he wondered if Schultz and his guys had also had something extra in them.

"Look, I ever blow a hit before? No. I tell you what, though, if the sonofabitch pulls through this, I'll pay him a visit in the hospital and personally stuff a pillow down his throat, okay?"

"Ain't necessary," Benny said in lieu of an apology. "I believe you. I'm just saying what you know Charlie's gonna."

Faolan lit a Camel and let Benny go on thinking he was steamed. Between that movie-star smile and those sad, Bing Crosby eyes, Benny could seem like the nicest, most unthreatening guy in the world. Women fell for it most, but skirts didn't mean anything to Benny.

Loyalty did.

Mess with one of his friends and you'd see Benny's famous temper, something a lot of people never lived through. Tonight, Benny was working that temper up over Faolan's involvement in a betrayal of Charlie a few years back. On Jack Diamond's orders, Faolan had organized a little ride for Charlie in 1929 that he wasn't supposed to survive. But he had survived and blamed the wrong gang for the attempt ... up until someone informed Charlie of Faolan's role.

Betrayals. Faolan's life had been a long series of them.

Him and Jack betrayed Dutch. Dutch betrayed them. Him and Jack betrayed Rothstein. Him and Jack betrayed Charlie. Dutch betrayed him. Jack betrayed him. His brother Tom betrayed him. He betrayed Jack. He betrayed Tom. He betrayed his wife Colleen. He betrayed Charlie. Charlie betrayed Dutch. Now Charlie and Benny were betraying him.

Life's grand pageant.

It's my own fault for trusting people, Faolan thought. *Fucking stupid to ever let anyone get their hooks into you like that. It just makes it harder when the time comes to betray them.*

Faolan glanced out at the dark tenements and shops along West Street and exhaled a cloud of smoke with a bitter smile. Charlie and Benny didn't realize that, revenge or no revenge, he'd still get the last laugh. That envelope he'd mailed tonight contained a detailed description of Charlie's operations as well as the names of some bitter old whores who'd be happy to testify against the Commission boss. Faolan figured Dewey would be eager to change his aim once the Dutchman was out of the picture.

After all, what was one more betrayal between friends?

"So where's this dock we're swinging by, anyhow?" he asked, just to say something.

"Couple more minutes," Benny said. "Won't take long. Hey, look back there—hasn't that same car been behind us since we got on West?"

"Who the fuck would be following us? Why, for that matter?" Faolan gave a cursory glance at his side mirror. They were being followed, all right, but there was no angle in tipping Benny.

"You're probably right."

"Hey, you ever been back to that Lombardi's place I took you and Charlie to, couple years back?" he asked. "You know, the one that makes them tomato pies?"

Benny chuckled. "Yeah, I remember. Pizzas, they was called. Pretty good for dago food." He glanced over at Faolan and went cold all the sudden. "Nah, I ain't been back there."

People who thought Benny was a stone killer had it all wrong. Sure, he could plug a stranger without any problem, but friends were something else. Benny needed a reason to kill a friend, a reason to hate them: a betrayal. Faolan's trip down memory lane made Benny remember the good times for a minute, messed with his effort to build up his hate.

It hurt stabbing an old friend in the back, Benny? Faolan thought, crushing out his Camel. *Your own fault for being weak.*

"Was thinking of them tomato pies before," Faolan continued. "On account of being sick, I ain't had nothing to eat in almost a week. I was thinking how I could go for one of them pies."

It wasn't tomato pies Faolan was hungry for at the moment, but it was something he'd thought about while he lay in his room with his guts twisted up in knots, burning with fever. Shitting and puking and stuffing pillows in his mouth to keep his screams from disturbing the neighbors, all the while thinking of tomato pies, chili dogs, chop suey, Del Monico steaks, ice cream, hot pastrami, and all the other favorites he'd never eat again.

"Nothing for a week. That's rough." Benny kept his eyes focused on the road. He slowed down and watched the car behind them pass. He flashed a smile, but it was tight. "Hey, can you believe that fucking series? I mean, if Greenberg didn't break his wrist in that second game, I guarantee you it never would have gone to six. Tigers act like it was no sweat when they won through by the skin of their teeth."

Hank Greenberg being the only Jewish star player in the majors made him a natural favorite of Benny's.

"You know me," Faolan said as Benny turned onto one of the piers, "if Brooklyn ain't in it, I couldn't give a rat's ass."

That made Benny snicker and shake his head. "You and them God-forsaken Dodgers. That club's got no future, mark my words."

"Hey, bite your tongue. Them's my bums you're running down."

There was a fog coming off the Hudson as Benny pulled to the front of one of the less ramshackle warehouses and set the parking brake.

"Like I said, this should only take a minute." Benny climbed out and Faolan waited.

This was the hard part. He wanted to fight back, wanted to knock Benny's ass to the ground and tear his throat out, but he had to take the dive.

His door jerked open and there was Benny, bared teeth and naked steel. In the half-second it took for Benny to shift position, Faolan could have had him.

Benny's blade punctured his navel, popping him open like a can. A professional job.

"Mother-fucking traitor!" Benny hissed, yanking the blade out. "Charlie says 'Thanks for the ride'!"

The next blows felt like weak punches in the stomach. Faolan's vision went gray, and he knew he couldn't fight back now if he wanted, so he let his body flop as his precious blood drizzled out of him.

Again and again Benny stabbed his stomach, cursing him, as everything went dark.

* * * * *

The sound of the foghorn stopped Benny Siegel a full minute later. He was huffing and sweating, his hand covered in blood. He'd gotten himself pretty worked up there. Got carried away. He loved the way the blood pumped in his veins when he got excited like that, the colors became more vivid and the world became more alive. Some fellas thought it was funny how he got carried away and called him "bugsy," but he wasn't no goddamned bughouse loony. He just got worked up.

Pushing a handful of his thick, black hair out of his face, Ben took a handkerchief out of his coat pocket and cleaned off the knife. Dipped the handkerchief in a puddle of rain water nearby and cleaned off his hand. Threw the bloody rag in the car and pocketed his knife.

He was good now, calm. Still excited, though. Doing somebody in, especially all close and personal like that, always got his blood going. He'd give some bimbo the *schtupping* of her life later.

Now to finish up with the body.

It was always "the body" after he was done. He had orders to make this one disappear, which was why he'd made Swiss cheese outta the belly. Kept the gasses from building up and bringing it to the surface like a balloon. Maybe he'd over-done it a little, but a wink was as good as a nod to a blind horse, eh?

Kneeling, he pulled the body forward so it flopped over his shoulder and carried it around to the driver side, laying it on the seat in a sitting position. More blood on his coat. Well, that's what he'd worn it for, wasn't it?

He popped the parking brake and gave the Ford a good shove from the back to get it going. He followed it, watched it roll. It veered to the right a little and went into the water a few yards short of the end, but that was close enough. The jalopy sank fast and, though he waited to be sure, he didn't see anything bubble up from it.

Ben Siegel removed his bloody rain coat, tossed it into the Hudson wrapped around the incriminating Colt, and found the back-up car waiting in the warehouse. Just like Charlie said.

Time for a little companionship of the female variety.

Chapter Two

Faolan O'Connor wanted to be somebody before he died.

He shivered under a pile of blankets, burning with fever on his sickbed as the snowy world outside prepared for 1932 to arrive. The bullet wound in his side tingled and burned. He thought it smelled funny, too. He had to remember to ask Colleen to hit it with more iodine when she changed the dressing tomorrow. He looked over at his watch—lying next to his prized Remington Model 51 on the small nightstand—and saw that it was only eleven at night. Colleen wouldn't be in to open her parent's café until five. He could call her if there was an emergency, but if the Dutchman's boys were watching her, she'd lead them right here. That's why she was at home and he was here in the vacant apartment above the café.

Actually, Dutch Schultz was the real reason he was here. After negotiating a very fair contract for the emotionally difficult task of killing his best friend and mentor Jack, Faolan was enraged that Dutch had the nerve to pull a double-cross. Only Faolan's instinct that something was fishy at the meeting and his skill with a pistol had allowed him to escape Dutch's death trap. Worse still, when Faolan had called Vincent Coll—Jack's frequent ally against Dutch—Coll had cursed him as a traitor and threatened to kill Faolan if he ever laid eyes on him again.

Dutch had spread the story. The rest of Jack's gang would go with Coll now. He was alone.

Then he heard footsteps on the stairs.

The only light came in through the closed dormer windows and he'd become accustomed to the creaks and groans of the house during his time here, so he recognized the sound of someone climbing the stairs. Faolan grabbed his Remington from the nightstand and dragged himself to a sitting position. Colleen wouldn't come over without calling first. The pistol already had a round in the chamber, so he released the safety as quietly as he could and aimed at the door. He thought about trying to hide under the bed, but knew he couldn't get down there fast enough in his current condition.

"Don't shoot, will ya?" came a voice from the other side of the door: a voice with a strong Irish accent that Faolan didn't recognize. The door opened and a short, skinny man strolled in like he didn't have a care in the world. He unbuttoned his camel hair coat now that he was in out of the cold and doffed a matching tan homburg as he moved closer, his soft-soled shoes making almost no noise on the wood floor.

He picked up the wooden chair Colleen always used and plunked it down at Faolan's bedside. He straddled the chair backwards and hung his hat on the back of the chair before resting his arms there. He was very pale and gaunt, but youthful looking despite the gray streaks in his straight black hair. His eyes had heavy lids that made him look sleepy; however, the hazel eyes beneath were bright and inquisitive. He was a man made up of contradictions. "You're a difficult man to find, Faolan O'Connor," he said with a smile.

Faolan lowered the pistol, but didn't let go of it. "Not difficult enough."

The stranger chuckled. "Sure, I've ways of learning things that most don't. Name's Byrne, by the by. Liam Byrne." He reached out his hand and Faolan shook it with his left, keeping his pistol ready. Despite the temperature outside, Byrne's hand was warm and he released Faolan's hand without trying anything. The gun didn't appear to bother him in the slightest. "I'm here to save your life, Faolan, if you agree to my terms."

"I can handle the Dutchman."

"Not in your current state, you can't," Byrne said. "Sure that wound's going septic, I can smell it. By the time your lass comes to check on you in the morning, I wager you'll be past saving. You could go to a hospital, but you know Dutch'll send someone in to finish you there."

Faolan found himself touching his wounded side and didn't like how tender and swollen it felt. "You some kinda doctor?"

"No, I'm a vampire."

Faolan laughed, but it turned into a cough. Byrne didn't laugh, he just smiled and opened his mouth. Faolan started to ask what he was doing when Byrne's canines *lengthened*. Faolan thought his eyes were playing tricks, but Byrne's teeth got longer, all right—and they looked sharp. He jumped back and stuck his pistol in Byrne's face. "What the fuck? Get outta here, you fucking freak!"

Byrne sighed and held his hands up. "Faolan, calm down for fucksake, will ya? I'm not here to hurt you, but I also don't have time to go through the usual shite—bringing you in gradual and all that. Or, I should say, *you* don't have time for that. So, yes, vampires are real and I am one, for sure, but it ain't like that cockamamie *Dracula* shite, okay? It's much more like the rackets that you're familiar with except, of course, we gotta be even more discreet."

Faolan lowered the pistol a little, but kept it aimed in Byrne's direction. His mind raced with possibilities, some ridiculous, but most very practical. Some of the mystical nonsense Jack used to mention began to fit a pattern and didn't seem so far fetched anymore: secret societies, psychic powers, and blood covenants. Still, this would take some getting used to. "So, if being a vampire ain't like *Dracula*, then what's it like?"

"Well, it's not so bad," Byrne said, spreading his hands as he spoke. "We're not dead, for one, that's pure baloney. There's something in our blood that makes us powerful and keeps us from aging and we do drink blood to live, but—oh, yes, sunlight is very uncomfortable, but we sleep right through the day. But that's most of it."

Somehow, Faolan realized he had already accepted the idea of vampires being real. Byrne's demonstration had been very effective, but Faolan also couldn't imagine why someone would make up such a story for him. So, the practical side of his mind took over. "Why save me?"

Byrne smiled. "Good man. Right to the heart of it. Well, it seems we had a mutual friend name of Jack Diamond—and I see what you're wondering now and the answer is yes, I know you killed him. Anyway, me boss and I had certain hopes for Jack, much as we do for Owney Madden, Vincent Coll, Vannie Higgins and other Irish businessmen of your acquaintance. Sure, I used to provide my blood to Jack and his brother Eddie, which prolonged Eddie's life in spite of his consumption, and helped Jack survive several tough scrapes. Now, in return for these services, Jack performed certain favors for me, but he'd began to stray upstate more and more of late and get himself tangled in legal troubles. The point being, I don't so much mind that you put poor Jack out of his misery. But, with Vannie still in the hospital from his latest scuffle and

Coll still under the cloud of killing that kid, surely I could use a replacement. And I figure you owe me."

The Remington 51 was a light gun for its caliber, but even the effort of holding it was taking its toll, so Faolan set it down beside him. He tingled with excitement, thinking of what this could mean if he played his cards right.

"So you vampires run things? Behind the scenes, like?" he asked.

Byrne reached into his coat and withdrew a case which, when opened, revealed a syringe. "We wield considerable influence, 'tis true, though to call it total control would be a bit of an exaggeration. Still, it's a long life of wealth, power, and vitality."

Faolan nodded. "Then I want in."

Byrne chuckled and stuck the syringe into his wrist to draw a full measure of dark, red blood. "We'll see about that, Faolan O'Connor. First I need you to prove yourself, but I will make you what we call a Dhampir and fix that wound of yours. Gimme your arm."

Faolan did and Byrne stuck the needle into Faolan's arm with expert precision and pushed the plunger down. "That's it?"

"You may feel strange in the next few hours, but come the morning you'll see a strong improvement in your wound. After you've healed fully, I'll give you another dose to keep you tip-top. What I want from you is for you to look up your old pal Luciano and see if you can join this commission of gang bosses he's building. I hear he's got Jews, eye-ties, and others all working together, but they been trying to push the Irish out of the rackets."

Faolan frowned, though part of his mind was already considering ways to approach Charlie. "So, wait, you want me to be a spy?"

"Aye. Perhaps more."

Faolan shifted uncomfortably and wondered if it was the blood or something else. "But, Charlie's a friend, you know?"

Byrne put the syringe and its case back in his pocket and leaned on the chair back with his hands clasped. "Look, lad, you know as well as I that friendship is for twats. This is a rough business we're in and it's not for the faint of heart. Where are your so-called friends now as you lay here dying? Luciano would serve you right up to the Dutchman if he was here and you know it for sure."

"Unless I make myself more useful to him alive," Faolan said.

Byrne smiled. "Exactly."

Sitting back, Faolan decided that Byrne had a good point. What had his loyalty to his friends brought him all these years but grief? All his life, he'd been forced to choose loyalty to one friend over another time and time again. All his years with Jack—all the men he'd killed for him—and it changed nothing. Jack was dead instead of in prison and Faolan O'Connor had nothing to show for it but a guilty conscience. Why not be the guy who made it to the top for once? Wasn't it his turn to succeed?

"You're right," he told Byrne. "I'm in." This was his chance, his last chance. He'd show this guy what he could do and he'd earn his fangs. Then he'd see what it took to climb the vampire ladder to the top.

Why not? I got forever now, don't I?

*****

He pitched forward and his head hit the steering wheel as the car hit the water.

Then darkness and noise: rushing water.

Faolan O'Connor, officially dead and woozy like a prize fighter in the thirteenth round, pried his bleary eyes open and did his best to shake it off. A splash of water on his face helped, but then ice-cold water moved up his legs to his balls. Now he was awake! Gaze darting around, he took in his situation and saw the Hudson River filling the small interior of the Ford. The water rose to his neck and he took the deepest breath he was capable of—

The searing pain in his abdomen doubled him over, plunging his head below the waves and almost forcing the breath out of him. Struggling just to move in the churning tide, he clutched the raw, healing flesh in terror that his intestines were about to snake out through his wounds.

There was no more air in the car. It sank toward the river bottom with a rocking motion like the Wonder Wheel cars at Coney Island. He heard nothing but the rapid pounding of his own heart. He felt squeezed from the outside and pushed from the inside by the remaining air in his lungs.

He had to get out while he could still think.

The Ford thumped to the bottom of the river, kicking up great billowing clouds of silt. He managed to get his door open just by leaning against it and tumbled half-out into the muck as the precious air he'd gulped blew out of him in a stream of bubbles. Clamping his mouth shut, he dragged his legs out of the car and pinched his nose to keep from sucking in a lungful of the polluted filth surrounding him.

He still couldn't see a damn thing, but he knew the muck he pushed against was down, so he rolled over— ignoring the feeling like his gut was fixing to rip right open—and pushed off with everything he had.

He kicked out and felt his foot smack metal. The car! That meant he'd made it—what?—five feet, maybe. That squeezing sensation was worse and he felt the river fighting him, shoving him around with a dozen sets of arms. His baggy clothes were holding him down. Cursing the effort, he thrashed out of his leaden overcoat and suit jacket.

Lighter, freer, he clawed at the blackness around him and kicked, dragging his way up inch by freezing inch. His lungs, having squandered their last breath of air only a minute before, pressed against his ribcage to demand another. His arms and legs were numb, but his chest was on fire.

Slowly, blackness gave way to gray and gray gave way to a rippling light and the pounding in his chest tripled as he realized that survival was only a few kicks away.

Something broke the surface above and fell toward him from a bundle. His first thought was to shove it aside and keep struggling upward, but he recognized it as it sank past his face.

The Colt.

Benny was still up there.

His instincts didn't give a shit, of course, and screamed at him to push forward before that blackness at the edges of his vision overwhelmed him. Before his lungs jumped into his mouth and forced him to suck in a deep, satisfying breath...

No! Didn't go through all this shit just to wind up dead for real!

Just ... a few ... feet ... over: the pier! His whole body tense and pleading for relief, he dragged himself beneath the sheltering darkness of the pier and felt his way through the tangle of beams and posts and supports, fading, looking for a way up, head getting fuzzy, trying to find the air that he thought was—

He almost didn't realize it as his head broke the surface and it took a second to remember how to breathe. Clutching a slimy support post, he sucked in huge gulps of moldy air and coughed and shook. He prayed that Benny couldn't hear him.

A few seconds later, when the worst of it had passed, Faolan heard the sound of a car engine: Benny driving away, or somebody picking him up, was his best guess.

God, he was tired. Fucking bone weary was the expression, though at that moment he could have believed he didn't possess any bones at all. He dragged himself from post to beam to post, all the while fighting to keep his eyes open. The water didn't seem so cold anymore. It was comfortable like a soft, warm bed.

He spotted the ladder and drifted toward it, coming out from under the darkness of the pier into the darkness of the night. When he grabbed the ladder the first time, his hand slipped right off. He tried again and got his fingers to close around the rung, but he had no strength to pull himself up.

Fucking ridiculous! It was only a couple rungs to climb and he'd be up on the pier, but it might as well have been a mountain. He was beyond exhaustion, beyond weakness, and beyond pain; he was numb all over and just couldn't summon the strength to lift his other arm out of the water.

His hand slipped off the rung.

His head lolled back and he floated...

His eyes slipped closed...

He tasted the river and sputtered, but it was a half-assed sputter...

His next breath brought water in with it...

* * * * *

He heard voices. Then a splash.

He sank, breathing in water, when something grabbed him. It drug him, clutching his chest...

Then he was vomiting up water, lying on the dock while someone rammed his tender gut. He heard voices—

"Holy cow, Rod, he looks terrible."

"...shived him pretty bad, he's lost a lot of blood—think his heart might have stopped for a few seconds." The smooth voice of a confident man shaken by concern, like a doctor on a radio drama.

"He gonna be okay?" The first voice was deferential, local accent.

The smooth voice (Rod?) sighed. "If he doesn't get blood soon, his body could start eating itself or just shut down for good. Lot of damage for somebody just turned ... hey, dammit, Enzo, you know the rules!"

"You rather bring back a corpse?"

Something warm and delicious touched Faolan's tongue—rich, thick, coppery blood—and he swallowed, wanting more and more and more again, but he didn't even have the strength to lift his head.

"He's supposed to haul his own load, remember? The boss already has you on his shit list."

"Just gave him a little. You know—just so he makes it through the night. You—you ain't gonna say nothing, are you?"

"You have to ask?"

"Sorry, I'm just nervous."

The trickle stopped, but Faolan kept swallowing out of reflex and hope. His eyes cracked open, but the light of the pier turned his rescuers into silhouettes.

"All right, let's hurry up and get this guy back." There was something beneath Rod's all-business tone. Maybe even dread.

Faolan felt himself being lifted and the moment of dizziness it produced was enough to put him out again.

* * * * *

Moving. A car.

He felt a little better, if you could call feeling slugged in the gut better than feeling kicked in the balls.

"...division of manpower I'm talking about," Rod said. Both were up front while Faolan lay across the backseat. "Everybody thinks we need more guys, but what we really need is to use the ones we've got more efficiently."

"Yeah."

The car stopped at a red light. The red of the light made Faolan ache again. Desperation welled up in him.

"Ever since they took out Byrne, what little we had in the way of operational strategy is gone. Now the boss just throws us around like a big street gang, which isn't the way you fight this kind of war."

Byrne. War. He knew these things—but, then, it was gone and he drifted out.

* * * * *

He came back up to the sound of laughter. They were moving again.

"... so I'se tol' Mister Frank I was regusted, absolutely regusted dat dey be treatin' us so shabby!"

It sounded like scheming old Kingfish from *Amos 'n' Andy*. But wasn't it a little late for it to be on? It was Rod up front doing just about the best imitation of Kingfish that Faolan had ever heard. Enzo laughed, doubled up in his seat and fighting for breath. He was an average-sized Sicilian with a head of curly hair worn short, bushy eyebrows, and an unremarkable face that was built for smiling.

Rod chuckled—flattered by his partner's enthusiastic reaction—and took a drag off his Chesterfield. Faolan only saw his profile, but he thought Rod could be a matinee idol. A tall fella with an athlete's build, he had those elegant features the dames went bonkers for. Faolan was reminded of Douglas Fairbanks Jr. or Charles Lindberg. Rod was even wearing one of those Lindy-style aviator jackets. His hair, however, still hung in wet locks.

So it had been Rod who dove in to fish him out while Enzo had slipped him the little pick-me-up against orders.

They both saved his life.

Watch it, he warned himself as Rod parked the car in a loading area at the back of the Empire State Building. *You don't know the score yet. What's to say you won't have to kill these two a week from now? Just sit tight and get the lay of the land.*

Faolan shut his eyes as the pair climbed out, intending only to play possum, but his head swam as Rod opened the back door and hoisted him as easy as a bag of feathers.

"… gotta put him downstairs?" Enzo asked, sounding like he was behind glass.

"Yeah," Rod's voice answered from far away. Faolan heard the impressionist's rapid heartbeat quicken. "Downstairs."

The darkness claimed him again.

* * * * *

He awoke by degrees.

Concrete beneath his back, probably a floor. He felt cold, stiff, and dry as a corn-husk doll. He kept his breathing deep and regular, as if he were still asleep. The air smelled of sweat, mildew, ammonia, blood, and fear.

He heard a heartbeat and breathing a few feet back and to his right. It was a small, fast beat: like a rabbit's. The breathing was shallow but slow; the breathing of someone trying not to be heard.

It was the fresh fear wafting over that convinced him to open his eyes and move. That turned out to be a mistake: the bare bulb in the ceiling scorched his eyes and he had to sit up fast to get away from it— that made his joints crack six ways to Sunday and gave him a nice shooting pain up his spine to replace the ones he'd left behind.

"Ah, fuck me!" He flexed his hands a few times to work out the stiffness and rubbed the gum and sand out of his sight. He cracked his neck and glanced over to where he heard breathing.

A boy pressed into the corner as far as he could, eyes wide and heart racing. A little ragamuffin in frayed clothes and a newsboy's cap that was too big for him—lucky his ears poked out enough to hold it up. He couldn't have been more than ten.

Faolan ignored him for the time being and stood to work more of his kinks out. The room wasn't more than fifteen feet square and could have been less, concrete floor and walls all painted a dirty gray. The single door appeared to be solid steel with a little viewing slot at eye level. The floor dipped a little at the center where a metal drain was set into the concrete.

Faolan knew a cell when he saw one.

The only furnishing in the cell was a battered oak desk against one wall. On the desk sat a glass of water.

"They said that water was for you," the kid mumbled, shrinking further back into the corner when Faolan looked at him. "I didn't drink none of it."

He opened his mouth to say thanks, but his throat was so rough you could have struck matches on it. That nagging pain, which he'd thought was just an ache from sleeping badly, was a burning thirst that had a hold on every part of him. Nodding, he grabbed the glass and gulped down half the contents in a few swallows before a realization made him stop.

He tumbled to why he and the kid were down here.

He set the glass down, though his thirst was far from satisfied, and ran his hand over his face while he considered options. The skin had tightened up a little more and he had the scattered peach fuzz that passed for a beard on him. *Nobody said nothing about a fucking kid.* "Who told you the water was for me?"

"Them two guys who brung me here. Told me they was looking for Gator's Candy Shop, and they'd buy me something if I showed them how to get there, so I gots in the car." The kid sounded more relaxed now and, after a pause, muttered, "Lying bastards."

Faolan laughed and the kid apologized, but he told him there wasn't anything for him to be sorry for. He patted himself down, but his Camels were gone. He could have used one right about now. He sat down against a wall away from the kid. He was still wearing the clothes he'd been fished out in, so he yanked off his tie and opened his loose shirt collar. He was burning up again.

"You sure must have been tired," the kid said after a moment.

"What do you mean?"

The kid sat down in the corner and squirmed a little. "I dunno, 'cause you was asleep when they put me in here and that was hours and hours ago."

So he'd slept straight through the day. Couldn't say he was surprised. Digging into his pockets, he found his lighter (he'd have to replace the wick before it'd strike again), his penknife, and a little spare change. He transferred the penknife into his shirt pocket and held onto a fifty-cent piece before pocketing the rest.

"Hey, uh, Mister?"

"Yeah?"

"H-How long do you figure them keeping us for?"

This was one hell of a kid. He'd known full-grown, experienced guys who wouldn't have kept it together so well.

"What's your name, kid?"

"Michael."

"I had a brother named Michael. He was in the Navy during the war. Got sunk by some Kraut boat." He flipped the half dollar up with his thumb and caught it with more panache than George Raft ever had. "Anyways, Michael, your best bet's to not even think about how long. Whole idea of keeping you waiting is to make you sweat, drive you bugshit."

The kid giggled at the term and Faolan smiled, concentrating on his coin flips. "You keep your mind on whatever you're doing right then. Whether it's counting ceiling tiles or seeing how long you can hold your breath, it don't matter so long as it keeps you from thinking about the future. They want you to worry yourself half to death so they got the advantage over you when they come around. But if you learn how to wait without getting worried, then you got the advantage."

The kid nodded, excited. "Yeah, I get it! That's smart. I bet I can hold my breath for five minutes, just watch!"

Faolan wasn't sure, but he thought the little slot in the door had opened a crack sometime in the last few minutes. He kept his attention on his hands.

After the next toss, he let the coin drop into his cuff and blew across his now empty palm.

The kid gave up holding his breath to watch.

Faking a cough, Faolan found the coin sitting back in his palm with an expression of mild surprise.

The kid smiled.

Faolan rolled the coin back and forth across his knuckles a few times, and then went back to flipping it.

The kid got up and walked over, pausing only a moment before plunking himself down on Faolan's right. Faolan tossed the coin to his left hand without missing a beat, draping his right around the kid. The coin rolled back and forth across the knuckles of his left hand before being flipped up and caught.

Then it disappeared.

The kid gave Faolan a knowing look. Faolan returned the look with a raised eyebrow. "Open your mouth."

When the kid did so, Faolan reached inside and produced the coin. "Shouldn't try swallowing something so big," he said. The kid giggled and Faolan flipped the coin toward him. "Catch."

When the kid leaned forward to do so, Faolan snapped his neck in a single blur of motion.

The coin rang off the concrete floor.

He didn't let himself think about what he'd just done—what he'd decided he was going to do as soon as he realized feeding on Michael was the only way he was getting out—he just took the penknife from his shirt and got to work.

He sliced the wrist open, because he could fit his mouth around it, and drank the blood his body demanded. The sensation was like liquid magic pouring down his throat. It was better than liquor, better than opium, better than cocaine, and better than the greatest sex he'd ever had. It might have been the newness and the intensity of his need that made it so strong, but entire minutes passed when he could think of nothing but drinking and was unaware of anything but the blood.

When the vein started going dry, Faolan shifted the body's position to let gravity help him out. He wouldn't allow himself to regret what he'd done, but he'd also be damned if he'd let a single drop of this blood go to waste. Michael deserved better, but his death would be worth that much, at least.

Could he have figured some way to trick their captors and get the kid out? Possibly. But he'd recognized the situation for the test it was and, since he was here by choice, had every intention of passing it.

In this world, heroics would get him nowhere.

When he finished, he laid Michael's body down—turned away toward the wall so he wouldn't have to look at the face—and got up. He could feel the blood working, rushing through him and energizing him, fixing him.

He walked over to the desk and drank the rest of the water to wash the taste out of his mouth. As he finished, he heard a bolt slide back, and the thick steel door opened.

Faolan found himself face to face with a dead man.

Chapter Three

Faolan might not have recognized the man at the door if it weren't for his good memory for faces. This one had lost weight, the skin had paled, and the brown eyes that used to twinkle with warmth and good humor were cold and flat. Hell, more than that, those eyes were plain dead. They reminded Faolan of the glass eyes of an automaton in a boardwalk museum.

Despite those changes, however, he recognized Frank Giordano, who came out of the Bronx with the Schultz mob before striking out with the Coll brothers and declaring war on the Dutchman. Frank Giordano who he'd met and liked when the Colls partnered up with Jack Diamond. Frank Giordano who helped Vince Coll shoot up a Harlem street full of kids and kill a five-year-old boy.

Frank Giordano who died in the electric chair three years ago.

"Hello, Faolan," Frank said without any expression in his face or voice.

Faolan hid his surprise. This wasn't the first person he'd seen rise from the dead since learning how vampires were real and ran damn-near everything.

Glancing back at Michael's body, Faolan's shock gave way to anger and he glared up the taller vampire.

"You have anything to do with putting this little test together, Frank?"

Frank's dead eyes fired up for a second and Faolan wondered what he would do if the larger vampire attacked him. Frank still looked to have at least a twenty pound advantage. But then the larger man blinked, very slowly, and his eyes went back to dead.

"No," he answered. Standing there in his black three-piece with a matching black tie and hat and those eyes, he looked like an unsympathetic undertaker.

Faolan studied him for a second and nodded. "Good. I want the kid's parents told, so he can get a decent burial and all. I'll pay for everything."

"We got funeral homes. The kid's body goes out with the trash collection, then it gets cremated and mixed in with other stiffs." Frank shrugged. "That's the rules. If I was you, I wouldn't try contacting the parents. It never helps."

Faolan swallowed his response along with his anger.

Frank turned to lead the way out then turned back. "Wait—did you want me to lie?"

"No."

Frank nodded and stepped aside so Faolan could exit the cell. He stepped through into a large utility closet with racks of wires on every wall and watched as Frank slid the cell's thick steel door shut. Frank then swung a hinged panel closed over the cell door. It clicked into place with magnets and was covered in wires and switches to match the rest of the closet interior, making the door behind it invisible. Faolan grunted in appreciation of the trick and followed Frank out into the hall.

"Schultz?" he asked as Frank locked the closet door behind them.

The taller vampire slipped his keys into his pocket. "In Newark Hospital dying of peritonitis and raving with fever. The rest of his boys are dead or dying. I heard Lulu kept demanding an ice-cream soda."

"You're kidding."

A smirk tugged the corner of Frank's liver-colored lips. "Death is funny sometimes." He headed down the gray basement corridor, and Faolan kept pace.

"All right, Frank, spill. What the fuck's with you walking around? I heard enough about this vampire thing to know it don't bring the dead back to life."

"The correct pronunciation is *Vahm-peer*. We're a species of living vampire," Frank corrected as they turned into a larger service hallway, their footsteps echoing. "But you're right, I was never dead. Rothstein picked me as his number two just before the Harlem incident. Him and Byrne grabbed some drifter to take my place—"

"Take your place? What the hell are you talking about?"

Frank stopped and glanced at Faolan, tapping the side of his head with his finger. "They used the whammy, see? Spend enough time talking to somebody and they can make them think anything. They made this chump think he was Frank Giordano, then they sent him out on the Mullins hit and saw to it that he went up for it."

"What about the baby killing? Somebody else did that?" The Frank he remembered had been pretty broken up over that incident. After the murder of his brother Peter by Dutch Schultz, an enraged Vincent Coll had loaded up a car full of men, including Frank, and gone out looking for the Dutchman to take vengeance. Instead, they had spotted Dutch's man Joey Rao outside the Helmar Social Club in Harlem and opened fire with shotguns and a Thompson. They missed Rao completely, wounded several young children, and killed a five-year-old boy named Michael

Vengalli. The story made papers across the country and earned Coll his "Mad Dog" nickname.

"No, I did that. Fucked everything up," Frank said, continuing toward the freight elevators. Faolan tried to read something from Frank's reaction, but got nothing.

"Byrne still had plans for Coll, so they had to rush with my stand-in and sabotage Coll's trial."

"So, that skinny runt I saw in the paper was your impostor? He didn't look nothing like you. I figured the papers made a mistake with the caption."

"That's what we hoped people would think." Frank hit the button to call the elevator down. "That picture wasn't supposed to happen, but we stopped any other pictures during the trial."

No pictures and rather scant coverage. Faolan had followed the case as it went along and had been surprised even then at how little ink was wasted on "Frank Giordano." The trial for the Mullins killing went almost unreported despite the fact that "Frank's" near-suicidal cooperation with the police sewed up the entire case—so much that one of the jurors even questioned his motives during the trial. Hell, the unprecedented legal move of bringing "Frank" down from Sing Sing's death row to stand trial with Coll only rated a three-inch column on page 31 of the *Times*. The comment about sabotaging Coll's baby murder trial was the only thing that made sense considering what a sham that had been: the state's main witness had a criminal record, lied under oath, and ended up committed to a psychiatric hospital. "Frank" and Coll got off, for all the good it did either of them. "Frank" went back to death row and Coll got turned into Swiss cheese by the Dutchman two months later.

"Hell of a fix," Faolan admitted, wondering what happened to the Frank Giordano he'd once known: the big, good-natured *goombah*. It was tempting to believe the real one had gone to the chair and this zombie beside him was the botched replacement. Being a Vampyr didn't suit Frank too well, physically-speaking. His face seemed like it was on too tight without any fat to soften it and his arms and legs had shrunk to sticks that didn't look like they could support his barrel chest. He was like a toy that somebody put together all wrong.

"We pulled that off when our gang ran nothing but the rackets and was not well liked by the other factions," Frank said as the elevator doors opened. They got inside and Frank punched three. "By the way, the original hierarchy of this city got wiped out about six months ago, and the powers that be are blaming us for it. We didn't do it, but there it is. So, now the rest of The Order is trying to wipe us out and we're fighting to keep the city that we rightfully stole. We own twelve floors of this building outright. Six are closed off for us while the three above and below our section contain companies we own or control. Banks, real estate holding companies, lawyers, investment firms, a detective agency, cleaning service, and political lobbying organizations—that's just in this building. Through our companies, we have hundreds of properties all over the state and employ thousands of people."

"So, who really wiped out the guys at the top?"

Frank had made his speech while staring straight ahead, but now turned to look into Faolan's eyes. "We don't know, but that doesn't matter," he said. "What matters is that tonight we're going into combat against vamps from every other city in the Northeast. I hope you're ready."

Faolan felt queasy under the intensity of Frank's fish-eye gaze and almost breathed a sigh of relief when the elevator doors opened on the third floor. Frank's head swiveled forward and he got out, indicating a door across the hall which was stenciled with the words: Empire Investments Service Entrance.

"This is the way we get to and from the sub-basement," he explained as the doors closed behind them. "I've got a key for this door, but I want to show you the main way you'll come up."

Faolan had been in the Empire State Building once or twice before, but as Frank led him around past the darkened offices and restaurants he admired the modern style of the building all over again. As home bases went, you sure could do worse.

"The floors we control are all served by the F Bank of elevators," Frank continued in his rapid monotone. "The lobby elevators can all access the buffer floors, but not the six that we operate out of. You take the stairs or an elevator to this office."

They reached the front of Empire Investments, Inc. and Faolan figured it for the kind of place he would have passed by without noticing. Nothing but blank walls and a door with a frosted panel bearing the company name.

"An investment company?"

"Can you think of a better way to scare people off during a depression?" Frank asked. He opened the door and invited Faolan in. "We designed it to look fly-by-night too, just to be sure. During the day, there's a whole set of grifters to keep up the false front and, at night, we explain our comings and goings by being employees and customers."

"At night?"

Frank shrugged, closing the door. "Overseas investing. Night here is day someplace else."

The inside of the place wasn't any more impressive. An old desk with an armed security guard (a regular ex-military bulldog by the look of him) and some second-hand waiting room furniture. To the left of the desk, a hall ran back to a narrow row of offices.

The guard rose to attention, but Frank spoke as if he wasn't there. "There's always a guard on duty at night. We own the company and they all know the score, so you don't have to be coy with them. Reason to come in the front is that if Stout here doesn't call up to the guard stations on our floors and inform them we're coming, we'll be met with an armed response." He turned to the guard at last. "This is Mister O'Connor: general access."

Stout nodded, still at attention.

Frank turned back to Faolan. "You ever find one of these guys asleep or they fail to show you the proper respect, you let me know. We don't pay them good money to fuck around. If you want to bust them up, that's fine too—just clear any permanent damage with me so I can make the necessary arrangements."

Faolan nodded and couldn't help sneaking a glance at Stout's expression. It hadn't changed. *Shit. Depression or no depression*, he thought, *you'd have to pay me a fucking fortune.*

Frank marched down the hall and Faolan followed. Behind them, Faolan heard Stout punch an intercom button and say, "Mister Giordano and Mister O'Connor."

Halfway down the hall of identical office doors, Frank led him through a door on the left marked "Storage." After navigating the piles of boxes and file cabinets, he opened a door labeled "Building Maintenance Only."

"The elevator back here is part of the F Bank, though it doesn't appear on any plans or schematics. This is our main route in and out of our floors."

"Right."

"Something on your mind?" Frank turned to face him.

Faolan hesitated. He didn't think he'd been obvious about his thoughts, so he realized he'd have to be more careful in the future. Frank may have started acting like a robot, but that big brain of his was as sharp as ever.

"Yeah, you're on my mind," Faolan said. "What the hell happened to you, Frank? We weren't never best buddies or nothing, but I remember how you used to be. Not only were you the only brain Coll's bunch had, but you were also his conscience. You always stuck up for the regular folks. That one time when his brother Peter wanted to bump that delivery man they thought might tip the cops about Jack's arsenal, remember that? You got right up in Vince Coll's face and told him it was a bum's move hitting some fella just making his living. That took guts, Frank. I always respected you for that."

Frank's expression didn't change and his eyes stayed dead, he just tilted his head to the side a little. "Thank you. It also takes guts to talk to me like that these days. You were always one for guts, though. That should serve you well here."

"Can't you talk like a normal goddamn person anymore?"

"Why?" Frank asked. "I'm not a normal person anymore, am I? That man you're referring to—devoted husband and the father of a five year-old girl—died in the electric chair on July first, nineteen thirty-two at eleven-oh-five p.m. Life is different here, Faolan. We have to be different. I had a hard time of it at first—"

Faolan heard the slight hitch in his voice, but held back from jumping on it. He still had to consider where this new Frank might fit into his plans.

"—and I want to make it easier for you if I can. I spoke up for you when Byrne first suggested you be brought in. I think you could do well here, but you have to let go of that old life. Are you prepared to do that?"

Faolan took a deep breath and made a show of thinking it over. "Yeah. Nothing much worth holding onto, really."

Frank nodded and led him down the hall to the secret elevator. It occurred to Faolan that he should have said his old life had been letting go of him for years. By the time the first dead man showed up at his door a week ago, the life he'd built had already fallen apart.

* * * * *

On October 18, 1935 Dutch Schultz was plotting his assassination of Thomas Dewey from the Chophouse in Newark, and Faolan O'Connor was still a Dhampir. He sat in his suite at the Waldorf listening to Duke Ellington on his Victrola, staring down at the remains of his poached salmon and caviar on the room service cart. The food here was world class, all right. Just in the last two weeks he'd had everything from veal piccatta, roast suckling pig and lamb chops to lobster, baked Alaska, and the famous Waldorf salad.

He didn't remember the taste of any of it.

Faolan sat in the green leather wing chair that had become his favorite and nursed a glass of Haig and Haig, the good twenty year old stuff in the pinch bottle. City lights shone in from both sets of large windows and the mellow piano and hollow horns of "Solitude" transitioned into the Duke's most popular swinger "It Don't Mean A Thing (If It Ain't Got That Swing)."

He knew he shouldn't just sit here in limbo. Charlie would call as soon as something was arranged or if any emergency came up. He could make his own use of his empty hours. Hit the Savoy or the Sky Room and see who was playing. Maybe take in that Gershwin show that just opened, *Porgy and Bess*. Go see a Cagney picture.

Instead, he sat and drank like he'd done almost every night for the past two months. His grand scheme to wash away his sorrows in luxury had proven a great big failure.

But that was him as always: Failin' O'Connor.

The record ran out and so did his whisky. He set the glass down on the cart next to the half-empty glass of expensive white wine the steward suggested to compliment his salmon. He'd only ordered the wine in the first place so he didn't look like some no-class bum. His first night here, he'd ordered up a bottle of that *Dom Perignon* all the snobs raved about. He'd thought it tasted like sweet needle beer with a shot of seltzer water and poured it down the toilet after one sip. The occasional beer aside, he'd never had much of a taste for booze. Not until things with Colleen hit the skids.

When he got tired of listening to the needle spin on nothing, he hoisted himself out of his chair and took the record off. His combination radio/record player, a couple suitcases of clothes, and his jazz records were all he'd taken from the house when he left.

Their house.

The real estate agent wasn't too enthusiastic about unloading a place that big with the market being so tight, but Faolan made it easy by telling him to take the first offer. Just so long as he never had to lay eyes on it again.

As he picked out his next selection, a knock came from the door. *'Bout time they sent the kid up for the cart*, he thought, digging into his pocket and peeling a buck off the roll. Then he opened the door and came face to face with his first dead man.

"Bang, bang," said Arnold Rothstein, shooting him with a finger gun.

Back in 1928, their positions had been reversed: Rothstein opening the hotel room door and Faolan plugging him in the gut. It was the first time Faolan had ever done somebody up close like that.

Faolan took an involuntary step backward and Rothstein smiled that rodent's grin of his. It looked even more predatory than usual on his pale, gaunt face with that big wedge of a nose and gleaming, narrow eyes. He strode into the suite, still wearing a black Chesterfield coat and Homburg. Then a much larger man stepped into view in the doorway.

"This is Mister Darcy Killian, the new Reeve of New York City," Rothstein announced.

The vamp entering behind Rothstein brought J.P. Morgan to Faolan's mind for some reason. Perhaps if Morgan were still in his forties and a heavyweight boxer, he might look like Darcy Killian. The Reeve's brown eyes danced with a furious light inside a strong, ruddy face and his lips stretched into a ready smile beneath his thick, gently curled mustache.

"Byrne's told me many good things, Mister O'Connor." His speech retained the rhythm of an Irish brogue beneath its more recent layer of Hell's Kitchen. He took Faolan's hand in a calloused, bone crushing grip and pumped it while removing his silk top hat. His stylish evening wear made Faolan feel underdressed in his shirt sleeves, pants, and socks.

"Well, thanks," Faolan managed. "That means a lot coming from Byrne."

"Byrne's dead," Rothstein added, strolling around the suite and examining the posh décor. "Philadelphia Reeve mailed us his head last week."

Killian threw a look at his companion, but elected to remain silent, taking a seat on the overstuffed floral sofa.

Rothstein's inspection of the suite was getting so thorough that Faolan began to wonder if the other man had come along just for decorating tips. "I'm told that you've tried to acquire a certain measure of refinement in these last few years, yet you inhabit this establishment like a rat in a nest of silk," Rothstein said, unable to keep his trademark smugness out of his nasal voice. "In any event, it appears that your famous luck has run out at last. Not only has the Vampyr who owned and protected you met an untimely end, but your friend Luciano just put out a contract on you. He was recently informed that it was you who took him for that unpleasant car trip back in twenty-nine."

"And I wonder who let him in on that," Faolan said. His read on Rothstein detected something not quite kosher in the gloating. His opponent was overplaying his hand a little, but Faolan wasn't sure about his own cards yet. Time to decide: call, raise, or fold.

"Who told him is beside the point, though it wasn't me," Rothstein said with a hasty glance at Killian. "What is very much the point, O'Connor, is that I have taken over the administration of Mister Byrne's responsibilities, including you. If I allow you to continue living, you will have to do so as a Vampyr and that means you will be under my command. I want to emphasize that this is a very big if—"

"Balls," Faolan said, turning his back on Rothstein and sitting down in one of the sofa's matching lounge chairs.

Fuck it. Might as well go down like a man.

Rothstein drew himself up to his full five-nine. "What did you just say to me?"

Killian leaned forward on the sofa: interested or ready to attack?

"I said balls, as in you got some pair if you think you can sell me that bag of wooden nickels." He sat back, dug out his silver cigarette case, and offered Killian a Camel. Killian declined with a wave of his hand, the sheer physicality of his presence leaping the distance between them like electricity. Faolan lit up and took a long drag. "Byrne mentioned you guys coming into power a few months back," he said, addressing himself to Killian. "So I know you're too busy to fuck around with me unless you wanted to check me out for yourself and make the decision. It's up to you whether I live or die, so you're the one I'll be taking orders from if I get the nod."

Killian fought not to show any reaction, but poker just wasn't his game. His eyebrows twitched and he leaned back ever so slightly. "And if I tell you to do as Rothstein says?"

Faolan shrugged. "Still your orders, what do I care if you pass them through Rothstein? If he managed to convince you to put him in charge of your guys, I'll bet you anything you care to wager he's got a strong right hand making his decisions for him."

"Really? How can you be so sure?"

"'Cause when he was human, Arnold Rothstein did only two things well: making money and playing big shot. He ain't been a vamp long enough to learn new tricks."

That got a genuine laugh out of Killian, which made Rothstein furious.

"You've got some nerve pretending you know anything about me!" He strode over to Faolan's chair, trying to make him feel like a kid summoned to the principal's office. "Why, you're nothing but a two-bit hood yourself, O'Connor. A gun for hire who usually winds up killing the people he works for!"

Faolan just sat and smoked while Rothstein pointed at him like a sideshow attraction. "Mister Killian, I watched this man for years back when he worked for Diamond. He's the reason we *lost* Diamond, for God's sake! Jack treated him like a brother and this ungrateful little coward shot him while he slept so he could try to take over—but he couldn't even manage that and had to let Coll run things instead. You saw how that worked out. Luciano made the mistake of trusting this guy and was nearly stabbed and beaten to death for it. Not knowing any better, Luciano trusted him again and brought him into his organization as a hitter and O'Connor snitched on him from day one. Granted, he did so for us, but think of the mentality that can betray a friend so easily and often. Hell, I've even heard it rumored that he killed his own brother! His own flesh and blood! Sure, he talks a good game, but he's nothing but a conniving trigger with delusions of grandeur. Don't let him play you for a sucker, too, Darcy."

Faolan took his time finishing his cigarette, letting the new Reeve of New York City look him over while Rothstein condemned him. He hadn't realized there were rumors about his brother. The knowledge brought back unpleasant memories of Tom. Things he'd been forcing down, trying to forget.

"Well, what about it, lad?" Killian asked. "There any truth to Mister Rothstein's claims?"

There's a rule of poker that says: play your opponent, not your hand. In this case, his opponent was not Rothstein, but Killian. In almost any other situation, the smart course would have been to lie as convincingly as he could. If his read on Killian was correct, however, he was better off telling the truth.

"There's truth to every one of Mister Rothstein's claims," Faolan answered, stabbing out the remains of his Camel in the ash tray. "Just gotta understand he's still got a beef with me 'cause he's one of the guys I plugged—and his sainted Jack Diamond was the one who ordered him hit."

He turned to face Killian head-on, eye to eye, and ignored Rothstein's looming figure. "It ain't too thrilling to hear my life laid out like some Walter Winchell column, but I'm not gonna sit here and make excuses. Aside from the Charleston or jitterbug, the only thing I ever had a real talent for was a gun. I did what I did to earn a living, to help my friends and, yeah, sometimes I hit somebody on account of them betraying me or because they were planning to betray me. I got no apologies to make about what I've done."

Killian let an approving smile slip as he asked: "Your brother?"

Jesus Christ, Faolan thought, careful not to let anything show. *This guy figures killing my own brother for a mark of guts or determination or something. Why is it always like this?* A feeling of disgust rose up in him which he stomped down mercilessly. *'Cause the folks who want to do things the decent way got no use for a killer, that's why.*

Faolan shrugged. "He was a cop. He didn't approve of how I made my living and tried to blackmail me into quitting."

Killian's eyebrows shot up, but he nodded. "That's a man's way. See what needs to be done, do it, and fuck the personal sentiments. So, the idea of being a God-cursed blood-drinker doesn't disturb you, then?"

"I don't believe my ears," Rothstein grumbled. They both ignored him.

Faolan sat back. "If there's a Hell, then my stay was booked and paid for a long time ago. Besides, I got eyes. The need for full-time hitters is drying up and nobody's breaking my door down to put me in charge of any rackets. I'm on my way out, regardless of Charlie and his little grudge. Maybe Byrne told you already, maybe he didn't, but I pushed away everything else in my life to do this Dhampir thing for you and him—"

"Don't blame us just because your wife killed herself," Rothstein said with a sneer. "She probably couldn't stand—"

Faolan's fist landed square on Rothstein's jaw even before the Vampyr noticed him spring out of the chair. Suddenly on the carpet, Rothstein bared his extended canines just in time for Faolan to stomp Rothstein's face. Rothstein rolled and scrambled up—

But then Killian was between them: a wall of muscle and bone. Faolan sat back down with a shrug. Rothstein glared at Faolan, then Killian, then back again. "He struck me! That—that *Dhampir* lifted a hand to a Vampyr!"

"A fist, actually," Faolan interjected.

"You know the rules, Killian, his life is forfeit!"

"Arnold. Sit the fuck down," Killian said.

Looking miserable and furious, Rothstein slinked over to the leather armchair. Faolan lit another Camel as Killian turned back to him with undisguised approval.

"As I was saying," said Faolan, all innocence, "if you're not gonna take me up into the big time with you then I'd prefer the quick death here and now. But if you need people killed, then I'm your man."

Killian grinned with an almost obscene number of teeth. "Fay-o-lan: the wolf. You're well named, sir, and I do indeed have many people that need killing. To begin with, your old sparring partner the Dutchman has gained himself some out of town backers during his recent trip upstate. What do you say to starting with him?"

Gee, he'd only been waiting to settle up with old Dutch for half a decade, right? Faolan gave his new boss a matching grin. "I say if you line them up, I'll knock them down…"

Chapter Four

"We've got close to sixty Vampyrs living in this building," Frank explained as the elevator stopped on the sixty-second floor of the Empire State Building. "The fifty-eighth and fifty-ninth are living quarters. Fifty-nine's the executive suites, eight's the barracks. You're down there for now. Your stuff's already set up in your room."

"Nice digs?"

"It's a place to sleep. There's a common area for sitting and a couple small kitchens for warming up bottled blood."

They emerged into a wide hall with granite tile floors, dark wood paneling, and deco brass wall sconces that went with the sunburst theme on the closing elevator doors. Faolan noticed that no pillars, furniture, or alcoves lay between the elevator and the guard station forty feet down: they'd have no cover from the guards' fire if they were hostile.

"Bottled blood?"

"Just like in a hospital," Frank said. "There's a company run by some old-timer in England that sells it by the crate. Probably comes from orphans, dope fiends, and lunatics, but it's good for emergency rations." He looked at Faolan and smiled that creepy smile again. "Didn't think you'd get kids for dinner every night, did you?"

Faolan scowled as they hung a left at the guard station and headed for a huge set of ornate doors. "Anyplace around here I can get a whisky?"

"The Indigo Lounge on sixty-one is stocked with alcohol-saturated blood. Boss has some in his study, too, but I wouldn't ask unless he offers."

"No, I mean straight booze. We can't eat solid food, I get that, but if I can drink water, why can't I take some whisky with it?"

Frank did that smile again but, thank God, didn't glance his way. "You can try it, but I guarantee you won't like it. Dehydration is a big problem, so avoid alcohol and caffeine. We can drink small amounts of anything with high water content: weak fruit juices, lemonade, etcetera. Something about the fermentation of beers and ales make them bad for us. Seltzer and soda pop are also out 'cause of the carbonation. Milk's too thick, tends to curdle and you get cramps. Human blood is what your body needs. Anything else is for blending and shouldn't exceed a glass a night."

"Damn," Faolan said. "Was hoping I wouldn't have to give it all up."

Frank shrugged. "You'll probably find it doesn't taste the same to you now, anyway." He opened the huge doors, revealing a short vestibule and an enormous reception room all done up in reds. "Welcome to Hell's Waiting Room," he proclaimed, something about his timing or inflection making the line fall flat.

Faolan put on a smirk anyway and followed him in. The maroon carpeting, burgundy drapes, and cherry furniture with blood-red upholstery and brass accents should have been hideous. Somehow, it fell just to the wild side of tasteful.

"This is Night Blondie, the boss' receptionist," Frank said, pointing at the delicious young blond (dressed in a cherry red dress, no less) behind a circular desk that was just a sail away from being a boat. "Her twin, Day Blondie, handles Everett."

"Why not hire redheads?"

Frank stared at him. "Because that would be ridiculous."

"Is he serious?" he asked the girl whose name plaque read Rose. She smiled, but it was tight, and Faolan figured she cared for Frank's "humor" about as much as he did. She shrugged. "Nice place you got here," Faolan told her, just to say something.

"Thanks," she said, her smile warming a bit for him.

He smiled back and then walked past her, drawn to the windows. He wasn't too good with women. When he was serious, he scared them and when he tried to be clever, he came off like a heel. Colleen had been a once in a lifetime thing and he still couldn't say he understood why she'd loved him.

Still, even if he'd been the world's biggest skirt chaser, that girl couldn't compete with the view behind her. A fifty-foot row of glass panes displayed New York City spread out beneath him in all her evening finery. From sixty stories up, the city was an ocean of blinking, dancing, swirling lights in every color imaginable. Towering above it all, Faolan thought: *Yeah, this is what I want.*

He was home.

"Boss available?"

"Yes, Mister Giordano, he's with Mister Rothstein, Mister Devlin, and Mister Everett, but you can both go right in."

"C'mon, Faolan, don't want to keep him waiting."

Tearing himself away from the majesty of the city, he followed Frank through another pair of tall, ornate doors into the biggest office he'd ever seen. Hell, it was bigger than any office he'd even imagined.

The place could have been a church if it had some pews, but it didn't. The emptiness of the space contributed to the impression of vastness. It had a hammered tin ceiling and a swath of red carpet running the sixty feet of gleaming dark wood to where it became an area rug beneath the massive desk where Killian and two others stood gathered. Another fabulous night view, this one of Fifth Avenue, lay behind them.

To either side of Faolan, ten foot tall smoked glass panels grabbed his attention. There were six in all and they angled to create a narrowing funnel of glass that moved you, inexorably, to the desk. The first set was etched with perfect front views of Daniel Chester French's "Manhattan" and "Brooklyn" sculptures. Faolan recognized them from outside the Brooklyn Museum of Art: Manhattan on her throne, head high with a skyscraper crown on her head and winged orb in hand, her foot resting arrogantly upon a beautiful chest while his beloved hometown was represented as a maternal angel, a crown of laurels on her head and a book-reading child at her feet.

Following after Frank, he saw the similar etchings of St. Patrick's Cathedral, the Brooklyn Bridge, Lady Liberty, and the Empire State Building itself, all rendered with such loving care that they were like magical doorways to the place itself rather than just glass. As a rule, Faolan didn't care much for pompous displays of wealth and power, but this place was so bold that he couldn't help being awed. This wasn't an office: it was a throne room for the King of New York City.

It was everything he'd ever dreamed of attaining.

"Ah ha! Your timing is im-fucking-peccable," Killian bellowed when Faolan had made it about halfway down the runner. Grinning, the Reeve came around from behind a massive cherry desk and let Frank and Faolan finish their walk to him. "I had a hunch you'd pass the test early."

Faolan saw Rothstein glare at him before turning away. A lanky cowboy in black at the desk's corner, however, remained watchful.

"Well?" Killian asked Frank. In an ironic contrast to the rich surroundings, Killian was as underdressed as Faolan tonight, wearing a collarless shirt with the sleeves rolled up to his elbows, heavy workman's trousers held up by suspenders, and boots. With his barbershop mustache and black hair combed down to either side of his head, he could have stepped out of some Wild West daguerreotype.

Frank glanced back at Faolan and removed his hat. "Made the kid feel comfy, snapped his neck, and drank him."

Killian nodded, giving Faolan a thorough looking over. "Good man. It bother you, snuffing a kid?"

Faolan took a breath and decided to roll the dice. He needed a reputation as a straight-shooter. "A little bit, yeah."

Killian's eyes widened a tad. "Well, just so long as it stays a little, that's your own affair. Understand, I'm not a cruel man by nature, but it's a cruel life we inhabit in The Order. That test serves well to give me a man's measure. Take Frank, here: I knew he had brains from what Rothstein and Byrne told me, but what a fighter! Sure, he balled and screamed and pleaded the entire first night, but then he got real quiet and just sat."

Frank showed no reaction at all to Killian's recital. Faolan watched hard for one, but he might as well have been watching a mannequin.

"He sat there for a *week*. Seven full nights," Killian continued. Then he laughed and clapped Frank hard on the shoulder. "Why, we thought he'd up and died! No man before or since ever held out so long and I was on the edge of pronouncing the test done when, on the eighth night, he just tears the girl's throat out, drinks her to the dregs ... and sits back down."

You think snuffing kids shows guts? One day, I'm gonna make you pay for that kid. It was lucky for Faolan that Killian was too busy grinning admiration at Frank to see Faolan's eyes, since they might have given him away right then.

"Anyhow, they say babe's blood is more nutritious for one like you who's not yet taken the brand."

"Brand?" Faolan asked.

"In The Order," Killian said. "Back in the olden times, see, a young vamp took a brand over his heart as part of his initiation ceremony. Meant he was done learning the ropes and had his full citizenship. We don't have time for such niceties these days, so I consider you fully initiated by passing the test. That means it's your responsibility to abide by the rules, follow?"

Faolan nodded. "Got it."

"So, I hear you scuffed the play on Schultz," Rothstein said, inspecting his manicure.

He had to stop himself from rolling his eyes. "Anybody got a smoke?"

A rough-skinned, bearded fellow with an athlete's build hidden beneath an expensive blue suit rose from his chair. He wore his dark hair parted without oil and down to the tops of his shoulders. He held a half-eaten apple in one hand and used the other to produce a cigarette case of intricately carved ivory which also held a lighter. The carvings on the case looked Chinese to Faolan's eyes and were very beautiful.

"Thanks," Faolan said, lighting one and handing the case back.

"No trouble at all," the bearded man said, pocketing the case and smiling to reveal a golden tooth. He reached out and gave Faolan a firm shake with a hand that had seen its share of labor. "Since Mister Killian has opted not to perform the honors, I'll make my own introduction. I'm Nathaniel Everett, Mister Killian's Adjutor and Dhampir. I oversee the operation of this organization during daylight hours and would be most interested in hearing your assessment of the Schultz-Luciano situation."

"Don't you reproach me before others, you salty prig," Killian said, smiling as he hopped up onto his desk. "O'Connor, that's Everett—he's my chief lackey. The undertaker in the steel-toe shit-kickers there is Johnny Devlin," he nodded toward the cowboy, "my bodyguard."

Devlin nodded with a ghost of a smile and lounged his lanky six-foot frame against the desk with a distracted air that didn't fool Faolan one bit. Those green eyes were as cold as death itself and aware of every movement in the room.

Faolan returned his nod.

"If we're done with all the introductions and stalling for time?" Rothstein prompted.

Everett took a loud bite out of his apple and sat down on the arm of his chair, oblivious to Rothstein's disdainful gaze. Faolan's opinion of the Dhampir went up another notch.

He exhaled the smoke from his last drag and addressed himself to Killian and Everett. "First off, the hit on the Dutchman went off as well as could be expected under the circumstances."

Rothstein snickered. "Yeah, says you."

"He's dying, ain't he?" Faolan shot back.

"Dead, in fact," Everett said, swallowing the last of his apple. "We just received the word."

Faolan nodded. "Then Luciano and his pals already have everything that matters. Now you just have to deal with his organization."

"And Luciano's still controlled by Philadelphia," Rothstein said.

He looked the gambler's way for the first time. "Would you mind letting me tell my own fucking story, please? With Schultz gone, this Dewey still needs a big target to make his headlines. He'll go after Luciano and you guys don't need to lift a finger except to keep Philadelphia from solving his problems."

Killian got to his feet again. "Is this what you think or what you know?"

Faolan returned his smile. "I know, 'cause before I went down to pull Schultz's plug, I sent Dewey everything he needs to end Charlie's luck but good."

"When?" Rothstein demanded.

"Whenever Dewey decides the time is right," Faolan shrugged. "I'm sure you got enough connections to know when it happens."

"But why not kill Luciano now?" Killian asked.

Faolan took a drag. "This is better. Ties him up for maybe a year or more and drags his backers into wasting time and money trying to win a game you already rigged. Meanwhile, you get that time to set up his replacement."

Killian chucked, glancing at Rothstein. "Satisfied?"

Rothstein turned to Frank instead. "Costello. He'll have to be ready sooner than we thought."

"Of course," Everett said with a wry smile. "This could all become academic depending on the night's events."

"You talking about this big fight Frank mentioned?" Faolan asked.

Killian's grin returned. He came over and hugged his arm around Faolan's shoulder. "Ah, Faolan, what a moment you've chosen to make the cross to the night!"

Killian led him over to the desk and used his free arm to indicate the map spread across its surface as well as the spectacular view. "In only two hours' time, Vampyrs from Boston, Philadelphia, Providence, Baltimore, and any other arsehole from which those cocksuckers have obtained men will meet us in honest battle for the rule of this fine city. The battle will surely be pitched, but it will decide my standing as Reeve once and for all."

"Them other cities don't appreciate the change in management, eh?"

That won him a chuckle. "Pre-cisely. It was they who have brought this unjust war upon our doorstep, but tonight we end it. I've no doubt that this army I've assembled can obliterate any force those aged dandies can muster, whether twice or even four times our number! Happy Frank has devised a strategy that should bring us victory if you are, in fact, the man I've come to believe you to be."

"Really?" Faolan asked, casual, as Killian turned to examine him.

"Oh, yes, young wolf. You and I will be out in the very front of it."

Chapter Five

"Still can't believe we're having a vampire gang war at Coney Island," Faolan said as Killian's sixty-Vampyr army marched across Surf Avenue down West Sixteenth toward the world famous boardwalk.

Frank had explained how it made sense, of course. The boardwalk was nice and isolated from civilians this time of year and the police had been paid to disregard any complaints for the night, just in case. It was also big enough to hold the battle, accessible for both sides, and the sound of the waves made for a natural muffler.

Still, it felt a bit weird.

"Maybe the boss and the leader of the other gang can run the Horse Race to decide it," his swimming partner Rod suggested from behind him.

Faolan grinned. He remembered how the Steeplechase Horse Race had been one of Benny's favorites back when they used to come here as kids. Any summer day when they had a few bucks in their pockets they would take the subway in from Brooklyn or the paddlewheel steamer from Manhattan. He remembered how they used to shoot Rock-Paper-Scissors for who got the faster horse on the inside track and then race those mechanical ponies hard, pretending they were Tom Mix or Billy the Kid.

"Yeah, that would be something. Loser gets chased out through the Insanitarium," he added. That was always great, too, going down that big ramp onto the stage where clowns waited to blow the ladies' skirts up with air hoses.

He'd seen ladies panties for the first time that way, just before another clown zapped his ass with a cattle prod.

"Fuck that," Killian growled from beside him. The boss had insisted on leading the battle and now pulled on a pair of the strangest gloves Faolan had ever seen: rough leather with razor sharp thimbles attached to each finger and a strip of spikes sewn across the knuckles. He held his gleaming digits up for Faolan's admiration. "Been years since my little friends and I had us a good brawl. Had them made special after I saw this gang whore name of Hellcat Maggie using them to great effect against some Plug Uglies."

"Kind of messy for my tastes, though," Faolan told him.

Killian chuckled. "Well, naturally, you being a gunman. I've nothing against guns, myself, but they're not the best weapon against Vampyrs. Stop the heart beating or rip it out, separate the brain from the body, burn them with sun or flames: those are the only sure ways. When I make a kill, I want to see the man die before my eyes. So don't you forget you got that short sword on you for when your pop-gun runs dry. I expect to find it bloodied come the battle's end."

According to Frank, there had been an attempt at peacefully resolving this whole issue of New York's leadership, but Killian had blown that at the peace talks. Apparently, Killian had been offended by the Governor's attitude—this was the vampire who ran the entire East Coast—and insulted the fuck out of him right in front of all the other Reeves before storming out. Maybe Killian had thought that he was scoring points as a tough negotiator, being used to negotiating with other gang leaders, but it had produced declarations of war instead.

Then again, from what Faolan had seen so far, maybe that had been Killian's intent.

"What you carry, anyhow, O'Connor?" asked a deep Texas drawl off to the other side of Killian. Faolan saw Devlin glancing his way. "One of them shiny little mechanized Colts?"

"Not if I can help it," he said. "Inaccurate as all hell, the action's sticky, and the ejection's bad so they're prone to jamming. But I think you already know that."

"That's a fact, mister. Tried one of them somebitches once and that was all I needed. Got my Peacemakers and I have yet to encounter any man who can touch me."

"I rather like the new Colt, meself," Stebbins piped in with his bright Dublin accent. The short blond grifter walked on Faolan's other side. He'd introduced himself during the ride down and seemed a cheerful fella. "Used one for years and never a spot of trouble."

"Didn't ask your opinion, pimp," Devlin growled.

Stebbins wasn't a pimp by trade (though he had a reputation as a serious skirt hound), but his duties included maintaining a building full of Dhampir whores known as "The Doll House" which Killian had devised to make feeding easy. Strange as it seemed, the fast healing of Dhampirs made them useful as long-term blood donors because they recovered faster. Also, by using girls who were already whores, the higher pay and better accommodations were usually enough to make them overlook the whole vampire thing.

The small man flashed a nervous smile. "Right. Closed conversation, then. Sorry."

Faolan gave Stebbins a quick smile and then turned his attention to Devlin. Had to be careful how he did this next bit. He wanted to impress the man, not make an enemy of him. "Peacemaker's probably the best single-action revolver ever made, no argument. Reliable, easy to maintain, four-inch barrel for quick-drawing, and a range of about fifty feet."

"I've made shots at sixty, but you do know your guns," Devlin admitted. "However, I recall asking you a question."

Faolan drew his weapon of choice, handing it to Devlin butt-first. "Browning Hi-Power. It's nine-millimeter, a brand new model. All the stopping power of a forty-five caliber with terrific accuracy right out of the box and an effective range of eighty feet. Action's smooth, the ejection never jams, and the grip is comfy. Not to mention you cock it once and fire continuously."

"One shot's all I need most times. This is light, though, and it does indeed grip nice," Devlin remarked. "Still, this here holds nine or ten shots? I get twelve with my pair and I reload quick."

Faolan smiled. "I get thirteen. Double-line staggered. And I reload them all at once."

Killian chuckled. "I think he may have you there, Johnny."

Devlin said nothing for a few seconds and Faolan thought he'd lost him, but then the cowboy handed the gun back with a smile. "I'll see how it does tonight, but I may indeed give it a twirl. Just imagine the damage I could do with two of those..."

Faolan only noticed Steeplechase Park on their right because of the Thunderbolt's distinctive outline. The streets he remembered packed with people seemed too big without them. Desolate, empty space. Muted streetlights and wetly glistening shadows. Rows of empty stands and steel gates that rattled with every breath of wind. Over the rooftops, he saw his old friend the Wonder Wheel spread across the sky like a giant spider's web.

He imagined he heard the spirits of dead children—like Michael from the cell—running and playing here while no one else was around to bother them. He shook the thought away as the boardwalk and pier came into view before them. Enzo ran up to report.

"Well?" Killian demanded.

Dressed like a longshoreman, the curly-haired Sicilian fidgeted under his boss's stare. "No traps or ambushes waiting here, Mister Killian. Our guys kept watch all day and I been patrolling with fresh replacements since I got here after dark. The other side sent some of their people out to do the same, but I figured it would be better not to interfere with them, you know, so long as they was just watching."

"You figured?" Killian repeated and Enzo went pale. Then the boss glanced at Frank, who nodded, and Killian said, "Well, for once you figured right. Where are they now?"

Faolan caught the look and the encouraging smile that passed between Rod and Enzo before the latter spoke. "They headed up the pier when they spotted the tugboat and barge. That was about twenty minutes ago."

They continued forward, Enzo falling in alongside Devlin. That meant he was also a gunman.

"Fucking kidding me," Faolan muttered, squinting as if he was gonna see the end of the 1600 foot pier at night. Still, he thought he could make out a silhouette there past the lights. Maybe his Vampyr eyes were that good, after all. "A barge?"

"What did you think?" Frank asked. "A hundred and fifty vamps were gonna ride the subway through hostile territory? Nobody notices a barge from Jersey and, best of all, the winner gets an instant way to dispose of the remains."

"A hundred and fifty guys? They really bringing that many?"

"At least," Killian confirmed. "I've no doubt they grabbed every available vamp in the Northeast and made some new ones besides. Still not bad odds, though. Every one of us kills two or three of them and we'll win."

Of course, just as he said this, they emerged from the shelter of the buildings onto the open expanse of boardwalk and the chill of the wind bit into every exposed inch of skin. At eighty feet across and over three miles long, the boardwalk was bigger than most streets, but its proximity to the water and lack of any windbreaks made it a frigid place to be in the off-season.

The noise of the waves was like constant thunder.

"And it ain't a fit night out for man or beast!" Rod declared in an uncanny W.C. Fields that drew a few chuckles from their crowd.

"Form up," Frank called and the group just spread out a little, since they were all near their assigned places. They marched down the boardwalk like soldiers.

Looking down the pier, Faolan made out the opposing army heading their way, swarming across the boards like ants. Christ, that pier was at least sixty feet wide and they had it filled side-to-side and back hundreds more feet.

"Reckon at least two hundred, maybe more," Devlin said as if commenting on the weather.

Killian trembled with excitement. "Aye, this will be a fight worth remembering, then."

Faolan glanced to the other side where the entrance to the Steeplechase pavilion stood. From signs everywhere, the park's mascot Smiley watched: a grinning loon whose forty-four teeth took up the lower half of his face, his hair was parted like Killian's except for the way it curled up at the sides like devil's horns. Tonight he looked neither silly nor benevolent, but like some rapacious cannibal god awaiting sacrifice.

The front line crossed onto Steeplechase Pier.

A battle cry went up from the other Vampyrs, a loud and terrifying sound that drowned out even the crashing of the waves. They charged.

A wave of reaction went through their group and Faolan heard muttering and grumblings as men hesitated or tried to ready weapons. Killian caught it and yelled, "Steady, lads! Step forward, but slowly! Let the bastards come to us! Keep to the plan if you can and stay together, but remember chiefly that you fight for your lives tonight! There'll be blood aplenty for the victors!"

The tense anticipation crackled around them all like static electricity, getting their blood up. Faolan smelled the anxiety turn to eagerness as the tinkling of swords, knives and brass knuckles mingled with the thumping of clubs and the clicks and twangs of pistols being readied. A popping of gunshots drifted across the distance to them as the charging mass surged closer.

Faolan settled into his killing groove.

He draws his Browning from its shoulder rig with the mindless ease of long practice, thumbing off the safety and pulling back the slide to chamber a round while scanning the front line of charging Vampyrs for his first target.

"Hold here!" Frank calls back and their gang shuffles to a halt.

Faolan notes that Frank stopped them from going beyond the expanse of the two-tone beach. Beside him, Stebbins moves over to the railing, giving himself more clearance to fire as well as providing multiple escape routes: this and his tense posture tell Faolan that the grifter is not experienced in large-scale gun battles and will probably retreat to safer ground at the earliest opportunity.

Faolan moves three steps closer to Stebbins to give him and Frank room to fire. On the other side of Killian, he sees Devlin, Enzo, and a gorilla named Little also spreading out.

He takes aim at the first man he's targeted as the charging, firing army closes to one hundred feet ... ninety...

Faolan fires, smiling when his target runs into the bullet's range. Sternum shattered, the vamp staggers and gets run over by the vamps behind him.

But Faolan's already shifted aim and shoots his next target right through the heart.

Stebbins blasts away as fast as his finger can pull the trigger. His target and the vamp behind fall.

His gun making hollow pops to his ringing ears, Faolan shatters a Vampyr's teeth at seventy feet.

Frank fires a .44 S&W with deliberate accuracy, taking a head here, a knee there...

Aim, fire. Faolan puts another one down.

Little just points two Colts and spits lead willy-nilly into the screaming horde.

Faolan's Browning parts a vamp's hair about an inch too low as bullets fall like hail around him.

Devlin punches holes through Vampyr faces one after another, knocking them down like tin cans on a fence.

Faolan makes another head-shot, already picking out his next target.

A shot whips past his cheek, striking the vamp behind him.

Stebbins goes empty. Without a moment's hesitation, he runs to the back of the group.

Enzo fires his Colt 1911A with rapid precision until an enemy bullet slams into his stomach. He doubles over, but raises his arm to continue firing.

They're almost close enough to spit at now, so close Faolan could make these shots blindfolded: they may be shooting back at him, but they're bouncing up and down and he's steady as rock. At this range, many of his shots are punching through one head and hitting the guy behind in a two-for-one deal.

To his left, Frank goes empty. The revolver clunks to the boards and Frank just stands there, waiting for death.

Faolan fires, feels a shot splinter wood near his feet, fires back and fires, fires, fires. His gun and his body and his mind are one lethal mechanism: his eyes see, his heart beats, his hand twitches, and someone drops.

The last of the enemy gunners is down, but behind him come knives and swords, row after row less than ten feet away.

Faolan fires. Head shot. Only one bullet left.

Chapter Six

"They'll put their tougher maniacs out front to charge our guns," Frank explained back on the bus as they made their way to Coney Island. "Their fiercest, most experienced fighters will be at the back to push the charge and—they think—slaughter whatever exhausted vamps survive the fodder waves. The fodder is the new vamps they'll stick in the middle: just Created, starving for blood, and given the choice to fight or die. Once you sharpshooters take out their front line, Little and I will break up the fodder some more with the B-A-Rs and everybody else goes in tight. Split them up and chop them down while the sharpshooters get to the back to pick off stragglers and help out where they can."

"Now!" Frank shouts. He reaches under his overcoat as the mob of enemy Vampyrs rush closer.

Keeping to the plan, Faolan darts to the side and follows the route Stebbins took moments before. He considers firing his last shot into some approaching vamp, but decides it's smarter to keep it in the chamber while he reloads. Moving backwards, he watches Frank move to the rail and unleash a full-auto storm of incendiary rounds from the cut-down Browning Automatic Rifles he and Little hid under their coats.

No artillery, machine guns, rifles, or shotguns: those were the terms both sides agreed to for the fight on account of noise. But, if they win, nobody will be alive to cry foul. If they lose, it won't matter. Faolan has no idea where they got hold of these military armaments and really couldn't care less. Though the BAR's magazine only holds twelve rounds, the effect is greater than all their pistol shots combined. The distinctive sound of the weapon stampedes through the echoing confines of the pier, slowing the opposing army as the artillery rounds punch through the front line, then the men behind them, and into the vamps three or four rows deep. Some of these last victims also suffer having their clothes catch fire from the incendiary rounds.

The moment the BAR's spray ceases, Killian and his sword-, knife-, and club-wielding army surges forward to sever heads, gore eyes, and stab hearts.

Faolan exchanges clips, watching as Frank does the same on his machine gun. Before the other man is finished, though, an enemy vamp charges him. Faolan has one shot, but Frank's large figure impedes his aim. Stebbins, Devlin, and Enzo all have their attention elsewhere.

Cool as a cucumber, Frank jams the heated barrel of his Browning into the enemy vamp's eye! The vamp stumbles back and collapses, screaming. Frank finishes reloading.

For the moment, all the fighting is going on further up the pier. Standing here, taking potshots at unsuspecting targets from a distance isn't going to build Faolan's reputation at all. He needs to get involved, needs to make a difference. This is a crucial battle, who knows when such an opportunity will come around again?

He scans for a target when movement on the water catches his attention. Could those be boats? Rushing to the railing, he looks down at the beach below and sees two small boats landing. They are the type the gangs used to use for rum running, but these hold men: six to a boat, all dressed in black and carrying what appear to be Thompson submachine guns.

They're gonna sneak around to the boardwalk and massacre us from behind. And if there's two more boats landing on the other side ... twenty-four guys firing full auto...

Firing down on them is out of the question. He'd never get them all before they took him out. He rushes up to where Frank fires a stream of bullets into a group of charging attackers.

"Frank! Frank!" He touches Frank's shoulder and jumps back to be recognized when the big man whips around. Rather than waste time and breath when the bigger vamp probably can't hear him anyway, Faolan just points beachside.

Glancing down, Frank takes stock of the situation and shouts over the din of battle and tide: "Get Little and Enzo down the other side with Devlin covering them! Leave Stebbins where he is! Then come back and cover me!"

Faolan nods, dashing around behind the fighting. One big vamp wielding a meat cleaver comes at him. Faolan puts a round between his beady eyes and keeps going, reloading his magazine and cocking the slide by habit.

He passes Stebbins, who still looks nervous as all hell when he glances at Faolan, but at least he's putting the bullets where they need to go. Faolan briefly wonders how the guy gets such reliability out of his Colt, but doesn't pause.

Enzo and Devlin both choose their shots well, picking from groups of enemy vamps who are trying to overpower one of their guys. Enzo's wound is healing and Devlin, who also looks to have taken a hit or two, covers him while he reloads. As Faolan hurries toward them, he looks for Little and sees the large vamp being mobbed during a reload.

"Little!" he cries for the benefit of Enzo and Devlin. The pair punch holes in the attacking group, but there are too many of them. Even as he aims, Faolan recognizes the futility. They want Little's BAR out of the picture and are willing to sacrifice ten men to do it.

He fires anyway, taking out the machete-wielding thug who holds Little's decapitated head aloft.

What now? It will take too long to fight through that crowd and recover the BAR before dispatching the gunners to the beach. Assuming the BAR is even in any shape to be used. Fuck it. Little's gone. The BAR's gone. They have to stop those beach landers.

"Devlin! There's machine gunners on the beach!" he shouts, getting the gunfighter's undivided attention. "Frank says to take Enzo and stop them! I'll get Stebbins to give you cover!"

Devlin and Enzo move to the railing. Spotting their targets, they fire a shot before leaping down, probably to their death. Faolan turns to find Stebbins already watching and gives him a few quick signals. Stebbins nods and hurries to the railing as Faolan rushes back to the other side, where Frank has already jumped down to the beach.

He expects to find Frank laying low, awaiting his arrival, but the big fucking loony's charging the guns! The landers take cover behind their boats, but Frank's high-caliber rounds have already shredded the first craft and a couple of the men. They know Frank's ammo is limited and are hoping to wait him out.

Faolan takes aim just as Frank's BAR goes empty and the first lander rises, Tommy gun ready. Faolan's shot blows the left side of his forehead away, leaving four defenders behind the first boat and six behind the second one.

Two more get up just as their companion collapses and Frank runs right toward them. *Dive, you fucking schmuck! You know I'm here now, so drop and reload!*

Running faster than a man his size should be capable of, especially across sand, Frank makes it within ten feet of his adversaries before one of the landers fires a burst into his chest.

Fucking suicidal—

But Frank doesn't stop. He doesn't even stagger. Still running full-bore, he leaps over the boat's hull and buries the barrel of his BAR into his assailant's chest as he tackles him.

The men in the second boat scramble up and make for the boardwalk, but Faolan changes their minds by putting shots into the first and second guys to step away from the boat. The rest rush back, dragging their wounded companions.

To Faolan's surprise, Frank's not dead yet. Rolling beneath his opponent, Frank manages to get his hands on the Thompson and fires it from the ground. The others dive away while Frank bites the other vamp and drinks from him.

Faolan splits the head of one of the divers, causing more panic among the remaining vamps. Frank rises, holding the body of his meal in front of him for a shield, the BAR still swinging from his chest like a gruesome pendulum, and one of the landers obligingly fires a burst into the unfortunate vamp.

Faolan puts a bullet through the lander's nose.

The men behind the second boat divide their fire between Frank and Faolan. Faolan ducks behind a post as the .45 caliber ammunition splinters wood in a ten foot radius of where he stands. He peeks out as soon as the shower stops and sees Frank firing back with a Thompson on each arm.

The last vamp from the first boat makes the mistake of trying to run for the second boat when his mates started shooting. Frank cuts him down by the time he makes it halfway.

As soon as Frank runs out of bullets—the landers are using the standard 30-round magazines rather than the famous but awkward hundred-round drums—Frank drops the Tommys and picks the pockets of the fallen for spare clips.

That's Faolan's cue. As soon as the last vamps poke their heads up from behind that Swiss cheese boat of theirs, Faolan puts a shot through one of them. He fires another two rounds into the boat just to keep them down and his slide pops back to indicate his gun's empty status. As he digs into his coat pocket for a full clip, he watches Frank fire a burst from a fresh Thompson to cover himself as he drags one of his kills around the other side of the boat for another little snack.

Jesus, that's disgusting, Faolan thinks, slapping his new clip in and chambering. *Eating our enemies like some kind of fucking island cannibals.*

The bullet whizzes past his head, missing his nose by a good six inches, but it makes him jump to the side—

Which allows the Bowie knife to whistle through his former space rather than slash open his neck. He jumps back again and points his Browning at the ugliest, boniest, and buggiest looking motherfucker he's ever laid eyes on. The guy's a skeleton with dirty skin stretched over him: he has no visible hair and wears no shirt, so you can count his ribs above his indentation of a gut.

Faolan fires.

Bony dodges by turning sideways. Peeling his lips back to grin with brown teeth, he swings inhumanly fast with his open hand, knocking the Browning out of Faolan's grip. The pistol bounces off the pier railing and falls down to the beach. Bony swipes the knife again and Faolan jumps, but this time it slices open his arm.

Then a bullet punches through one side of the shriveled ribcage and out the other. Bony flinches and snaps his eyes to the direction of the bullet. It's enough distraction for Faolan to yank the gladiator sword he was given for backup out of his belt as Stebbins appears in his peripheral vision, Colt in hand.

Bony circles, forcing Faolan to block Stebbins' shot with his body, and then comes in for a slash at Faolan's belly. Rather than try to dodge or block with his sword, Faolan steps into the attack and brings the sword down.

Bony ducks out to the left, away from Stebbins, and manages to give Faolan a good stab to the kidney as he twirls away. But Faolan cuts his swing left to follow him—in a move not unlike swinging a baseball bat—and chops off his business arm.

Bony screams, slumping against the railing and clutching at the bleeding stump. Stebbins comes around to finish him, but Faolan stops the grifter with a look. Eyes darting, Bony searches for someplace to run even as Faolan hacks the thick blade into the junction of his neck and shoulder. Blood spurting in thick, syrupy gouts, Bony collapses and tumbles through the bottom of the railing and drops to the sands below.

Oh, well, fuck it. He wasn't about to drink from that disgusting bastard, anyway.

Looking down to the beach, he notices that Devlin and Enzo have joined Frank in mopping up the remaining landers. That explains Stebbins' presence.

"How did you guys take out the ones on the other side so fast?" he asks, clutching his kidney wound.

Stebbins lets out a nervous laugh as he reloads his Colt. "Surprisingly easy, as it happened. Buggers was already halfway to the boardwalk when we opened up, so they had no cover at all. Picked them off like pigeons, we did."

Faolan studies the dark sand below, but doesn't see his Browning even with his swell new Vampyr eyes. *Fuck!* "So, what was the big idea of throwing that bullet past my head, anyhow? Don't get me wrong, I appreciate the warning, but you could have just shot the fucker."

"Well, uh," Stebbins says, flashing a sheepish smile. "I-I was shooting at him, you see. I missed. Sorry."

Faolan sighs. "Fucking Colts."

Looking around, he's surprised by how far down the pier the fighting has moved. He and Stebbins stand beyond the furthest outskirts. Within its area, however, the fighting is still brutal and intense:

A 280 lb. former wrestler called Cuddles presses an opponent into the railing, crushing the guy's skull between his meaty hands, while another vamp whacks his back with a baseball bat to no effect.

The bantam-weight boxer, Daniels, smashes his brass knuckles into a vamp's jaw and hits a second attacker with a left jab to the gut before a third guy jumps him from behind with a piano-wire garrote. The other two rush back in and all three grab themselves a vein.

Ed "Crowbar" Charnas, a former strikebreaker who now oversees Killian's manufacturing and labor interests, pushes an enemy vamp to the ground with his foot and employs his namesake weapon as a fish-hook, tearing the skin from half of his opponent's skull before bashing said skull in with the downswing.

Faolan spots Rod emerging from the middle of the throng, dueling with a pair of enemy swordsman. Not only does the guy look like a movie star, but he swash-buckles like one, too! He whips his marine dress sword around in a blur of motion, driving his opponents back with a tireless hail of full-strength attacks. He's also grinning like a kid playing pirates.

As Faolan watches, a third vamp breaks from the crowd to come at Rod's back. He's just about to tell Stebbins to put a bullet in the guy when Rod spins and jumps into the air to deliver a kick to the vamp's chin! Before Faolan can wonder what the hell kind of move that was, Rod lands with perfect poise and runs one of his opponents through as the guy tries an attack. The other moves to Rod's side and tries to take advantage of the fact that Rod's sword is now stuck in his friend's heart. The guy comes in for a head strike, but Rod dodges, knocks the guy's sword aside with his bare hand, kicks him in the chest, pulls his sword free, and slashes the guy's throat open in *one smooth series of motions*!

Then, without so much as a pause to catch his breath, Mister Spectacular chases his would-be backstabber back into the fray.

"That Mister Chambers is something else, eh?" Stebbins asks, echoing his thoughts.

"Rod Chambers? No way that's his real name," Faolan says.

Stebbins gives him a queer look. "Sure it is. Navy man, he was. Says he was stationed in the Far East for a time. Good mate to have at your back."

"It's a put-on. You're talking to a guy once bought hotdogs from Cary Grant at Nathan's when he was called Archie Leach."

Just then, he notices Killian leap onto the back of a giant vamp from the other side and gouge his eyes out with those hellish gloves. The giant bucks him, but the boss digs his claws into the giant's shoulders and sinks his teeth into his neck. The giant grabs at him, dropping to his knees, but Killian's on like a tick. That's when three other vamps come out of the crowd with knives and bury them in Killian's back and sides.

Killian stops drinking long enough to cry out and smash in the teeth of one of his assailants with his elbow, but the other two throw him to the deck, daggers high. More of their friends come from the crowd to join in.

Back when they were in the Five Points Gang together, Charlie Luciano told Faolan that he was the only Irishman he'd ever met who schemed like a Sicilian. Charlie meant it as a compliment. Faolan's reminded of that compliment now as he takes a second to decide whether he should let Killian die. What will do him the most good right now and in the immediate future, Killian or no Killian? In the split second it takes his mind to ask the question, he realizes his position in the gang isn't stable enough yet. He's got a reputation with Killian and a basic understanding of how the man operates. With Killian gone, who knows what could happen? Better to be the guy who saves the boss, the man the boss comes to trust above everybody else.

The pain from his wound has faded to a background ache, so he should be able to move okay. He'd rather have his Browning, but the sword in his hand will just have to do.

As he takes off at a run, he hears Stebbins yell after him, "What're you doing? They'll be bringing the Tommy's 'round in a tic!"

Exactly. Not much glory to be had when you're just one among many packing superior firepower.

He lets loose a battle cry of fury and exhilaration as he gets within striking distance of the group, just to make one of the fuckers turn. He takes a page from Rod's book and kicks the first vamp dead in the balls before bringing the gladiator sword down onto the back of his neck—
thwack!

The sword takes that head off with surprising ease and the strength of Faolan's swing jams the point into the seam between two of the boards.

"Ah, fuck!"

Two more vamps come at him: a shrimp with a dagger and a gorilla with an ax. As the shrimp darts in with his dagger, Faolan yanks the sword free and gets it up in time to deflect the first swipe. He swings wide, making both the shrimp and his gorilla partner retreat back a few steps. That's when the pair start playing the old circle-in-opposite-directions game.

The trick here is to move on one of them before they can fully synchronize their efforts. Most would think going for the shrimp is the smarter option: he's quicker but weak and you can probably take him out in the time it takes the big lummox to come to his rescue, right?

Faolan's not fooled. The shrimp is a distraction. He'll feint and dodge you right onto the chopping block if you let him. Sword raised to chest level, Faolan rushes the gorilla in the clown suit. Like magic, the gorilla snaps into motion and deflects Faolan's thrust with a one-handed swing of his ax. Prepared for the deflect, Faolan whips the sword back quicker than his opponent can bring back that ax and hacks the gorilla's leg to the bone.

He jumps sideways as the gorilla lashes at him with the ax, bringing his blade up to his shoulder and spinning just in time to catch the shrimp coming up for a back-stab. Too close to get away, the shrimp makes the only move available and tries to stab him.

"Sa-wing batter, batter," Faolan says as the thick blade jams itself between two of the shrimp's ribs and deflates a lung. Yanking the blade out, he sees the gorilla limping their way and hauls the shrimp up by his jacket. Not easy while holding a sword, but the shrimp don't weigh much. He throws the shrimp at the gorilla full-force and waits to see what the gorilla does.

Unable to dodge because of his leg and more interested in seeking revenge than helping his partner, the gorilla knocks the shrimp aside with his free arm and does his best to keep his ax ready. So, when Faolan rushes at him with a high feint, he's still able to give a good swing back—but that's okay, because now he's badly balanced. When Faolan drops flat on his back and kicks his knees, the gorilla can't keep from falling right onto Faolan's waiting sword.

He rolls out, of course, before the gorilla finishes making his way down the blade and makes use of the handy ax to decapitate the gorilla before retrieving his sword.

Sword in one hand and ax in the other, he charges back to the crowd.

There's a nice dog-pile, but with enough wrestling going on to make him think Killian's still alive. Not having much experience with axes, Faolan just buries his in the head of the first vamp he comes upon.

This causes a second vamp to raise his head, so Faolan chops it off with the sword.

Two vamps who were trying to hold Killian down leap up to fight. Faolan runs the first one through the heart before he can get his weapon out and Killian trips the other guy by accident while he thrashes with his remaining two foes. With his sword stuck in the other guy, Faolan just grabs the tripped vamp in a headlock, punches him a couple times to stun him, and breaks his neck, paralyzing him.

Killian and his two remaining attackers are thrashing around on the planks like rabid dogs and Faolan considers taking a moment to indulge in his first taste of Vampyr blood. But then he spots Rod heading his way with the obvious intention of helping out. Dropping the paralyzed vamp, Faolan points urgently at some random group of vamps and waves him on. Rod nods, giving him a grin and a big thumbs-up, and charges into the fray.

Damned if he's gonna let Mister Hollywood steal his credit.

Pulling his sword out of the now-dead vamp, he spots an opening and stabs one of Killian's attackers through the back. Before Faolan can even think of finishing him off, Killian drags himself and his remaining opponent to their feet and Faolan is too stunned to move.

The boss of New York is a living nightmare from Hell itself: he wears little more than bloody rags and is missing chunks of flesh from perhaps a dozen spots on his body. Both ears have been torn off and one of his eyes is pulped. There's even a dagger sticking out from his gut, but the inferno of energy within hasn't dampened a bit.

Punching one of his claw-gloves into the throat of his attacker, Killian pushes the vamp's jaw back with his other hand and *pulls*—ripping the guy's breast-bone out!

Not completely, of course, and that's the worst part. It dangles from the guy, dripping little bits of bone and guts and the poor bastard shrieks like nothing Faolan's ever heard. Mouth wide, Killian jams his face into the vamp's open chest and feasts.

"Life is different here, Faolan. We have to be different."

Swallowing his revulsion, Faolan pulls his wounded vamp up to his knees. When Killian pulls his face out and throws his meal aside, Faolan cleaves the vamp's head from his body and jogs over to the boss. Killian leaps at him, knocks his sword aside, grabs his throat, and draws back his clawed fingers for a strike—

"Boss, it's me! Faolan!"

Killian's intact eye focuses and examines him for a second before his hand lets go. "Well, what are you standing around waiting for, a fucking medal?"

"Came to see if you was okay is all."

"I feel positively capital!" the walking slaughterhouse roars.

"Well, uh, you got a knife in your gut there, boss."

"Oh? So I do." He pulls it out, glances around at the fighting still taking place, and turns back. "So, lad, what do you say we get us a few good kills in while there's still men willing to fight back?"

In his killing groove, he always assumes he's going to die. Years ago in the Five Pointers, it was a way to combat his fear by accepting his worst fears as fact. Now it's become a part of him and—for just a second—he always feels a tiny prick of disappointment when he finds he's survived another battle.

Faolan forces a smile and readies his sword. "Sounds like fucking Christmas to me."

He gets a big, blood-stained grin for that and they head for the biggest knot of enemy vamps they can see.

The man said it's a different life here and yet, somehow, it all just feels so familiar.

Chapter Seven

He ended up the hero of the battle, publicly proclaimed by Killian with the whole gang of cannibalizing Vampyrs as witnesses. He even got presented with two untouched enemy vamps for his first taste of "the gods' nectar" as Killian called it. It felt thick, like trying to drink a glass of maple syrup, and had an unpleasant bite to it like strong cough medicine. He'd been told Vampyr blood was more concentrated, had more energy and nutrients in it, and made you stronger. He drank both guys down to the dregs while everybody cheered.

Unpleasant or not, it was the taste of victory and Faolan intended to get used to it.

It was Frank who got him named hero, though the slaughtering they had done together at the battle's end might have already put Killian in a mind to do it. When the boss asked for reports of extraordinary feats that should be recognized, Frank came forward and stated that Faolan had saved the battle for them. With his trademark monotone, he went on to explain how Faolan's spotting of the machine gunners and immediate understanding of their tactical significance had kept Killian's forces from being massacred. Turned out, Frank had never spoken up for anyone before.

Hard to believe, him being such a people person.
* * * * *
"I always wanted to be a Wild West outlaw," Faolan said.

The faces watching him around the table all seemed to get the idea to smile at the same time and, likewise, the urge to try to repress it without success. Enzo broke first, no surprise there, and Rod followed before Devlin finally allowed his lips to quirk up.

"I'm serious," he continued. "I watched all them cliffhangers when I was a kid and read every dime novel about cowboys I could get my hands on. Me and Benny even used to practice our quick draws together and patrolled the street vendors we collected protection from like we was town sheriff and deputy."

Devlin sipped from a glass of bourbon-laced blood. "Ever' one of them pictures I seen was nothing but a pack of horseshit. Never once in my life did I see fellas wearing them kind of dude outfits outside of a Buffalo Bill show. And that stand-and-draw in the middle of the street nonsense..."

"What?" Enzo said. "Guys never really did that?"

Devlin gave him a look like he'd grown a second head. "Do you? It's a pure invention of novelists. You stood still when you shot, sure enough, 'cause most of them guns weren't accurate to any distance, but when you went about shooting a man, you did it same as you might today. You get the drop on the some-bitch and you put lead in him. Come up in a gunfight, it was accuracy and steadiness that counted, not speed. All that fast-draw nonsense, why I can't tell you how many times some little cocksucker's made me put a bullet in his head by drawing on me in jest."

The gunfighter turned back to Faolan, raising his glass in salute. "You did some fine shooting tonight, O'Connor. You got a steady hand under fire and might have made yourself a name in the old days."

Faolan grinned, feeling almost bashful. How often in his childhood had he dreamed of meeting a real, live Old West gunfighter? If he could get this guy to switch over to his side, the things they could accomplish. Not to mention how much he'd love to sit around swapping stories with someone who could really understand the way he felt sometimes.

Rod and Enzo seconded Devlin's opinion.

"Well, thanks, guys. That means a lot."

"It's not a compliment I bestow lightly, to be sure." Devlin tossed the rest of his drink back and grabbed for the bottle.

Did he feel it, too? That inexpressible sense of letdown after the high of the kill? The isolation from everyone around you, like you were watching life from inside a glass box that you carried with you everywhere? Did Devlin understand? Faolan suspected he did.

This wasn't the right time to have that talk, however.

"Thanks for getting my gun back, too," he told Enzo just to move the conversation in another direction.

Enzo shrugged. "Don't mention it."

Faolan and Devlin sat on a banquette, Rod and Enzo in chairs, just a bit away from the main entrance in what they called the Indigo Lounge. It took up nearly half of the sixty-first floor of the Empire State Building and, while not as big as the Savoy or as fancy as some places he'd been in, it had style to spare. Midnight blue carpeting covered the floor and continued in the heavy velvet drapes that blocked out the building's many windows. Silk wallpaper in indigo matched the upholstery, but the tables and dance floor were glossy blond oak accented with silver.

"So, Rod, they teach you them fancy moves in the Navy?" Faolan asked.

Rod flashed his boyish grin and tapped off his cigar in the nearby ashtray. "Not hardly. I ended up in Hong Kong for most of my enlistment. I was a Marine, so I was ashore more than most guarding warehouses for American companies while our ship protected the trade routes. This was a few years before the Boxer Rebellion, you understand."

"Wait," Faolan said. "I didn't think any of you guys went that far back aside from Devlin."

Rod nodded, but it was Enzo who sat forward and said, "Well, see, a couple guys like me, Rod, and Everett the Dhampir are hold-overs from the earlier ... uh—"

"Administration," Rod supplied.

So that explained it. Faolan hadn't been able to figure how the hell a couple of Happy Jacks like these could make it through Killian's recruitment program.

"As I was saying," Rod continued. "These warehouse workers were a big mix of races and nationalities and once I started to learn a little Chinese, I got friendly with a few of them, too—"

"What in the world you want to get friendly with a chink for?" Devlin asked, clearly not enthralled by Rod's tale. "Ain't nothing worthwhile gonna come out of one of them."

"Afraid I have to disagree with you there, Mister Devlin," Rod said, either not noticing or ignoring the edge in the gunfighter's tone. "They have a very interesting way of looking at the world if you're willing to forgive some of their more non-Christian notions. Now, I'm not saying I subscribe to all or even most of it, but the effectiveness of their unarmed fighting techniques is obvious. Any people who can develop such—"

"All them girlie jumps and chorus-line kicks help you fend off a bullet?" Devlin sneered, taking another drink.

Faolan saw how things were heading and decided to try his hand at peacemaking. "Maybe this ain't the right place for a philosophical discussion, Rod. But I'd be interested in taking it up again some other time. Maybe you could show me some of them moves."

Rod glanced at Devlin for a second, then smiled like nothing had happened and agreed. Enzo nodded. His smile a little less enthusiastic than his partner's.

Everybody was spread out in little buddy groups at tables, the radio lounges, the card room, the billiard room, or at the bar. Over mounted speakers, Benny Goodman and his orchestra played on the "Let's Dance" broadcast, but nobody was taking the hint. The place deserved a live band and a more swinging crowd, but otherwise it was a pretty swell joint.

"So, Rod," Faolan said, just for conversation. "You like this jazz music?"

Rod finished his drink. "It's not bad. I prefer John Phillip Sousa, but this is pleasant enough."

"I like it," Enzo added. "I listened to the opera and Italian singers a lot growing up, but I like dancing to this hot stuff."

Rod nodded. "Good point. Nothing better for a night on the town."

"Show tunes," Devlin said, almost to himself. "Them old minstrel shows. Don't cotton much to this race music."

And that brought another awkward silence. Faolan took a puff on his cigar, adding to the room's general haze, and glanced over a few feet to where Killian's group sat at a set of chairs in the corner. Rothstein, Frank, and Everett were all there with him, discussing the ramifications of the night's victory. The party wouldn't kick into high gear until Stebbins got here with the girls. Until then, the place could pass for a high society gentlemen's club if you ignored the absence of true gentlemen.

Just then, the doors opened and a flood of girls poured in, dressed for a party. They came in all flavors of beautiful: blonde, brunette, red-haired, black-haired, white, Chinese, Negro, Latin, Italian, Irish, Jewish, French, English, Southern, short, tall, and medium-sized. The visible ages ranged from barely-out-of-school all the way up to mature ladies.

Turning to look around the frosted glass screen that separated the bar section, Faolan saw that an equal inundation of women were entering from those doors. Easily enough for every vamp in the place to take two.

"About time," Rod said. "I was beginning to think I'd have to drag one of you guys into the closet."

Enzo giggled. "You know I like you as a friend and all, but—"

"See, that's where the Navy training comes in," Faolan said, getting laughs from all.

A pack of the women headed toward them and Rod, Enzo, and Faolan rose to greet them. Devlin remained glued to his seat, bottle in hand and eyes narrowed like he was anticipating an assassination attempt. It was an idea Faolan had toyed with years before, since an attractive female could get close to people in a way no man could, but Devlin was in a bad position to go for his guns.

A petite Italian girl with a head of curls down to her shoulders and the biggest brown eyes this side of Betty Boop made straight for Enzo and slipped her arms around his. "Hey there, kiddo."

Enzo's face went red, but he grinned while Cupid sucker-punched him. "Hi, Angie."

After introducing Angie around, the pair drifted away toward a private booth.

Like the others, Faolan was all spiffed up for the party. Most of the physical side-effects of his Creation had smoothed out and he'd even put some oil in his hair, despite the fact it made his scalp itch like mad. He looked about as good as possible for him and still couldn't hold a candle to Rod. Suave as a prince, Mister Hollywood greeted those he knew and met the few he didn't, kissing the backs of hands like an expert. The women waited with hopeful smiles until Rod selected a perky, busty blond and an elegant French redhead in her thirties.

Interesting mix, Faolan noted as the trio took their places: Rod in his seat, the blond in his lap, and the redhead perched on the wide armrest with her arms around him. They were cozy as old friends in moments.

Meanwhile, the other women turned their best professional smiles on him and Devlin.

"Any of you new?" the gunfighter asked, finishing another glass. There was a careful slowness to his words that made Faolan suspect he was a little drunk.

A wisp of a blond with skin that matched her ivory dress raised her hand and took a demure step forward.

"Well, get on over here then, girl," Devlin drawled, patting his leg. The girl sidled over with just a trifle of uncertainty and made herself comfortable.

Looking over the rest, Faolan just couldn't find any desire in him at all. Usually, surviving a fight made him randy as a goat. His blood was going and, after that weird depression, he always wanted to celebrate being alive. Maybe it had something to do with becoming a Vampyr.

"Sorry girls," he said with an awkward shrug. "I just don't seem to have no appetite."

After assuring them he was serious and sitting back down, they broke up and headed for different parts of the club. Glancing over, he watched Devlin's girl ask and receive the gunfighter's name and was struck by her resemblance to his wife Colleen.

Just for an instant, the memory returned: a bathtub of blood surrounding a face in peaceful repose as her golden waves drifted out around her like the once-white wedding dress she wore.

He stared at the carpet. *That's all in the past, so fucking forget about it already.*

"Haven't lost your stomach yet."

He looked up at Rod. "Huh?"

"Your appetite," the other explained as his blond began kissing her way around his neck and his French companion toyed with his tie. "Your stomach hasn't shrunk yet, so it's still holding all that cream you had at the pier. Just give it some time to absorb, you'll get hungry again."

"Oh, right. Thanks."

In his peripheral vision, Faolan saw something happening between Devlin and his girl. He looked angry and she was frightened but trying to keep her smile. "Maybe we should go back to your room, honey," she whispered.

"And maybe you best do what I tell you," Devlin growled and pushed her off his leg onto the floor in front of him. "Go on and get to work now, girl, before you get me puckered."

Dropping any pretense, the blond glanced around at Faolan and Rod.

"N'mind them, you put a shake on," Devlin said, bringing his empty bottle into view. "I want everyone to see what a likely little hussy I got here. Don't make out like it's your first time."

Fast as a rattlesnake strike, he grabbed the girl by the hair and yanked her up toward him, making her yelp. Eyes filling with tears, she did her best to unbutton Devlin's fly with trembling hands.

Faolan sighed. "C'mon, Devlin…"

"Now, don't go getting worked up over some whore," Devlin said. "I'm just giving her some instruction in the realities of her position—"

"Hey," Rod said in a voice thick with controlled anger. The swordsman rose from his chair, his two women ready to move in and help the blond once they had the all-clear. "Devlin, you stop this right now. There's no reason for this kind of indecency. You've had a little too much to drink and—"

"Correction, sir, I have not yet begun to drink." Devlin's smile was cruel, his tone dripping malice despite the flippancy of his words. "You know the rules, so don't stand there and make like you're gonna lift a hand to stop me. This little bitch here is my property for the evening and I have every right to use her in any manner I take a fancy to—and man alive, woman, ain't you never pulled a prick from a set of britches before? There, that's got it."

The girl lowered a face full of tears to begin servicing him. Faolan turned his head away, a small voice inside demanding that he join Rod in condemning the gunfighter while the rest of him understood that there was no real gain in antagonizing Killian's bodyguard.

So what if the girl resembled Colleen?

She wasn't Colleen. His wife was dead and was never coming back. He'd given up the real thing for the sake of making his mark in the world, why risk his newly-earned esteem just for some girl with a familiar face?

What surprised him was the sincerity of Rod's fury. "Dammit, you son of a bitch, what are you trying to prove? I *will* not stand by and watch a lady be treated that way, rules be damned. Stand up."

Devlin just stared back, a cold fury of his own visible in the hard, angular lines of his face and those intense green eyes. "This ain't no lady, boy. This here's pussy. She sells her body and that makes her property. As a man for hire and yet another form of prostitute, I'm qualified to speak on such matters. You don't see me prancing around all high-falutin like I'm some kind of gentleman and *I* will not stand for a little harlot like this—

or them rented cunts you got hanging off your arms—doing so neither."

"She is not your property," Rod spat. "She's a young lady trying to make a living. Now let her go!"

"You want proof?" Devlin asked, speaking as much to the girl as Rod. He drew one of his Peacemakers and slid the barrel into the girl's ear, which just made her sobbing more frantic. "I could shoot her right now and only have to pay her pimp two hundred dollars compensation." He chuckled, looking down at the girl. "Hear that, sweet cheeks? That's what the life of a half-vampire whore is worth. You're paid up for the night already, all included, so how's about I fuck you in the ass for the enjoyment of all these fine folks after you finish sucking your monthly dose of immortality from my prick? How's that grand salary you're getting measure up then, huh?"

Rod moved his women into the growing crowd and they scurried away with a mixture of disgust and relief. Faolan stepped aside, too, seeing the look on Rod's face. "Get up off that bench now or, so help me God, I'll drag you off by your heels!"

"What the fuck is the meaning of all this ruckus?" shouted Killian.

The crowd now included Enzo, his girl Angie, and Stebbins. Everyone turned to where the boss of New York was also enjoying the attention of two women.

Devlin shrugged. "I was just explaining to Mister Chambers here that my position as your hired man keeps me from meeting him in a gentleman's duel of honor. Seems he's taken offense at my chosen pleasure."

"Sir—" Rod began, but Killian barked right over him.

"Rod, go wet your dick and mind your own fucking business! I won't have any fighting among my guys, follow?"

It took a second, but Rod swallowed his pride, muttered "Yes sir" through clenched teeth, and strode out. His two chosen women followed, as did Enzo and Angie.

Some of the crowd remained to watch Devlin put the girl through her paces, but Faolan had seen enough and drifted away. Business was business and politics was politics, but he didn't think he and Devlin would ever have their little heart-to-heart now.

Chapter Eight

In addition to the Indigo Lounge, the sixty-first floor contained a full gymnasium, library, room for pool and billiards, card room, firing range, and even a private theater that had all the latest movies as well as old favorites. He considered hitting all of them.

He ended up at the lounge's bar, nursing a lemon water.

"Let's Dance" had ended a few minutes before and some Goodtime Charlie was up on the stage banging away at the piano while his lady of the evening warbled Jolson's "You Made Me Love You" off-key and half a beat too slow. Faolan's deep love and respect for music urged him to open fire, but he didn't want to risk starting a bar fight.

"I hate to bother a man enjoying a quiet moment with a drink," said a rich female voice with a smile in it, "but can I trouble you for a light?"

He turned on his stool to find a tall, shapely, amber-haired woman standing beside him. Her simple evening gown matched the sapphire pendant around her long neck as well as the full-length opera gloves that held a cigarette holder like high-society types favored.

He obliged with his lighter. "Mind doing me a favor in return?"

"It depends on the favor." Her greenish-blue eyes sparkled with a wicked excitement that gave the lie to her cautious answer.

"I want you to jam that holder in my ears until you draw blood." He pulled a Camel from his cigarette case and lit up. "I'd appreciate being deaf for a while."

The woman smiled, casting a glance at the stage. "We try to keep Dolores away from the booze to avoid just this sort of thing. Shame, really. She's fine when she's sober."

"Remembers how to stay on key, eh?"

"No, she remembers that she can't sing. I think she might go all the way to Gershwin tonight, though." She took a drag through her cigarette holder and offered it to him. "Here, I can't stand to see a grown man cry."

He turned back to the bar, catching his own eyes reflected in the mirror behind the shelves. "On second thought, keep it. Listening to her makes for a fine act of contrition."

"Oh?" She slid up onto a stool beside him and leaned closer. "Been a bad boy tonight?"

Faolan dropped his eyes to the bar's surface, her smiling reflection in the mirror dredging up all kinds of impulses he felt were best left buried. He sipped his water. "Lady, I'm a creep. In fact, I'm a creep with a side order of bad penny. Nothing good has ever come to anyone associating with me and—in most cases—it's a fucking death sentence. See, told you I wasn't a gentleman. Go find somebody worth your time."

She chuckled. "As if I could leave after a build-up like that." When the bartender came over, she ordered and received a sidecar. "Now what makes you think you're qualified to determine who is and isn't worth my time? I'm a blood donor on retainer—sometimes referred to as a cow or sheep, but I don't find those terms particularly flattering—and you are a client in need of my services. Stephanie Chandler, courtesan extraordinaire."

She reached out her hand to be shaken like a man, so he obliged her. "Faolan O'Connor: killer of men, women, children, and disregarder of damsels in distress. What makes you so sure I'm in need of your services?"

"Your color, for one," she said without any teasing. "Your complexion's pale with a little blotchiness. You're still a teether, so you need blood more often than the average vamp."

"Teether?"

She smirked. "Get with the lingo, fella. Newborn vamp whose body's still adjusting, growing into his teeth and so on."

"Cute." He tried to keep from squirming by taking another sip of his water. Fear and desire mingled in his gut with an intensity that was getting uncomfortable. "I just don't feel hungry, is all I'm saying. Rod says my stomach—"

Stephanie touched his cheek with her gloved hand and leaned close so he was engulfed in the scents of her light lilac perfume, her smooth skin, her radiant hair, and the sweetness of the drink on her breath. "Rod's a terrific fella, but he's not exactly the world's deepest thinker if you catch my drift. Let me show you how to do it without hurting anybody, okay? It can be a very enjoyable experience for both parties…"

She smiled again, knowing but kind. Faolan had always had good relationships with prostitutes. In fact, he'd paid for every girl he'd ever been with except for Colleen and, honestly, he had no regrets. Why ruin the reputation or break the heart of a normal girl if all you were after was sex? Maybe Devlin was right about shooters being just another kind of prostitute, but instead of resenting whores, Faolan appreciated their professionalism.

"Sure," he said after a second. "That sounds all right."

She led him over to a big banquette against the wall as Dolores opted to forgo the Gershwin and jumped right into the classics. First up was "I'm Just Wild About Harry." Usually a song that could stand up to a good amount of abuse, but not when some bent bimbo got a notion to throw in bad scat singing. Looked like the man upstairs wasn't gonna let him off easy tonight.

"Here we go," Stephanie said, sliding into position beside him on the blue leather of the banquette. They set their drinks onto the table and she put an arm around him, sliding closer. "No need to be bashful. It's what everyone's here for, after all." She kissed the corners of his lips and lingered, licked his fresh-shaved chin and giggled, slid her other hand up the inside of his leg and whispered something in a language that sounded like French.

This time he did squirm a little, but he got himself to start kissing back. Her skin was unbearably soft and tasted even better than it smelled. he felt his canines push down into his mouth and felt a sudden stirring as something deep inside finally woke and woke hungry. What the hell was he so tense for, anyhow? Wasn't like he was a virgin in either the sex or blood-drinking department, so what the fuck?

"That's more like it," Stephanie murmured, easing back a bit. She took her hand back and went into her purse for a small scalpel. "Most guys get drinking mixed up with sex, but I find it's better to think of it as foreplay. You don't really need as much as you might think, so take it slow. Draw it out like a nice, long kiss."

She slipped the top of her dress down a half-inch or so to expose a little more cleavage and Faolan saw the delicate blue tracery of veins lying just under the surface of her skin. She brought the scalpel to a small junction of veins with long practiced movements and slipped the blade across, just like that. She drew in a breath between her teeth, but the sound wasn't without a certain amount of pleasure. "They call this mother's milk," she whispered as the blood bubbled to the surface.

Mother's milk? That was ... appropriate, he supposed, if you didn't mind being reminded of your mother at a time like this. Still, the blood enticed him closer and, when he licked the wound, she shuddered and pressed him to her, whispering, "That a boy." He really did think of Ma and the way she used to hold him to her when he was little and the Old Man had given him a thrashing for playing hooky or finding a large amount of cash in his pockets and then he thought of the way Ma must have looked at his bother Tom's funeral with no one but a few daughters to comfort her and then he saw the bloody waters of Colleen's last bath again and this time he could taste them and they tasted just like the blood of that kid Michael—

He pulled back, wanting like hell to spit and get the taste out of his mouth, but he made himself choke it down. His eyes filled with tears and he turned away from Stephanie, ashamed, trying to wipe them dry.

"Hey, hey there, what's wrong?" she asked, not sounding upset or annoyed like he figured she had every right to be. She touched his shoulders and he jumped like she'd been carrying an electric charge.

"I—" he started and stopped when he heard how tight and weepy he sounded. He sniffled, swallowed, and forced himself to suck in a deep breath. "It's nothing, I just ... I ain't been romantic with anybody since my wife ... passed a few months back."

Stephanie hugged him from the back, laying her head on his shoulder. "I'm sorry. I shouldn't have been so forward. I thought ... well, never mind. C'mon and turn around, would you?"

Jesus, why couldn't he shut off the fucking water works? Fine, so he missed his wife and felt bad about the kid. So what? He didn't need to make a goddamn production out of it.

"I thought you couldn't stand—"

"I lied. Couldn't have you taking advantage of my sentimental nature, could I?"

He turned quick, so she wouldn't see his face, and pressed into the warm softness of her neck. The tears kept coming. It was the stress of the night letting itself out, that was all. That damn whore of Devlin's got under his skin and made him feel all maudlin.

"That's it," she said, enveloping him in a private world of soft textures, sweet scents, and comforting warmth. "Let it out."

He started to wonder what she was talking about, then it hit him: he'd never really let himself cry for Colleen. Sure, he'd shed a few shocked tears after finding her, but he had to put those away before the cops showed up to grill him. After that, well, it just seemed more important to keep up a strong front.

Of all the people he'd done wrong in his life, she was the least deserving.

After another minute, he pried himself up off Stephanie's shoulder and wiped his eyes. "I'm sorry," he told her after clearing his throat. "I guess I'm just not ready to f—uh, to be with a woman yet ... in that way. Christ, is that 'Don't Mean A Thing' she's murdering now? Penance is penance, but I'm thinking a line's gotta be drawn somewhere."

Stephanie glanced up at the stage, shook her head, and turned back to him with a faint smile. Her wound was scabbed over already and she adjusted her dress to cover most of it. "You okay?"

"Not really. But I'm better for meeting you. Thanks."

"Anytime. Shall we try the straight-forward approach this time?"

He agreed and she removed one of her long opera gloves and nicked herself just under her inner elbow like in blood transfusions. Taking hold gingerly, he pressed his mouth to the wound and drank without any serious problems. He couldn't stop himself from remembering Michael, but he supposed that might never go away. It was okay, too, because that little bit of guilt made him careful and patient.

With Stephanie's guidance, he learned the trick of letting the blood come of its own accord rather than trying to suck it out (which hurt the donor and might collapse the vein). A gentle brush with his tongue now and then was all it took to keep the wound flowing and make Stephanie purr like a kitten as she laid against him, toying with the hair on the back of his neck. Also, she explained to him, this method kept his instincts from kicking in and turning him into a savage. When they finished, she snuggled up under his arm as he lounged back. Dolores had gotten parched a few minutes before and left to find lubrication, so the clumsy pianist was doodling around with "Rhapsody in Blue."

"Hey, Stephanie?"

"Mmm?"

"What is a cort-a-san, anyhow?"

She chuckled. "They were high society prostitutes in France, back before the Revolution. They were the only women who were allowed to be educated and speak their mind. they could go where they pleased without a husband and often discussed politics or social movements with the men they entertained. Sometimes they even sang or played instruments. I like thinking of myself as a modern courtesan, but some fellas don't get the distinction."

"I think you're every bit a modern courtesan," Faolan told her. "You've got real class and, when I do decide I'm ready for sex again—"

"I'd be honored. Just promise you won't go all goo-goo eyed and try to make an honest women out of me."

That made him laugh. "Don't worry. putting my personal feelings ahead of business has never been my problem. Besides, I think you'd be too much woman for me to handle full-time."

"At least you're smart enough to realize it."

He sat for a second, just glancing around, but felt his wheels turning again. "You know, I used to have this idea about having a group of sharp operators like you keeping your eyes and ears open while on a job. maybe pass things along for a little something extra..."

Now it was her turn to laugh. "Boy, you and Stebbins would make quite a pair!"

It figured he wasn't the first guy in town to work that angle. "You happy with him?"

Stephanie sat up, put a new cigarette into her holder (which he lit for her), and took on a more business-like demeanor. "This the part where you're a creep again?"

"Yeah."

She nodded. "Well, I count anything he gives me twice, but he's been smart enough to play square with me and runs as clean an operation as you could expect under the present regime. I don't want to see him hurt, if that's what you're asking."

So, Stebbins should be kept on friendly terms, but not too close. For the time being, at least. Faolan gave her his most easy-going smile. "You say he's a right guy. then he's right by me. I'm not looking to take his place, I'm just looking to subscribe to the same wire service and keep my business off the line."

She studied him for a few seconds and mulled it over. She was wondering now if everything that had happened between them had been an act, just like he would have if their positions were reversed. But she was also experienced enough to know what he'd shown her before was no act. "Okay. I'm gonna play the odds and believe you until you give me a reason not to. Hundred dollars a month plus bonuses for anything particularly helpful and I decide what counts as news. I don't spread catty gossip like sexual hang-ups or things of a purely personal nature. For instance, when Stebbins asks what our little scene was about—which he will because you're new—I'll tell him you felt guilty about that business in the basement."

He let his surprise show.

"It's a more common reaction than you'd think and it'll make him trust you more if he knows you're not made of stone."

Sure, nothing more appealing to a grifter than human weakness. Faolan just smiled and said, "His mistake."

Stephanie rolled her eyes. "Yeah, yeah, you're a creep and a bad penny, I remember. Are we clear on the terms?"

"I need to know how many other subscribers you got."

"You and Stebbins. Too many people get wise to something like this and it dies."

He nodded. "Along with the three of us." His billfold had been waiting for him in his room when he'd gone to get changed, so he pulled out a c-note and handed it to her. "This cover Killian and Rothstein or is that extra?"

Her eyes widened a bit, but she made the bill disappear and dropped her voice. "You're more ambitious than I thought. I never get much on them except second-hand. Killian never uses the same girl twice and doesn't discuss anything but what he wants done. Rothstein's a cold fish: never used a girl at all as far as I know. He's got his own live-in chef who makes gourmet meals from blood. everywhere else, he drinks it plain from unopened bottles. The only one who ever gets into his suite is that ghoul, Giordano."

He knew it wouldn't be easy. it rarely was. Frank was still a question mark, but even if Rothstein was immune to the charms of the ladies, maybe his chef wasn't. He'd broach the subject of doing more than eavesdropping with Stephanie when the time was right. A little poison in one of those blood dishes, perhaps.

Watching her sit there all business-like, Faolan thought how nice the warmth of her curled beside him had been with the scent of her hair in every breath. He wondered again why he couldn't just let a moment like that alone, why he felt compelled to exploit each and every opportunity he found.

Because this game was for keeps and the pot in the center of the table was what he'd been dreaming of since he was in short pants. Ambitious, she'd called him. *Sister, you got no fucking idea.*

He was about to suggest that they settle back down and forget their business arrangement for the rest of the evening when the blond who reminded him of Colleen came running from around the frosted glass partition. She clutched her torn dress to herself as she hurried down the stairs to the hall, sobbing the whole way.

Stephanie watched her go and rose. "I better go and talk her down. That fucking Devlin. We've got girls that like that kind of play…"

"Yeah." Faolan got up, too. "So, uh, I'll give you a ring sometime and we can maybe take in a show or something."

She smiled, but it was preoccupied. "Sounds great. And I'll give you an account where you can deposit the money from now on."

She kissed him on the cheek and headed out after the girl, leaving him with the lingering scent of lilacs. He sat back down and finished his lemon water as Dolores of the golden throat climbed back up onto the stage.

He lit a Camel and leaned back in the banquette to think, but before he could get a real good brood going, the Dhampir Everett came through the doors followed by the most unusual woman Faolan had ever seen.

Chapter Nine

She was tall, maybe five-nine or even ten, and built like the proverbial brick outhouse. he'd never seen a woman toting so much muscle. Her thick legs strode with a man's assurance in their worn Levis with engineer boots clomping across the floor, and her wide chest looked as flat as any man's under her blue work shirt. She wore a dark pea coat without the usual knit cap, but her copper-colored hair was pulled back in a ponytail so practical it made Faolan wonder why she didn't just cut it off.

He figured she was one of those dykes he'd heard about, these broads who acted like men right down to having a taste for other women. The notion was interesting enough to get him out of his seat and back to Killian's table where Everett brought her for presentation. Faolan wasn't the only one who crowded around to see the show.

Killian raised his face from the bloody breast of one of his girls and studied the newcomer with his intact eye. Everett returned to his seat and introduced her as Miranda Matheson, a rogue Vampyr who had arrived earlier to inquire about open positions and had been advised to return later in the evening.

"Let me guess," Killian said, drawing the words out. "You're a dancing girl?"

That got a big laugh from the half-drunken crowd, a little more than the joke deserved, but Miranda seemed accustomed to such teasing and smiled.

Seeing her closer, her face surprised Faolan. Rather than the battle-ax he'd expected, she looked like a cherub who had fallen on hard times. Even with the fat burned away, her face still had more curves than angles and her fair skin with its smattering of freckles seemed almost delicate. Her smile fit it well and reached her pale green eyes. She struck Faolan as a woman who did nothing halfway.

"I've been known to cut a few steps," she said when the laughter subsided. She had a heavy, fresh-off-the-boat burr that was duskier than Colleen's had been. Her first sentence came out sounding like "Oy've bin knowin ti cot affyoo stips."

At some signal from Killian, one of the goons at the back slipped in behind her and went for a backstab—

She sidestepped with surprising grace and moved back into him, smashed an elbow into his nose, and put his head in a lock. Before the guy could even begin to bring his knife back, Miranda hopped up and twisted, breaking his neck. She dropped him and stepped back to her previous spot, still smiling.

"All right," Killian allowed, still not smiling. "You got more wit than the average road agent, and certainly you're a likely enough brute, but I've those a-plenty already. What else are you offering?"

The guards came down and carried the unfortunate attacker back down to his room to heal while Miranda drew herself up an inch or two, planted her hands on her hips, and dropped her smile. "Well, sir, I was Mistress of Arms to the Duke of Northern Ireland less than ten years after taking the brand. I counseled him on strategy, enforced his will upon his Reeves, and led his forces in campaigns. We was always a smallish group, though, and not looked upon kindly by them in power, so we eventually came up buggered by a back-hander. Me and a few of me old fangs went to ground a few years, then did what we could to avenge our Lordship's betrayal. I organized our human and Dhampir fighters into what came to be the IRA, but that proved our undoing. After he got Collins, His Nibs began running us down and we that was left skipped to the continent on our back seam. But, as Europe isn't a friend to the vagabond vamp, I decided to try my luck across the pond. I got three languages solid and can get by in two more. I know my way around most pistols, rifles, swords, knives, and a few artillery pieces. I'm also a fair hand with bombs and such." She indicated Everett. "Your man here gave the impression this is a city at war. I can help on either a permanent or mercenary basis."

Faolan drew on his cigarette to mask his reaction. If this broad was half as useful as she sounded, then she was a real catch. He'd need to make an alliance with her as soon as possible or they'd end up fighting for the lieutenant's spot. He wasn't sure he could take her. He glanced over and watched Killian dismiss his girls as Frank whispered into his ear, then Rothstein. Obviously, Killian wondered if this Miranda was too good to be true and Faolan considered that too, but decided it'd be worth taking the time to find out.

What could he say? Dyke or not, he liked her moxie.

Killian rose, smiling for the first time, and took a second to straighten his disheveled evening clothes. "Well, Miranda Matheson, you have indeed stumbled into a city that could use someone of your experience. One that, by chance, is even run by a fellow Irishman—though Matheson isn't an Irish name."

She nodded and met his eyes as he strolled over to her. "I'm Scottish by birth, sir, but raised to call Ireland home."

He nodded, his smile broadening, and clapped a hand on one of her thick shoulders. "Well, manly wench though you are, we've enough of the other kind already. I'd say that your luck has most certainly changed—"

He slugged her in the belly.

Quick as she was, Miranda didn't see Killian's strike coming and doubled over as the wind rushed out of her. Faolan and a few others took a step forward, but Killian ignored them and, grabbing a handful of Miranda's hair, shot his knee up into her face.

"Move!" he shouted, lifting her up by her crotch and neck.

Seeing his intention, Faolan and the others on his side scattered. Killian hurled the bulky woman nearly fifteen feet to where she crashed against the edge of the band stand.

Faolan leapt a table, landing only a few strides from where Miranda fell. A glance at her face showed her to be shocked, hurt, and thoroughly steamed. She was putting herself back together already.

"Nobody fucking touch her!" Killian commanded, his strides eating the distance to her.

Faolan stepped back as Killian jogged in to kick her head football-style. His foot whipped out, but Miranda rolled, regained her feet, and slammed into him like a charging bull. They crashed back into the very table Faolan had just vaulted and Miranda turned the bigger vamp's upper body into a weight bag. She kept her head low, her piston-arms punching out a rabbit's heartbeat on his kidneys.

The crowd rushed around from everywhere in the lounge to watch, hooting and cheering Killian on, but

Faolan kept himself close to the action. Standing away from the others, casual, Frank and Rothstein watched. Rothstein betrayed a little nervousness, but also had that air of wishing he could get away with taking bets on the fight. Frank studied the match, then caught Faolan's glance. Faolan turned back to the fight before Frank could get a read. He hoped.

Killian clapped Miranda's ears with cupped palms, stunning her, then used the break to bring his elbows down into the insides of her collarbone—something cracked, but Miranda ignored it and threw a few alternating hooks into Killian's gut. She knew what she was doing: her considerable body weight went into every one of those hits.

Then, her *coup de grace*: a head-butt.

Except Killian saw it coming and met her halfway, their skulls colliding with a hollow popping sound that went through the room. She staggered back a few steps and Killian followed, looking almost as he had back on the pier. He kicked again, right below Miranda's kneecap—

She howled as the leg bent backwards, collapsed under her weight, and she spilled down onto the polished wood of the dance floor.

Jesus Christ, Faolan thought, lowering his eyes for a moment. Then he caught Frank studying him out of the corner of his eye and made himself keep watching.

"You've some sand in you, you kilty bitch, to think you could worm into my organization on the very night I've whipped my own weight in wildcats!" Killian bellowed at her, following.

Dragging her broken leg, Miranda slid away from him, face pale and gushing sweat.

"Did you think to find me dead, a simpleton, or had you intended to arrive before the ba—?"

Faolan watched, awestruck, as she somehow leapt up to tackle Killian despite her useless leg. They rolled, biting and punching, until she took a chunk out of his shoulder and he flipped her back into the band stand again.

After that, it was just a thrashing.

Killian pinned her up against that stand and kicked her teeth in, then he kicked his way down her chest to be sure he broke each and every rib in her body. Then he dragged her out flat and stomped on her hands to bust them up, too.

You could only tell she breathed because of the bubbling blood around her nose and mouth.

"Why don't you go on and drink her, boss?" Crowbar Charnas suggested. A chorus of seconds and thirds came from the crowd and a chant of "drink, drink, drink" began.

"Shut up!" Killian shouted, raising his arms and silencing the place. "I had enough of Boston's vintage for one night and we got better uses for this would-be in-fill-traitor."

Frank moved to the edge of the dance floor. "I'll take her down to the basement for questioning."

"Not worth it," Faolan said, almost without realizing he was going to. Maybe it was Rod's gallantry making him feel like such a shitheel before, but he was sick of watching women get beat on. "Tough as she seemed, she'd have been part of their crew at the pier if she was somebody they trusted. They grabbed her off the boat and sent her right down here."

He'd made all that up just now, but it sounded plausible enough. Frank said nothing, though there were a couple of counter-arguments he could have made. Faolan waited, hoping he hadn't miscalculated.

Killian looked at both of them in turn with his remaining eye. Dead calm now. "I think the new man's got the right of it, Frank. I want the bearded lady here shipped back to her cocksucking pals in Boston care of Mister Edward fucking Moore."

Faolan stepped down, casual. "Let me do the honors, then. I got a couple dirty limericks I been working on."

Killian guffawed.

"I'll help you," Frank said.

"Nah, I'll get Rod to point me to the right guys," he said, hoping he didn't sound as scared as he was. He walked over and moved Miranda's limbs into position to be trussed up. "If I can't handle something this easy, I got no business being around here in the first place."

Killian nodded. "Well put."

Then Rothstein came forward. "Darcy, don't make this kind of amateur mistake. Let Frank get whatever he can out of her and keep Moore in the dark. Or, better yet, send disinformation back. There's no angle in tipping our hand just for a gag."

Faolan lit a cigarette and pretended not to give a shit either way. Rothstein spoke perfect sense just then, but his timing was the pits. All Killian saw was Rothstein being a Nervous Nelly and, worst of all, telling him he didn't know shit from Shine-o-la in public.

Rothstein realized it a second later when Killian growled: "You watch those fucking words of yours, Arnold, unless you want a helping of what this cunt just got. I'm through being on the receiving end of this war. Imagine being Moore: not one living soul made it off that pier to report back what happened, and then his cunning spy shows up on his door like this only days later—maybe even leaps right out of the crate at him from hunger! What do you think that's bound to do to Moore's puffed up fucking chest?"

Killian was really hitting on all cylinders now, nothing less than an evangelist. "Don't you realize that the mind is where all fights are won or lost? The flesh is nothing but the instrument of the spirit and there ain't nothing in the physical world that can't be guided by a strong enough will! This is a goddamned psychic attack we're striking with! Once that crusty old cocksucker starts thinking he might lose this war, he starts losing it in physical fact!"

Faolan thought back, just for a moment, to when his friend Jack first started taking the blood. He'd gone mystical, too, talking about destiny and powers of the mind. Jack even went so far as to practice meditation in an attempt to "awaken his Chakras." He'd attributed his many miraculous survivals to the power he gained that way, even though it had more to do with Byrne's blood.

Jack's Eastern mumbo-jumbo may have been an amusing eccentricity, but Killian's brand of cunning and madness spooked Faolan. Fanatics were dangerous.

"It's decided," Killian declared. He turned to Faolan with a nasty smile. "You want to lick her wounds a little, that's fine, just remember I want her living when she goes in that crate."

Faolan nodded and threw in a smirk to sell the idea.

Killian strode to the doors and the crowd parted like the Red Sea. "Send my whores up to my rooms in a few minutes."

Faolan borrowed some cuffs from the guards for Miranda's wrists, tied her ankles, and did his best to ignore Rothstein and Frank's analyzing stares.

* * * * *

He pulled over as soon as he turned off Fifth Avenue.

"Where did you stash your gear?" he asked the bound woman in the back. It was near four in the morning and the street was as close to deserted as Manhattan ever got. He lit a Camel and waited a minute. "Miranda—mind if I call you Miranda?—Miranda, I know you ain't still unconscious back there. Experienced professional such as yourself, I'm sure you know that breathing and heartbeat don't sound the same asleep and awake, so quit playacting."

Still nothing.

"Don't make me fucking stick a knife or bullet in you to prove you're awake, okay? I know you didn't come into a city like this naked, so tell me where your stash is and you can take it with you. Ten seconds, then I start driving and it's finder's keepers."

He got to seven before a frustrated sigh drifted out of the back and her muffled brogue said, "Fucking locker at Grand Central."

He tried not to laugh, but it was tough. Her 'fucking' sounded like 'fuh-kin', which he thought sounded cute in a way few women did when they swore.

"Grand Central it is, Madame."

"Up your arse."

The trip to Grand Central was quick and uneventful. After gagging his passenger, he used the key he dug out of her pocket to obtain a duffel bag packed with a nice, bare-bones selection of survival equipment, weapons, and explosives. He tossed the bag in the trunk of the Lincoln sedan he'd been given and climbed in back to find Miranda still as he'd left her.

Checking her hands, he found the bones were still too broken for her to get much use out of them. He knelt on the back of her legs as he got out his keys and she started to buck. "Easy, now. I remember about your knee, but I don't need you kicking me. There."

As soon as he popped her cuffs, he slid back out and drew his piece. Miranda thrashed a bit as she turned over, but settled for quiet seething when she saw he wasn't doing anything else. She reached down to try untying her legs despite her busted hands.

"Don't be stubborn," he said, pulling out his jackknife with his left hand. "Sit back. There, see, now we can be civilized. Can you get to the front seat on that leg?"

She nodded slowly.

"Don't try running or coming at me, okay? You're fucking crippled and I'm armed and low on patience."

He watched her slide out of the back seat and hobble around to the front. He jumped behind the wheel and opened the door for her. she studied the interior before easing in, eyeing him the whole time.

"There's a bottle of blood-whisky under the seat," he said as he started the car. "I won't bother telling you it ain't spiked, since you wouldn't believe me and I figure you to be smart enough to realize I could have just left you fucking tied if I was gonna drug you."

"Maybe you just like your girls to lie still." She tried to make the line mocking, but her voice wavered with genuine fear. The fear stopped him from getting steamed at her. She'd probably had things like that done to her before.

"What can I say? I been crazy in love since I first laid eyes on you. So, what do you say, toots? You, me, Niagra Falls?"

She glared at him, but he gave her his best lovestruck eye flutter and she ducked to grab the bottle so he wouldn't see the smile fighting to break onto her face. "Well, push on if you're going to, then, you fucking bagpipe."

"Not 'till I know what the fuck you just called me."

Holding the bottle in her crippled hands, she pulled the cork out with her teeth and spit it. "Bag-fucking-pipe. Fucking saucy dodger like you who prattles on to no fucking end."

"You swear an awful fucking lot, you know that?"

"Stuff it up your fucking arse."

Grinning, Faolan holstered his Browning, shifted into gear, and made for the Holland Tunnel while Miranda drank her blood.

"What's your game?" she asked when they entered the Tunnel toward Jersey.

"Poker. How's that whisky doing for you?"

"Tastes like dog piss, but it's doing okay."

"You're welcome."

"First let's see if I've anything to be thankful for, right?"

Faolan took out a cigarette and offered her one, which she took, then lit them both up. "Let's just say I thought you got a bad beat tonight and I still owed a good deed for the day."

She whirled toward him and seemed about to use her empty bottle as a weapon when pain made her wince and fall back against the door. The bottle dropped onto the floor and rolled under the seat as a tear spilled down her reddening face. "Fuck! So, poor little fucking girl can't take care of herself and you want to play white fucking knight? Well, fuck you! I never asked for your fucking pity!"

"Well, fuck you, too," he said. "I never said a fucking word about pity. I got no pity for anybody, least of all some bitch who should fucking know better but times her infiltration so badly she might as well have carried a sign saying: 'I'm a fucking spy'!"

"I'm not no fucking spy!"

Faolan took his cigarette out of his mouth and pointing it at her like a finger while he answered. "Yes you are. Don't take me for some fucking chump just 'cause this looks like a chump move. You spying for Boston is the only thing that fits all the facts. Problem is, you're an honest, straight-ahead kind of gal and having a secret agenda don't sit right with you. Killian spotted it, but he didn't play it right. I would have let you in, checked you out, and seen if you could be turned to our side. See, I don't think you felt too obliged to stay loyal to Boston."

More he thought about it, in fact, the more he thought Killian had seen Miranda's usefulness, he just couldn't abide such a strong woman. Probably had a similar blind spot when it came to Negroes, Chinese, Latinos, and other "inferiors." Faolan had come up in Little Augie's mob, a polyglot of Irish, Italians, Jews, Polish, Germans, Russians, and almost every other stripe you could name. He'd learned the value of diverse backgrounds there as well as the stupidity of lumping people together. You never knew who might turn out useful.

He took his eyes off the road and glanced over to check her expression. "I was right. You were just looking for a place to settle in, you didn't care where. You could have helped us plenty."

"Not anymore."

"I suppose not," he said as Fourteenth Street became Route One South. "So, anyways, I don't see any gain from shipping you to Boston. Either they kill you or you join them for real and then you attack here someday and I gotta kill you."

She snorted. "You think so, eh?"

Faolan shrugged. "Rather not find out. I plan to drop you off a short walk from Newark Penn Station, from which you can catch trains going most anywhere. Figure you owe me one and if the road ain't been too kind after a few years, you can check back here and square up with me. If not, I still ain't lost nothing."

"Why would I?" she asked, more curious than belligerent.

"Because in a few years I'll be running this city."

She laughed, but he just smiled and finished his cigarette.

"All right," she said a few minutes later when Faolan pulled over on Market Street in Newark. "I suppose I trust selfish motives as much as I trust anything."

This area was all industrial lofts with a few brick tenements scattered about and no one but bums roaming. Working streetlights were sporatic, making the area perfect for feeding.

He took out his billfold and gave her the two hundred and change he had left in it. "Here. That'll get you some clothes, a sleeper car to anywhere the trains run, and some walking-around money. The next street up is West Raymond, turn right and you can't miss the station. There's bums around some of these buildings, just avoid the cops."

"What about other vamps?"

He smiled. "Pansies. Avoid them if you can, kill them if you can't. Newark's neutral from what I understand, so I don't give a fuck, but you can't stay here. Get away from this whole fucking war, okay?"

She nodded and climbed out. Her knee seemed better, at least good enough for her to walk. She leaned back in the car and asked, "What's your name, anyhow?"

"Faolan O'Connor."

"Failin'? Don't auger too well for your plans, does it? Well, Faolan O'Connor, as it happens I pay my debts, so don't you fucking get yourself killed before I come back to settle up."

"Deal."

She closed the door and vanished into the darkness while he sat and smoked and wondered whether he'd just made a fatal mistake. After all, it was always the good deeds that came back to bite him on the ass.

Still, this had been one hell of a first night.

PART TWO

ACES IN THE HOLE
November, 1935:

My colleague, my crony, my cohort, my friend
Companions, confederates, chums to the end
Like meat and potatoes, or salt and tomatoes
      Boy, what a blend!
  - Bing Crosby, "Put it there, Pal"

Chapter Ten

"You're under the gun, O'Connor," Rothstein said.

The cards slapped the table with the sound of a .22 in an alley: *snap, snap, snap.*

"Thought that was up to the cards," Faolan said, keeping his tone neutral.

Rothstein continued his deal, throwing cards with mechanical precision to Stebbins, Enzo, Rod, Frank, Devlin, and then himself. "In regular play, yes. Call it the price of admission, since you don't have the rank of these other men."

So Rothstein, as last to act, granted himself the prime position. Faolan, perpetually first to act, was in a bad spot. Faolan shrugged. "Your game, A.R."

"And don't you forget it," the gambler warned with a cold stare. "In this instance, however, my aim is educational rather than malicious. I choose Seven-stud because I feel it most accurately represents the structured nature of The Order and features more betting rounds than standard stud poker, indicating the longer commitment and increased number of choices necessary in undertaking any enterprise within that framework. The seating at this table is reflective of our status relative to each other. In The Order, position and status are everything. One hundred bring-in."

"High stakes," Faolan commented.

"Always," Rothstein said, challenging him with a stare. "Everything we do in The Order carries the potential of life or death consequences. Being the lowest man here, you commit yourself first by bringing-in. If that doesn't agree with you, then now's the time to take your cash and scurry home."

With the successful defense of the city at Coney Island, Killian figured the heads of his various departments should all get a crash course in the big picture so they could conduct his affairs accordingly.

Faolan's presence at the game, battle hero or not, seemed to be Killian's obvious way of marking him for bigger things.

Faolan had the smallest pile of cash in front of him, having bought in with the grand that was his weekly pay. He had to win some pots quick or the bring-in would chip him down to nothing within a few hands. He wouldn't have much time to play tight and study his opponents.

No problem. Loose had always been his style.

Tossing his hundred into the pot, he noted his door card was a ten of spades and checked his hole cards: a fucking five and deuce off-suit. Even with money already committed, he couldn't see staying around for Fourth Street and slid his bricks in Rothstein's direction.

"The new man folds," Rothstein announced, breaking standard poker etiquette by peeking at the discards. "With this hand, probably a smart move."

They sat in a corner of Rothstein's swank office, a large but comfortable room of dark wood paneling, fine furnishings, and tasteful accessories. Unlike Killian's cavernous, intimidating space, this had a warmth to it that was almost at odds with its owner. Of course, his being a shitheel notwithstanding, A.R. had always been a class act.

Faolan admired Rothstein's ensemble while Stebbins opened with five hundred. the gray smoking jacket and maroon ascot would have looked ridiculous on anybody else at the table, but the gambler carried it off like John Barrymore.

Charlie always credited Rothstein with teaching him how to dress classy and conduct himself in high society. Rothstein had also passed on some of his wisdom to Jack Diamond and now Faolan heard he was giving Killian the polish. Back when he'd first started with Jack, Faolan tried to get Rothstein to throw some tips his way, but the gambler had given him the brush.

"The structure of The Order is feudal in construction, but ingeniously fluid in practice," Rothstein said, his eyes following the movements of each player as they folded, bet, or raised. Faolan watched him absorb every fidget, every change in posture or expression, every nervous fingering of cash while thinking, every hesitation and show of eagerness. Rothstein absorbed it all, assessed it in that famous brain of his, and called an aggressive raise from Devlin. "At the very top sits the Hegemony, or Council of Hegemons, composed of each Domain's rulers."

"What, you mean like a League of Nations for vampires?" Crowbar Charnas asked, giving up on his pair of threes rather than cough up another grand. The square-headed vamp with the drill sergeant's haircut chewed his cigar in irritation.

"Not in the least," Rothstein told him, dealing Fifth Street. "Domains are not nations." *Snap, snap, snap.* "Nations are the temporary political creations of human whim. Domains hold nations within them as the U.S. holds states." The gambler's eyes lost their focus, looking inward, while his voice took on a tone of reverence. "The Roman Empire or maybe Charlemagne's kingdom represent the kind of power we're speaking of when we talk about Domains." Then he was back, his eyes sharp. "Well, Stebbins, what's your play: bet or fold?"

Beside Faolan, Stebbins nodded. Grabbing a stack of hundreds, he smacked them down into the center with a showy bravado that had to be a bluff. "Two thousand."

Enzo threw his cards in. "This is why I prefer five-card draw."

"Draw poker is a child's game," Rothstein said. "One might as well play Go Fish."

"Personally, I prefer strip poker in mixed company," Faolan added, earning grins from Rod, Stebbins, and Devlin.

"So where does the U.S. fit in terms of Domains?" Rod asked, fingering his greenbacks in silent debate.

Rothstein smiled, eyeing the pot as though it were already his. "America is an unusual case, Mister Chambers. The Hegemon of North America is something of an eccentric by The Order's standards, a man who appreciates freedom so much that he's even willing to let his subjects have some. Thus, we have our federalist republic—now, would you kindly make up your mind?"

With a sigh, Rod pushed his cards to the center.

Rothstein snatched them up, peeked, and continued. "From my admittedly imperfect understanding of the history, the Territories of America grew, changed, divided, and reformed with the ebb and flow of the country's growth."

"Well, shit," Devlin said, throwing ten thousand in with a flick of his wrist. "I might could've told you that much from *my* imperfect understanding of history. Ten thousand."

Faolan tried not to let his surprise show. The gunfighter had just risked nearly half his bankroll with nothing showing but an off-suit king, six, and nine. Hard play for the first hand of a game.

"You've bet out of turn, Mister Devlin," Rothstein told him. "Remove your money from the pot and wait until Mister Giordano has played."

"You know, I truly forgot he was even there," Devlin said, grabbing one of the expensive-smelling cigars out of Rothstein's engraved silver humidor. "But I made my bet, so what's done is done. Just tell your ghoul to make his move and we'll continue on as before."

Frank made no move to indicate he'd even heard the exchange, just sat and waited with his blank, dead eyes.

Rothstein set his hands flat onto the green felt and turned the full force of his cold, implacable calm on Devlin. "No, Mister Devlin, what we'll do is observe the etiquette of the game. Your unique status in this organization doesn't negate mine and, while you remain free to carry your personal anarchy with you, I won't permit it to infect the purity of what we do here. Therefore, you'll either show the proper respect for both the game and your fellow players or I'll ask you to leave."

"You just go ahead and try to throw me out, you cocksucking little sheeny." Devlin sat back enough to reach his guns, but met Rothstein's gaze.

The whole table went still, but Rothstein let the insult wash right over him. "While I may have no direct authority over you, Mister Devlin, you play here at my sufferance. If you refuse to conduct yourself in a civilized manner, I'll be forced to interrupt Mister Killian's leisure to ask him to remove you."

Faolan had nearly forgotten what it was like to see Rothstein back in his element. He was a king here: cool as ice and in complete control. Just like when Faolan first met him. Apparently, Devlin had never met this Rothstein, judging from the way he took a few moments to reevaluate.

"O'Connor," Devlin said without looking his way. "How's about we go down to that shooting range and put on a little contest?"

"Another time, maybe," Faolan told him. "Boss made a special point of including me here, so I better stick around and learn."

He thought he saw the faintest of smiles on Rothstein's lips as Devlin took his time lighting his cigar. Finally, the gunfighter grabbed his bills out of the pot. "Well, suppose I'll stick around then. None of them cocksuckers downstairs got the balls to play against me."

With a nod from Rothstein, Frank folded his cards as if the interruption hadn't taken place. Faolan wondered if the knowledge of Devlin's intended raise had spooked him, since he had a pair of queens showing. Rothstein must have thought the same thing, since he peeked at Frank's hole cards and raised a questioning eyebrow, then shook his head.

Pot odds, Faolan realized, looking down at the table. Stebbins' bet was almost double the money in the pot, which wouldn't have stopped most players with a strong two pair, but was enough to trigger Frank's caution. Fella played that tight all his life, he might as well be an insurance underwriter and leave the cards alone. Such Laydown Sally behavior didn't quite fit with Frank's reckless bravery at Steeplechase Pier, though, did it?

Then it was Devlin's turn (again) and the gunman folded his straight draw, just to be contrary. "Now, how d'ya like that, Hymie?"

"Don't you have a civil bone in you, Devlin?" Rod asked with genuine indignation. "Apologize to Mister Rothstein."

"Suck my prick."

"Gentlemen," Rothstein called. "There is no need. Mister Devlin, your racial epithets are misdirected. I'm not a Jew by practice or blood. I am a Vampyr, the same as everyone at this table."

Devlin looked disgusted by the thought, but Faolan realized he'd never considered the deeper implications of his transformation. Every Vampyr in this building was part of the same race, if not a bonafide blood relation.

But this wasn't the time to dwell on it.

"So, getting back to the game," Rothstein said, scooping the cards into the pile. "The hands we play are the possibilities for power and position which our membership in The Order gives us. When we take one of these opportunities, when we play rather than fold, we put ourselves in competition with any other members who are chasing an opportunity. We also expose ourselves to potential loss of our political clout, our social status, and even our lives, which are all represented here by money." Grabbing a stack of cash, Rothstein raised to ten thousand, five times Stebbins' initial bet. "You have odds of four and a half to one against making that flush, Mister Stebbins. You see my tens and you must be wondering if I have a third in the hole. If I do, my odds of making a full house are one and a half to one. You like those odds?"

Stebbins didn't sweat, but he blinked something fierce. Still, he smiled that devil-may-care smile and pushed eighteen thousand into the center. "I feel lucky."

Rothstein met the re-raise without hesitation. "Luck is for fools. a real player relies on skill." *Or by having a big enough bankroll to afford to stick around until the odds turn around*, Faolan added in his head, remembering Rothstein's human tactics.

Another card went down in front of each, *snap, snap*: Stebbins got hit with an off-suit five while Rothstein picked up a second seven to go with his tens. If there was indeed a third ten in his hole, then the gambler had just made his full house.

"So," Rothstein said. "You ready to call it quits or do you feel lucky enough to have a showdown with me?"

Faolan couldn't see what Stebbins could possibly have to beat the gambler. After a few seconds of nervous fidgeting, the grifter pushed his hand to the center.

His dark brown eyes gleaming, Rothstein pulled the cash to him in a lover's embrace. Whatever changes Vampyrism may have brought about in the man, the elimination of his avarice was not one of them. "While one is engaged in the pursuit of advancement, it's possible to show only certain elements of one's position. However, once one gets defeated in confrontation, everything becomes clear." Flipping over Stebbins' hole cards, he revealed an off-suit pair of fives. Three of a kind. Better than the flush draw he'd been representing, but not enough to beat a full house. Rothstein smiled. "So you see," he added, revealing his own hole cards to be nothing more than an ace and deuce, "sometimes position and the appearance of power is enough."

Rothstein held nothing but a lousy two pair.

* * * * *

"Fuck you, anyhow, O'Connor!" Crowbar Charnas growled, putting on his coat. The former strike breaker had made a bold play against Faolan in the previous hand and lost. "You ain't nothing but a lousy cheat!" When no one bothered to look up from the deal, Charnas got the message and stomped out.

"So, gentlemen," Rothstein continued as if Charnas' outburst hadn't happened. "I'm sorry to report that, for all our efforts at Coney Island, we all remain outlaws under sentence of death."

Everyone else folded to Faolan's raise, but Rod had enough confidence in his hole cards to meet it. Probably another king to match the one he had showing. The chivalrous swordsman was many things, but subtle didn't make the list. If he had a third king hiding under there, he would have re-raised.

"Wait, why outlaws? We won, didn't we?" Enzo asked from the sidelines. The kid was conservative, but unexpectedly shrewd. His tight play and honest personality made his rare bluffs very effective. Faolan's respect for him had bumped a few notches tonight.

Devlin had thrown his money away with suicidal abandon a few hours ago and left. In those hours, Faolan had doubled up a number of times against Frank, Charnas, Stebbins, and Rod. Frank had proven such a slave to the odds that Faolan had yet to showdown against the man, but had easily bluffed him out of some large pots that even a beginner would have contested. Stebbins was nearly the opposite, generally believing that luck would see him through and chasing pots long after a sensible man would have thrown the hand away. Having blown his wad a few hands ago, Stebbins just borrowed five g's from Rothstein to "make his comeback" and then proceeded to lose all but seven hundred of it.

Through it all, Rothstein won a few hands, folded out of a few, watched the plays, peeked at the discards, and lectured. He described how The Order dated back thousands of years and was pretty much the grandmother of all secret societies. The Hegemons each controlled a continent or major area of the globe and together they formed a ruling council. He speculated that The Hegemony might have started as the original name for The Order, but that everyone now thought of the Hegemony as referring to the council itself. Adjutor was a term for assistant, so you could find Adjutors to Hegemons, Governors, and Reeves. Most Adjutors were Dhampirs, since the position was kind of like a secretary, but some of the higher-ups had Vampyr Adjutors because of their status. Seven Governors controlled North America: two in Canada, one in Mexico, and four in the U.S. whose territories were now laid out more or less along the Time Zones. The exception to this was the so-called Executive Governor, who controlled Washington D.C. and the Federal government because of a compromise back during the days of the founding fathers.

Finally, Rothstein had described how Reeves technically controlled major cities, but in practice certain Reeves made themselves "first among equals" and controlled vast areas within a Governor's territory. One such individual was Edward Moore, the Reeve of Boston and Killian's sworn enemy. Prior to Killian's seizing of power, the entire Northeast had danced to Moore's tune, and he more than anyone else wanted to see New York's new hierarchy eliminated.

Rothstein watched now as Faolan faced Rod with a potential ace-high straight, showing a ten, ace, and king. Rod had his king, a jack, and the ace of hearts to boot, but he hesitated. Rod wasn't stupid, but he made the mistake of playing his cards rather than his opponent. He had that kind of straight-forward intelligence that trusted what he saw to be what it looked like. In a game of bluffs like poker, this was a problem for him and so he compensated by worrying about what he couldn't see.

From his earliest games against the gang he ran with as a kid, Faolan had never bothered worrying much about the cards or the odds or any of that. He'd always seen the game as a way of learning about the people you played: how a man made decisions, the kind of personality he had, what his instincts were under pressure, his talent for deception, how he dealt with loss and success. It was all there in poker if you knew what to look for. Once you knew how the other guy played his hands, the cards and the money were just instruments for manipulating him this way and that.

The only thing that told you as much was their preferred method of killing.

Rothstein snapped down a card each for Faolan and Rod: a queen for Faolan, another king for Rod. Now Rod had the three of a kind and maybe a full house if that second hole card of his was another ace.

Faolan, meanwhile, didn't even have the straight he represented. his hole cards were a ten and two which gave him a pair of tens with no possibility he would catch the jack to complete his straight: Rod held one, Enzo had folded a pair earlier, and Stebbins had one showing before he folded. Rod hadn't noticed or had forgotten those, but Rothstein hadn't. The gambler watched their contest like a buzzard waiting to see which desert traveler dropped first.

"What you got left there, Rod?" Faolan asked.

Rod's joy at achieving his trip kings drained in a moment as the swordsman did a quick count. "About, uh, seven thousand."

There was no ace in Rod's hole.

Faolan counted seven grand off his stack and tossed it into the pot without hesitation, then leaned back and lit a cigarette. "C'mon, Rod. I want to see if you can catch that ace."

Rothstein would have needled Rod to hurry up and decide, but that would be a mistake. Rod had solid instincts and, if pushed to a decision, would usually make the right one. Faolan was content to sit back, wait, and let the man second-guess himself out of the smart play.

"Go on with what you was saying about that death sentence, A.R.," he said, the picture of confidence.

Enzo perked up. "Yeah, I thought the *pessanovante*—that Governor, uh, what's his name?"

"Burlington," Rod supplied, still fingering his cards.

"That's him. I thought he was just waiting till the dust settled 'tween us and them other cities to see if we was still standing."

"Would that it were so, Mister Carreras," Rothstein sighed, rising. He went over to the wet bar cleverly hidden inside a large cabinet, poured himself a small glass of water, and added a squeeze of lemon. A teetotaler when human, Rothstein now seemed to be just as fussy with his blood drinking habits. "Would anyone care for another drink?"

"Sure," Faolan said. "Hit me with some more of that juiced-up AB Negative."

The others declined and Rothstein began filling a glass with "milk" from the veins of some well-pickled soul. "When our organization filled the vacuum left by the mysterious disappearance of New York's previous power structure, we assumed the suspicion of responsibility, or at least complicity, for that disappearance. Despite all attempts to convince Governor Burlington otherwise, the accusation stands because we have not relinquished power as ordered."

"Why not?" Rod asked, his tone indicating he'd wanted to ask for a while. "If we are, in fact, innocent, then why not surrender and prove our case?"

Rothstein stared down at Rod like that was the stupidest thing he'd ever heard. "Fold a competitive hand? Haven't you heard anything I've said? Never give up power once you have it! If we surrendered, they would execute us all without trial simply to satisfy the possibility of guilt and clear the way for whatever puppet regime the local powers wished to install. You only bargain from strength in The Order or you get run over: that's why we're at war."

"I fold."

Faolan turned back to where Rod pushed his cards away.

"God save us all from the naiveté of the honorable," Rothstein sneered as he set Faolan's drink down in front of him and continued to his spot at the head of the table.

Rod hung his head, smiling sheepishly. "I know, but I wanted to keep some for the rest of the week. Anyway, you had the straight, didn't you, Faolan?"

Looking across at the big lug, he just couldn't go through with revealing the bluff like he'd planned. "Yeah, made it on the queen. I would've busted you."

Rothstein snorted, gathering the cards. "You're a good loser, Chambers."

"Thanks."

"Wasn't a compliment," the gambler said, beginning his shuffle. "A good loser's a frequent loser. Get out of the habit of accepting defeat if you ever want to amount to something."

Stung or not, Rod didn't show it. He just nodded with a thoughtful expression and said, "Yes, sir. I'll keep that in mind."

"On your way, now," Rothstein said, cutting the deck. The cards crackled like distant thunder as he riffled the two stacks together. "As my first dealer used to say: 'If you ain't playin', you ain't stayin'.'"

Rod made his goodbyes, offering to wait downstairs for anybody who felt like going out later. Rothstein didn't spare another word for his waterfront lieutenant as he pushed the deck.

Faolan tossed in his three hundred, ready to bust the smug little bastard.

"Old Moore in Boston and Hamilton in Philly didn't expect us to be so organized so soon after taking power," Rothstein explained as he tossed in his ante and snapped the first card down in front of each man. "They figured they could destroy us subtly, so they infiltrated, procured the services of Luciano and Schultz to eliminate our influences, and quietly took out our people when opportunities arose." The second cards came down all around. "They caught one hell of a break when they got our Mister Byrne and might have ground us into dust if they'd been patient enough for the slow play, but they got impatient and tried for a quick resolution instead."

"Coney Island," Faolan said as his door card snapped down: an eight of clubs. Not very impressive but, when he checked his hole, he found pocket jacks in diamond and spade.

Rothstein showed a queen of spades. "Favors were called in and promises were made and damn near every city north of Virginia contributed a soldier or two. They sent us envoys with formal documents promising that if our force prevailed on the field of battle that our rights would be recognized, certain that their army couldn't be stopped."

"Except it was. We was all there for this part, so you can skip ahead, A.R." Faolan counted off five thousand and tossed it onto the bring-in. that ought to be enough to scare everyone else out except Rothstein, who wouldn't abide Faolan stealing the pot unchallenged. "Five thousand."

"Yeah," Rothstein said, annoyed at having his thunder stolen. "What you didn't see is them welching on us, claiming Burlington never signed off on the deal and oh, ain't that a crying shame."

"Call five thousand," Stebbins said, showing the king of hearts and scribbling on a scrap of paper. "And raise five ... my marker's good enough, right?"

Rothstein nodded. "Another five grand you'll owe me."

Stebbins grinned. "Not this time."

Damn, the grifter thought the others would fold and that he could beat whatever Faolan had. Maybe he did have two more kings under there.

Enzo folded his seven of clubs. Taking a peek at his own hole cards, Frank also folded without a word. Rothstein checked his hole, glanced once at Faolan and then Stebbins, and picked up his cash. "Call ten and raise another ten. So, here we stand, our enemies and us, each having learned a valuable lesson: them, not to underestimate us and us, not to trust their word. For the moment, they have exhausted themselves and probably won't attempt another frontal assault. However, their refusal to honor the terms of their offer tells us in no uncertain terms that they will strike at us again."

Faolan finished his cigarette, considering, while Rothstein peeked at all the discards. Facing a raise and re-raise with a pair of jacks wasn't exactly the strongest position to be in, but his gut told him Rothstein was just looking for a chance to crow—he'd turn over a fucking ace high or something and make some smarmy remark about how he'd lost his nerve.

"That's twenty to you, O'Connor."

Stebbins—hell, Stebbins was just looking to grab a pot before somebody outdrew him. Faolan knew he could beat those kings.

"Call twenty."

Stebbins called right behind him, writing out another IOU.

"So, why don't the boss call another sit-down? We'd be dealing from strength, wouldn't we?" Enzo asked.

"For the moment, yes," Rothstein allowed.

Snap, snap, snap: the jack of clubs for Faolan, a six for Stebbins, and the king of spades to go with Rothstein's queen.

"However," he continued. "Mister Killian refuses to apologize for the insult he gave Governor Burlington at their meeting, believing it's a sign of weakness. Governor Burlington has demanded the apology as the first step toward any negotiations."

He'd made three of a kind and Rothstein's king proved that Stebbins wouldn't get any more than three. Rothstein looked to be chasing a royal flush, but Faolan already held the jack he'd need to complete it. He wanted to throw all his money in right now, but knew that would scare the seasoned gambler out.

He was gonna bust the sonofabitch for everything he could.

"I check," he managed, faking weakness. "So, where's that leave us?"

"Up a certain creek without a certain necessary item," Stebbins quipped. "Check."

"Another five," Rothstein said, putting his money in. "The Governor's official neutrality could be to our advantage, given the right circumstances and our correct plays under those circumstances. Though he hasn't endorsed us yet, his refusal to directly make war upon us means that he believes we have a chance at winning."

"So, why don't he just back the others and squash us?" Faolan asked.

"Because Governors rule by holding power, not by popular consent. If he sent his personal forces against us and lost, he himself would become vulnerable to attack. The Hegemon, of course, would need to support him and thereby put his own position at potential risk. So, you see, what began as a simple dispute over a city could escalate into a Domain-wide revolution. On the other hand, Burlington needs the support of his strongest cities to maintain order, so he will not thwart their designs on this city lightly."

"In short, this is a tournament-style game," Faolan said. "We're in 'till we bust everybody else or get busted."

"Correct. What's your play, O'Connor?"

"Call five thousand."

Stebbins scribbled another marker.

Enzo watched from the edge of his seat. "So, uh, how do you figure them coming at us, Mister Rothstein?"

Faolan noticed that Frank's attention was on him alone.

Snap, snap, snap.

"From all sides, Mister Carreras. From all sides."

A useless nine for Faolan, a deuce for Stebbins, and the ace of spades for Rothstein.

"Twelve thousand," Faolan said. Let them worry about the nine rather than the jack that preceded it. Now he could catch another four or nine for a full house or get really lucky and hit the fourth jack. either way, Rothstein was drawing dead. "By 'all sides,' you mean they're gonna go back to fighting through humans and trying to take over our rackets?"

Rothstein favored him with a cold smile as Stebbins wrote another marker. "I meant exactly what I said. They will attack us politically, economically, through influence, and through direct attack. They will do everything within their power to sabotage our efforts to run this city effectively. Call twelve thousand."

Snap.

The jack of hearts winked up at Faolan.

Frank traced the movements of his face with those dead eyes.

Faolan held himself immobile.

Snap.

Stebbins caught a second six and spent a moment remembering how to breathe.

Snap.

A five of diamonds broke Rothstein's streak. The gambler was too good to let any hint of a reaction show. "That, gentlemen, is the assault we must prepare ourselves to weather. Any strong loss, any public incident, any stumble from which we do not immediately recover will signal our doom to The Order's upper ranks. They will descend in full force then and annihilate us. In short, not only must we ultimately win the war, but we also can't afford to ever lose a battle." He turned and locked gazes with Faolan. "Do you understand the necessity of keeping our defenses air-tight now?"

Faolan just smiled and tossed the last of his winnings into the pot, knowing he'd be getting it back times three. He leaned back, letting everyone see his confidence. Stebbins had no reason to think he was beat and those markers would make for good leverage against a rainy day. As for Rothstein's money, he'd put some of it to work building himself a network, maybe tuck the rest away for safety.

Though there was that new model Cord he'd had his eye on.

"As air-tight as the coffin you locked that big bull dyke in, get it?" Frank added.

The flat voice held no hint of any hidden meaning, but Faolan felt a cold fist grab his stomach anyway. Was Frank just stirring the water to see what floated to the surface or did the fucker really *know*?

More importantly: did Rothstein?

Was this all some kind of set-up?

"What's your play, O'Connor?"

Faolan forced a smile, ignoring Frank. "How much you got left there, A.R?"

Rothstein didn't blink. "Fifty two thousand, seven hundred. I wouldn't normally take a marker from a guy like you, no collateral and such, but I'll make an exception this time."

Faolan accepted one of Stebbins' scraps with thanks and wrote it out, signing his name beneath. "You ought to keep out of this one, Stebbins. Friendly warning."

Stebbins considered him suspiciously, and then smiled with a shrug. "In for a penny and so on."

"Are those really Houdini's handcuffs?" Enzo asked, pointing to one of the items displayed in Rothstein's walnut curio cabinet.

The gambler paused, confused, before turning around and noticing what Enzo was talking about. "Authenticated as one of many pairs he used in his stage act. They've appreciated significantly in value since I acquired them."

"I always loved Houdini," Enzo said. "Do you ever just put them on for fun?"

"Of course not. Handling them might lower their value." Rothstein slapped his dough down into the center and picked up the deck. "Since we're all fully committed, I propose we show our hole cards before the deal."

Faolan turned over his jacks. "Four of a kind, jacks."

"Ah, fuck balls!" Stebbins shouted, burying his face in his hands.

"Which beats Stebbins' full house if I'm not mistaken," Rothstein said. He turned over his hole cards.

A pair of aces.

"Three of a kind, aces."

Faolan sat forward with surprise. The fucking royal flush had been a ruse—the sonofabitch was building aces!

The cards came, face down this time.

Snap, snap, snap.

All he had to do was hold. If Rothstein didn't catch that last ace, Faolan had him. He turned over his river card, not that it mattered. Another nine—too bad there was no such thing as a Very Full House.

Stebbins had pulled himself together enough to flip his card over and reveal a meaningless eight.

Rothstein turned his card.

Faolan collapsed back into his chair, feeling the wind rush out of him. He couldn't believe his eyes: the ace of clubs.

"And so ends the lesson, gentlemen," Rothstein said, gathering up the money and IOUs. "Stebbins, the usual interest will apply starting tomorrow night."

Stebbins rose, mopping his brow. "Right you are, Mister Rothstein. Um ... you wouldn't, by any chance, happen to have any solid tips on tomorrow's races at Belmont or Saratoga, eh?"

"Come see me later. As for you, O'Connor," the gambler began, rising to look down at him. "I'd say it's high time you left the big moves to the big boys."

Without a word to anyone, Faolan got up and walked out.

Chapter Eleven

Faolan followed the music down Lenox Avenue.

He'd told the cabbie to let him out a few blocks from his destination so he could walk. Being in Harlem again was like coming home. It was better, really, since his childhood home across the river in Brooklyn held nothing but lost opportunities and bad memories. Harlem had been a place of refuge for him during bad times.

Despite the end of the "New Negro Movement" as it had been called, the air here still felt alive with creation and possibility. It was the spirit of the whole community infused in the bricks of the tenement buildings and the stones of the shops, a sensation in the air like echoes of the day's laughter and song. The scents of perfume, car exhaust, wood smoke, tobacco and marijuana wafted toward him on the breeze. Above all that, the sweet sass of trumpets, trombones, clarinets, and saxophones pulled him hypnotically down the street toward "The Home of Happy Feet."

As he neared his destination, the crowd grew a bit thicker, the laughter louder, and the movements more graceful. Two o'clock in the morning and the Savoy Ballroom still swung, exhausted folks staggering out the door for some air and, moments later, dancing on the sidewalk just for the irresistible joy of it. The second floor windows, open to let heat out of the always-crowded ballroom, issued the toe-tapping, brassy thump of "Midnite in Harlem." Chick Webb was in fine form tonight.

His stride having long since fallen into the rhythm, Faolan greeted the folks outside who enthusiastically greeted him back. There was no color here, just people united by the brotherhood of jazz. The idea of all Vampyrs being one big family was a nice thought, but he'd only ever seen that kind of togetherness achieved in the dance halls and rent parties of Harlem. Just up the street was the more famous Cotton Club where Negro entertainers entered through the back to perform for all white audiences, but this little pocket of culture had no such separations.

God, he hadn't realized how much he'd missed this inclusive world until Rothstein's little lesson knocked the last of his stuffing out. He strode up and broke his last buck on the thirty-cent admission even though he had his Old Timer's Club membership right in his billfold that would have saved him a nickel. With a smile, he tossed the kid at the counter a dime from his change and glided up the wide marble stairway to the second floor.

The music tugged at him as strong as the scent of blood.

He tried to shake that image as he came out into the mad, dancing throng of the ballroom. The Savoy was as lively and vibrant a place as he'd ever seen, its pinks and greens and mirrored walls like the jewels and tassels of a chorus girl. Lindy-Hopping dancers of all races filled the fifty by two hundred foot dance floor known as The Track, flipping and spinning in their best dancing clothes. The biggest dance floor he knew of in New York, The Track was made of polished and spring-loaded black maple which got so much use they had to replace it every three years. At each end sat bandstands with colored spotlights for the two bands the place employed so the music never stopped. he'd been here for some of the legendary battles where bands from out of town or rival clubs would come to try to take the crown from the Savoy's own King of Swing, Chick Webb.

Chick was bringing it hard: "Go Harlem."

This was what he'd come for, to lose himself in dancing like the old days. To lose himself in life.

Fresh, hot, vibrant life.

His canines pushed down out of his gums—

Shit! What was wrong with him? He backed up against the wall to catch his breath. Was he so fucking depraved that just being near people and enjoying himself would make him attack them for blood?

Maybe losing himself wasn't such a sharp idea, after all.

"Hey, hey, Fay-man!"

Faolan turned at the familiar voice of Gordon "Jelly" Thompson as the tall, slender Negro trucked over. Jelly had skin the smoothness and hue of a ripe eggplant which made his polished white grin seem that much brighter. The small diamond mounted into his right incisor caught a spot from the bandstand and sparkled like a miniature flashbulb as he reached out a long hand covered in rubies and diamonds. "Harp cat, the original rug-cutter himself! Gimme some skin, my friend! Where you been hiding yourself?"

Jelly's deep voice carried a faint accent from some Caribbean island and, as usual, he was draped down in a tailored maroon pinstripe with matching tie and hat, oxblood loafers, and a big white carnation on his lapel to match his shirt and teeth.

"I been caught up all over," Faolan said, shaking his hand. "Couldn't get uptown to save my life."

"You are very pale and you have lost weight, my friend, but it suits you. You are lean and hungry once again, eh? I have remained so, as well." He laughed, waving at the

Lindy Hoppers. "A good crowd tonight! Have you come to show these young people how a rug is cut, my friend?"

Faolan swallowed. "Nah, I'm feeling a little rusty. I just needed to bask in the groove a little to get my head on straight."

"Come, then. Come sit with me and let me buy you a drink."

He nodded and let Jelly lead him to an open table at the edge of The Track. It felt good to see someone like Jelly again and just talk. they'd never been more than business associates, but the man made everyone feel like an old friend. When the waiter in the white tuxedo made it over to their table, Faolan ordered lemonade while Jelly got rum.

"Lemonade? You have not changed in the least, my friend," Jelly said with a chuckle.

"Trust me, I've changed a little." Faolan tossed his hat on the table, smoothing down the hair that had finally grown back in. "How 'bout you? How's business?"

Jelly removed his own wide-brimmed fedora to reveal his gleaming shaved head and made a face. "Things are a bit uncertain now that the Dutchman is dead, so I wait to see who comes to take his place."

"It'll be Luciano and the dagos picking up Schultz's rackets," Faolan told him, glancing out toward the bandstand. "Go see them before they start looking for you, might get a better place in line that way. Don't mention my name, though. Me and Charlie are on the outs."

"Ah, I see. That is unfortunate. But thank you for the tip, it's appreciated."

"Is that the Fitzgerald girl singing? I been hearing about her for months. Man, look at her! Is it true she's only seventeen fucking years old?"

Jelly grinned. "Hard to believe, I know, but very true. Her voice is like the fairest angel in heaven, yes?"

"I wouldn't disagree with you. She looks like she ought to be home in bed for school tomorrow, but the kid's fantastic."

The drinks came and Faolan found his lemonade surprisingly refreshing. Maybe Frank had been wrong about the whole taste change thing or maybe his just hadn't changed yet.

"Will you be coming uptown more often now?" Jelly asked, sipping his drink. "If so, perhaps you will bring your lovely wife again next time, eh?"

Before he could stop himself, he saw them out on the dance floor again as if it were happening before his eyes. Two ghosts, young and sparkling with happiness, doing the jitterbug with such exuberant passion that the dancers nearby actually stopped to watch and shout encouragement. It took Faolan another moment to recognize that the same song had been playing then as now: "Clap Hands, Here Comes Charley."

"What's wrong?"

Faolan glanced over at him and busied himself getting a cigarette. "Colleen died about, uh, six months ago."

Jelly sighed. "I am very sad to hear that, my friend. I could see that something bothered you from first glance and yet I still manage to stick my foot in my mouth. Forgive me."

Faolan waved off the apology and took a drag on his Camel. He wondered again if coming here had been such a smart idea, but he could still feel a groove here. Not his killing groove, which comforted him in its numbing coldness, but a sharper kind of groove full of life and pain and truth.

Chick Webb had gotten TB of the spine as a baby which had twisted him into something like a hunchbacked dwarf. The story went that, at three years old, his doctors had prescribed drumming as a way for him to soothe his stiff joints and so he started banging away on pots and pans. Whatever the truth, this tiny man who couldn't even reach a drum set without a special rig had built himself into one of the world's great drummers through the determination of his spirit and what Faolan's Ma would have termed "God-granted ability." This man lived with pain like Creation every day of his life and still came out smiling each night to do battle. And he was "just" a human.

What's my excuse?

He watched Webb and the Fitzgerald girl producing music that seemed to come straight from their souls and was ashamed at the audacity that had allowed him to feel sorry for himself. What he really wanted was just to know what his "God-granted ability" was, assuming he had one at all. Was he nothing but a skilled killer as he'd believed for the last few years? Was he destined for power and glory or should he give up now and spend his immortality here, appreciating the beauty of a life he'd foolishly given up?

"Perhaps I should leave you now to your thoughts," Jelly said.

"No," he said. "I could use the company. My thoughts ain't the kind of things I want to face alone."

Jelly smiled and started to say something, then trailed off. Faolan felt it, too: a change in the atmosphere, like an ice cube dropped into a warm bath. Glancing up, he saw Frank walking toward their table as club patrons moved away from him and the black cloud he carried.

Frank stopped at Jelly's chair without taking his eyes off Faolan and muttered, "Excuse us."

"I'll see you around sometime, my friend," Jelly said, taking his drink and hat. "I don't want to neglect the ladies."

Faolan nodded goodbye and jerked his head toward the vacant seat for Frank's benefit. "Hurry up and sit down, goon squad, the bouncers are getting jumpy."

In fact, there were quite a few people casting looks in their direction now, so Faolan did his best to look apologetic as Frank sat down. "You shouldn't be associating with people from your old life," he said.

"Jelly's good people."

Frank just gave him that thousand-yard stare. "Jelly Thompson rolls over with every change of the wind."

"That's why he's still alive and making money," Faolan said, still not looking in Frank's direction.

"Not for much longer. My guy Bennett's got someone primed to take over."

"Why throw away a good guy like Jelly? He's never done us a bad turn, which is more than I can say about some of our people. Besides, he's liked in the community and he don't ruffle any feathers downtown." He knew he was pleading a hopeless case, but he didn't like seeing decent guys go down, especially decent criminals. They were a rare breed.

"He's soft," Frank declared, needing only a gavel to sound more final. "Boss's orders are to plug any potential leaks and strengthen any potential weak spots before another attack comes, so we replace Jelly. We figure there's more money to be squeezed out of this area if people can still afford to come to places like this."

Faolan glared at him. "They come to places like this because things are bad. As bad as this depression is everywhere else, it's worse here. Make-believe hope like drugs and numbers only feel good for a little while, but places like this are different. There's something real here."

"Maybe to you. You're trying to recapture something that's lost in the past," Frank said. "Leave it there."

Yeah, just what he needed: a lesson in life from the Frankenstein Monster. He took another sip of lemonade and got Frank water when the waiter tip-toed over. Fitzgerald and the band slipped into the brisk favorite "Anything Goes."

"Can we go somewhere quieter?" Frank asked. "This music annoys me."

"You used to like it."

"Stop doing that."

"Doing what?"

He glanced at Frank as the big man leaned across toward him. "You keep trying to remind me of who I was. I told you before, that guy's dead. I don't enjoy listening to music anymore and that's that."

Faolan shook his head. "Man who doesn't listen to music is a man who's lost his soul."

Frank sat back and considered for a few moments. "Do you really think so?" he asked, his calm tone making it impossible to tell whether the idea thrilled or horrified him.

Faolan turned away and repressed a shudder as the scheming part of his mind clicked into action without an invitation. Frank was bluffing, his instincts said, showing strength to conceal weakness. What it meant for his plans right now he couldn't say, but he filed it away for future use. *Fuck it all, anyway*, he told himself. Colleen once asked him why he didn't pursue dancing or something and he'd told her that no man ever made a million bucks dancing. Truth was, though, that the thrill of the life called to him as much as the money, maybe even more. He wasn't part of this life anymore and would never be again. He would watch, take what he needed, and go back to his schemes and his killing groove.

Whatever the truth of his God-granted ability, he'd already made too many sacrifices on this road to turn off now. He watched the dancers spin and blew his regrets out in a cloud of smooth Turkish blend. "You want to talk to me, we talk here."

"Fine. Tell me why I'm here first," Frank said.

Faolan mocked him with a raised eyebrow. "Don't you know?"

"I need to know that you know."

He sighed. "Maybe Rothstein cheated me in that game and you were so tormented with guilt that you had to come right down after me and return my dough."

"He did cheat, that's true, but that's not why I'm here."

Faolan didn't even hear the second part. "What? You telling me he fucking cheated? That sonofabitch, I should have fucking called him on it! How's anybody pull four fucking aces against four jacks anyhow? How'd he do it? I watched him like a fucking hawk!"

"Forget about it," Frank said. "Suffice it to say me and Rothstein played as a team which, combined with all the other advantages he gave himself, is enough to sink even the best player. He only grifted that last hand because he wanted to make sure he busted you. Anyway, that's not the point. The point—"

"Yeah, yeah," he said, stabbing out his Camel. "I know why you fucking came here. You're here to offer me a helping hand up off the floor now that I've been knocked down, but you're probably just a ringer for Rothstein looking to get close so you can fuck me."

"You're probably right," Frank answered. "But that doesn't mean I intend to go through with it. So, let's talk."

"So you can run back and rat me out for plotting against the boss?"

Frank smiled that creepy smile of his. "I can run back and rat you out whether we talk or not. Doesn't matter if Killian believes me. You know he'll kill you just in case."

"Yeah, he's a fucking sweetheart, all right."

"Or I could just tell him about how you let that Scottish dyke go."

Faolan leaned in. "Look, that's the second time you've dropped a cute line about that. Do you fucking know something or are you just fishing?"

"I know you took her into Jersey against orders. You need to be more cautious in the future. there's lots of our guys who would love to shine up to Killian at your expense. Did you drink her? It doesn't matter, but I'm curious."

"No, I took her out of the situation, keeping Boston in the dark and maybe setting her up for use later on. She owes me one."

Frank nodded. "I hoped as much, though the odds of her returning to help are negligible. Terror tactics like what the boss was thinking of are only effective when there's an emotional attachment to the victim. As admirable as some of his methods are, he's got a few ideas that are just plain bughouse."

"Only a few? I'd say that's awful fucking generous." He took a sip of his lemonade.

Frank shook his head. "Don't let him fool you. he's not crazy or stupid. He spent most of his life running street gangs and, yes, that can be done through brute strength and reckless bravery, but Killian has much more going on upstairs than he lets on. Remember that you've only known him for two weeks and I've had a few years of close contact. I know you're an unusually good reader of people, but isn't it likely I'd have a better read in this situation?"

"Maybe."

"Darcy Killian cares about two, and only two, things with regard to this city: strength and control. Everything he does, everything he says, and every decision he makes increases one or the other for him."

Faolan lit up another cigarette. "He worries more about what race a fella belongs to than what that fella can do, so how's he expect to get good people? Not to mention his fucking paranoia and all that controlling and strength-building bullshit of his does nothing to get him loyalty."

"He doesn't need it," Frank said. "A fair and rational ruler gets questioned, gets argued with and disobeyed. A compassionate and cautious ruler has to surround himself with like-minded men or they'll take advantage of his fondness and doubts to destroy him. This is a society of predators we belong to now. Killian has to establish and maintain dominance in order to rule. Why do you think he insisted on going to Coney Island? It wasn't fatalism or the urge for a good brawl. It was because every one of us had to witness his ferocity, endurance, and relentlessness. Then, just in case anyone missed it the first time, he leaps—wounded and exhausted—into single combat against a fresh behemoth of a Vampyr and breaks her in an act of pure savagery. That creates an impression in each of our minds about what kind of force it would take to bring him down. Knowing he's only going to get more dangerous with age and experience, fear of his personal strength now weakens any plot against him."

"Yeah, okay, I get the tough-guy routine. I had that figured, but I also think it won't be tough to rally the men against him—"

"If you could get close enough to Killian, would you sacrifice yourself to take him out?" Frank asked.

"No, but I'd sacrifice somebody else."

Frank smiled his creepy smile again. "Now you're on the right track. Still, you see how effective this style of leadership is? If the boss is an eight-minute egg who will kill at the first sign of disloyalty, failure, or disagreement, then most of the gang is too busy keeping their heads down and trying to avoid screw-ups to think about plotting against him. Throw in a little fanning of natural rivalries and, instead of plotting against the boss, everybody's busy trying to get the boss' help to eliminate their competition for his favor. It's a classic set-up, aided by the fact that Killian isn't some human gang leader you can put a well-placed bullet into and call it a day. Especially not with a shadow like Johnny Devlin. Taking Killian and Rothstein down will take a well-planned and concerted effort."

"Any chance of bribing Devlin into turning assassin or taking a powder some night?"

"None," Frank said. "Killian controls his blood supply and his money. He's the only one Devlin respects, and—since Devlin can't help picking at people—he knows Killian's the only thing keeping him alive here. Then there's his reputation, which seems to be the only thing that really matters to the man. If Killian died while under his protection, his name wouldn't be worth shit in the mercenary trade anymore."

"All right," Faolan said, blowing a cloud of smoke. "What's your plan, then, genius?"

Frank shrugged. "I don't have one."

That made Faolan relax just a bit. He figured if a guy like Frank came to a guy like him with a fully mapped-out and bulletproof plan, then it was definitely a set-up.

The ghoul seemed to read Faolan's unspoken response. "I've been keeping my eyes open, cataloguing, while I waited for somebody with potential to join up."

"Why? You're in a pretty sweet spot, Frank. What exactly do you get out of plotting against Killian and Rothstein?"

Frank sipped his water for the first time, stalling. He had to know this was the make or break answer. "I've got personal reasons that wouldn't mean a thing to you. Mostly, though, I need to make my position stronger. I'm not particularly well-liked—"

"And you being such a charmer."

"Yeah. I have no irreplaceable skills or leverage on Rothstein or Killian to keep myself alive if they ever decide to bump me," Frank continued. "I'm also in a perfect position if Killian ever needs to scare Rothstein back into line. Killing me would inconvenience Rothstein just enough to send the message, but not enough to disrupt the operation."

It all fit perfectly with Frank's performance at the table, his obsession with the odds, the way he always made the safe move. "Maybe he'd kill Rothstein and promote you. He seems to like you well enough."

Frank shook his head. "I don't have A.R.'s contacts or his social graces. Killian sees Rothstein as a society gentleman who can move in criminal circles and the Jew world. We both know it's a bullshit image Rothstein created, but Killian bought it. He also figures that Rothstein's Jew blood makes it impossible for him to go anywhere in The Order without him, which makes him the perfect toady. Killian won't ditch Rothstein anytime soon with all the schemes they've got going together."

It was just too damn neat.

"Like what?" Faolan demanded.

"A new World's Fair is the big one," Frank answered without hesitation. "Won't be for a few years, at least, but they got an office for it set up in the building and Rothstein's hunting up backers. It's gonna be Killian's demonstration that his New York is a world power. Like the way he pushed through the construction of the Empire State Building in spite of a depression and the hostility of the Vampyr power structure of New York. Killian likes his statements big and bold."

Chick and Ella started in on "I Want To Be Happy." Faolan finished his lemonade and lit another Camel. "All right, so how come you picked me out of everybody? Or are you making this proposal to everybody and just waiting to see who bites first?"

"You're right, you're not the first." Frank leaned across the table. "I was just getting started with Byrne before Killian smelled a rat—or maybe he just got paranoid that Byrne was strong enough, smart enough, and well-liked enough to stage a successful coup. At any rate, somebody tipped off Philly to where they could find Byrne that night. Keep that in mind in your future dealings with Killian."

Faolan nodded, more surprised that he hadn't pieced that together himself than by the revelation.

Frank continued, "I remembered you from the old gang, so when your name came up as a potential recruit, I put in a good word. When I saw you again, I could see you were even better than I remembered. Harder, more ambitious and determined. You've got a good head for schemes, which I need—I've got a great eye for the big picture, seeing how everything fits together and I can see what needs to happen to change things, but I'm not good with the details of getting it done. I'm also not real good at getting people to do what I want except by coming right out and telling them, but I remember how you used to work people. You got a knack for thinking on your feet and you've got great instincts, both of which I need for this to work. Lastly, and most importantly, I've got something on you and, when we're done, I'll know where all the bodies are buried."

"So I can't just kill you after you help me take over."

"Exactly."

Faolan considered. "How can I trust you not to just kill me after we take over?"

"Trust doesn't factor into this," Frank said. "That's why it will work. It's a partnership based on mutual need.

You know I can't try to be Reeve myself. I don't have the strength to fight off all challengers and I don't have the personality to get others to fight them off for me. You, on the other hand, could be a very successful leader with the right advisors. With me playing the heavy for you—enforcing discipline, punishing disloyalty, preaching the hard truths and so on—you could have all the benefits of Killian's fear tactics while remaining popularly supported. You're too good a figurehead for me to want to eliminate you."

It was perfect, really. Everything fit together so nicely, he couldn't have worked it out any better himself.

Damn shame it was all a fucking con job.

Frank had stuck close enough to the truth to make it very hard to see any inconsistencies. He'd been waiting for a guy like him, all right: the perfect patsy.

Rothstein wanted to use him as a torpedo against Killian. Then Frank would kill him and Rothstein would take over New York.

"What about Rod?" Faolan asked, just to keep Frank from reading into his silence. "He's popular."

"Rod has no talent for manipulation or deception. You saw that tonight."

"What about Charnas? Or Fingers Martin for that matter?"

"Charnas is a bully and he's stupid. He'd be worse than Killian," Frank said, leaning back. "Martin doesn't have the stomach. Quit stalling, you know why I picked you and you know there's nobody else I could make this work with."

Faolan smiled and finished his Camel. "You're right. It just sounds too good to be true."

"Oh, sure. We just have to keep Killian, Rothstein, and everybody else from getting suspicious while we form a plan of action, execute it flawlessly, and deal with any unforeseen events all while fighting a successful war against every Vampyr in the Northeast. It's a fucking cakewalk."

"Well," he said, extending his hand, "since you put it that way, I suppose you can count me interested."

Frank shook his hand gravely, studying him. Then, without a word, he put on his hat and left. Faolan sat back and considered his options as Chick and his orchestra finished up the night's selections with the instrumental "Spinnin' the Webb." Complex and brassy, but slow in tempo, it made good scheming music.

Could he go directly to Killian and report Frank's little proposal without getting himself killed on suspicion? Even if he had to make his accusations in Rothstein's presence, he was pretty sure he could sway the boss to his side. The problem was Frank. Faolan's word against both Rothstein's and Frank's would be too tricky. Besides, if Frank mysteriously vanished without reporting back to Rothstein, A.R.'s credibility and ability to run his operations would take a big hit, leaving openings for Faolan to exploit later. That settled, he rose and grabbed his hat.

Frank had to die.

Chapter Twelve

Outside the Savoy, there was no sign of the big vampire.

Cinching up his light raincoat, Faolan went over to the nearest group of stragglers. "Hey, any of you folks see where the big ugly white guy went? Came out just a minute ago?"

"Friend of yours?" asked a scarred, wiry fella through teeth clenching a joint. The look in his eyes was suspicious bordering on hostile.

"No. I got something to settle with him, though."

Scarface considered, glancing around at his companions, and said: "Biggity motherfucker shoved me and my lady friend out the way so he could grab a hack, like he was The Man hisself."

Faolan glanced over at two more cabs parked at the curb. Drivers looking to make a few last fares often came down here as the Savoy emptied out. "You happen to catch the destination?"

"Station at One Twenty-Fifth and Lexington," Scarface said and then grinned wickedly. "You settle up with him good, hear?"

Faolan nodded, hopped in the nearest cab and headed off. By car, it was a short trip, but between the fare, the tip, and the subway, he'd be down to his last nickel by the end of it.

Of course, he'd be able to roll Frank for some cash when he was done.

He stared out the window as they rode down Lenox and sighed. Harlem was changing. The proud old row houses were looking a little less proud these days, the shops a little less prosperous, the streets a little less clean, and the people a little less hopeful. Away from the lights and music of the Savoy, what he'd said to Frank about Harlem came back to him like a fortuneteller's pronouncement of doom. This was a place Roosevelt's New Deal had yet to reach and it bothered him to think of so much potential destroyed by simple neglect.

As they turned onto 125th, the scenery transformed into a prosperous street lined with hotels, movie houses, real-estate offices, banks, and automats. Though folks from the area regularly shopped here, the businesses were all white-owned and many refused to even hire blacks. This was where the riot had happened back at the beginning of the year, though he couldn't see any signs of the violence that had led desperate storeowners to post signs advertising "We Employ Negro Workers" in the windows to avoid looting and vandalism. It had been an ugly incident, a stain on the thriving community he'd come to love and, as he'd found out after the fact, a strategic maneuver in Killian's campaign against Vandergriff, the former Reeve. All it had taken was an accusation of theft and some rumors to fan community outrage and produce looting, fires, and three Negro deaths.

Maybe he could make some changes once he had some power.

When the driver pulled to a stop, Faolan paid and got out. He waited at the head of the stairs until his improved hearing picked up the sound of the approaching subway and crept down the stairs. He spotted Frank at the platform, alone, and waited behind a column for the train to come thundering in before paying his fare and entering. Frank made the mistake of entering his empty car immediately, letting Faolan cross behind a group of night cleaning women leaving a rear car. Waiting until the last second to be sure Frank didn't hop off, Faolan got in the furthermost car and off they went.

He'd gotten his first report from Stephanie a few nights ago and, according to her, Frank spent his days at a secret residence in the city. Faolan hoped he was about to discover where.

He debated exactly how he should take Frank out when they reached his destination: a simple shot to the head followed by a nice long drink or something more flamboyant like burning down Frank's house with him in it. The difference lay mostly in the effect each would cause: a simple disappearance left a mystery he might choose to "solve" later while the torch-job suggested Frank faking his own death and skipping town, possibly to join their enemies. That added touch of paranoia could be very helpful in weakening Rothstein's credibility and would give Faolan a scapegoat to blame future intelligence failures on.

It was a good thing he stayed near the window at the first stop and watched to the very moment the doors closed, because that's when Frank got off. As soon as the train cleared the station, Faolan yanked the emergency stop cord and forced the doors of his car open as it squealed to a halt. Leaping out onto the tunnel floor, he ignored the shouts of the engineer as he ran back to the station, leapt back onto the platform, and jogged to the stairs. If Frank heard the sudden braking and was now waiting in ambush, then so be it. He'd finish up here while getting some good wounds to corroborate his story of Frank attacking him at Rothstein's direction or whatever cockamamie yarn he invented to explain the night's events.

He drew his trusted Browning as he crept up the last few steps, eyes darting and ears sharp for any hint of attack. Instead, he spotted Frank heading south down Lexington, still unaware of his presence. This area was primarily Puerto Rican as he could see from the brightly painted Spanish signs of the many *bodegas*, music shops, *canicieras* and bars. Lexington was much darker than Lenox, but he didn't put it past Frank's night vision to spot him, so he holstered his piece and moved into the shadows of a stone tenement's fire escape to wait.

When this kind of thing had become a routine part of his work, he'd hired a respected PI firm to instruct him on the tricks of the trade to avoid screwing up hits or recons by getting made. He'd learned that effectively tailing a walking target required a team of three or four guys working together, placing themselves in one of several patterns around the person and switching positions often. Simple disguises and props also came in very handy to keep from being recognized and it was assumed there would be other people out on the street to blend in with.

He didn't have any of that tonight.

On general principle, he'd taken to wearing soft-soled shoes years ago, so at least the sound of his footfalls didn't carry, but that was his main advantage. Frank's movements seemed edgier and he glanced around more. The Italian neighborhoods weren't far. They were probably close to home.

When Frank got two blocks up, Faolan darted out and moved with him a bit, keeping close to the buildings and their protective niches. The clattering of an old, open-bed truck made him spring into the bright yellow doorway of a Spanish restaurant, knowing the headlights would expose him just as Frank turned at the sound. As the truck rumbled past on the cracked and pitted street, Faolan saw that the back held cages of roosters and a Puerto Rican boy of about eight or nine who watched them.

Cock-fighting roosters, Faolan guessed, having been to two such matches in his time, both held in somebody's basement. The kid and his old man had to be on their way home at this hour.

Frank, illuminated in the truck's lights for a moment, continued down Lexington. As it beat him to the next intersection, the truck hit a bump or pothole and bounced one of its rooster cages off onto the street. The driver hadn't noticed yet and rattled along. The kid threw off his blanket and leapt off the truck to grab the cage.

That's when the battered Ford coup came racing around the corner onto Lexington, right toward where the kid was bent down wrestling with the cage. The lights hadn't hit the kid yet and, by the time they did, the Ford would have no time to stop.

Shit, he was too far!

Just as Faolan started to move, he saw something that made him freeze in his tracks: Frank rushing across the street on all cylinders, grabbing the kid (and the rooster cage he held), and carrying him out of harm's way as the Ford swerved to the curb, horn bleating.

As soon as the kid was safe, Frank dropped him and the two just stood and looked at each other for a second until the kid's father shouted from where he'd brought the truck to a stop. The kid, clutching his precious passenger, ran up the block to where his old man gave him nine kinds of hell before hugging him tightly.

Frank watched them until they continued on their way, nothing showing in his face or body that Faolan could read. Meanwhile, the driver of the Ford got out, looking both soused and terrified. He rushed across the street to Frank, babbling out his worries and relief about the kid with a good share of excuses mixed in for good measure.

Frank said nothing, hardly even seemed to be paying attention to the guy as he glanced around and walked back toward the Ford. The drunk followed like a puppy, calming down now but still going on about what a close call and no need to bother the police and so on. Frank just kept checking the area, but nobody else seemed to have heard the disturbance or was interested enough to look out their window.

So Frank snapped the drunk's neck.

Faolan wasn't sure he'd seen it right, but Frank just shot his hands out and *snap!* The guy didn't even have time to stop talking before he was a heap in Frank's arms. Frank didn't drink him. he just shoved the body back into the seat of the car, looked around again, and hurried his pace down Lexington.

Faolan followed, eager to get past the corpse in the car before some beat cop came along. They'd crossed some invisible border and entered the older, Italian area. exposed red brick replaced stone on the buildings, building-front fire escapes gave way to plain-fronted tenements, muted Italian and English signs replaced the vibrant Spanish, and dry-goods stores and tailoring shops took the places of the music stores. The bars remained bars. He felt a pent-up breath blow out of him in relief when Frank made the right at 107th Street and he could run flat-out and close some distance.

107th . The Helmar Social Club had been on 107th! They were almost at the spot where Frank and Coll had shot the Vengalli kid!

Everything clicked, all at once, and Faolan had to force himself not to burst out laughing. He'd seen Frank's hole cards now and understood what all those mixed signals had been about. Frank had a guilty conscience, but didn't want anyone to know it. If he wanted revenge for being locked up with a kid like Faolan had been, then maybe he was sincere about his offer and was just playing along with Rothstein.

Faolan might not have to kill him, after all.

Peeking around the corner, he saw Frank halfway down the block and spotted a convenient hiding place behind a stoop. He snuck over to it and waited until Frank cleared the block before repeating the process. Finally, as they reached the block where the Helmar Social Club had been, Frank stopped. Faolan ducked behind a parked car and watched Frank check the deserted street one last time before fishing out a set of keys and climbing the steps of a gray, freestanding tenement that looked almost indistinguishable from any of the others on the block.

Just for kicks, he decided to make a dramatic entrance. Stepping onto the sidewalk, he lit a well-earned Camel and the *click-snick* of his Zippo shattered the glassy silence.

Frank froze, key in the lock.

"Looks like we both got something on each other now," Faolan said, strolling toward him.

Frank turned before Faolan could say another word, ran across the stoop's small concrete ledge, and leapt at him. Faolan reached into his jacket for the Browning, but got fouled on his raincoat as Frank tackled him, fangs bared for striking—

Chapter Thirteen

Ironically, it was his tangled arm that saved him, creating an elbow-wedge that kept Frank's mouth from making it to his neck. Before Frank's greater weight could finish settling on him, he twisted his hips hard and rolled, but Frank pulled him close and held. Those big, meaty hands on their long, wiry arms wrapped around his throat and began to squeeze.

Strangulation wasn't as easy as they made it look in the movies, Faolan knew, and it was even more difficult to strangle somebody from below, but Frank was making a pretty good try of it. Still, Faolan could see the other vamp wasn't using that big, rational brain of his and that was an advantage. Struggling his way to his knees before he started seeing spots or going weak forced Frank to extend his arms to their full reach. Knowing from experience that you never mess with the hands in a situation like this, Faolan swung his fists down hard on Frank's locked elbows. The first time had no effect, but the second time he felt those long arms buckle a little and saw the wince on Frank's face. That's when he pushed off with his legs, breaking out of Frank's grip and shot to his feet. He kicked like a football player, nailing Frank solidly in the nuts and jumped back as the bigger man curled up.

Only when his Browning was out and aimed squarely at Frank's head did he let himself rub his sore neck. "Christ, did I fucking spook you, Frank?"

"Don't you think you got the bite on me," Frank growled from the sidewalk, his voice all choked up. "I'm not letting you bleed me over this. I'll put myself out in the sun first!"

Faolan inched closer and squatted down, lowering his piece but keeping it handy. "Frank, don't go screwy on me. I'll keep your secret."

Frank sat up, but said nothing. Looking closely, Faolan thought he saw a spark in the normally lifeless eyes. "Do you understand that if Killian found out, he wouldn't kill me for it?" Frank asked with a cold, dull voice. He didn't move and he didn't look at Faolan. He stared straight ahead.

But he blinked rapidly.

"He'd try to ... fix me," he continued. "He'd put me in the cell over and over again, kid after kid, until I break completely or I get past it. I know I should let him or I ought to do it myself—I want to be stronger. I want to be sleek and cold and practical like you. When I saw the way you handled that kid: quick and business-like, but with no unnecessary cruelty, like a tiger or a scorpion—just strike and feed. You did what you had to and moved on with no looking back. I get so scared of going through the cell again, so sick with fear—"

"I understand," Faolan interrupted, putting his hand on the bigger man's shoulder while unobtrusively slipping his pistol into his coat pocket. It was hard to imagine what was going on inside Frank: emotion that he wasn't used to and didn't know how to express. His cold monotone had no relation to the words marching out of his face. It sounded like some speech he'd committed to memory without any attempt at understanding, but it made sense to Faolan. He'd known a few guys who'd come home from the war the same way: shell-shocked. He believed what he was hearing and realized Frank had been waiting for a moment like this to come whether he knew it or not. Probably for years now.

Frank didn't acknowledge the hand on his shoulder and his eyes didn't lose their thousand-yard stare. "I saw that Vengalli kid go down that day with Coll. I thought I sprayed above the kids' heads, to get them down while Coll went to work with the street-sweeper, but I saw right away that I hit the boy. I felt terrible, of course, but it's not like I fell apart. I was gonna be turning into a vampire, after all. When they made that chump think he was Frank Giordano, I remember wondering if maybe somehow God would be fooled. That because this man believed he was me and because my flesh and blood would be completely transformed that maybe my sins would somehow transubstantiate onto him the way the host wafers and wine becomes the flesh and blood of Christ during Holy Communion. That my soul would pass to him and be judged when he died in the chair."

Faolan sat down on the curb next to him and reached his arm around the big man's shoulders. Frank didn't react. "I kept thinking about that. For days and nights I dwelled on the idea until it seemed very real and so much more horrible than even being damned for all eternity. That I would be a creature beyond sin or divine judgment. That if I ever stood before God, He wouldn't even know who or what I was. I wrestled with it all during my Creation process, but before I had a chance to work any of it out, Killian and Rothstein put me in the room we used to use for the tests and there he was..."

"God?"

"Michael Vengalli. Just the same as the day I shot him. I never saw that little girl Killian talks about. It was always him. He talked the whole time, telling me I was right about Vampyrs being soulless creations that exist outside the grace of God. I don't remember all of it because my mind tore itself apart during those eight days and reconstructed itself and some things got lost. I've been trying to purge myself of these echoes of Frank Giordano, these feelings that haunt me and make me do impractical things like saving that kid and living as close as I can to where the Vengalli boy died."

Faolan gave his shoulder a squeeze. "It's just guilt, Frank."

"No!" Frank's voice rose for the first time. He glanced at Faolan moved out from his arm. "I don't feel guilt. A predator doesn't feel sorry for the prey it kills to survive."

"Ah balls," he said. "Don't you start with Killian's predator bullshit. We ain't just a couple of lions in the jungle, Frank, we're people. I'm no expert, but feeling guilt seems like a pretty good argument that you still got a soul. Don't try to get rid of that guilt, Frank. Sometimes that pain is all we've got to let us know we're alive. You think snuffing a kid didn't bother the fuck out of me? That all the lousy shit I've done in my life don't hurt? It keeps me awake all hours sometimes, haunting me so I never forget all the dues I've already paid. The way I figure it, a great man who's done some terrible things is still a great man, while a nobody who does terrible things is just a scumbag. So I got to keep pushing for greatness. How 'bout you?"

Frank looked at him and considered for a moment before speaking. "That person I used to be is gone for good. I know I can't ever get him back, but I can make Killian and Rothstein pay for what they did to him."

Faolan nodded, lighting a cigarette. "Now that's a motive I can trust." He brought out his warmest smile, stood, and held out his hand. "Let's get your revenge and mine both, but let's be smart about it. Let's forget about having something on each other and be a real team. Let's shoot for greatness together."

He watched the spark in Frank's eyes turn into honest human uncertainty for a second, and then warmth, and he knew that he'd won him. Even as the life retreated from Frank's eyes and the big man rose without taking his hand, Faolan was confident in his read. Frank had burned out so many of his emotions that the few he still possessed worked into everything, regardless of how little he let show. A big smile and enthusiastic handshake would have been an act and told Faolan he'd blown it. No, Frank had felt the hooks go in and it scared him, hence the sudden cold front. If his new partner didn't try to kill him before the night was out, Faolan figured the man was completely his.

"Come inside," Frank said as he picked up their hats from the porch steps where they had wound up. "There's a few hours left before sunrise. we should discuss our first steps."

"You really live in a tenement apartment?" he asked as Frank led him up the stairs. A plaque beside the door proclaimed the building to be some doctor's private research facility. Through the front window, Faolan could see a furnished office with diplomas on the wall, a desk, and filing cabinets.

"I own the entire building through intermediaries and one of my Dhampirs runs the place and conducts all the business needed for its upkeep," Frank said, unlocking the door and waiting until Faolan entered the vestibule so he could lock it behind them. "My position allows me the freedom to live outside the Empire State Building and I need someplace where I can conduct my studies without giving my thoughts away. Don't believe for a moment that you're safe or have any privacy while you're living under Killian's roof. Think of your place there as a set, like in a theater. it should show Killian and his people exactly what you want them to think of you."

Bypassing the door to the office entirely, Frank unlocked another door at the far end and led Faolan into an unadorned hall. "I had the insides gutted and rebuilt for my purposes."

The hall was a row of unfinished doors leading to a staircase, all exposed slats and sub-flooring and bare light bulbs. "Love the décor," Faolan said. "Very chic."

He heard strange noises coming from one of the floors above.

Frank opened the first door on the left. "As long as it works, I don't care how things look. Step into my parlor."

The smell hit Faolan first, his sensitive Vampyr nose recoiling at the alien scent. Frank flipped on the lights and entered, Faolan behind him. Was that a tree there in the corner? It was, planted in dirt and sitting behind a sheet of glass that took up the whole corner. The room was empty except for a bunch of glass tanks around the perimeter and a wheeled chair, apparently for watching whatever was in the tanks. The exterior walls still had scraps of wallpaper clinging to them and the cracked linoleum on the floor suggested this had once been a kitchen or washroom. He saw something move in the tank next to him and leaned closer for a look.

"Spiders?" he asked, straightening back up. "What, you planning on opening the world's creepiest pet shop or something?"

Frank joined him. "I needed models from the natural world to help me determine what Vampyrs should be in our purest form. The one in front of you is an *Atrax Robustus* or Sydney Funnel-web. They're poisonous and have fangs that can penetrate a child's fingernail, but the smaller male's venom is five times more potent than the female's. Strong enough to kill a man. The big one in the web is the female and I have a male who has a burrow under those rocks. I'm hoping to watch them mate when they're mature and then the female will most likely kill the male."

"Like one of them Black Widows, eh?" Ugly fuckers, he thought, watching the black, cockroach-sized monster move around in its white tubular web.

"Not really," Frank said. "That spider's poorly named. Look around you, Faolan, and learn. Spiders are among the most adaptable creatures on Earth: there are tens of thousands of species existing in every corner of the globe under every environmental condition. Even though they're not technically blood-drinkers, they possess fangs which they use to hunt prey and their digestive system is similar to ours. Most species also re-grow lost limbs like we do—"

"Wait, you mean like if somebody chops my arm off, I can grow it back?"

"As long as your heart is circulating blood," Frank said. "It usually takes a month or two, depending on the size of the missing piece and the amount of blood consumed. Properly nursed, it's even possible for Vampyrs to survive your famous bullet between the eyes, so always make sure to stop the heart."

Frank went over to a large tank filled with an intricate gold web, bent down to a cabinet beneath, and brought out a box of chirping crickets. "Like us, spiders have to feed on live prey. Most have poisons to paralyze or webs to immobilize them, which we don't, but I find much to admire in their hunting behaviors." Reaching in and pinching out a couple crickets between his fingers, he dropped them into the tank. "Have you noticed that Vampyrs aren't a well-designed species? As predators, we're lacking in natural adaptations for successful hunting. We're a little stronger, our senses are a bit more acute, and we're more robust, but our most successful technique is socializing with our prey or using human tools, concepts, and institutions to make them amenable to feeding. Then there's our extreme vulnerability to ultraviolet radiation, which makes no sense from an evolutionary standpoint. I don't believe that our species evolved in the Darwinian sense. I've read the writings of some Order scholars who believe we're either demon-tainted descendants of Adam's first wife, Lilith, or the Nephilim who the Bible mentions being wiped out by the Great Flood. Others claim we descend from Lamia of Greek myth."

"Yeah, that's one hell of a family tree, all right," Faolan muttered, wondering whether it was better being related to spiders or demons. "Where do you learn all this, anyhow?"

"Rothstein and Everett both have large and eclectic libraries. Do you like my *sitticus palustris*?"

"Yeah, it's swell." The spider in question was about the size of a quarter and had a black upper body with short black legs and a bright red abdomen. From across the tank, it sprang up onto the glass and Faolan jumped back, suppressing a shiver.

"He's beautiful. Jumping spiders stalk their prey from a distance and then pounce. they can leap forty times the length of their own body. These creatures are absolute masters of industry, economy, and patience. Most of them are nocturnal hunters, though, so it's better to watch them with the lights off."

Faolan shook his head. "You must have a waiting list miles long. So, what's in the tree, a vampire bat?"

"No."

"Of course not." He lit a Camel.

"I keep the vampires down in the basement in a special room that replicates a cave," Frank explained. "I've set up a dark room beside it where I can watch them feed on pigs. Occasionally humans. They're very subtle creatures, masters of stealth and the delicate touch."

At first Faolan thought this was another bad attempt at humor, but something in those dark, dead eyes told him otherwise. He decided to ignore the bit about the people. "And here I thought bats were just for belfries."

Frank kept on like it was the most sensible thing in the world. "Naturally, it's too difficult to buy live pigs regularly, so I had to start breeding them."

"Naturally."

"I converted the third story into a pen with an industrial elevator to carry the pigs directly from the third floor to the basement. With my Dhampir here to see to their daily requirements, they're doing quite well. Would you like to watch the bats feed on one?"

"No."

"What about a person?"

"Fuck no."

"You're right, we're straying off the point," Frank said. "Killian and Rothstein are trying to create their own web out of the Empire State Building and, eventually, all of New York City: a protected, well-constructed web that traps and entangles any prey or enemy that tries to challenge them."

"So we tear it down and squash them before they finish putting it together, right?" Faolan paced a few steps in each direction, not wanting to get too close to any of the tanks. He'd never been particularly bothered by spiders before, but this place was starting to give him the willies.

Frank stared at him a moment with eyes as unreadable as those of one of his spiders and cocked his head to the side. "Do you know the differences between true spiders and tarantulas?"

He shrugged. "Grooming?"

Frank did his creepy smile. "In a way. Here, let me show you."

Frank opened a door into the next room, walked in, and turned on an amber-painted light. Faolan noticed a difference in the temperature: this room was hotter. As expected, the first terrarium he saw on his right featured your standard black and brown tarantula lounging on some desert-type rocks. Frank, box in hand, opened the feeding slot on top of the tank and dropped in a cricket. As Faolan watched, the hairy bug skittered over and made with the fangs while the cricket was still getting its bearings.

"See? No real strategy, just a strong and direct attack," Frank said, closing the slot and walking over to a larger tank that appeared to be empty except for a foot's worth of clay-heavy soil. Dropping another few crickets inside, he motioned Faolan closer. Reluctantly, Faolan came over in time to see one of the crickets disappear.

"What—"

Frank shushed him and Faolan watched the second cricket more closely. Getting itself together, the little insect made an experimental hop ... and a piece of the ground popped open and the cricket disappeared in a flash of writhing legs.

"Holy shit!"

"Trap-door spider, of which I have a few varieties," Frank explained. "The engineers of the tarantula family. Some of their lairs are ingenious, but outside the protection of their tunnels they're extremely timid and vulnerable."

Setting the crickets down, Frank stepped over to the largest of the terrariums: nearly four feet square and filled with jungle plants and a sprinkler valve up top for watering them. Frank opened up the cabinet beneath the tank and Faolan heard the rattling of a metal box and an angry hissing.

Thinking Frank had finally gotten around to the snakes, he took an involuntary step back in shock when Frank turned around holding the biggest spider Faolan had ever seen. The damn thing was bigger than his hand! Held by its front legs, the hairy brown monster twitched and flexed while Frank admired it with ghoulish pride.

Swear to Christ, if he tosses that thing at me, I'll blow the motherfucker apart in mid-air!

This was definitely the last time they were meeting at Frank's place. Ever.

"*Theraphosa Blondi*," Frank declared. "The Goliath Bird-Eating Spider from the jungles of South America. This is a male on the youthful side of maturity—five or six-years-old, I think. he's very aggressive and hungry from being locked up and holding him like this is only going to fire him up more."

"Blondie, did you say?" Faolan asked, trying to force himself to relax and finish his Camel. "Looks more like an auburn brunette to me."

"Let's pretend this feisty fella is you, Faolan. Open the top of the terrarium for me, would you?"

Just what I always wanted in a namesake, he thought, moving toward the tank with uncharacteristic hesitation. "Move back a little, Frank, I don't want you touching me with that fucking thing."

"Its venom is harmless to humans and Vampyrs."

"I don't give a fuck!"

Frank moved back and Faolan slid open a panel in the top, stepping back quick when Frank came forward to lower the struggling beast into the tank. "So, let's say that your savage and direct tarantula plan works and we tear down Killian and Rothstein's web before they finish constructing it. Let's pretend further that your partner, Frank the Tree Dwelling Funnel-web, managed to get the best of a scorpion named Devlin that was roaming around this tank, guarding its master. Rothstein, a trap-door spider, is hiding around here somewhere, but he won't be a factor in this fight. So, that just leaves…"

As the auburn-haired arachnid waved its legs at Frank's retreating arms, another Goliath emerged from a burrow beneath a small log: it was dark brown, had fangs like a cobra, and was nearly twice the size of the first with a leg-span a full foot across!

"Killian: the older male guarding his territory."

The two monstrosities rubbed their front legs together, and reared back on their hind legs to spread their thick, hairy arms out and up. He didn't know if they were intimidating each other, but he sure as hell wanted nothing to do with either. The Faolan-spider broke first, racing at the bigger guy and trying to topple him onto his back, or maybe just to get a good bite in on his underside.

Whatever the idea, it didn't work. The darker one brought his legs down before auburn could get beneath him and the two spent the next few seconds grappling legs and trying to get close enough for a strike.

"C'mon, small-fry. Don't fight him on his terms. You gotta get behind him, climb on top of him—that's it!" he called at the tank. Frank gave him a look like *he* was the weirdo. "So I want him to win now, what of it?"

Just when it looked like the little auburn spider was going to pull it off, it was over: the big brown bastard reared up and slammed down on the smaller guy, pinning the front legs, and jammed his fangs into auburn's back. He held auburn down for a second before scrambling back to wait while the loser curled up like a fist.

"So, that's what happens when a smaller tarantula tries to challenge an older, larger tarantula." Frank said. "Now Killian takes Faolan back down into the lair to devour at his leisure."

Faolan turned away and took a seat in the room's observation chair. "Okay, very cute. But what would you have said if the little guy pulled it off?"

"That was a possibility," Frank admitted. "If it happened, I would have told you how a bird named Burlington, attracted by the disturbance, makes a meal of both spiders, leaving the prized burrow open for that sneaky little trap-door spider that waited in hiding."

"Rothstein's plan," he said.

Frank nodded. "Have I mentioned that even a Goliath is extremely vulnerable when it's molting—that is, when it's shedding its old skin to grow larger? When his new exoskeleton is fresh and soft, even a wasp or poisonous ant might kill it."

The weirdest thing was that Faolan followed Frank's convoluted train of thought. "Grooming. When I said that, you told me I was right ... so, Rothstein has been starting to groom Killian, to help him fit better into the big picture—helping him shed his skin and grow into a new one, so to speak. You're saying that's when he'll be vulnerable."

"Exactly," Frank said, his face animated for a moment with pride. The big man knelt down in front of him, channeling urgency with his eyes. "Let them build their carefully-constructed tunnels and their water-tight trap-door to hide behind. You have to maintain Killian's affection, make him believe that you live to do things for him, get him to carry you on his back like a mother Wolf Spider, and raise you to a position where you're his natural successor. Peasant revolutions scare the upper echelons of The Order, they don't like to see someone rise up from the crowd and strike down a leader—the illusion of hierarchy has to be maintained."

"That's the same game Byrne was playing, wasn't it?" Faolan asked, running his hands through his hair and leaning back. "Didn't work too well for him."

"That's because he moved too fast, trying to build himself up by openly disagreeing with Killian and thinking he could convince the men to support him against the boss. We won't make that mistake. Nobody joins this coup but us and we make Rothstein think his plan is working for as long as possible." Frank smiled and leaned closer, making the hairs on the back of Faolan's neck stand up. "We take a lesson from the bat and move silently, we sit gently upon our prey and bite painlessly with razor-sharp fangs, then bleed him slowly without alerting him."

Faolan tried not to smile. "All while sitting on his back like a baby Wolf Spider?"

"Right. Then, once he's done molting and we're in position to inherit the lair free and clear, we strike!"

It wasn't a bad start, really: his personality and instincts, Frank's brains, a war to blame things on, and even some unwitting assistance from Rothstein.

"At which point I'd be a grown up Wolf Spider," Faolan added. "What are they like, anyhow?"

Frank didn't get that he was being ribbed. "They're wonderful. They're small for tarantulas, but they have eyes all around their heads, they can hunt in the open or make traps like a trap-door spider which makes them very adaptable, and their venom causes a necrosis that eats through flesh and tissue all the way to the bone. Nothing can stop it!"

"Yeah, sounds just like me," he muttered.

"I see myself as an *Atrax Formidabilis*, the tree-dwelling cousin to the Sydney Funnel-web you were looking at," Frank continued, talking mostly to himself. "They create very well-designed and practical webs, though the male tends to lead a more wandering existence. The Tree-Dweller is extremely aggressive and one of the most lethal spiders in the world. one bite can easily kill a full-sized man. Though, I also like to think I've got just a bit of tarantula in me."

Faolan sighed and got up to leave. "We gotta get you a new fucking hobby, Frank."

Chapter Fourteen

Arnold Rothstein's visitor entered the suite through the gallery, a formal central foyer that connected several rooms and provided a display for several of the most impressive pieces in A.R.'s collection. Dove gray walls with eggshell trim created a neutral backdrop that showcased his Picasso, his Renoir, his Van Gogh—originals, of course—and his Ming vases. At least, that was what the decorator had told him. He'd trusted the decorator's judgment in such matters because he really had no eye for that garbage. "Whatever makes the pictures look the best," he'd said when he cut the check. Most had been gifts from the same society snobs that used to look down their noses at him, tributes to the power he now wielded.

The ornate grandfather clock out in the gallery chimed five o'clock a.m. and Arnold's visitor paused a moment in his approach. Then the footsteps resumed, the strides slow and measured as they echoed on the black and white checkerboard marble tile. Arnold could have looked up and watched him approach, but he didn't.

Arnold was enjoying a late dessert in his dining room. Well, "enjoying" may not have been the best way to describe it, since his meal consisted of a blood-based pudding his chef had prepared incorporating some sort of citrus blend for flavor. The chef was a special Order-trained culinary artist specializing in the difficult art of transforming ordinary human blood into new and interesting meals within the limited digestive confines of the Vampyr. They were very hard to acquire and extremely prestigious to own—even Killian himself didn't have one—but Arnold had managed. His chef was a second-rater, of course, since New York's outlaw position made getting someone better impossible, but even a second-rate blood chef was not something a city Steward had access to under normal circumstances. He let that thought cheer him a bit as he scooped another spoonful of the viscous maroon custard from the crystal parfait dish and transferred it to his mouth. Something in the combination of flavors was too sour for his liking tonight—the chef had made this dish before and he'd enjoyed it, but the blood was off tonight or perhaps he'd used too much grapefruit juice or lime juice or whatever.

His choice to eat during this visit was deliberate, of course, as was everything he did. Not only was forcing another to stand and wait while you took your ease and busied yourself with some other task an effective method of reinforcing your superior status, it also gave him the ability to show off the fact that he had a live-in blood chef. It didn't particularly matter if the visitor was impressed or not, because it was the statement that mattered. Arnold wasn't looking for compliments, just acknowledgement. It was the same reason he conducted the poker games here in his suite or in his office. He didn't surround himself with all these luxurious and lovely things because he needed them. He was no hedonist, he could have lived comfortably in a simple suite with a bed, a desk, and the other necessities of his nightly duties, but that wouldn't be fitting. It wasn't about having, it was about being *seen* to have. Others had to be made aware of your value or they would quickly come to doubt whether you had any at all.

The visitor entered the dining room through the archway where the marble gave way to gleaming oak. Arnold had seated himself at the head of the table on the opposite side of the room against the large windows and city backdrop which were framed by royal blue damask curtains with gold piping. The same pattern appeared on the napkins and place settings on the hand-carved twenty foot rectangular table that could seat eighteen people but never had. The only light in the huge room came from the four gold candelabras positioned at intervals upon the table surface and the large, ornate fireplace to Arnold's left.

He'd gotten the candelabras from a respected old society dowager in payment for her son's gambling debts and his agreement to take no more bets from him. He still remembered just how much effort it had taken the old girl to maintain a civil façade as she invited him into her home and granted him an audience. Her good-for-nothing son could disappear for all she cared, but when word began to spread that he had debts he couldn't pay, well, that was a different situation all together. The old dowager didn't have nearly the kind of money she pretended anymore, so he'd made sure to stick it to her and take the candelabras—which were worth far more than the debts he'd bought—because he knew she couldn't come up with the cash.

Nobody treated Arnold Rothstein like that without paying the price.

Which brought him back to his present situation with the O'Connor punk. Of all the people to bring into the organization, why O'Connor? What was it that made Killian throw caution to the wind and take an unnecessary chance on a disrespectful little *goniff* like him? Did O'Connor remind Killian of himself as a younger man? It had to be some kind of silly sentimentality like that, since it made no logical sense at all. A man with a history of treachery and disrespect for authority like that and Killian somehow thought the leopard was going to change his spots? Maybe it was an Irish thing. He'd had the same problems with Jack Diamond and his brother and, really, wasn't O'Connor just an extension of that same problem?

Back when he was still human, Arnold Rothstein had dental problems. Soft teeth. All his life they were an issue until he finally spent an entire day at the dentist getting the damn things pulled one by one. He'd brought his ledgers with him, of course, and conducted his business over the dentist's phone between drillings and spitting out mouthfuls of blood. Money was money, after all, and the day was already costly enough without loosing a full day's action in the bargain. When he was done, he had a sore jaw to beat the band and a new set of firm dentures and that was that. Or so he'd thought. Didn't it just figure that, while becoming a Vampyr, lo and behold what should happen but his teeth should grow back! His *soft* teeth! Killian and his flunkies had laughed and made jokes for months at his difficulty with feeding. What could he do? The damn teeth just wouldn't take a point, so he was forced to find another way. For years it was needles and razors like some dirty hop-head until he'd finally arranged for his chef.

Some problems just kept coming back again and again.

Like his teeth.

Like O'Connor.

It had been very satisfying to put the gunman in his place earlier this evening, but Arnold didn't think for a second that his little demonstration had done more than tweak O'Connor's nose. No, O'Connor was a problem that was going to be around for a while and—like his teeth giving him the need to hire the chef—he'd decided to make the disadvantage of O'Connor's presence work in his favor. That was why his visitor was here now, after all.

Arnold was eager to hear the news, but made a point of restraining himself through a few more spoonfuls of the too-sour blood pudding, thinking all the while of how much he would have liked to be having a good steak at Lindy's as various associates, cronies, and patronage-seekers came to his table to pay their respects and run their propositions by him or seek his aid or counsel. He lost himself for just a few moments, reveling in the memories, which wasn't like him at all. Still, it was tempting to go back to a time before all the blood (both literal and figurative), back to a time when he was just a man with a loving wife, a mistress, his money, his horses…back to when a card game was just a card game. Back before everything turned so sour.

Pulling himself from his reverie, he set down the spoon, took a sip of water from the crystal water glass, and dabbed his lips with a napkin before turning to his visitor, who stood beside his chair. "Well, how'd it go?"

"He's in the web," answered Frank Giordano. "Now we just gotta wait till he moves around enough to get stuck."

PART THREE

EARLY POSITION
December, 1936

Have you seen the well to do up and down Park Avenue?
On that famous thoroughfare with their noses in the air
High hats and arrowed collars, wide spats and fifteen dollars
Spending every dime for a wonderful time
- Judy Garland, "Putting on the Ritz"

Chapter Fifteen

"You sure they're coming tonight?" Paulie King asked. "I'm gonna feel like a fucking *jah-drool* if I sat out here all night for nothing."

"What do you want I should tell you, Paulie?" Faolan said, finishing his cigarette. "My plants in Philly said tonight, so we're out waiting tonight."

"Yeah, but you said they'd be here early."

Faolan sighed. He was trying to listen to the live Duke Ellington broadcast over the radio, since Enzo's Packard had one. It was one of the Duke's first shows since the death of his mother last year and Faolan hoped he'd perform that new "Reminiscing in Tempo" he'd written in her honor. Faolan thought it was a beautiful piece and longed to hear it live without all the changing of records it normally required.

"I said if it was me, I'd try to slip through very early or very late. Actually, if I thought they had anything like this set up, I'd get crated up in trucks during the day and have one of my Dhampirs drive us in."

"Damn, that's sneaky," Enzo said, glancing away from the steady stream of cars exiting the Holland Tunnel. "You don't think they did that, do you?"

"Ah, sweet Christ, this is a waste of time," Paulie whined.

Rod took his eye away from the viewer of his fancy new Leica camera with its long telescopic attachment. The former Marine had taken to the photography craze with gusto, but at least the camera could serve multiple purposes. "Would you give it a rest, Paulie? My people in the Port Authority inspected all the warehouses that got shipments today."

"Even the ones that always get shipments?"

"Especially those."

Before anybody could say anything more, Frank's voice crackled over the other radio: "This is Funnel-web calling Wolf Spider, any sightings yet? Over."

The military style two-way radio resting under the dash of Enzo's Packard Twelve, which a few cities' police forces had begun experimenting with, was the most expensive brainstorm he and Frank had come up with to improve New York's defenses. Using the antennas of the Empire State Building as a central hub, they had put up "repeaters" to amplify their signal all across the city, spinning a web of sound that connected all their teams together. And although they used channels that most of the ham radio crowd didn't frequent, they still had to be very careful about what went over the air. Frank's transmission caused the car's receiver to break up, so Faolan shut it off just as Ellington was starting in on "Sophisticated Lady."

He grabbed the little microphone off the floor and pressed the button. "Nothing yet, there, uh, Funnel-web, but it's still pretty early." He set the microphone down, then remembered the protocols Frank had drilled into his head and picked it up again. "Uh, over."

They listened as Frank went through the same routine with all the other teams.

It had taken a few months for their enemies to recover from the enormous losses they'd suffered at Coney Island, but they'd done so quicker than expected. By the time Moore had enough spare men Created and trained, winter had given way to spring and fending off the Northeast's financial assaults were taking most of the organization's time and attention. Despite Rothstein's best efforts, many of their real estate holdings suffered banking errors and were vandalized or foreclosed upon while their companies were audited, sued, or subjected to hostile takeovers. During all this, Faolan stepped up and organized the scant resources Rothstein begrudged him, managing to capture or kill every infiltration team the Northeast sent their way and thwart attempts by Crowbar Charnas to steal his credit. Finally, by the time summer's long days and short nights provided a slowdown in the frequency and scale of attacks, Killian promoted Faolan to acting Street Boss. Faolan and Frank had quickly agreed that, in a city of millions, only coordination of efforts would provide any chance against the many possible routes of attack, but it had cost them a mint. If Killian was impressed come the year's end, the job would be his and he'd be where he needed to be. If he blew it, he'd be dead.

"Wolf Spider, you there?" The distorted voice of Marty Rice crackled over the radio, interrupting a debate between the swordsman "Slash Gordon" Romkey and Paulie over the relative physical attributes of Greta Garbo and Jean Harlow. "This is Golden Orb and we got a sighting at the toll plaza. Six guys in a dark green Lincoln sedan, over."

Faolan grabbed the microphone as everyone else in the car clammed up. Golden Orb was Crowbar Charnas' team. Ed Charnas was Rothstein's man and Faolan's only real competition for the Street Boss position. Faolan needed this plan to work to put Charnas in his place. "He's sure? Over."

"Our spotter says yes. All six have the look and there's a shiner in the bunch. You sure you don't want us to just knock them off the bridge? Over."

Given the burning of body fat that happened when a Vampyr got Created, it wasn't hard to pick one out from a crowd if you knew what you were looking for. One skinny guy might not mean anything, but a car full of skeletons? Not likely. The other giveaway was the cat-like eye-shine some vamps developed for some reason. An experienced spotter could pick them out nine times in ten and Faolan's crew was getting to be awful experienced.

"Just stick to the plan. Funnel-Web, you got the rest of the web in position? Over."

"That's affirmative," came Frank's reply. "You still want to hold the south in reserve? Over."

"Yeah. Over."

Once the enemy car was on the New York side, Charnas' team would get on their tails and stick there while the rest of their guys, all haunting various areas of Manhattan like police patrol cars, moved in to block any attempts by the enemy car to flee.

Charnas' bunch was the team he'd placed at the George Washington Bridge. With their spotter posing as a Port Authority agent watching the toll plaza in Fort Lee, Frank would have at least five good minutes to move the other pieces into place. Frank and his spotters back at headquarters (Dhampirs on the observation deck with telescopes) had a much better view of the big picture.

"So, uh, ain't we gonna get going?" asked Paulie as Frank directed each of their cars stationed above 59th Street into intercept positions based on his calculations of the Philly car's likely movements.

"No," said Faolan.

"How come?" Paulie asked. Paulie King was a wiry Sicilian with slicked back hair, a pencil mustache, and bulging eyes. He oversaw the narcotics trade and dealt with Luciano's Commission.

Faolan's eyes never left the stream of cars exiting the Holland Tunnel onto Canal Street as he spoke, betraying a little of the tension building within him. "Cause

I got a hunch that this bunch ain't it. That good enough for you, Paulie?"

Rod took his eye away from the viewer of the camera he used to get a closer look at the emerging cars and their passengers. "Look, Paul, we're near certain that Philadelphia's agents are going to try entering the city from multiple locations to increase their odds of getting a team implanted. They did a dry run last night—"

Both Paulie and Slash Gordon expressed surprise. "What do you mean? I didn't hear nothing about that," Paulie said.

Faolan lit a Camel, watching the tunnel with eyes that were sharp and cold. There was a reason nobody but those who absolutely had to know had been told.

They had a traitor in the gang.

"It was kept quiet," Rod explained. "They sent people in on the ferries, through the tunnel, the bridge, the trains and subways, everything. They came through at all different times of the night—a man, a woman, always alone—but we spotted them."

Paulie sniffed. "Far as you know, anyway."

Enzo turned in his seat to face the wiry narcotics chief. "No, we know 'cause Faolan's plants gave a count of how many they sent out and we accounted for them all."

"Right," Rod said, picking up the thought. "The teams at Grand Central, Penn Station, and the subways used dogs to sniff them out because we wanted Philly to give up on those routes. My people in the Port Authority took one down on the Staten Island Ferry and we let their agents spot a few of our patrol cars. The rest were tailed to whatever safe houses their people had set up and allowed to report in. So, now Hamilton in Philadelphia thinks he's got our security cracked and it's safe to send more in."

On the radio, Rice announced visual confirmation of the green Lincoln that they'd begun tailing. As expected, they'd been made and now the Lincoln was moving fast down St. Nicholas to try to shake them.

"What about the ones who are now here inside?" asked Gordon. His slight Russian pronunciation made the question ominous.

"We sent Dhampirs to bring them in today while they slept. The boss is interrogating them," Rod said, going back to watching the tunnel exit with his camera.

"They're scared now for sure," said Rice on the radio. "They're moving right, get me? They're gonna try to cut onto One Fifty-Fifth!"

Collins, whose car had been patrolling that section of Harlem, said: "Don't worry, I got him." A half-minute later, his satisfied chuckle could be heard. "Yeah, that scared him but good. Over."

"Keep on them, Trap-Door," Frank ordered. "They'll try to pull over now that they see how we're hemming them in. Over."

"Don't worry," Collins answered. "I'll run up the curb and take their door off if'n they try it. Over."

"We're gonna miss it," Paulie complained, nervousness creeping into his voice. "C'mon, nobody else is coming this way."

"Quiet," Rod told him.

Faolan just sat and smoked and scanned the endless line of cars and trucks that poured onto Canal Street. He rolled his window down an inch to let some of the frigid winter breeze in. Vampyr bodies ran hot and, even with the heater set to low, the air in the car was getting close. The radio reported that the Lincoln was now surrounded as their progress towards the destination was slowed by the thick midtown traffic.

A minute later, a new voice came over the radio: "Holland to Wolf Spider, Holland to Wolf Spider, I have a group of eight lean individuals in the toll plaza. They're in a brown Chevrolet Carry-all Suburban. license plate Whisky Delta Four Three Eight Foxtrot. Over."

Faolan snatched up the microphone and handed it to Rod, who said: "We copy, Holland, excellent work. Just keep it up, since they may try to sneak another car in behind this one. Over."

"Understood, sir. Over."

"All right," said Paulie as Rod handed the microphone back to Faolan. "It's about fucking time."

Faolan stabbed his cigarette out in the Packard's ashtray and pressed the send button on the microphone as Rod resumed his camera vigil. "Okay, you heard him. Everybody below Fifty-Ninth, get in position. We're gonna herd them up Sixth, so I want cars waiting at every major intersection. Over."

Faolan kept his eyes glued to the tunnel opening as the cars on their half of the island acknowledged or warned of possible traffic delays. Enzo's Packard sat in the parking lot of a small chop suey joint near the intersection of Canal and Sixth Avenue, lights off and motor purring. This part of the Village held a lot of Chinese. Neon signs bearing the strange symbols of their language hung on storefronts and sat in windows all around them as if they'd been deposited into an alien world.

In the silence that followed the last check-in, Faolan set the microphone down on the seat, drew his trusted Hi-Power, and screwed on the silencer.

Paulie, seated directly behind him, pulled the Remington revolver he favored and nervously checked the chambers.

Rod remained ready to give the word the moment the Suburban came into view.

Enzo wiped his brow with the back of his coat sleeve and rested his right hand on the gear shift while his left clenched and unclenched the wheel.

Slash Gordon—who looked like a circus strong man right down to the bald head and handlebar mustache—sat still and calm and seemingly unmindful of the cut-down double-barrel shotgun resting between his knees alongside his beloved Arabian scimitar.

Cars and trucks and buses and still more cars spewed from the electric glow of the tunnel into the darkness of the street in wave after wave of headlights.

The plan was simple: force the Suburban up Sixth Avenue and keep it there by virtue of the cars placed at all the cross streets. The idea was to push the invaders into Central Park, which was also where Charnas and the northern group were herding the Lincoln. At this time of year, the park was empty, as isolated an area as you could get in Manhattan, and had a big dug up section where the Reservoir used to be that would swallow bodies nicely.

"There they are," Rod said.

Faolan cranked his window down and the cold blasted in. "Roll 'em down!"

Enzo shifted and the Packard rolled forward as Gordon and Paulie complied.

Faolan scanned the oncoming cars as Rod dropped the camera, grabbed the microphone, and sat back. "You see them, Enzo?"

"I see them." Cool and confident now, the kid was in his element. "Might as well've used a bus."

Faolan spotted the Suburban riding behind a panel truck. Long and rounded, he'd seen other models outfitted like delivery wagons, but mostly it was the sort of car you'd pack up for a long weekend of camping. He braced himself as Enzo drove under the elevated train tracks and into a small gap in the traffic, cutting across both lanes to the sound of squealing brakes and bleating horns.

Enzo jammed the Packard's nose right in behind the panel truck—forcing the Suburban to cut toward the curb as it skidded to a stop—while Faolan slipped through the open window and aimed his Browning across the roof at the vamp in the enemy's passenger seat.

To his credit, the driver of the Suburban had already thrown it into reverse and begun backing up for the left onto Sixth Avenue, but Faolan put two slugs through the left panel of the divided windshield as further motivation. The Suburban clipped the Ford behind it and sped north onto Sixth Avenue as Faolan slipped back inside and the Packard raced over the curb in pursuit.

"They're coming your way, Wilson," Rod warned their nearest car. He forgot to use Frank's daffy spider codename in his excitement.

Traffic on Sixth was too heavy to make much speed so, sure enough, the Suburban tried to make the easy merge onto Sullivan Street but encountered Charlie Wilson in his bright red Studebaker. Wilson was probably the best driver in the gang after Enzo and timed his cut into the oncoming lane to give the big Suburban time to react, then gunned it left onto Broome to stop the Suburban from trying that route of escape.

But the Suburban's driver had other ideas.

Shooting forward under the elevated train tracks, the Suburban jumped left and caused a gaily-painted Ford roadster to stop short, blocking Enzo from following.

"He's gonna try Spring," Faolan said as Enzo sped into the space the Suburban had left. He had to shout over the noise of the El passing overhead like an enormous mechanical heartbeat.

"Farren, are you on Spring Street?" Rod demanded into the microphone. "Damn it, is anybody covering Spring?"

Any answer was drowned out by the passing train. As Enzo hustled around the Ford, the Suburban swung a hard left onto Spring Street and just missed getting broadsided by a laundry truck. They couldn't possibly follow without slamming on the brakes to wait and causing a pile-up. Enzo kept going.

Then the train passed and they heard Rice announce that somebody in the Lincoln just blew off Collins' head with a shotgun so they could make a break into Spanish Harlem.

"Son of a bitch!" Faolan shouted.

"Oh, Jesus—"

"Don't you say a fucking word, Paulie," Faolan ordered. "Not one fucking word!"

But Enzo wasn't fazed. "This joker wants to play cute? I can play cute."

Taking advantage of the slowing of southbound traffic caused by the Suburban's maneuver on Spring, Enzo turned left onto Vandam, the next cross-street.

Which only went in the opposite direction.

"What—no, take Charlton!" Faolan told him.

"Are you crazy, Enzo?" Rod cried.

Laying on the horn and grinning like a savage, Enzo flew toward the oncoming headlights like a man possessed. "Don't worry. They always clear a path!"

Vandam was mostly tenements and bars with very few cars parked along the curbs, which was lucky because the first car they passed just honked until Enzo drove up onto the curb to avoid him. The second had the good sense to adhere to Enzo's prediction and make way.

Slash Gordon laughed. "This is very good!"

"Well, so long as you're happy," Faolan growled.

"Oh, yes, I love this!"

"It's them!" Rod said, pointing ahead to where the Suburban was just about to turn toward them.

Faolan glanced over at Enzo appreciatively. The Suburban had been planning to double back and the kid figured it out!

The Suburban spotted them and Faolan saw the fellow he'd shot earlier getting ready to return the favor with a pistol as the Suburban roared around an awkward U-turn. A second later, Faolan heard his shots as the Packard closed the distance and whipped around the corner.

"Rod, who else is in the area?" Faolan called back, but before Rod could check, the radio started blaring away again with Frank and the uptown cars trying to coordinate the corralling of the Lincoln.

By the time the Suburban made the short run back to Spring Street, Enzo was right on their tail and Charlie Wilson could be seen approaching. Having no choice, the Suburban swung right and headed for the river. Enzo stayed on them tight and Wilson followed. "Get up alongside them so we can push them uptown." Faolan told Enzo, "Wilson can pick up the tail. We'll take them up Greenwich to Eighth Avenue."

We can still make this work, Faolan reassured himself.

Enzo nodded and moved the Packard parallel to the Suburban as Wilson took the cue and slid in behind their quarry. Westbound traffic on Spring Street was light and Faolan started looking ahead to gauge the traffic on Greenwich Street when Paulie cried out.

A shot clipped Faolan's ear and punched into the glove-box even as he caught the gunman's movement out of the corner of his eye. At the same instant, more bullets tore into Paulie's back as he tried to turn away and a machine gun opened up from the Suburban's tailgate, shredding the grille and windshield of Wilson's Studebaker.

Enzo swerved away while Faolan clutched the side of his head and the Suburban put on a burst of speed to fly through a stop signal. The bright red Studebaker veered right, crashed into the brick front wall of a small café, and was still.

Teeth clenched, Enzo shifted the Packard into high gear and hit the gas. The others were voicing their shock or outrage, but Faolan couldn't make out anything. He concentrated on suppressing the pain as they closed the gap on the Suburban.

He'd noticed that Vampyrs didn't feel pain for as long as humans did. It was like the nerves shut down after a few seconds of intense pain or something. Whatever it was, at this moment it couldn't happen fast enough to suit him. His hearing came back just as the Suburban flew through another stop sign and Faolan heard Rod on the radio reporting what just happened and asking if Wilson could hear him.

Faolan couldn't have cared less about Wilson just then. He only had eyes for the little shit kneeling backwards on the Suburban's third row seat and pointing the Thompson at them. Enzo slid right just in time to avoid a stream of automatic fire.

Faolan leaned out the window, took his aim, and squeezed the trigger twice. The gunner's neck exploded over his companions in a thick red spray as the gunner's head lolled back. The Thompson tumbled down to the open tailgate and bounced out onto the street.

The big Suburban moved into the shadows of West Street beneath the Miller Elevated Highway and lurched right around a corner like a fat drunkard trying to maintain his balance. The Packard came right behind, fast and sure as a jungle cat.

North and south, all four of West Street's icy lanes were crowded with cars beneath the dark canopy of the highway above. Faolan knew both groups would keep the guns stashed until they got somewhere more private, since nobody wanted the hassle of police involvement. Frank had somebody at home base monitoring WPEG, the police radio station, just to make sure that phone calls about their activities were being ignored. The big problem would be if they passed a squad car.

In the back, Slash Gordon pulled bullets out of Paulie's back while Paulie cried out and muttered. Rice's voice came back over the radio saying that the wayward Lincoln had been brought to heel and was once again under escort to Central Park.

While Rod reported their position, Faolan watched the Suburban close up its tail and struggle to find somewhere to go in the heavy traffic. There was no chance of saving the original plan at this point, so they'd have to go another route. "I think they're gonna try to go up onto the highway. Can you make like you're trying not to let them, but give them an opening at the last minute?"

Enzo smiled. "No problem, boss."

"You sure you'll be able to catch up after?"

"Yeah. This guy ain't half bad, but he ain't me. This is a Thirty Four Packard, not one of them new heaps they been putting out on the cheap. Twelve valves and a four and a half to one axle ratio. She can get from first gear to ninety in less than twenty seconds. That bucket up there couldn't get away from me if it was on a train."

Faolan turned to Rod. "Get the boys in position."

Chapter Sixteen

Completed only five years earlier, the Miller Elevated Highway (also called the Westside Highway) was constructed as a scenic car path along the Hudson. With its three narrow, cobblestone lanes in each direction, high concrete railings, sharp curves, and poor drainage, however, it was quickly developing a reputation for flooding, icy patches, and all-around unfriendly driving conditions.

It was a fine place for a game of tag.

Once up the ramp and onto the bumpy highway, Enzo's powerful Packard had no problem catching up to the Suburban. The brown beast raced toward the next exit at Fourteenth Street, traveling at well beyond the official forty mile speed limit and weaving through the lighter traffic. Enzo shifted with expert precision as he accelerated, moving the Packard smoothly up to sixty while deftly avoiding the worst frozen puddles. At that speed, the cobblestones beneath played hell with both the suspension and their nerves, but Faolan hoped that the plan could now be salvaged. While Rod coordinated the other cars and freezing December winds assaulted them through the open windows, Faolan sang "Mack the Knife."

They overtook the Suburban and Enzo moved into the right lane so he could block any attempt by the enemy to exit the highway. As the two cars crossed from the Village into Chelsea, the Suburban tried to pull ahead—despite the fact that the rattling from the roadway beneath must have been even more unbearable in the wagon—but the Packard easily matched them. They tried to pop a few shots and muscle their way over, but two broadsides from Gordon's street sweeper, a good smack from the Packard, and a 9mm warning from Faolan's Browning across the driver's nose persuaded them to reconsider the idea. When both cars had to slow for the first of the highway's reverse-S curves, the Suburban tried to be gutsy and move ahead again—which was a mistake, since a large frozen puddle at the bottom of a drop nearly sent them flying into the concrete median strip. The visitors from Philly then tried to use the near-accident to their advantage, slowing and then making a play to get in behind the Packard, but Enzo blocked them without breaking a sweat.

The sweatshops, Catholic churches, and theaters of Chelsea soon transitioned into the freight yards, factories, stock pens, and tenements of Hell's Kitchen. Whatever ruse Frank had employed, it proved enough to keep them from encountering any police interference.

Around Thirty-Eighth Street, the highway widened out a bit and they could see the ongoing construction for the new Lincoln Tunnel that would soon connect Manhattan to Weehawken. The Suburban moved over into the left-most lane and waited, but Enzo didn't rise to the bait. So they waited until there was a decent bit of traffic between and began to slow, dropping further back. Just for kicks, Faolan had Enzo let them get some distance and nodded to Rod, who gave Newman the signal over the radio.

Once the Packard crawled past the Forty-Second Street exit with the Suburban trailing behind in the far lane, the Philly driver made his break to the right, diving for the exit. Shad Newman's blue Ford flew up the on-ramp just in time to queer the play and give the Suburban a bump into the center lane for good measure. When Enzo moved the

Packard into the far left lane and dropped back to meet them, the guys in the Suburban fell back in line.

As they passed over Forty-Eighth Street, they saw the big ocean liners docked at the Passenger Ship Terminal all lit up like floating birthday cakes. The radio announced the spotting of a third car team coming over the Goethals Bridge into Staten Island and Faolan told Frank to let their boys on Staten Island handle it however they thought best. There was no realistic way to shepherd those mooks all the way over to Central Manhattan from there.

"Christ, it's a fucking invasion," Paulie said, now holding the shotgun so he could cover the Suburban. "They must've rounded up every sucker in Pennsylvania, Jersey, and Delaware for this!"

"New Jersey's neutral," Rod reminded him.

Paulie snorted. "Yeah, like fuck they are. We just ain't caught one of them in the act yet."

Faolan said nothing. Paulie didn't know what he, Frank, and Rothstein knew about the secret phone calls to Jersey, the security leaks, and the sabotage. He did make an interesting point, though. Six vamps in the Lincoln, eight in the Suburban, plus however many in the Goethals team, not to mention the fifteen individual agents they'd sent in the previous night. That was a lot to recruit, train, and feed in one year when you were talking about places like Jersey, Delaware, and Pennsylvania. Since they were marked for infiltration duty, they couldn't even be used to run cities. They were just dead weight to carry. Even the biggest cities in those states couldn't support anything close to the numbers New York could.

They're all-in on this hand, Faolan thought. He took a drag from his Camel and smiled a cold and predatory smile. *We take these fish in the showdown tonight and they're tap city.*

"Christ, I'm starving," Paulie whined. "I gotta get some blood in me soon or I'm gonna go bugsy."

"I too am very hungry," added Slash Gordon.

Faolan cast a glance over at the other Vampyrs in the Suburban. "Don't worry, fellas, we'll be eating like kings in a little bit."

Rod checked in with the other teams for the final bit.

"Everybody in position on Fifty-Ninth and the circle, Rod?" Faolan asked as they slowed for the final reverse-S curve. His jaw ached from the constant vibration of the cobblestone surface.

Rod nodded. "Everyone's set."

He looked over at Enzo. "Hey, kid, that was some damn good wheel work back there."

Enzo smiled. "Thanks. I just always loved cars, you know? My pop used to take me for rides in his Model T and let me drive it when I got big enough to reach the pedals. In the war, I drove the officers back and forth from the front lines. When I came home, I spent a couple years driving a hack all over the city." He reached out and rubbed the dashboard affectionately. "The right car's important, though, and this here's a good car."

Faolan smiled, nodded, smoked, and thought about the tricky part that was still to come. He hoped the kid was up to it. "That's the kind I want," Faolan said, indicating a white Cord convertible off in the far right lane. Now that he'd finally finished paying off Rothstein from that crooked poker game of his, he could save up enough to get himself a swell ride like he'd been wanting. "Except I think I'd get it in red. What do you think of the Cord, Enzo?"

"They're okay," Enzo allowed. "Fast, light, but they ain't as responsive as I like and they ain't engineered too sturdy, you know? They don't take much punishment."

"True, but the dames love them," Faolan mused, letting his thoughts turn to Stephanie Chandler for a moment.

Rod leaned forward. "Faolan, a man with your looks, wealth, and charming personality should have no problem interesting many quality ladies."

"Flower sellers, maybe," added Enzo, unable to hide his smile.

"Or cigarette girls," said Rod.

"Laundry women," Enzo said.

Faolan shook his head, smiling. "Yeah, maybe if I wasn't always associating with bums like youse."

While the others pretended to be hurt, Enzo said, "Hey, I think—"

Just then, Faolan noticed the Suburban drop behind them. Traffic on the highway had thickened a little as they neared midtown and, with horns bleating, the cars behind the Suburban wasted no time in pulling around them, which stymied Enzo and Newman's attempts to reverse.

Knowing the game, Enzo moved them up a little ahead of the Suburban as they neared the Fifty-Ninth Street exit. The Suburban unwittingly obliged their plans by jumping off at Fifty-Ninth as soon as it looked like Enzo wouldn't be able to follow.

However, Newman dropped back enough for Enzo to whip across the lanes and make the narrow exit ramp with bare inches to spare. Once on Fifty-Ninth, the Suburban found itself between the Central Railroad yards to their left and a set of warehouses on the right. They were once again caught in the stop-and-start crawl of midtown traffic and Enzo was able to maneuver the Packard onto the Suburban's right while Newman's Ford resumed its close tail.

Here the slums of Hell's Kitchen gave way to the theaters, hotels, cafes, and neon that radiated from the epicenter of Times Square. Hemmed in by respectable citizens as they were, the time for guns was over, so Paulie tried to give the sweeper back to Slash Gordon, but the bald man told him to keep it.

From the radio, Marty Rice announced that they had reached Central Park with the Lincoln. He then added that the Philly crew had quit their vehicle and begun the battle by firebombing two of New York's cars. After that message, Frank's requests for updates went unanswered and Frank ordered more of their lone patrol boys to move in.

"Jesus, I hope they're all right," Rod said. Enzo made the sign of the cross.

Faolan said nothing. Losing Charnas and his boys to the enemy would be an easy enough price to pay for a victory like this.

* * * * *

Central Park in December was a winter wilderness in the middle of the urban metropolis of New York City. Here the snow from several nights before remained white and undisturbed in large expanses, the monuments and buildings wore sparkling garlands of ice, and the trees stood naked, skeletal. On Frank's orders, the drives had been plowed clear the night before last and the cops had run off the homeless and tore down their shanty towns in preparation.

Under the imposing gazes of Christopher Columbus and the General Motors building, Faolan's people had arranged themselves to block the Suburban from taking Broadway, Eighth Avenue, or continuing on Fifty-Ninth so that their only option was to pass between the grand marble pylons of Merchant's Gate into Central Park. Newman remained behind at the entrance to keep the curious out and make certain the Suburban couldn't backtrack.

The Suburban raced up the center drive toward the east rather than the closer west drive, the same route their teammates in the Lincoln had opted for a few minutes earlier. If they were hoping to make it through to Fifth Avenue before Faolan and his crew had time to set up the roadblocks, they were in for a surprise.

"Keep on them, kid," Faolan told Enzo as the Suburban tried to make some distance. Enzo nodded and kicked up their speed a bit. The drives in the park were twisty, being meant for leisurely scenic cruising and, like the highway, icy patches and blowing snow combined to make for dangerous driving at any speed. The Suburban had weight on its side.

"We've got all the exits blocked, don't worry," Rod reminded him as they passed over the first of the transverse roads and neared the large expanse of lawns and strolling paths known as The Mall.

"Ain't them getting out I'm thinking of. I don't want them getting so far ahead that they can stop and set up an ambush."

Far off to their left, they could see the lights of Tavern On The Green where the well-to-do society types sat around eating porterhouse steaks while imagining they were on some kind of picnic. Meantime, the poor bastards who actually had to live in the park rummaged through the garbage outside hoping to find enough meat left on the bones to make soup.

And then they get booted out of their little makeshift homes so some vampires can have a rumble, Faolan thought with a wry smile. He checked his clip and found he still had six shots left. That should be enough, since the pistol wouldn't be his primary weapon come the fight.

The radio announced that victory had been achieved on Staten Island. No enemy survivors. Frank told them to split up and send people to cover the Holland Tunnel and

Washington Bridge on the slight chance that their enemies got cute and sent another batch tonight. Faolan doubted that possibility, though.

The south end of the park was playgrounds and open greens, all of which were covered in blankets of snow made gray by the occasional frosted street light and the cold, dim moon. Both prey and pursuer appeared to move across narrow streaks of darkness in an otherwise dead and washed-out limbo.

Enzo pulled beside the Suburban just in time to keep it from taking the east drive and the Philly Vampyrs threw a few shots at them before making a dash toward the lake.

Gordon shouted curses in his native language, clutching his newly wounded side. Not a fatal wound for a Vampyr, but damned inconveniencing.

"Where'd Rice say the other bunch stopped?" Faolan called back, rolling his window down.

Rod ministered to Slash Gordon while he answered. "Said they spun out just passed the Eighty-Fifth Street Transverse. Near the Reservoir."

That was perfect. The Reservoir had been drained earlier that year in preparation for another big lawn with a new reservoir planned on the other side of the transverse road. It was nothing but a big mud pie and a perfect grave site. "Bring the boys in closer, Rod. I don't want them assholes going nowhere but the Reservoir."

"Attention all park perimeter cars, move in to block all exit routes from the east drive," Rod transmitted.

Outside Faolan's window playgrounds waited for spring beneath mounds of drift snow. The slides, swings, and monkey bars stood backlit by the filtered glow of Fifth Avenue as a strong gust of wind set the swings to moving. For a moment, he imagined his former cell companion, Michael, running through the chains and pushing them this way and that. A chill cut through him that he blamed on the wind. He turned away to watch the Suburban's progress. He tasted blood in his mouth.

Chapter Seventeen

Once over the second transverse road, they heard the party still going full swing.

"Looks like cheese and crackers, boys," Faolan said as he leaned out the window.

"I don't get that one," Rod said.

Paulie snickered. "Crackers are machine guns, get it, and they—"

"They turn guys into Swiss cheese, yeah, I get it now."

The torched cars appeared to have burned down to smoldering heaps while the fighting had moved to the torn-up ditch that used to be the Reservoir. Faolan took careful aim and fired.

A few lengths ahead, the Suburban accelerated across the overpass at the top of the hill just as Faolan's bullet blew the right front tire.

The big wagon whipped around and slid backwards down the slope.

The Packard mounted the hill and, cresting the overpass, they saw where the Suburban had fallen off the road onto the snowy hillside near Cleopatra's Needle. Already the occupants scrambled out of the toppled vehicle and made haste for the eighty foot obelisk and the clusters of skeleton trees around it.

Enzo parked, pointing the headlights in the direction of the men struggling up the hill through the snow, and everyone climbed out. "Pop the trunk, Enzo," Faolan said as he lined up a shot on the vamp furthest up the hillside.

The blood and brains on the snow looked black under the moonlight as the vamp's body dropped, rolled once, and lay still.

The rest dropped down and belly-crawled after that.

Slash Gordon twirled his Arabian scimitar and gave chase to the others with a hearty laugh that belied his slow, staggered run.

"Gordon, hold on!" Rod cried as Enzo opened up the back and began distributing the shotguns and Thompsons they'd laid in store along with the digging implements.

"Crazy fucking Cossak," Paulie said, slinging a second shotgun over his shoulder before jogging after Gordon with the other still in hand. He stopped at the tumbled Suburban and shouted back, "Hey, the driver is still in here! Looks like he's been bashed up pretty good!"

Faolan nodded, holstering the Hi-Power. He and Rod took Thompsons while Enzo got a street sweeper. All the shotguns were loaded with the standard deer slugs to give them better range and power than buckshot.

"Go check the driver," he told Enzo. "Sit on him if he ain't a memory and, if he is, just cover Gordon and Paulie."

"Gotcha," Enzo said and took off. Faolan climbed into the driver's seat of the Packard, Rod got in beside him, and they drove a few hundred feet further up the road while Rod reported their progress. Ahead, they could see the large collection of cars all around the smoldering heaps that represented the arrival of Charnas' reinforcements. He just hoped that Frank would be able to keep the cops away for a while longer. Once on the other side of the Needle, Faolan positioned the Packard to put maximum light on the monument and they got out with their machine guns.

The long, gray, stone mausoleum that was the Metropolitan Museum of Art sat on the other side of the road while Cleopatra's Needle stretched before them like the world's tallest tombstone. In the car's lights, Faolan could just make out the hieroglyphs that covered its sandy surface and the giant bronze crabs standing vigil all around it like monstrous gatekeepers. Further on, just on the horizon across a small lake, the gray stone towers and turrets of Belvedere Castle sat watching over everything like some transported Transylvanian despot. Another greedy vampire ruler awaiting a blood sacrifice.

"Christ, I hate this fucking place," he muttered. Rod gave him a curious look and Faolan shrugged, feigning nonchalance as he cocked his rifle. "All this bizarre shit thrown together here. Only rich folks can afford to be this fucking morbid, am I right?"

Good old Mister Even Keel smiled uncertainly and shrugged, letting it drift. Faolan sucked in a deep breath and took a firmer hold of his thoughts. He found the escape he needed in his killing groove as they began the approach to the obelisk. They stayed out of the light, moving only in darkness.

The first of their slaughters ended quickly, with only one loss to their side. Slash Gordon went for the vamp Faolan had shot, hoping for an easy feast, and fell victim to a deadly crossfire instead. Paulie managed to keep them busy while Faolan and Rod came up on them from behind, taking one quietly by hand and chopping the other down with the Thompson when the bronze crab he'd taken refuge behind took no interest in protecting him. That left the *schmucks* in the trees caught between Paulie and Enzo below and Faolan and Rod above.

Their blood was sweet with fear.

The last four boys from the Lincoln were tougher and better armed, but they were hopelessly outnumbered and it was only a matter of crawling through the snow behind the small ditch where the survivors from Charnas' team had them pinned. They had lookouts at their back, of course, but Rod spotted them before they spotted him and that was the end of the lookouts. So the two left in the hole decided it was time to use their last whisky bottle firebomb, but they held it up too high and Faolan blew it apart in the guy's hand, spraying whisky all over them. Then Rod brought out the Coast Guard signal-gun he sometimes carried and gave the gents a light.

Then it was Happy Hour again.

Faolan finished the last of the lookouts and sat back in the blood-spattered snow when Crowbar Charnas—unfortunately still alive and no worse for wear—marched up with his guys. "O'Connor, you greedy fuck, what's the idea? You knowed these yegs was ours! Hell, that's just—"

"Dammit, Rod," Paulie complained, dropping the body of the second burn victim back into the ditch. "Why'd you have to go and burn these ones?"

"—common fucking manners, ain't it? We spotted them, we—"

"What's the matter, Paulie? You don't like them well-done?" Faolan asked with the giddiness he always got from over-indulging in Vampyr blood. He gave no attention to Charnas' presence at all.

"First come, first served," Rod told Charnas, having finished the other lookout.

"—fucking carried them down here 'cause of your loony plan and got shot at for our trouble—hey, fucko, I'm talking to you!" Charnas' taut leather box of a head was bright red beneath his drill sergeant's haircut as he shouted and kicked Faolan's resting foot.

The merriment vanished from Faolan's eyes.

Faolan kicked with both feet in one of the moves Rod had taught him, hitting the beefy Vampyr in the ankles. As Charnas fell forward, Faolan rolled aside and sprang up in one fluid motion. The Browning came out of its holster and Faolan pressed it against the base of Charnas' skull before the other could even push himself up. In such a location, a single bullet could sever all the nerve connections between the head and body. Death even for a Vampyr.

"You wanna talk, Charnas? Then talk. You wanna give orders? Then you buy yourself some flunkies to push around. You ever bark at me like a dog again, and I'm gonna put you through fucking obedience school, you get me?"

Silence. The crowd stood immobile.

Charnas squirmed beneath the barrel.

Faolan thumbed back the hammer.

"I get you," Charnas said through gritted teeth.

"That's good," Faolan said, glancing around at the others. "It's important that you understand how things stand between us, Eddie, 'cause I hear things. Like how you think you oughtta be the one calling the shots, and you figure you got the support to come after me. Except, here we are away from the boss and surrounded by just the men. You know what, Eddie? I don't see nobody trying to save you." He stood up, lowering the Browning. "You think about that, Eddie. You think real hard."

He turned away and looked over the gathered crowd while Charnas picked himself up and glared daggers at his back. Faolan waited, hoping Charnas would try something, but after a few seconds it became clear that Charnas wasn't going to boil over "But while you're doing all that thinking, Ed, go get the picks and shovels out of the Packard. We need all these bodies tucked away out there in the Reservoir tonight, so pick out a couple guys to help you. Rod, go let Frank know what happened and arrange for the cars to be towed. Oh, and have Enzo bring that driver over."

Rod nodded and jogged up the hill.

Faolan pretended not to notice that Charnas hadn't moved as he spotted the guy he was looking for and called out: "Hey, Rice, you think you're gonna pull through over there?"

Marty Rice, one of Rothstein's money men whose primary responsibilities lay in the stock market and the gang's real estate holdings, sat off to the side nursing a gun wound in his leg. He was a short, middle-aged guy with a receding hairline and glasses. He had dressed for this battle in a Herringbone patterned brown tweed suit. He chuckled. "Yeah, Mister O'Connor, I'll be aces in another few minutes. Don't worry about me."

Faolan shot him in the stomach.

Aside from a few jumps and gasps, there wasn't quite the surprised reaction Faolan had expected. Maybe things had been too tense for anyone to be surprised by much. Well, almost anyone.

"What the fuck are you doing?" Charnas asked, too shocked to be angry as Rice rolled around on the ground and squealed.

Faolan strode over to where Rice flopped around. "I told you I hear things, Ed, and one of the things I heard from the boss was that we got a traitor among us. Tag, Marty! You're it."

"No, please! It's not true, I swear—!" he screamed, shaking as he tried to find a position that didn't hurt.

"Don't even bother, you little shit," Faolan shouted down at him as the crowd drew closer, drawn like sharks by the blood and weakness. "You don't think we're gonna catch on when most of your stock picks turn out losers and you sell short over and over again? You been sabotaging us, you fuck!"

"No! They were honest mistakes!"

Faolan watched the crowd, directing his arguments to them. "Me and Frank been logging your calls for a month, shit-head. Awful lot of calls to Jersey." As a matter of fact, Killian's policy had always been to have all the calls from the building logged during the night, but there was no reason to let the others know it. "Every time we put a new plan in effect, you call the same exchange in Atlantic City. Every time you get ready to tank one of our investments, you call that exchange. Who is it, Marty? I know already, but I want the boys to hear it straight from the traitor's mouth. Who's running you from Atlantic City?"

Rice began to cry. A full-blown blubbering that made him difficult to understand. "My sister! It's—it's true...they, please, they got my kid sister! I had to do what they said! I think he's from Philly, but he'll kill her and her whole family if I don't play ball! Please, don't kill me!"

"Is Rothstein in on this with you?"

"No! It's just me! I swear!"

Damn. He knew the little accountant would be ready to roll over on anybody by now, but he'd also known the chances of Rothstein's involvement were minimal. Much as he had hoped otherwise. Faolan looked at the others, including Enzo and the Philly driver he'd just brought over. Rod had known about Rice's betrayal and Faolan's plan for exposing him, but Enzo hadn't. The kid looked like he was about to lose his lunch, even though he'd refused to partake in their cannibalistic victory feast.

"You see, fellas," Faolan said, "this is why we cut all ties with people from our other lives. Because it makes you weak, makes you vulnerable. Just like this little rat fuck piece of shit here!"

Faolan fired.

The investor's right kneecap exploded.

Again.

The left kneecap.

A third shot. A fourth.

Rice lost both elbows.

A high, keening shriek came from somewhere deep in Marty Rice's chest as he trembled and shook on the ground. But he'd survive, given time. Vampyr bodies were incredibly resilient.

Faolan holstered his spent pistol and turned to regard Charnas. "You understand now, Eddie?" he asked with perfect, deadly calm. "I hear everything."

Charnas stared down at the man he'd known for years and yet, had never really known. He nodded and left to get the tools.

"Nobody kills him," Faolan warned the others, gratified by the new fear in their eyes. "When the hole is ready, you bury this turn-coat rat with his buddies." Faolan knelt down next to Rice's face, took out a cigarette, and waited until the man's watering, bulging eyes found him. "You're gonna live a long time yet, Marty, but I want you to know you did it all for nothing. I had a couple of Lepke's boys pay your sister a visit this afternoon."

Rice's screams got louder as Faolan lit his cigarette, rose, and strolled over to where Enzo covered the driver with his shotgun.

Enzo looked over at the traitor and back to Faolan. "Did you…? I mean, was that true about the sister?"

The kid was too soft for this kind of racket, really, but here he was. Faolan looked at him evenly for a moment while he smoked and said: "We do what we gotta do, kid. It's a war."

The remaining color drained from Enzo's face. Faolan was lying, of course, since there was no angle in hitting some broad in Jersey that no longer meant anything to anybody, but neither Marty nor Enzo needed to know that.

"Go on, kid, give Rod a hand. I want to talk to my new pal here alone."

Enzo nodded and wandered away.

The driver from Philly was in pretty bad shape, but he tried not to show it. He was a medium sized fella with dark hair, deep set eyes, and a five o'clock shadow. He had the kind of looks that were improved by the gauntness of Vampyrism. His face was bruised and slashed up where he'd hit the steering wheel and then the windshield, his hat was gone, and his gray suit was crumpled, bloody, and torn. He favored his left leg in a way that made Faolan suspect a break. Still, for all that, his brown eyes were clear and unafraid, his breathing slow and regular.

Faolan led him over to a small, broken slab of concrete that rested just high enough to be a reasonable seat. "Smoke?"

"Thanks," the driver said, accepting a Camel and a light.

"What's your name?"

The other Vampyr took a long drag and slow exhale before answering. "Davidson. Bill Davidson."

"Faolan O'Connor. Call you Bill?"

Bill shrugged. "Don't see why not."

Faolan noticed that a few of the guys were grabbing bottles of liquor-laced blood from their cars to lighten the mood a bit. He called to one of the boys and got one brought over. He opened it and passed it over to Bill, who thanked him again and took a few healthy swallows.

"Well, Bill, I got to start by saying that I think you're okay. I don't always warm to people so quick, but I like what I seen so far. You're a pretty good hand with a car, that's for sure."

Bill smiled ruefully. "Your man's better. No question."

Faolan laughed. "Lucky for us. Still, I'm betting you knew that early in the game, but you didn't throw in the towel. You put up a struggle every goddamn chance you got, which makes me believe you ain't a quitter and that this composure I'm seeing here ain't just a— whaddayacallit—fatalistic kind of walk to the gallows."

Bill swallowed another sip and turned to search his face. "Isn't it?"

"Well," Faolan said, "it don't have to be, Bill. I mean, it depends on you is what I'm trying to say. I'd rather gain a friend than lose an enemy if I can and I hope that you're not too wrapped up in some personal code or loyalty to your Reeve that you'd shoot down a good opportunity just on principle."

"A man without principles doesn't have much to stand on, does he?" Bill asked. Faolan smoked and waited while the other Vampyr smoked and weighed whatever he had to weigh. After a minute or so, Bill Davidson sighed. "I'm not a man who changes allegiances every time the wind blows from a different direction, O'Connor, and I mean that. But I also don't pretend I'm eager to die a martyr. Not for a pig like Josiah Hamilton, anyway." Hamilton was the Reeve of Philadelphia and Boston's most steadfast ally in the war. "What's your offer?"

"First of all, can you contact Hamilton? Arrange a meeting, like, if you found out something important?"

Bill nodded. "Yeah, I was in charge of this infiltration. I knew your set-up looked too sloppy, but Jersey's getting cold feet and the rest of Pennsylvania wants out of the whole war, so Hamilton had to make it big. Pompous ass wouldn't listen to any concerns, just pushed us out the door. Anyway, I'm supposed to report in by tomorrow night. I can send back phony information if that's what you want."

Faolan glanced around at the men he had assembled, trying to contain his growing excitement. He glanced down at his watch. Frank and Rothstein would be irritated by his little improvisation, but that was an acceptable risk. There were still plenty of hours left before dawn and he was going to need every one.

"So?" Bill prompted. "C'mon, man, give. What's the deal?"

Faolan stood, flicked his cigarette away, and smiled down at his lucky find. "Bill, how'd you like to be the Reeve of Philadelphia?"

Chapter Eighteen

"Where the hell have you been?" Frank demanded the moment Faolan stepped off the elevator onto the third floor of the Empire State Building. "Rothstein has been calling me every half-hour wanting to know where you are."

Faolan shrugged. "That's why I didn't tell you. Save you the trouble of lying."

"Well, thanks for your consideration. Now, for the second time, where the hell have you been?" Frank's monotone never changed, but Faolan picked up the slight increase in intensity.

"I been out winning friends and influencing people," he replied, moving past Frank toward their sham investment office.

"Elaborate," Frank said, keeping pace.

"I don't want to repeat myself, Frank. You'll ask a bunch of questions that'll take me time to answer. You know how the boss feels about waiting—"

Frank shook his head. "No dice. Killian's already steamed about your little disappearing act and Rothstein's had all night to piss in his ear about it."

Faolan kept walking, the damp squish of his soft-soled shoes a marked contrast to the strident clap of Frank's hard rubber heels in the wide, empty halls. "Rothstein still with him?"

"Yeah. In Killian's suite as of half an hour ago. So spill."

"I'd rather just tell youse at the same time," he said, opening the door of Empire Investments. Behind the desk, the guard Stout rose to attention as always. Easy to take a guy like that for granted, but Faolan knew that what guards saw and heard got around. What he was seeing now would be tension and possible mistrust between the supremely self-assured Faolan strolling in the lead and the worried Frank dogging his heels.

That quiet talk about him being Frank's puppet had to stop.

"Faolan, drop the cute remarks and listen to me," Frank said, dropping his volume to a near-whisper as Faolan gave Stout a playful salute and continued down the hall toward the secret elevator. "You grabbed three-quarters of our people and left the city without any explanation or permission." Frank's voice was steady, but he walked like his muscles had been twisted up into sailor's knots. "Do you understand what you're walking into up there?"

Faolan pushed the button and the elevator door opened. He got a Camel from his pack and stepped inside while fishing for his Zippo. Frank stepped in behind him. The tall Vampyr waited. He did not insert his executive key. The door closed as Faolan lit his cigarette. Frank was a silent, immobile, black-clad monolith whose empty eyes were able to stare at every part of Faolan at the same time.

"Time's wasting, Frank," he said, taking a drag.

Then Frank was on him, covering the space of the elevator car in one quick step. Before Faolan could exhale, Frank grabbed his arms in a monstrous grip, yanked him off the floor, and slammed him back into the solid oak paneling.

"Are you trying to fuck me, Faolan? Is that your game?" Frank asked, trying hard to keep his tone from climbing out of its usual coldness.

Faolan knew then that Frank was completely his.

This was as worked up as he'd seen Frank since that nervous breakdown outside *Chez Spider* a year ago. If Frank really thought he was setting him up for a fall, then the ghoul would have out-flanked him with a counter-move and let him walk right into the trap. This routine here was just a play for attention and reassurance, much like a dame bursting into tears and packing her bags for a trip to mother's.

Ain't love grand?

"Jesus, Frank, stop acting like a chump and put me down." He kept his voice calm. Frank hesitated, but set him down.

Faolan flexed his arms to push Frank's big hands away and took the cigarette out of his mouth. "I thought you understood this sort of thing. It looks better if I come straight up to Killian with the explanation, right? If I stop to tell you first, how's he supposed to know that you weren't in on this from the get-go?"

Frank took a moment to consider and compose before responding. "So you want Rothstein and Killian to suspect friction between us? That's what this is about?"

Faolan smiled. "Sure, they shouldn't think that you always know what I'm gonna do. If tonight backfires, it should be my fuck-up for going above and beyond the plan—"

"And not a problem with the plan itself," Frank finished for him.

"You see now how I'm looking out for you?" Faolan said, putting his hand on Frank's shoulder. "Got to learn to trust me."

"Not a fucking chance," Frank said as he stepped away and pushed the hand off. "Trust doesn't enter into this, so don't get any cute ideas."

Faolan laughed. "Christ, I didn't say I wanted to marry you, Frank, I said I trust you to do right by me and you can trust me to do right by you. Like you said at the beginning, we need each other."

He said the words casually, but could see them striking home in Frank's malformed little excuse for a heart. The more the big ghoul played up that ice-water-for-blood routine, the more cracks there were in the dam.

Frank turned and put his key in the elevator, pressing the button for the executive floor. After a moment he said without turning around, "Trust is a dangerous thing, Faolan. Knowing someone is different from trusting them: one is based on facts and observations. The other is a tangle of emotions and perceptions. Trust gets Vampyrs killed."

Faolan hid his smile as he watched the dial climb.

* * * * *

By the time they got to Killian's office, Faolan had filled Frank in on the events in Central Park, his dealing with Charnas, and the end of Marty Rice without revealing his talk with the Philly driver or its results. Sweethearts again, they agreed to promote the wrestler Cuddles to fill the gap left by Slash Gordon's demise. Since the wrestler had less attachment to Charnas than the other street enforcers, there was an excellent chance that Faolan could win or buy his loyalty.

From Killian's office, Frank led him through a cherry wood door on the distant left wall. This took them into an enormous paneled library complete with the majestic fireplace, floor-to-ceiling bookcases filled with leather-bound volumes nobody ever read, and every other expensive world-traveler antique you'd expect. It was all wealth and power and tradition, designed to impress with just a touch more comfort and informality than the office.

At the far corner of the library, directly ahead of them, stood a pool table of cherry finish and green felt lit by a Tiffany glass light fixture. Darcy Killian and Arnold Rothstein played and the air periodically echoed the clap of the balls.

Killian's bodyguard Johnny Devlin watched them enter from his vantage point at the bar against the far left wall. The gunman sat with studied casualness upon a stool and nursed a glass of heated blood, but his cool green eyes remained locked on Faolan during his walk toward the pool table. During the last year, Devlin and Faolan had settled into a wary amiability that was the closest thing to friendship Devlin had managed among the members of Killian's gang. They often competed in shooting matches in the building's indoor firing range and, though Devlin consistently beat him in both speed and accuracy, Faolan continued in the hopes of spotting some weakness he could use. The fact that Devlin now clocked his movements without giving him the slightest of greetings confirmed Frank's earlier assessment of the general mood.

Everett, the Dhampir, raised a glass of wine and nodded his head in greeting. He sat on a brown leather sofa between them and the pool table, his back to the wonderful view of Fifth Avenue beyond the large windows. Between the couch and one of the many tufted leather wing chairs that completed the seating area stood the floor model radio that currently filled the air with the strings and horns of a symphony. Although the chairs were empty, Frank made no move to sit and Faolan decided to follow his example.

"Don't you ever sleep, Nate?" Faolan asked the Dhampir.

Everett shrugged. "Chronic insomniac, I'm afraid." He took another sip of his wine and scratched his beard with a sly smile. "Besides, I couldn't bear to miss this."

He hoped the Dhampir meant his explanation. "What's the game?"

"Eight ball. So far Mister Rothstein's won six of the eight games they've played tonight."

While Faolan watched, Rothstein made a difficult combo shot from against the rail and followed by dropping three more balls in a row. His fumbling of the fourth shot struck Faolan as deliberate. He could have run the table. "Never knew he played."

"A.R. made his first bankroll hustling pool," Frank said, keeping his voice low so as not to draw the attention of the players. "He played a set of games in Nineteen-oh-Nine against Jack Conway that went on for more than thirty-four hours. He won over ten grand."

Neither Killian nor Rothstein, however, paid them any attention whatsoever. These days, on Rothstein's advice, the Reeve wore mostly three-piece double-breasted tweeds in browns or grays with ties in varying shades of green. Tonight the suit was chestnut brown with an emerald tie. For ease of play, he'd hung up his jacket and Faolan thought the gold watch chain looping from the pocket of his vest was a nice detail. He'd also trimmed down his mustache in order to achieve a more current look. The smaller mustache didn't suit him, though, and Faolan felt he was just taking baby steps toward eliminating it entirely.

The Goliath spider had begun to shed his skin.

Killian followed Rothstein's shot by sinking a tough one into the corner, but scuffed the final shot that would have won the match. He held onto his temper, but tension radiated out from him and Rothstein knew better than to try throwing the game a second time. He sank the last striped ball into a side pocket with an anticlimactic *thunk*. Killian forced a smile, complimented Rothstein on a well-played game, replaced his cue in the rack, and slipped on his jacket. He took up the curved wooden pipe he'd adopted a month or so ago and loaded it with tobacco.

Rothstein buttoned his own jacket of steel gray and tightened the knot in his cobalt silk tie. "So, Frank, when did the Artful Dodger here find his way home?"

"Ten minutes ago. We came straight up."

"Your idea or his?"

Frank didn't hesitate. "His. Said he didn't want to answer the same questions a bunch of times."

"Sensible enough," Rothstein allowed with a glance at Killian, who had lit his pipe and now sat in the wingchair nearest Everett. "Though, if we'd known what kind of appearance he'd make, a brief delay for a shower and change of clothes might have been permitted."

Faolan smiled, glancing down at his dirty, bloody denim work clothes and the battered overcoat that framed them. He'd lost his hat sometime during the night's activities and knew that his blond hair hung in a scattered mess around his bruised face, but he wouldn't have cleaned himself up for presentation even if he'd been able. He looked exactly like someone who'd spent a rough night mixing it up in the streets should look and expected Killian to appreciate that. However, the boss just sat and smoked his pipe, giving no visible hint to his feelings.

"Well, O'Connor," Rothstein continued, "to give you your due, let me first congratulate you on overseeing the elimination of tonight's infiltration force."

"Thanks."

"You brought us no new prisoners, I take it?"

"Nope."

"Too bad. The prisoners your Dhampirs brought in during the day gave us a little information, but mostly minor details that will be outdated by next month. The

Vampyrs you fought would have known considerably more, but I suppose you just couldn't take any of them alive."

Faolan said nothing. He knew he still had the best hand, but Rothstein was playing his cards perfectly for a change. Any denials he tried to make would just sound like excuses and Killian's patience appeared paper thin.

Rothstein poked his stick at the few remaining balls atop the pool table. "Still, whatever unsanctioned activities you engaged in after your costly victory, at least you've demonstrated the effectiveness of our radio system. Next time, of course, you'll know better than to try arranging our cars all over Manhattan to chase enemy teams up and down crowded streets, throwing bullets like confetti. Still, it was a large group that came in, so you bought us a little time. Which reminds me: Frank, how much did you have to lay out in bribes and damages for tonight's festivities?"

"Forty-eight grand total in police bribes, but that covers it top to—"

"We got a bargain there," Rothstein commented.

Frank went on: "Another ten cleans up the park, repairs the statues and things, replaces a couple windows in the MET, and keeps the staff and museum director quiet. It isn't really much more than—"

"So almost sixty thousand dollars," Rothstein interrupted, feigning surprise. "And how many men did we lose?"

"Two," Frank answered. "Romkey and Collins."

"We lost four," Faolan corrected.

"No, Wilson survived," Frank told him. "He's healing. Rice doesn't count."

"I ain't talking about Rice or Wilson. I lost Farren and Sizemore after the park," Faolan said, deciding it was time to take control of the conversation. Killian stopped smoking and looked steamed enough to throw him out one of the windows without waiting to hear his side.

As he hoped, the revelation threw Rothstein off his script and he strode forward incredulously, pointing his pool cue like a fencing blade. "You mean you left this city completely defenseless for an entire night and got two more of our men killed *after* the fighting was over so you could—what? Bump off a few random *schmucks* in Philadelphia? Knock over a couple of operations? Maybe leave some men behind to spy?"

Faolan answered: "So I could end the war on our southern borders."

Killian rose to his feet and Everett sat forward while Rothstein and Frank went still. Faolan reached into his coat's inner pocket and pulled out the photos Rod had developed earlier, taking the camera negatives from the outer pocket with his other hand, and set both down onto the coffee table before anyone could recover. "The guy getting drained dry is Josiah Hamilton, formerly the Reeve of Philadelphia, while the guy doing the drinking is Bill Davidson. Davidson was the only survivor from the other team in the park, so I had a chat with him and learned that Philly could be completely taken if we moved quick. So I did—"

"Without getting permission from me, your superior, or your Reeve," Rothstein injected. "This could have been a set-up—"

"Balls," Faolan said. "The whole Northeast couldn't afford to throw away twenty vamps just to bait a fucking hook and you know it." He addressed Killian, ignoring Rothstein's attempts to butt in. "You were still working on the guys from last night and I didn't want to see an opportunity like this lost because Rothstein got cold feet. For two years, he hasn't taken the fight to them and it ain't got us nowhere but barely holding onto what we started with! You put me in charge of defending this city and, the way I see it, the best defense we can have is fewer enemies and more friends. I—"

"Just tell me what you did," Killian said without taking his eyes off the photographs. His tone was firm, but curiously lacking in any strong emotion.

Faolan took a breath and let it out. He'd gone all-in and been called, so he hoped his read was good. "I made you the proud owner of the new Reeve of Philadelphia, that's what. Once I got Davidson to see the sense in working with us, he lured Hamilton and his main guys to a rendezvous and we took them down, though not without a fight—which is where we lost Farren and Sizemore. I decided to make Davidson personally finish Hamilton, just to make it all legal and tidy, and had Rod take those pictures to make sure Davidson stays bought." Though they'd been drinking other vamps as a regular part of their spoils since the beginning, it was still a crime punishable by death in The Order and such photo evidence would be enough to bring down anybody, anytime, no matter how big or well-connected they might eventually get.

"We spent the next few hours rounding up every other vamp in Philly and getting them sworn to Davidson," Faolan continued. "I left Cuddles and the enforcers there to keep the transfer of power smooth and deal with any problems that pop up."

"You gave our enforcers to Philly indefinitely?" Rothstein asked.

Faolan ignored him. "Enzo spent the night going through the files and questioning the mugs, so we've got a full list of who's who in Pennsylvania, Jersey, Delaware, and Maryland, along with the major players in Rhode Island, Massachusetts, Connecticut, and New Hampshire. Turns out the allies were spying on each other as much as us, so we even got a few addresses to use for spying or hitting." He pushed his hand through his hair. "So, sure, I took things into my own hands and went outside of my authority, but I think you can see that I had a good reason and that it was worth it."

Rothstein tossed his cue onto the green felt of the table in a gesture of derision, but didn't say anything.

"What do you say to all this, Frank?" Killian asked, having long ago dropped the formality of asking Rothstein tactical questions when Frank was present. His mood was significantly brighter than it had been, but still wary.

Faolan glanced at his partner as he answered, but Frank gave away his usual nothing. "If we have Philadelphia, then Pittsburg and Harrisburg will lay down for whatever terms we give them."

Assuming an air of complete confidence, Faolan strolled away from the group and took a closer look at the items in the boss' display cabinet. According to Frank, Killian had been drafted into one of New York's Irish regiments in the Civil War shortly after getting off the boat. Inside the cabinet sat a collection of pipes, knives, and uniform patches from that time as well as a scarred Kentucky rifle with detachable bayonet and an ornate cavalry sword he'd supposedly taken in hand-fighting from a Southern Colonel at Shiloh.

Frank was still speaking: "As for those pissants in Jersey, they'll switch over to us as fast as they can now. We'll be able to squeeze them for men, money, equipment, and information, and they can't cry to nobody."

The reflection in the glass of the case told Faolan that Devlin was still following his every move.

"Also," Frank continued without pause, "I'd lay odds on Delaware and Maryland going neutral now since they were never very enthused about supporting this war. If we can make this all happen quickly, say a week or two, there's also a good chance to get Albany and Buffalo to swing over to us or go neutral. If we play it right, Faolan's play could net us three states and cost Moore five."

That made Killian smile. "Which might be enough to end this whole thing." He looked at Rothstein, Frank, and Everett. "Well, gentlemen, how do we play it right?"

Rothstein joined him, glancing down at the photos. "We insist that Jersey, the rest of Pennsylvania, and upstate New York support this guy Davidson for Reeve as a condition of alliance. That'll show us how much their support is really worth to Governor Burlington."

"Makes sense," Killian said. "But what's the chance Burlington tells them all to go fuck themselves?"

"He can't afford to," Rothstein told him. "Having a major city like New York in open rebellion looks bad enough, but let it spread to two and he'll get pressure from the Hegemon."

"Along with challenges from every Reeve on the East Coast who thinks they can do a better job and has enough support to make a play," Frank added.

"So, is this enough for us to force that cocksucker to give me the nod?" Killian asked.

"Doubtful, sir," Everett replied. "Unless, of course, you've reconsidered making an apology to the Governor for your remarks at that meeting—"

"I do not apologize to that puffed up little bag of shit!" Killian shouted. "Never. I meant every goddamn word I said, do you hear me?"

Everett adjusted his posture a bit. "Yes, sir. My apologies. However, that aside, Reeve Moore will likely persuade the Governor to grant Philadelphia legitimacy while continuing to withhold it from us."

Rothstein stepped in to rescue the Dhampir. "It's not the end of the war, but I admit it's a big step forward. Now it will be us and our allies against Moore and his allies."

"So now we can take the war to them," Frank added.

Faolan—who had tired of studying the illustrated aerial view of the Five Points area in 1880 that hung above the cabinet—turned to face them. "You're welcome."

Killian smiled at him, spreading his arms wide. "I've not forgotten that it was your cleverness that has turned this war for us, Faolan." Then, still smiling, he turned to Devlin and nodded.

Faolan shoved his hand into his pocket, gripping his Browning even as he turned. Thumbing the safety, he didn't bother trying to draw, just pointed through the pocket—

Devlin's bullet punched through his forearm before he'd finished bringing the gun up.

Chapter Nineteen

The Browning slipped from between his suddenly numb and boneless fingers as blood poured down his twitching hand. Then Frank was there, gripping the wound in his powerful grip to slow the flow as the flesh began the process of knitting back together.

Faolan fought the urge to drop to his knees as his mind raced, but supported himself by leaning against the cabinet as Killian approached, motioning Frank away. The large, ruddy face smiled at him once again and the big, callused hand squeezed his shoulder. "Now, don't worry, lad, you'll heal that up in short order. Your move did put the city at risk for a time, 'specially as I knew nothing about it, you see? So, I gave you a slap on the wrist to learn you."

He was watching expectantly, so Faolan swallowed his anger as best he could and nodded. "Yeah, I get it now. I'm sorry for keeping you in the dark."

Killian nodded magnanimously. "You're young and eager, I understand. And it was a hell of a clever move. Devlin, bring a bottle of the good stuff for my new Street Boss!" He grinned that feral, savage grin of his, saying, "You've certainly earned the position, son, and I'm glad to see that my confidence in you was not misplaced."

Faolan nodded, smiling, even as he imagined taking Killian apart joint by joint like Marty Rice.

Devlin gave him a courteous nod and handed him an open bottle of Vampyr blood that had once belonged to some rival of Killian's. "I went for the muscle so's it wouldn't bleed so much," he said by way of apology.

"I appreciate it," Faolan said and took a long swig of blood. In his periphery, he saw Rothstein dig into his pocket and hand Everett a hundred dollar bill which the Dhampir smugly pocketed.

Nice to know somebody had been betting on him.

* * * * *

A few minutes later, after Rothstein and Everett left to begin organizing the diplomacy necessary to make the promised alliances a reality and Frank was sent off to move the new Street Boss's stuff into Byrne's old suite on the executive floor, Killian asked Faolan to follow him. "I have something I want to show you," he said and gestured for Devlin to remain behind.

They moved from the parlor into Killian's bedroom, which was practically Spartan. A king-size bed with intricate carvings on the head and footboards and a chair were the only furnishings aside from a large mat where two large Doberman Pinschers lay. The dogs sprang to alertness at Faolan's presence, but became docile at a gesture from their master.

"You want to clean up a bit first?" the boss asked.

"No thanks, I'll wait and break in my new private bathroom." He was looking forward to having his own place after months of communal living. No more paying off Stebbins for an awkward date at Stephanie's room in the Doll House, or petting sessions in the gang's private movie theater, or having to make do with a quickie in some deserted corner of the Indigo Lounge.

He was on his way to being a real somebody now.

"I thought you might," Killian said, leading him further to a door on the opposite side of the room. "I'll see you get an appointment with the barber tomorrow night, though. Hair's getting a little long."

"Thanks." A few months ago, Killian had instituted a dress and grooming code for his "employees" so as to keep from being embarrassed further by the lack of style possessed by some of his killers. Since Faolan was an executive now the building's barber, dentist, and tailor who operated at night for them would bump a regular mug's appointment to accommodate him.

"You wanna get your teeth sharpened, too?" Killian asked as they crossed from the bedroom into a full woodworking shop that any craftsman would be proud to call his.

"Nah," he said. "I still gotta mingle with the normals too often to have the fangs showing. Nice place you got here."

Killian smiled with genuine warmth, gazing around. Saws, lathes, drills, lumber, and a variety of hand tools were spread through a linoleum-floored space that was easily twenty-five feet wide by sixty long. A single upholstered chair on casters sat beside one of the workbenches, a box of fine detail tools open and in easy reach.

"This is where I come when I need to think," he explained. "Or sometimes just to relax and not think about anything, follow?"

Faolan smiled. "Never figured you for a whittler."

"Whittler? Hell, I used to be a furniture maker back in Ireland. Had my own shop, even an apprentice. Good quality stuff for manor homes, too, not that cheap shit you see most places. Damn famine ruined everything, of course, and over here I couldn't get anything going on account of there being so much feeling against us Irish."

"You do your bed?"

Killian nodded, picking up a half-finished carving of some building Faolan didn't recognize from the workbench. "And most all the pieces in my rooms. There's nothing like building something with your own two hands, Faolan, believe me. Taking a pile of lumber or some scrap of wood and forging it into something fine: smoothing every surface, fitting every joint, carving every line until you've created exactly what you set out to. It's a feeling to beat all others. That's partly why I asked you back here. Come on upstairs."

At the workshop's center, a wrought iron spiral staircase wound its way up to the next floor. Setting the carving down, Killian ascended the stairs at a brisk pace and Faolan followed.

"Well, since you mention it," Faolan called ahead of him as he clomped up the iron steps. "I need some materials to build this Street Boss position you gave me..."

He trailed off when he saw what awaited on the floor. His first impression was of the vastness of the space, the empty and unfinished state of it. There were no walls except for the building exterior, nothing dividing the entire floor except for the regularly spaced iron support posts and the bank of elevators in the center. The city lights shone in from the unobstructed windows and the widely-spaced bare bulbs in the ceiling. The floor was covered in speckled green linoleum and on that floor rested dozens of wheeled tables.

On those table tops sat the isle of Manhattan.

Killian grinned at Faolan's reaction, proud as a rooster, and hung his jacket on the back of an office chair. "Aye, it's a sight to take your breath away, isn't it?"

The enormous wooden model of their island city ran nearly the length of the floor, from where the Bronx swelled above Killian's parlor below to where Faolan stood (looking over at the green rectangle of Central Park) and down to the knife-point of Battery Park, at least fifty feet total length and maybe as much as fifty five. The map was constructed in chunks to fit the five-by-ten tables which were placed to avoid the support posts and allow access to each section. The detail was impressive, given the scale. Faolan had no problem recognizing the Empire State Building, the Chrysler Building, Woolworth's, Rockefeller Center, and every other notable structure. Most of the smaller tenement areas were bare wood blocks, but many buildings were painted red or yellow or blue. Judging by the places he recognized, the red represented things they owned or controlled outright, yellow was stuff they influenced indirectly or through human agents, and the few spots of blue had to be known areas of enemy influence.

Faolan whistled. "It's pretty swell, all right. You need a hand with Brooklyn?"

"Already got Brooklyn and Queens behind you."

He turned and saw his hometown and its northern sister replicated on tables set twenty feet wide by maybe thirty long, but without the level of detail of Manhattan. "And you did all this by hand?"

"Yes." Killian stood where Harlem was widest, represented in about twelve feet of table space, and gazed at the expanse of his domain like Zeus on Olympus. "I started nearly fifteen years ago now, just as a lark to occupy myself." He flashed Faolan a conspiratorial smile. "A man can only build so many spare highboys, after all."

Just beyond him sat a detailed model of the George Washington Bridge made of matchsticks, shims, and fishing line. Killian loomed over it like a colossus, his wide brown eyes devouring every detail. "But I've always known it was my destiny to rule this city, to shape it with my will in the direction of the future," he said.

Faolan pushed his dirty hair off his face and stepped closer. It was always dicey trying to steer the boss away from one of his crazy speeches, but he wasn't in the mood for any of that mystical mumbo-jumbo tonight. "Yeah, I get you. So, like I was saying, I need to be outside—"

"The strong shape the world to their will while the weak submit to the will of the world," Killian continued, ignoring his attempt.

"That's clever," Faolan said, suppressing his frustration. The boss always responded well to flattery. "Who said that?"

"I fucking said that," he met Faolan's eyes as if daring him to challenge the assertion and, seeing none, nodded. "See, Faolan, I needed to know whether you were just playing at strength or if you were the genuine article. If you don't have strength, then you've gotta know your place and accept it. A man who plays at being strong ain't sticking to his place. Now, I knew you were a slick operator, of course. You're quick on your feet and you got a way about you that ain't fancy, but it makes people believe what you say and want to trust you. But that's not strength, that's just charm."

Faolan felt the back of his neck prickle and his fingers itched to feel the Browning in their grasp, despite that his arm probably couldn't support the weight. He fought to keep his expression bland.

Killian stared into him, his hands casually on his hips. His eyes stared into Faolan's across the short distance as if none existed. "I know about your little games, don't kid yourself," he said.

Faolan said nothing, showed nothing.

His heartbeat increased.

If the other Vampyr attacked, the first move would be to throw out one of these tables to block him. Get to his gun.

How could he have tipped his hand?

Killian's teeth came out in a smile that was savage, predatory, and triumphant. "You and Rothstein both. I let it drift so long as it didn't hurt my efforts. After all, a little rivalry usually brings out the best in people and it has here as well."

Slowly, so as not to be obvious, Faolan let out the breath he'd been holding.

"You bent the world to your will tonight and steered the course of events toward the outcome I've already plotted. Strength and vision, Faolan: the two qualities I need in a right hand. Rothstein has vision, but not strength while you have shown tonight that you have strength. I brought you here to see if you also possess vision."

And if I do, does that make me a threat? Faolan wondered. It was easy to see that him and Rothstein pecking at each other all the time suited Darcy Killian just fine.

New York's unofficial Reeve pushed two of the wheeled tables apart and split the city like Moses parting the Red Sea so he could stride through, heading into the elevator corridor. Faolan decided to show a little more respect and ambled around Battery Park—taking a quick look at the Brooklyn model to see if he could pick out the row-house he'd grown up in on Division Avenue—and followed through the corridor to the other side of the floor. There was another set of table saws, horses, and a wood planer beneath a huge street map of the city tacked to the back wall. Killian passed these by and led him toward the building's southwest corner where Faolan saw a city unlike anything he'd ever imagined.

Fifteen feet wide and thirty feet long, this model was scaled differently than the others. Every detail was painstakingly rendered, from the painted streets and tiny pipe-cleaner trees to the miniature cars, and all labeled in small, neat block letters: Ford Building, Westinghouse Building, Dupont Building, Court of Communication, Court of Power, Commerce Circle, Plaza of Light, City

Hall Square, Great White Way, and on and on like someplace out of Buck Rogers.

On the wall a huge banner proclaimed: BUILDING THE WORLD OF TOMORROW WITH THE TOOLS OF TODAY!

What Faolan saw was a spacious place, a place of color-coding and clear delineations that was geometric, ordered, and clean to the point of sterility.

"What's this?" he asked quietly.

Killian put an arm around his shoulder and said proudly, "This is the future."

It was as far removed from the color, chaos, grime, and vibrant energy of New York City as any place could be.

Faolan hated it.

"Behold the World's Fair of 1939," Killian announced. "My demonstration to the entire Order that New York City is now a world-class power to be reckoned with: a city following a vision that supports the Vampyr power structure, but lights the way to firmer control and greater influence. Rothstein and me have been putting this together since I first took power, and nothing will interfere with it. If we haven't won this war outright by the time the Fair opens, then the breathtaking scope of my vision will make them understand that I can't be denied any longer!"

Faolan held still, keeping his breathing slow and regular, working the angles.

Like an echo in his mind, he heard his old friend Jack Diamond going on about the Catskills: *"It's wide open up here, Faolan. A man like me with power and guts and enough guns could build an empire up here. Before long, I could control all of upstate New York! That's the state government, Saratoga, and all the bootleg routes down from Canada! They'd all have to pay us their respects—and taxes. Like having my own little kingdom..."*

All so familiar.

If only he weren't so fucking weak from that damn bullet and all the night's running around! He'd never have a better chance to take out Killian than this!

Yes you fucking will if you just keep your head and play it smart, he berated himself.

"You mean like them expositions in Chicago and St. Louis?" he asked to keep from saying anything that Killian might take for criticism.

"Bigger," the other Vampyr assured him, taking his arm away as quickly as it had come down so he could strut around his little city of the future and point things out. "General Motors has got a model of what cities will be like by 1960 complete with radio controlled cars that can go a hundred miles an hour on a super-highway and skyscrapers a quarter of a mile tall and floating hangers for dirigibles! AT&T's bringing a machine that can create a human voice with electronics and then there's something called a television in the White Owl building that can send filmed news and sports live like a radio! This depression's been a real son of a bitch for everybody and now that the weather's finally beginning to clear, people want things easier and that's just what we'll show them. Borden's got something called a Rotolactor that can milk a hundred and fifty cows twice a day all by itself! Automation, you see, the way of the future!"

"Well, sure, everybody likes seeing new inventions and stuff," Faolan commented. He wasn't seeing what Killian's excitement was about yet and that bothered him. There had to be something beneath this kiddie fantasy or why was the sweat dripping cold down his back?

"The guys at the top of The Order have always controlled governments, so it's natural for them to make the government bigger and stronger like they're doing with Roosevelt and his programs, right?" Killian asked as he rested his hands on the area marked in red that held pavilions for sixty other nations and twenty-four represented states. "But what did Prohibition teach everybody?"

Faolan smiled, catching on. "That the G can pass laws, but it can't change what folks want."

"Yes!" Killian cried, slapping the table surface so that the whole Fair model rattled. "Having the power to make the rules ain't the same as having control! And The Order is all about control, what with having our food supply running around armed and outnumbering us by thousands to one. See, mob guys like you know about using the rackets to control little businesses with money and fear, right? But if we control those huge companies like the ones I've got on board for the Fair, we can lobby politicians in Washington, control what's available for people to buy, and control the lives of millions."

A dark suspicion crept through Faolan's mind as the pit of his stomach went cold, but he played it slow for safety's sake. "But them companies still answer to the feds, don't they?"

Killian sighed. "That's where the vision comes in, Faolan. You remember when Morgan bailed the government out of that gold squeeze back before Teddy fucking Roosevelt went trust-busting? One man able to put the whole country right just by reaching into his pocket! Money is power and there's nobody out there who doesn't want more of it. My will and vision is gonna allow The Order to take advantage of that." He began to pace back and forth, his eyes alight with that mad inner fire. "When you're the one that pays a man's wage, puts food on his table, then you've got leverage on him. Suppose you also own the bank that holds the note on his house? Then you've got even more say in what he does, who he associates with ... how he votes—you see where I'm going with this now?"

"Sure," Faolan agreed. Control enough votes and you control the politicians. That was common sense, but no single company could really control that many people. So that meant controlling lots of companies, which meant a lot of coordination, a lot of dough spent keeping control, and a lot of time fighting off attempts to push you out. "But ain't that a lot more work than just putting the bite on whoever gets elected? Or using our boys to make sure the guys we want get elected?"

Killian's excitement was like an aura of crackling electricity around him, dying down for no particular reason only to lash back out farther than before. "Of course it is, at first. Laying the groundwork for a social revolution ain't something to be accomplished without a lot of time and effort. It was Frank, I think, who first mentioned what the fascists are doing over in Italy, but me and Rothstein made it work for America. The state oversees and supports large corporations—I'm talking about huge corporations, now, like the kind we used to have before Teddy fucking Roosevelt, with a near monopoly on their product—and the corporations support the state by promoting patriotism and giving the government all kinds of economic breaks that Rothstein can explain better than I can."

"I get it," Faolan said, taking out a cigarette and lighting it. "We get control of the companies at the Fair and help them gobble up other companies until they become unstoppable. The higher-ups make the feds cooperate and not go after us while we give them votes to keep their lackeys in office. And, later, when we've got partnerships with other Reeves in key cities and our companies are too powerful for the G to buck—"

"We start dictating the terms to them!" Killian finished with delight. "Now you see the power of the vision, its grand scale and ambitious scope!"

Faolan looked down at the Fair model again. He saw, all right. He saw the grocers, delicatessens, and bakeries of every neighborhood in New York City gone, replaced by those new super-markets. He saw shops and stores all swallowed up inside giant department stores with no restaurants, pushcarts, greasy spoon diners, or ice-cream parlors. just giant automats on every corner. He saw wide, clean, open streets filled with the fast-flying, radio-controlled limousines of the Order and its puppets (white men, naturally) on their way to the Court of Power while the working stiffs who held up the pyramid (Negroes, Jews, Puerto Ricans, Chinese, and other immigrants, naturally) filed in orderly lines from Residence Square down the Great White Way into the Plaza of Production to punch the clock at their assembly-line factory of choice and keep the wheels moving ever forward. He saw the women file down to the Commerce Circle to put the family earnings right back into the economy by purchasing many fine, can't-live-without-them products as instructed by the advertisers in the Court of Communication, their hearts swelling with patriotic pride.

And behind Killian's vision he saw Arnold Rothstein's brain.

Even all laid out it still sounded like a hair-brained scheme, but Faolan figured that was because of Killian's giddy over-simplification. Rothstein had the details all worked out in that big, greedy account book of a mind—the answers to the questions Faolan didn't even know to ask: the who's, the how's, and the when's. And in Darcy Killian, he'd found the perfect front man and backer.

"Building the world of tomorrow with the tools of today," Faolan said as he blew the smoke from his lungs out between his lips in a slow creep. "It's sure a hell of a plan, boss, but I'm behind you two-hundred percent."

Killian grinned and Faolan found himself reminded of Smiley from Coney Island: the vampire god awaiting sacrifice. "Outstanding. Your readiness to employ technological innovation impressed me and, of all the men who could general my war, I felt that you would be the quickest to appreciate what I've begun here."

Faolan nodded and took another drag from his Camel. "But you still ain't gonna let me bump Rothstein, are you?"

The ruddy-faced Vampyr's grin became a gentle smile as he stoked his trimmed-down mustache absently with a meaty forefinger. He walked around the table and rested his arm upon Faolan's shoulder. "Well, you understand that that's a complicated matter, don't you? Believe me, I've no more love for that scheming little sheeny than you do, Faolan, but he's sharp as a Philadelphia lawyer. I need him for the foreseeable future, since he knows the ins and outs of so many of these city and business people we're having to deal with on the Fair."

Faolan put on his most amiable smile and shrugged. "That's fine, but wouldn't he have more time to devote to fulfilling your vision if he didn't also have the rackets, the street forces, and the war crowding up his plate?"

The boss' smile faltered as he considered, removing his hand. He turned and paced a few steps, then turned back and said, "Yes, yes he would. He won't like it, though. Once Arnold has something in his hands, you have the devil of a time taking it away. He'll want to know why you can't run it night-to-night with him overseeing."

The Killian he'd first met would have made his decision and told A.R. to go take a walk in the sun if it didn't suit him. Rothstein had sunk his hooks deep into the man, it seemed. Putting Killian on the defensive by taking the obvious shot at his ego would backfire, as would telling him he didn't need Rothstein. Faolan would have to show him.

"Let me play him for it," Faolan said quickly. He could feel the morning lethargy beginning to grip him, sapping his energy and focus. Glancing down to the eastern side of the floor, he could see the horizon getting lighter outside the windows.

"How so?"

"A poker game," Faolan explained. "Just him and me. Winner gets his way. He wins, I stay under his thumb and run things his way. If I win, then I get it all: the rackets, the men, the money, and the authority to use my own plans. I report directly to you and he keeps his fucking nose out of my business. He can stay your advisor and handle the Fair for as long as you need him."

Killian's large brown eyes narrowed in thought and his gaze darted to where the sun was announcing its imminent arrival. He smiled again and turned his attention back to Faolan. "It does sound fair enough, certainly. No one who calls himself a man could refuse as long as there would be no dishonesty."

Faolan locked eyes with Killian, his expression one of utmost gravity. "I don't have to cheat to beat Rothstein."

But he and Frank were going to, anyway, just to make sure. One good fix deserved another, after all.

"That's fine, then," Killian declared. "But I can't let him lose his financial influences, the legitimate ones, I mean. Nobody can work money like a Jew."

"Fine," Faolan agreed, hiding his irritation behind his growing fatigue. "Well, I think I'm gonna go break in my new private suite."

Killian nodded, smiling. "You've earned it. I'll go tell Rothstein what's what."

Faolan walked toward the elevator, glancing back at the model of the World's Fair as he went.

More than ever, he felt like he needed a shower.

Chapter Twenty

In the shower the next evening, Faolan became aware that he was no longer alone in his new apartment. There was a sound that could have been his front door unlocking, but it was difficult to tell over the rush of the water. Then there were occasional creaks that could have been the building settling. All of these could have been dismissed, but not his intuition. His intuition told him that someone else moved and breathed within his territory.

Without turning off the water, he slipped past the shower curtain onto the shaggy black mat and listened.

Nothing.

He took the Browning from where it rested on the toilet, within easy reach of the tub, and gripped it tight as he slipped his black silk robe on over his wet body. When human, he'd always enjoyed cotton terrycloth, but the heat of his Vampyr body demanded the thin silk. Once he was sure that his feet were dry enough not to slip on the black-and-white hexagonal tile that covered the floor, he took an experimental step toward the door and placed his free hand onto the cut glass knob.

He waited, listening.

After a few moments, he heard an unmistakable creak of movement from the direction of the living room. Faolan twisted the knob simultaneously with the creak and eased the door open, shoving the Browning's muzzle into the opening in case the intruder came into the bedroom.

The sounds of movement—slight shifts of weight on the floorboards and brushes of fabric—remained in the living room.

Sliding sideways through the doorway into the bedroom, Faolan exhaled slowly, and moved to the bedroom door. He drew another slow breath, crouched low, and spun into the doorway, Browning aimed and ready.

Stephanie Chandler stood by the window with her back to him and busied herself flipping through the uppermost box of his record collection. The backless green number that hugged her curves snugly and stopped just below her knees gave him no reason to complain about the rear view and he rose, smiling. He thumbed on the Browning's safety, but kept it trained on her.

"Hold still," he ordered. "Get your hands where I can see them."

A slight twitch was the only hint she gave of being startled. Her hands came up slowly and her eyes rose to meet his reflection in the glass, a wry smile twisting her lips. "You always shower with your gun?"

"I lost my rubber ducky. Besides, never know when I might have to get the jump on a record thief," he said, crossing to her. She began to turn, opening her lips to speak, but he gestured with the gun and said: "Keep still, now. When a man finds an intruder in his place, he can't be too careful."

In the glass, he saw her arch an eyebrow. "You better be thorough, then. I always carry concealed."

"Yeah, you seem a dangerous sort."

He placed the barrel of the gun against the small of her exposed back and she shivered as goose-bumps traveled up her creamy skin. "Mmm-hmmm," she murmured.

He brought his free hand down to the back of her ankle and brushed it slowly up her stocking to the knee, then pushed her dress up as he slid the hand over the outside of her bare thigh. She leaned back into him a bit and sighed, her breath quickening. Navigating around the garter belt, his fingers stroked her belly and then traced down the front of her panties before finding their way to the inside of her thigh. Her head tilted back and her rich chestnut hair fell in a cascade that ended mere inches from the gun. He stepped in even closer, searching carefully up and down her hips and thighs while she squirmed and pressed her body back into him.

"Nah, this is no good," he whispered, his lips beside her ear. "How's a fella supposed to be thorough with all this fabric in the way?"

He tossed the Browning onto the armchair behind him and set both hands to negotiating the tight green dress up her cooperative body.

"I'd think twice about losing the rod," she whispered back, smiling wickedly. "I give no quarter to unarmed men."

"Don't get any ideas, sweetheart." Faolan paused to kiss her full, parted lips before sliding the dress up over her raised arms. His hands settled onto her hips. "I got a back-up."

* * * * *

"I like your place," Stephanie said, her head resting on his bare chest, her nude body curled around him as they lay together on the long brown leather sofa.

"Thanks for helping me break it in."

She smiled. "The furniture really compliments the architecture. Did you have the ceiling painted silver?"

"Yeah. I saw it in somebody's place one time and liked it." Actually, most of the furniture and decoration had been Byrne's, but it suited him. Faolan lit a Camel and took a deep drag.

"Well, I'll be damned, there's some taste lurking inside that loutish exterior after all."

"Try and keep that under your hat, would you?"

"My lips are sealed."

"Well, I wouldn't do *that*." He pulled her closer and she tilted her head up to meet his kiss, long and slow. When their lips parted and their tongues met again, Faolan's spine actually tingled. He'd never been with another woman who could do as many things with a kiss as Stephanie. Each time was like the first time with a brand new woman and he'd come to look forward to the time spent before and after sex with her even more than the act itself. And she was no slouch when it came to sex.

"Your shower's still running," she said after another moment.

"Let it."

"So, you got plans for that big empty area over there?" she asked, pointing toward the wide expanse of hardwood between the couch and his bedroom.

"That's where the poker table's going, maybe a little bar."

"Why not just use the dining table for games?"

"I ain't putting anything in the dining room," he said between puffs. "What? It ain't like I throw lavish dinner parties anyhow. I'm using it for my exercise. I found this little rubber ball that I play wall ball with in there, keep my reflexes sharp, and me and Rod can use it for my lessons."

She arched an eyebrow. "Lessons?"

He smiled sheepishly. "Yeah, he's been showing me how to do some of them fancy kicks and punches he does. It's really something. Instead of just ducking a guy's fist, he's showing me how to grab it and flip the guy over with it."

"Fascinating. But why do it in your dining room? There's the gym downstairs."

"Nah. I don't want nobody to know 'bout it, just in case."

"Well, your secret's safe with me. Even if I do think it's the daffiest idea I ever heard."

Stephanie borrowed his cigarette for a drag and then got up to put on some music. Faolan pushed the front of his robe closed and lay back to admire the way the city lights and shadows of the window played across the sweat-slick skin of her back, around the curves of her little round tush, and down her long slender legs. It still tickled him how she could just walk around in the buff all perfectly comfortable and relaxed. His wife Colleen hadn't been able to get out of bed in anything less than a nightgown and robe, not even to use the john. He used to joke that she showered in her bathing costume.

He turned his attention back to Stephanie, who was tossing her hair out of her way and selecting an album. He found himself thinking about Colleen less often these days, but it always happened when he was with Stephanie. He couldn't tell if it was guilt or just his natural tendency to compare things that made it happen. Was it a good thing or bad thing that he could see himself settling down with Stephanie the way he had with Colleen? Or that he could picture it working out better than things had with Colleen? Faolan took another drag of his cigarette and considered the question of whether you could be unfaithful to a memory.

"How many Armstrong records you got, anyhow?" Stephanie asked.

Faolan smiled. "Just about all of them. Been collecting since I heard him play with Fletcher Henderson at the Roseland."

"You ever meet him?"

"Yeah, I used to slip backstage sometimes after shows and we'd smoke some muggles and talk music—"

Stephanie selected a record and cranked the turntable. "Muggles?"

"Yeah, you know, reefer. Like the song, 'Muggles.'"

"Never heard it." She set the needle and the speaker played the opening notes to Fats Waller's "Ain't Misbehavin'," except this was Armstrong's rendition.

"Pops is always happy to see me, 'cause I always make sure to bring him the really good stuff. Well, hell, he always seems like he's happy to see everybody. I never met a cooler cat."

"I saw him doing *Hot Chocolates* at Connie's Inn and fell in love." She began doing a sexy little improvised dance, turning around to face him as she swayed her hips and slid her hands up and down her gorgeous body. Faolan chuckled and got up to join her, crushing out his cigarette. "I always liked this song," she continued, sliding her hands into the opening of his robe and setting them onto his hips. "But he put so much joy into the way he sang it that he just won me over completely."

He smiled and swayed his hips in time with hers, reaching his hands around to cup her behind. She snuggled up closer to him and it didn't matter to him that they weren't in tempo with the song. It didn't matter that they were slow dancing naked in front of a window. Nothing mattered except her nearness, the feel of her hands on him, and the feel of his hands on her. "Well, he's a joyful sort of fella," Faolan told her.

"Good," she said, resting her head on his shoulders. Her voice was wistful, holding no glibness or flippancy as she said: "People ought to be happy."

The song ended. The needle hissed and spun along the record's edge. It didn't matter because they were still holding each other. Still swaying.

Still together.

Then the hissing of the needle made Faolan decide that there was no reason to ruin the needle's point. He took one of his hands from Stephanie's body and reached out and set the arm back up on the stand. He remembered that he had his big game with Rothstein in an hour and he should get ready soon. He tried to push that thought away and go back to holding Stephanie, but he felt the hollowness of the act. Thoughts of Rothstein led to thoughts of Killian and that kooky scheme of his. Thoughts of the scheme led back to his unresolved thoughts about what he and Frank could do to work the World's Fair into their own plans. Thoughts of their plans led to reviewing Frank's arrangements for the poker game tonight. On and on it went like that, trains of thought kicking each other off like branches of tumbling dominoes.

Stephanie felt the change, glanced into his eyes, and disengaged herself.

Faolan closed his robe, replaced the fragile shellac record in the sleeve of the big album he kept his Armstrongs in, closed the book, and slipped it back into the box. He said: "You know, now that the Dutchman ain't around to harass him no more, Pops has been playing New York again. How's about you and me go see him sometime? I'll even take you backstage and introduce youse."

"Sure," Stephanie said, getting her stockings and panties in place. "That sounds swell."

Faolan sat down beside her on the couch and grabbed a Camel out of his pack along with his lighter. "Yeah, we could maybe—"

"So, I hear you've got—" she began at the same time. "Sorry."

"Nah, it's okay," he said, lighting the cigarette. "Go ahead."

"Well," she said with a touch of awkwardness as she stood and slipped her dress over her head. She tugged it down over her breasts and let it drop the rest of the way. "I was just saying that I heard there's some kind of important game going on tonight and so I thought maybe you needed to get ready for that..." She let it hang while she smoothed out wrinkles in her dress and began fussing her hair back into place.

"I got time yet," he told her. "Stick around."

She smiled, half-embarrassed and half-relieved, and sat back down on his left. "Oh. All right."

Faolan offered her a cigarette and lit it for her when she accepted. He felt agitated now and he didn't know why. He took a drag and exhaled slowly to stall. "So, uh, yeah, me and Rothstein are playing tonight to see who gets to general the war."

"You nervous?"

"Hell no. I got this locked." She reached around to put her hand on his right shoulder, resting her cheek gently on his left. He remained still except for the arm that carried the cigarette to and from his lips, his sharp blue eyes staring across the room at the blank wall. "That big-talking swindler's getting paid off in spades tonight, I'll tell you that. Practically my whole life this guy's been riding me, needling me, trying to torpedo me, and he don't think I'm gonna square up with him one day?"

He sat and smoked with unfocused eyes as memories paraded through his head. From the very first, Rothstein had been there. The first time he'd met Jack Diamond—his first step out of the petty street gangs of his youth into the world of serious operators like Little Augie—A.R. had been there to turn his big nose up at Faolan. Rothstein had never wanted him around and he could never figure out why. It wasn't like he'd ever insulted the man. It didn't seem likely that Rothstein disliked him for being Irish, since Jack and his brother Eddie had been trusted bodyguards of his for years, and they'd been just as Irish. It made no sense, but there it was: no matter how many times Jack spoke up for Faolan, no matter how many solid plays he made for the team, no matter how much Faolan cleaned up his act and tried to be classy like Jack and Charlie Luck, that high-handed prick still wouldn't give him the time of day. Even at the end (or what he'd thought of as the end before seeing Rothstein alive and well as a Vampyr), when Faolan plugged him in the gut, his last words had been nothing but a contemptuous dismissal: *"Oh ... he would have to send you."*

"Some people are just that way," Stephanie said in a soothing tone, stroking his shoulder through the silk of his robe. "No reason to it."

"Yeah, I suppose."

"So, what are you gonna do if you win this game tonight?"

"If? I told you, doll, I got it locked."

"Okay, fine, *when* you win. What happens next?"

He glanced over at her, smirking. "You angling for a dinner invitation?"

"No, I mean what's the next step in the big plan?" She smiled. "Of course, if you wanted to take me out with you afterward to celebrate, I might be able to find a few spare hours."

"It's a date," he told her. "So, you mean after I rub Arnie's nose in his defeat a little? Well, after that there's gonna be a lot of weeding out Rothstein's rats, busting heads, and generally getting everything into the shape we want."

"We?"

"Yeah, Frank and me."

"Of course. You and The Ghoul are thick as thieves now."

Faolan smiled, oddly pleased by her jealousy. "Yeah, but I always come home to you don't I? Anyways, once I've got a free hand to fight the war my way, there's plenty of ideas we've cooked up to keep the city safer and start taking the war into Moore's turf. Then Killian'll see what I can do and, eventually, when he's confident and smug in his victory and everybody else is behind me, then we'll make our play and win the pot." He finished his cigarette and imagined what it would be like to be Reeve.

"Then what?" Stephanie asked.

Faolan blinked out of his revere and looked at her. "What do you mean? Then we've won. Killian, Rothstein, and Devlin'll be dead or chased out, I'll be the Reeve, and I'll put Frank in Rothstein's place. Probably keep Everett around if we can manage it. maybe make Rod the Street Boss—"

"No, I mean what about you? What are you gonna do differently than Killian?"

He smiled. "Well, I might put in that elevator you been wanting at the Doll House." The building that housed Stephanie and all the other girls was five floors and all stairs. Stephanie had been campaigning for an elevator for months now.

The corners of her mouth tugged briefly upward. "Yeah, well, I hope we don't have to wait that long. No offense. But, seriously, what changes would you make, do you think?"

"I don't know," Faolan said, shrugging. "We're mostly concentrating on how to win this thing, you know? Ain't like we sat down and wrote up a constitution. What's it to you, anyhow?" He considered her a moment and felt suspicion sneak into the back of his thoughts like a malevolent shadow. Why would his practical, sensible Stephanie want to know about the plans him and Frank had been making? Had somebody turned her into their stoolie?

Rothstein? Killian? Stebbins? Was she trying to work him now?

She smiled. "Well, I'm going to be living here, right? Besides, I would have thought that you'd have all kinds of grand ideas by now. I mean, as much as you're always thinking about this stuff, it doesn't seem possible that you never considered what you'd do after you won."

He had an itch for another cigarette, felt like his skin was crawling, wanted to tear Stephanie's head open and dig through everything she thought and felt and knew so he could be sure about her. His guts squirmed in revulsion that he could have let somebody get so close, let her slip under his defenses like she had and stay so blind to the possibility of treachery. What was it Frank told him last night? *"Knowing someone is different from trusting them: one is based on facts and observations. the other is a tangle of emotions and perceptions. Trust gets Vampyrs killed."*

"I had ideas," he said, getting to his feet and walking over to his radio, a new model that had a record player built into the top. "Naturally, I've daydreamed about it sometimes, but like I said it ain't something that's been a high priority."

Frank knew that Dracula trick, the whammy, that way certain Vampyrs had for getting into a person's head and opening it up. Maybe he could arrange for Frank to have a little heart-to-heart with Stephanie so they could know for sure.

Stephanie glanced at the floor, her smile gone. "So you really haven't made any plans for the future? Or just not ones you want to share with me?"

He shrugged, his insides squirming a little now. "I guess I just always been a little superstitious about planning too far ahead, you know? Most of the dreams I had when I was a kid never worked out, so somewhere along the line I suppose I just stopped trying to think that far ahead."

She arched her brow, but with a soft sympathy in her eyes. "But if you don't ever set a few goals, you'll never know when you've gotten there, will you? You'll just keep trying to climb forever."

Faolan sat down, sighed. "I used to figure that's what I had to do. Just keep climbing as high as the world would let me until I died."

She chuckled. "Honey, I wouldn't know what to do with the whole world if I could have it. I'll settle for a life of comfort and occasional excitement with someone I can trust."

He looked at her for a few seconds, really looked at her. There was nothing he saw that he didn't like and it scared him. It scared him a lot. "Trust is a hard thing to come by."

She must have heard the deeper meaning in his tone, because she didn't laugh the comment off. She met his eyes and let him see everything behind them as she reached up to stroke his cheek. "You can trust me, Faolan. Just tell me I'm not alone in this."

She didn't have to say what "this" was because he knew. That's what scared him so much. "I think I do trust you, Steph, but trust is a dangerous thing. Love, too, but everybody knows that. I trusted Jack, right up to when he went crazy, but I loved him long after that. I killed him, but I loved him—do you get that?"

"I think so," she answered.

He grabbed a cigarette from his case and lit it, passing Stephanie one of hers and lighting it for her. "He was going to prison—Jack, I mean. The fix was in and I knew it, but he was stir-crazy from his time in the Army. He couldn't take it. So, I went to Schultz and negotiated the contract. I figured I was doing him a favor, that it should be somebody who cared who finally did it rather than some stooge." He laughed, a short bitter chuckle. "Of course, the fucking Dutchman tried to kill me when I went to collect my money, but one good turn deserves another, right?"

He took a long pull off his Camel and exhaled. "Luciano sends my best friend from growing up to bump me off because I took him for a ride back in twenty-nine and tried to kill him. That was on Jack's orders—the dope business, you know? I didn't like it, but Jack was counting on me. Then there was my brother, Tom … he tried to blackmail me with the Luciano thing into going straight, but he didn't know, he couldn't know … see, I was already a Dhampir by then. I already made my deal with Byrne and there was no backing out of it, but Tom just wouldn't listen, he…"

He choked on the words, swallowed, and took another hit from his cigarette. Stephanie put her arm around his shoulders and they sat there, sharing silence and smoke together for a minute. The fall out from his last betrayal had seen Dewey bring Luciano to trial with the evidence he'd provided and more that the prosecutor had dug up himself. With Philadelphia no longer an enemy, the original objective of that particular move had become moot, but his old pal Charlie went down hard on pandering charges and was now up at Sing Sing making appeals.

"I didn't start out trying to be a turncoat is what I think I'm trying to explain," he said. "I ain't saying I haven't done wrong by plenty of people, but it just always seems like the only play that makes sense at the time. Sometimes, it just feels like I'm cursed. Like no matter what I want to do, what I always end up doing is killing somebody close to me … so it just started making sense not to have nobody close to me."

Stephanie squeezed his shoulder and lay her head down on his other one. "Yeah, but then you just wind up a monster like Killian or Devlin. Maybe you ought to give the honest approach a chance sometime."

He put his arm around her and pulled her into him. "Around here, honesty is the one thing guaranteed to get me killed. Just look how many times Rod's nearly talked himself into a grave with that upstanding gentleman routine of his."

"It takes guts to stand up around guys like Killian," she said.

Faolan shook his head. "My old man was an honest cop, if you can believe that. Wouldn't take a bribe, never shook nobody down, and never looked the other way." He took another drag of his cigarette. "First it got him transferred to Brooklyn and then it got him killed. No witnesses in two whole tenements full of people and no real investigation by the cops. Of course, Tom idolized the old man and went right down the same road and came to the same end. That's the honest approach in my book, babe. Nah, I gotta keep playing this the way that makes sense. It ain't even just about me being in charge, either. Killian's a fucking mad dog under all that Rothstein polish and somebody needs to put him down."

Stephanie lifted her head. "Really? This sounds new. Do tell."

As well as he could, he explained about the World's Fair and Killian's crazy obsession with the future and corporations controlling everything, trying hard to get across just how wrong it felt to him. In the end, he wasn't sure he succeeded, but Stephanie said: "That doesn't sound much like any future I'd want to be part of, either."

"Yeah. Me, I love this city just the way it is," he said. "Not that there ain't no room for improvements, of course, but I figure we can keep what works and just try to fix what don't."

Stephanie smiled. "So there's your goal."

He looked at her skeptically. "That's too simple to be a goal."

"Not necessarily. Just focus it a little, make it into a genuine plan of action. If Killian's got his vision, he's got something to fight for. That's what you need, too."

He smiled, shaking his head gently, and gave her a kiss. He stood, closed the front of his robe, and belted it. "Anyway, it's about time I shut off that shower and got dressed. I got a city to win tonight."

Chapter Twenty-One

Snap, snap, snap.

Arnold Rothstein studied the cards he'd dealt: an ace, a jack, and a seven of clubs. He saw nothing amiss with any of them. They had no foreign materials on them, his fingers had told him that much, and as his eyes scrutinized every inch of their front and back surfaces, he couldn't make out a single defect or mark.

The only mark tonight was him.

Snap, snap, snap.

He just couldn't figure out how. He'd examined every bit of the card room in the Indigo Lounge where he had played O'Connor. Where O'Connor had beaten him. Scratch that, where O'Connor had *cheated* him! So, he sat in Killian's library going through the deck, card by card, and checking it while he waited for Killian to get done carving whatever new piece he needed for that glorified model train set upstairs. Between Killian with his temper tantrums and his building blocks, Devlin's schoolyard bully routine, Rod Chambers playing pirate, and O'Connor running around playing at being Jimmy Cagney with his pop gun, Arnold sometimes felt like he was surrounded by children.

Well, that wasn't quite fair. Arnold liked children.

Snap, snap ...

Then, not for the first time, he pondered whether his Carolyn would have stayed if he'd given her children.

The third card plopped to the table.

Dammit, how many times am I gonna put myself

through this? he wondered. But it was already too late and, also not for the first time, he desperately wished that there was some way he could talk to her again. She was his rock, his best friend. Carolyn understood him in a way that nobody else did. He could talk to her about anything, and she would understand. Even after the divorce, they had remained close. He would call her when something went wrong, and they would just talk. No bitterness, no recriminations. Just old friends who understood each other. Of course, sometimes he called to tell her about something wonderful that had happened, but more often than not during that last year after the divorce, he called to receive comfort when he felt blue.

But she would never understand where he was now and the troubles he had here. Not only would his darling Carolyn be completely unhinged by the notion of her ex-husband having returned from the dead, but his enemies would know and report his indiscretion to Killian. They watched him constantly, O'Connor and his people, looking for some weakness or mistake they could exploit to bring him down. He knew. He'd always been a private person, but now he had to be entirely circumspect in all his dealings or risk destruction. Not to mention what that animal Killian would do to Carolyn if he made the slightest effort to contact or assist her. His silence protected her.

His silence was something she had never completely understood about him. Or was it his coolness? His aloof demeanor, his unflappability, and his constant calculation had protected him since childhood. These qualities had helped him succeed and prosper in a world that attacked him and wanted him to fail. Hadn't he proved his love for her? Hadn't he defied his father and his father's faith by marrying her? His orthodox father had sat Shiva for him as if he were dead the day Arnold wed Carolyn and the two men had rarely spoken afterward. Arnold had bought his wife everything she could want. In his quiet way, he'd worshiped her.

She had written a book about him a few years ago, despite the strings he'd pulled to keep it under wraps. He had a copy of it on a shelf in his room, but he'd never read it. They had even made a movie out of it—with Spencer Tracy, no less!—and he hadn't watched that, either. He supposed it was cowardly of him, but he didn't want to find that she'd written unkind things about him. He preferred to remember their relationship the way he did.

Tonight had been especially bad. Arnold hated to lose at anything, but it really burned him to get cheated. As often as he'd been accused of cheating, often out of simple anti-Semitism, he had to be very careful. That was his secret: he played careful. He didn't make wagers he wasn't sure of and when he did wager, he used strategies to maximize the profit of his investment. What others called gambling, he considered business. A man who wagered without researching the prospects, working the numbers, or undertaking the due diligence, was just throwing money away. He looked for opportunities others missed and exploited them. He was no pool room hustler or grifter, he was a businessman and gambling was his business. Had been his business, anyhow.

It didn't matter that O'Connor's little ploy still benefited him in the end. Hell, without the load of the gangland position weighing on his shoulders, Arnold would have more free time trying to transform that grotesque beast Killian into a gentleman able to mix among his betters. Long enough, at least. Long enough to gain the legitimacy and title of Reeve. Once that occurred, Killian's death would bring about a succession protocol rather than gangland anarchy and this city would be Arnold's.

Governor Burlington had an unusual reputation among the Vampyrs of the North American Domain. Some said he was a Virginian idealist in the Jeffersonian mold while others maintained that he was a wolf in sheep's clothing, hiding a ruthless political acumen behind a facade of Southern gentility and enlightenment. Either way, Arnold was willing to wager his future that Burlington wouldn't allow a bias against Jews to keep the most qualified Vampyr in New York from taking over as Reeve once Killian was dead. Arnold had studied the history, he had the social nuance, he had the political connections, and he was the true architect of a plan to increase The Order's control and while minimizing chaos and disruption.

O'Connor, meanwhile, had just won himself a tangled mess to deal with and the thankless task of defending the city. If he succeeded, he'd gain no accolades, but if he failed significantly enough to come to Killian's attention, then O'Connor would either be killed or have more motivation to eliminate Killian. Then Arnold would see that the Governor executed O'Connor for the murder, leaving Arnold clear to inherit the Reeveship.

However, Arnold realized that he might have to consider that plan compromised, since Frank had gone over to O'Connor's side with knowledge of that scheme. Having exhausted all the other possibilities, he was left with only one inescapable conclusion and that was that Frank Giordano had turned against him. That was unfortunate since, as much as the Golem-like Vampyr disturbed him, he'd come to rely on Frank's consistency. He'd trusted Frank in an odd way. It was that damn inexplicable charm that O'Connor seemed to have been gifted with! It was uncanny. Why in the world did people warm to that grimy gun-for-hire so quickly and so often? Arnold had never felt the need to be liked and had never pursued it, but that didn't mean he didn't recognize its usefulness. Or that he didn't occasionally wish he possessed such a quality.

Carolyn would have understood. God, he missed

her at times like this!

"You still trying to figure out if Faolan Jewed you over in that card game?" asked Darcy Killian with a laugh, striding into the enormous room. Arnold smiled tolerantly, having long since become accustomed to Killian's open racism. As he'd told Devlin, he didn't consider himself a Jew in anything but the genetic sense, so comments like Killian's annoyed him primarily at the intellectual level. He just didn't see the purpose or the practical value in lumping groups of people together by something so arbitrary as race. Why despise Killian for being Irish when it was much more sensible to despise him for being an unsophisticated buffoon?

"Your Honor," he said, rising and using the proper honorific for an American Reeve.

"All right," Killian said as he sat down on the green leather tufted sofa across from the identical sofa Arnold occupied. He'd shaved off the last traces of the mustache, Arnold noticed. Good. "I'm ready for my lesson, schoolmaster."

Arnold gathered the cards up and worked them back into a solid deck with nimble fingers. "Tonight I thought it would be appropriate to get into the practice of learning and using the proper titles and forms of address for the city positions."

"Since we have ourselves a new Street Boss, you mean?" Killian's eyes glinted with mischief. He seemed to relish tweaking Arnold's nose over the evening's events.

"Marshal," Arnold corrected without missing a beat. "The correct term for Mister O'Connor's position is Marshal. I am now the Steward. Both the Steward and the Marshal have Bailiffs who are responsible for the direct supervision of an aspect of the city—"

Killian nodded. "Right, that's Chambers and Charnas and Frank and such."

"Correct. Reporting to the Bailiffs are the Squires—"

"You know," Killian interrupted. "This all sounds awful damn English."

Arnold sighed. "Well, yes, that's because it's based on the Yeoman ranks from feudal England. In the Empire, apparently, they still use the titles of nobility while America chose to adopt the peasant titles to distinguish itself. So, to continue ..."

Damn you, O'Connor, Arnold seethed as he rattled off the information he'd memorized. *Nobody cheats Arnold Rothstein! Sooner or later you're gonna slip and, when you do, I'll be there to bust you!*

*****

Faolan took the Jamaica Line out to the Marcy Avenue station, wondering all the while what in the hell had possessed him. He should be celebrating with Stephanie, Rod, Enzo, Stebbins and the rest of the boys, not wandering the streets of Brooklyn. Stepping off the train onto the elevated platform, he could see the tops of the Williamsburg Bridge, the grand green dome of the Williamsburg Savings Bank, the striking Williamsburg Trust Company building over on Roebling across from the statue of George Washington, a sign for Peter Luger's Steak House, the reddish brick tower of St. Paul's Church where his sister got married, and a sprinkling of street lights and delivery truck traffic. It was nearly two o'clock in the morning and the platform was empty. He wasn't really cold, but he pulled up the collar on his overcoat anyway as he walked to the stairs and took them down to street level.

Behind him, the normally constant roar of the bridge traffic was reduced by the hour to the intermittent sound of trucks and cars rumbling beneath the train as it hissed and chugged itself up to speed and away. It was a short walk across the old trolley and bus turnaround to Marcy Avenue, less than half a block, but with each step Faolan's apprehension grew. *What the fuck are you doing here?* He asked himself for the dozenth time and, for the dozenth time, he had no sensible answer to give. His fifty dollar ox-blood shoes clapped the pavement, echoing down the emptiness of Marcy Avenue. *This is worse than a fucking waste of time,* he berated himself. *It's a waste of time that's gonna do more harm than good. Is she gonna be impressed now, tough guy, after all this time? You think you're gonna walk into some tearful reunion like in the movies? Or are you just such a glutton for punishment that you want to finally give the old gal a chance to spit in your face? That gonna make you feel better?*

The night air smelled of caramel, thanks to the Domino Sugar factory over on Kent near the waterfront. God, how that smell brought back memories! His first adventures had occurred on these streets, back before his old man was killed, back before his sisters got married, before he dropped out of school, back before a thousand other things. He saw the spot under the L-train tracks where his old man had caught him and Benny smoking cigarettes (he'd always believed his brother Tom had ratted him out) and remembered the beating the old man had given him for that. Of course, he reflected, it really wasn't so different from the beatings the old man had given him for every other crime he'd been accused of, real or imagined. His superior night vision allowed him to spot the collection of bums huddled under that space now, sleeping.

He hadn't thought of his old man in years and shook his head as he continued toward the corner. He reached the three way intersection at Division Avenue, his street. Maybe it was just to spite the memory of the old man that he drew a Camel out from his pack and fired it up. Then again, maybe it was just because he needed a cigarette. The squat two-story brick edifice of the Williamsburg Public Library stood behind him as he crossed Marcy and then Williamsburg Street. He'd never had too much use for the library growing up except when hiding out from truant officers and in winter where it could be a good place to pick the pockets of coats and purses left unattended.

The neighborhood took on a strange and ominous quality in the dead of night and, Vampyr or not, Faolan found himself feeling oddly apprehensive as he strode these once-familiar streets. So many familiar old storefronts were boarded up and labeled for sale by the bank, so many houses seemed neglected and undecorated. Inside these abandoned buildings, he could hear the sounds of people moving about furtively or shifting in their sleep. In the daylight the streets would be packed, friends and neighbors would sit together on stoops and talk, and vendors with produce carts would fill the sidewalks to disguise how desperate everything was, but right now, under the clouded moonlight, Williamsburg looked desolate.

What was the matter with him tonight, anyhow? He'd beaten Rothstein, publicly and at his own game—of course he and Frank had cheated to make sure it would happen—but he'd accomplished his goal, hadn't he? He was Killian's Street Boss. He didn't have to answer to Rothstein at all now and he could do things his way. Cause for fucking celebration, right? So, why, instead of celebrating at the Doll House with Rod, Enzo, Stephanie, Stebbins, and the others, was he moping around here on the street where he grew up? What was he hoping to find here? Wasn't there a reason he'd stayed away from here all these years?

He had a big wad of dough in his pocket, just over ten grand, and figured the very least he would do was slip the money in through the mail slot if he couldn't go through with waking Ma up and speaking to her. He hoped she would speak to him, though, no matter how much she hated him or cursed him. He deserved it, but he needed to get some kind of footing. That's really why he was here, wasn't it? To figure out where the hell he was now.

He'd wiped the floor with Rothstein in their poker game, just as he'd known he would. Rothstein was furious and probably knocking himself out trying to figure out how he'd done it, checking the cards, looking for mirrors and all that kind of fancy shit. In fact, it had been the simplest thing: Frank just stood in the crowd behind Rothstein where he could see his cards and, when Rothstein had a good hand, Frank would do something. No obvious signal or sign, but with a guy who could stand as still and blank as Frank, it was easy to identify any shift of weight, any change of posture, or movement of his hands. So, when Frank did anything, Faolan knew Rothstein was holding something. A minor advantage, but for a player of Faolan's skill, that was all he needed to confirm his instincts and expose Rothstein's bluffs. It was a moment he'd been waiting to have for over ten years now.

But he hadn't felt anything near the satisfaction he'd been expecting. He'd gone out with everybody to celebrate like he'd planned, but each passing hour of wearing that fake smile and hearing the congratulations had grated and he'd finally excused himself and fled ... here. Home.

Except it wasn't his home anymore.

Stephanie's questions from the beginning of the night kept nagging at him. What had he really won? Now he was in charge of the war like he'd wanted—so now what? It didn't take a genius to figure that, by some perspectives, he'd moved from the frying pan into the proverbial fire. He was free from Rothstein, but he also couldn't blame his failures on Rothstein any more. Killian would be expecting results and if he didn't get them quick and on a regular basis, Faolan knew his shine would start to wear off.

An odd combination of dread and anticipation grew inside him as he neared 203 Division Avenue, the two story brick row-house near the corner of Havemeyer that had been home from his birth until his late teens when he started working with Jack. The street seemed dirtier than he remembered, with more trash lying around on the street than back when he was a kid.

There it was.

When the house and its neighbors finally came into view, he stopped dead in his tracks for a minute. His heart pounded like it hadn't done since the days when he was still a kid heading for a rumble with some other gang. He kept imagining scenes over and over in his mind: his mother slamming the door in his face or him pleading tearfully while she just stood there and then spit at him or her breaking into tears at the sight of him and embracing him without a word or her fainting dead at the sight of him—all the various ways this could play out. He remembered how happy she had been at his wedding—they all had, even Tom—and he tried to push the memories of Tom out of his head, but it was like trying not to think of an elephant once somebody said it.

His whole life seemed like nothing more than a pile of fuck-ups when he looked at it the wrong way—or the right way—and yet here he was, still alive when so many of his pals were dead. Guys who had been smarter, faster, better-connected, and even more deserving. They were all in the ground while he still walked around with a shot at running the whole city someday. *Do you think that she's gonna be able to tell you why?* a cynical voice asked inside his head. *You think maybe you got this far because you was special? Maybe because of that magic St. Paddy's necklace she gave you? Is she gonna absolve you of your sins so you can pursue your cheap hoodlum dreams with a clean conscience?*

No, that was stupid. Maybe he was alive because of dumb luck and maybe it meant something and maybe it didn't matter why he was alive and they weren't. He figured maybe he just needed to try to make some kind of peace with the past before he continued. He'd need a clear head in the weeks and months ahead if he was gonna take on Killian and Rothstein and that crazy inhuman future they had planned for his city, that's all. It made sense. It was practical. Nothing sentimental or superstitious about it. Just a man doing some mental house cleaning so he could make a clean start.

His feet still wouldn't move.

He lit another Camel and smoked it, watching the house, and started picking out little details that were wrong: the front window had no curtains and Ma always had curtains in the windows, the front stoop hadn't been painted in a few years and was peeling, and the little welcome mat Ma always kept at the door for wiping your feet wasn't there. A chill ran down Faolan's back and settled around his stomach. Had she moved? He couldn't imagine anything that would make his Ma leave that house. She loved that house and wanted to pass it on to her grandkids! He didn't want to think what else this could—

He heard a toilet flush inside the house.

There was someone inside. There was someone inside his mother's house!

Inside *his* fucking house!

Flicking the cigarette aside, he drew his Browning out of his coat without even really thinking about it and started moving to the cement steps, flying up them in a leap and setting his free hand gently on the door. He focused his improved hearing to the rooms beyond the door and heard indistinct, quiet movement in several places. He gingerly twisted the knob on the front door and found it still locked. Burglars? Oh, if these were burglars robbing his mother's house while she was out, were they in for some serious trouble!

He had to move fast, though, since he knew there would be a beat cop strolling by sometime soon. He hadn't seen one yet, which was lucky, but the flat-foot's routine had to bring him back through here sometime in the next couple of hours even if Faolan had just missed him. And if not him, then the milk man or the garbage man or some early morning dock worker or some fucking body was gonna pass by eventually.

The back door into the kitchen was his best bet. Lucky for him, one of the big selling features of this house had been the fact that it was semi-detached, featuring an alleyway on the left side that held the gas meter and other odds and ends. His parents had shared walls with two sets of very noisy neighbors back in Hell's Kitchen and so the idea of only sharing one wall (with the quiet old widow Donnelly, no less) had seemed like heaven. He didn't hear anything on the street except the wind and some cars a few blocks away. He looked around to be sure and, seeing nothing, jumped off the porch into the side alley. He sprinted down the length and hopped the back fence just like he had as a kid.

The back yard looked to be in bad shape, too. Behind the painted wooden fence, the grass hadn't been cut in weeks, maybe months, and Ma's little flower bed was over-run with weeds. There used to be a garden back here, back when he was little, where they used to grow a few vegetables like tomatoes and peppers and cabbage to help stretch the food money. It wasn't big, of course—the whole backyard was only as wide as the house and went back maybe thirty feet—but it had still been nice eating fresh tomatoes from his back yard growing up.

Faolan shook off his reverie, readied his gun, and climbed the concrete steps to the kitchen door. When he tried the knob on this door, he found it unlocked and, with a smile that promised pain, eased the door open slow and silent, and listened ...

Movement upstairs.

The sight of the kitchen stopped him cold as his night attuned eyes swept across the wrongness of it all: the new electric icebox that he'd bought for Ma years back sat silent and open in the corner, half the cabinets were hanging open and the shelves were bare, and the big kitchen table was gone. In the center of the room where the table had been was a big burned coffee tin with an old grill over top, like for cooking. *Squatters*, he thought. A bunch of lousy fucking hobos had busted in and were squatting in his mother's house!

The cold in the pit of his stomach returned, sharp and fierce. He drifted into the empty wasteland that had been his mother's kitchen and stopped when he heard someone walking upstairs, heading toward the stairs. The cold slowly warmed up, replaced by a hot rage, and he marched out of the kitchen, out into the big front room where apple crates and newspapers and trash had replaced the parlor couches, chairs, and tables he'd grown up with. On the wall where the stairs came down, Ma's china hutch still stood, dust on the shelves, but the good Irish china she'd inherited from her mother was gone.

He could have forced himself to accept that she had moved away, maybe due to too many memories or maybe his sister Catherine had taken her in when the house became too much for her alone, but this ... she wouldn't have left her china hutch behind.

The footsteps creaked down the stairs. Tentative and slow.

His stomach tightening up till he felt like he was about to vomit, Faolan charged over to the bottom landing of the stairs, pistol raised high at the shadowy figure he saw descending, and shouted: "Get the fuck down here, you fucking vagrant! All of youse, anybody upstairs, you get your asses down here now! I gotta come find you, you're gonna be awful sorry!"

The man on the stairs dropped backwards onto the stairs and began begging him not to shoot throughout Faolan's diatribe. "Please, officer, don't shoot! I'm coming," he said again when Faolan finished and very slowly eased himself down the stairs in a strange kind of crab-walk using both his legs and one hand while holding the other out. Upstairs, there was a flurry of noises: calls, running feet, items being dropped but no one else appeared.

As soon as the hobo on the stairs got close enough, Faolan reached out and yanked him to his feet by his outstretched hand, then propelled him off the stairs and into the empty living room. The man was a little shorter than Faolan, unshaven and balding, middle forties, and dressed in just his wrinkled undershirt, stained brown trousers, and socks.

Faolan pointed the Browning at him again to fix him in place, and then turned his attention back to the stairs. "You got till the count of five, then I start shooting!"

"Oh, God, please, officer! It's just me and my family! Th-they're just scared, is all!"

This time Faolan caught the title. It annoyed and amused him at the same time to be mistaken for a flat-foot. "I ain't no cop, pal. This here's my fucking house and youse ain't welcome, so you take your family and get out!"

The man held both hands up, palms out. "Okay, okay, we're leaving, just please don't hurt anyone! Barbara, c'mon honey, get the kids together and come downstairs! Hurry!"

Faolan heard more movement and what sounded like a little girl's voice followed by a woman's hurried whisper. He glanced over at the man again and realized that he recognized the face.

"Jimmy Hammett?" he asked.

The man stopped glancing desperately back and forth from the stairs to Faolan's gun and really looked at Faolan's face for the first time. His shock was obvious. "Oh, my goodness ... you—you're Missus O'Connor's youngest! Franklin, was it?"

"Faolan." The gun lowered to his side and Faolan stepped off the landing, suddenly unsure what to do. The man standing before him was the son of old Mr. Hammett, an acquaintance of his mother's who had run a corner grocery store a few blocks down for as long as he could remember. The son had helped out for his father for years before taking over just before Faolan had left the neighborhood for good. They weren't friends, really, since the boy had been almost ten years Faolan's senior, but he couldn't count how many times he had picked up his Ma's shopping from that store or how often Mr. Hammett had given him a gumball or some licorice bits on the house.

He was neighborhood.

"Everybody said you were dead," Mister Hammett's son said.

"We're coming!" shouted a woman's voice from upstairs, followed by the sound of several sets of feet moving along the upstairs hall. "We're coming down! Please don't shoot, there are children!"

Saved from having to answer the man's last statement, Faolan stepped away from the stairs and absently shoved his gun back into its holster. He didn't figure needing it now. Yanking the fedora off his head, he shoved his fingers through his hair and took a deep breath.

Sensing a change in the atmosphere, Hammett moved cautiously over to the stairway landing as his family—twin girls in their early teens and a plump woman with disheveled gray-brown hair—piled down the stairs, all looking as if they had hastily dressed. The father quieted them down and soothed the two girls' tears while his wife stared at Faolan with a combination of terror and loathing.

Faolan just kept pacing inside the archway between the stairs and the outer wall, mind racing ahead of his emotions, terrified of the possibilities that were presenting themselves in his mind. "How—how long have youse all been living here like this? And what happened to my—" the word caught in his throat, as if saying it would make the worst possibility a reality. "What happened to Mrs. O'Connor? Do you know where she went?"

Jimmy and his wife exchanged a fearful glance and just the expression of cautious sympathy on the man's face was enough to clench his gut up like he'd been slugged. "Aw, I'm …I'm really sorry, Fa—Mister O'Connor." He couldn't meet Faolan's gaze. "She passed a while back, must be over a year now."

Faolan couldn't breathe. His hat slipped from between his fingers and fell to the floor. His hands, his face, everywhere went numb and he stood there on rubber legs that felt like they wouldn't hold him and yet somehow they did. He swayed for a moment, but he didn't fall. He'd known, hadn't he? From the moment he saw the missing curtains, he had known and just refused to believe it.

Hammett continued talking, throwing out words to keep the silence at bay. "Her daughter, Cathy—your sister—she and her husband came down to settle things and I helped them move some of the furniture and boxes out of here. She wanted to sell the place—she tried, but everybody's moving out of Williamsburg, and there's so many empty houses—so she let us stay here while it was on the market, you know, to keep the house neat for buyers. The bank took my father's store about a year ago, and we needed a place, see. After a few months, though, the bank took this place too, and the cops threw us out—we just snuck back in a few weeks ago when we saw that nobody had moved in. We mostly just live upstairs so the cops can't tell, you see. Please, sir, please just let us stay here for a little while—there ain't anyplace else we can go and it's gonna be winter soon…"

Whether Jimmy Hammett stopped talking or Faolan just stopped hearing him, he couldn't tell. A year, he'd said. Right about the time he disappeared after his ride with Benny. A few months after he'd killed his brother Tom. First her cherished daughter-in-law Colleen—he knew Ma had been torn up about that and worried for him because Tom had told him—and then her beloved straight-arrow son, both gone. The good one, the pride of the O'Connor family. Not that other one nobody talked about, the one everybody knew was headed for a bad end. Detective Thomas O'Connor of the NYPD: the apple of his mother's eye. Had she known he'd done it? Could she have imagined that their life-long differences might actually end in murder? He hadn't come to see her afterward—he just couldn't—and he hadn't gone to the funeral.

Of course she had known.

His sister would have looked in on her at first, neighbors too, but after a month or so who would notice if she barely ate, if she didn't go out, if she just let herself get weaker until the first strong illness came along to carry her off? Did she curse him at the end? Did she die hating him?

He looked up to find the Hammett family staring at him, all huddled up together at the stairs afraid to move or speak. He wanted to cry. He wanted to scream. He could feel the pressure building up in his chest and behind his eyes, but he couldn't. He wouldn't. Not in front of these people, these strangers. It occurred to him that he ought to slaughter the entire family, just drink them dry and burn this place to the ground. The neighbors might already be calling the police because of the noise and it wasn't safe to leave these normal folks knowing he wasn't dead.

He looked down at the two girls, staring at him in naked terror ... no, not terror, he realized with a start. Sympathy. Those tears in their eyes were for him. Of all the screwy reactions he'd ever seen! Here he was, about to kick them to the curb, and they felt sorry for *him*? They should save their sympathy for themselves, he thought. they were just the right age for some smooth-talking pimp to swindle them away from their old man and into a life in the brothels. Making money for guys like him and Killian.

It was just too much all of the sudden. Stumbling over to one of the apple crates on the floor—he figured they must go out and sell apples and flowers and other stuff during the day like others he'd passed by for years now—he sat down heavily and felt something like a dry heave come over him. His body seized up a few times and he thought he would start vomiting blood up all over the floor, but he didn't. Finally, he was going to cry.

But he didn't.

He just sat there silently trembling and trying to make something happen, but nothing did.

"Mister O'Connor ... are you okay? Can I get you a glass of water?" Hammett asked.

Jesus, what was he doing here anyway? He'd come here for some screwball reason that didn't make any good sense and now he was gonna do something that made even less sense. He couldn't spill blood in his mother's house. What if some part of her was still here somehow? What if she was watching him from heaven? He wasn't sure if he believed in heaven or not, but if it existed, there was no question his Ma belonged there. There was also no question what she would do. What she'd want him to do.

They were neighborhood, after all.

Pulling himself together, Faolan took a deep breath. "Don't worry 'bout me. I'm aces. Just caught me off guard, is all."

"I'm so sorry to be the one to tell you."

"It's all right," he said, pushing himself to his feet and brushing his hair back out of his eyes again. "Listen, I'm sorry I, uh, came busting in here like this. You guys don't need to go nowhere. Go ahead and stay here."

Their relief would have been comical if it hadn't been so genuine. They hugged, the wife started crying, and Jimmy Hammett pumped his hand and thanked him several times over and Faolan didn't think he'd ever felt so low. Looking at them, he felt shame rising in him like he hadn't felt in decades. What was he really giving them except what they already had? He'd never been so desperate in his life as this family. He'd always had food, always had a roof over his head, and when he ever ran low on spending money, he just stole more or killed someone. Yet he'd never been as happy as this poor vagrant family was right now.

Killian would slaughter them without a second thought, burn the house, and then punish him for ever being here in the first place. Rothstein would ignore them while they were ground down along with thousands just like them. There was no place in their grand vision of the future for people like this.

Well, fuck Killian and fuck Rothstein, Faolan thought. *I ain't them.*

He reached into his pocket and pulled out the wad of bills he had brought with him. "Here, take this. There's ten grand in there. Tomorrow, somebody from the bank'll come out here with the paperwork for you to pay the back taxes on this place."

Jimmy took the money like it might bite him. "I—this is too—I don't even know what to say, Mister—"

"Don't say nothing," Faolan told him. "Just forget I was ever here, understand? Fix this place up, raise your family here. Maybe spread some of that dough out around the neighborhood, okay? Get your store back or something. I gotta go now, so, like I said, I was never here. You found that money in a shoe box in the attic …"

Christ, he couldn't even bear to look at them, they were so grateful. The twin girls were smiling and jumping up and down and, for some reason, all he could think of was Michael down in the cell. He'd won that ten grand cheating at poker with Rothstein: a night's earnings for him and these folks had probably never seen that kind of dough in their lives. He grabbed his hat off the floor and strode toward the kitchen.

"Mister O'Connor," Barbara Hammett called. He stopped and glanced back to see her looking at him with tears in her eyes. "Thank you."

He nodded, feeling sick to his stomach again, and hurried out before they started singing "For He's A Jolly Good Fellow" or something. Rather than go back onto Division, he went through a neighbor's yard and out onto Broadway just in case.

He made it halfway to Marcy Avenue before he couldn't hold the tears in anymore.

PART FOUR

ACES AND JACKS
September, 1938 – March, 1939

Don't you hit that chick, that's my broad!
Where'd you get that stuff at?
Why, I'll knock you to your knees, what?
Put this cat out of here, what?
Get rid of that pistol, get rid of that pistol!
- Fats Waller, "This Joint is Jumping"

Chapter Twenty-Two

Faolan had taken out Frank, Enzo, and Paulie before they'd made it to Fourth Street, while Bennett and Martin had given up back at the door. Now, on Fourth Street, Faolan found himself confronted by Stephanie, Rod, Stebbins, and his big German enforcer Hans "Cuddles" Saberhagen.

"All right," Faolan said. "You asked for it, so here it comes."

"I'm dead," declared Stebbins in a miserable tone.

Stephanie's tone was confident. "He can't win against all of us."

Faolan fired.

Snap, snap, snap, snap, snap.

Saberhagen got the eight of clubs, which stopped his two pair a card short of being the full house he needed to win. Stebbins fared little better, catching a jack of diamonds that didn't complete the inside straight he'd been building. Rod, who had absently pushed his money in and paid more attention to the radio than the game, caught a two of hearts that did nothing to improve the jack-high straight he had already completed. Stephanie, however, got the queen of hearts and completed her flush to the queen. But all eyes were on Faolan's hand where a king of spades had transformed his flush from queen high to king high, besting them all.

Stebbins just shook his head. Saberhagen, who didn't particularly care for the nickname Cuddles, tossed his cards on the table with a bit more force than necessary and sat back in his chair. Rod continued listening to the radio broadcast, which had changed from music to news a minute or so ago.

They were sitting around a large corner booth in The Wolf, the night club Faolan had opened about a year ago. It served both as an alternative to the Indigo Lounge and as a headquarters away from the Empire State Building. He had bought out the location that used to house Jack Diamond's old Hotsy Totsy Club near the corner of 57th and Seventh Avenue. Stephanie had put up some of the money to buy the place, so he'd made her the manager. He was happy to give her the responsibility and he trusted her to run the place. He'd also left the decorating to her and was pleased with the result: the whole place was very modern and jazzy.

Faolan put himself in charge of booking the acts, of course, and so far he'd managed to get Chick Webb and his band, Louis Armstrong and Jack Teagarden, Benny Goodman, Fats Waller (now that had been a night to remember!), and a bunch of young up-and-comers. The best perk of the job, of course, was being able to shoot the breeze with the cats after their sets. Unlike certain other Manhattan clubs, he refused to separate out the other races or any of that shit. Right from the first, that was a big priority for him with The Wolf. There were black and white waiters, bands, and a mixed crowd and anybody who didn't like it could go fuck themselves. Sure, it cost him some business, but he just figured that was business he didn't need and Stephanie agreed.

"Dammit," Stephanie said, smacking her fingers on the edge of the table. "If I didn't know better, I'd say you were a lousy cheat."

Faolan smiled as he raked in the money from the center. "Yeah, but you do know better, so why bother bringing it up?"

Stephanie got a cigarette out of her gold case, tapped the end a few times and put it in her mouth. Sure enough, Rod was there with a lighter before she'd finished putting it between her lips. When he'd first started doing that, Faolan had gotten annoyed and told him to knock it off, but such gallantry was second nature to Rod. It was so awkward for him not to do it, in fact, that Faolan didn't even bother to go for his lighter anymore when Rod was around.

"I'm just letting you know I still keep my eye on you," she answered.

"You looking to get put across my knee?"

Stephanie raised an eyebrow. "Just try it, buster."

It was funny in a way, Faolan mused. She knew as well as he did that everything he won at the poker game got donated out to the various charities and soup kitchens they had been supporting for the past two years, but she still got sore when she lost. Their charity work began a little while after Faolan had come back from that visit to his mother's house. She had gotten the story out of him and, to his surprise, she'd been proud of what he'd done and encouraged him to keep it up. They had even gone out that year on Christmas Eve and volunteered some time at a soup kitchen in Harlem. It felt really strange at first, but after a bit, he'd really begun to enjoy the feeling of doing some honest work that he knew was helping people. They had continued the tradition last year and their help had been needed even more than before because of something called a recession, which apparently turned back the clock on a bunch of the progress the country had made since the start of the depression. Faolan didn't understand it.

He had also checked up on his adopted vagrants periodically. The Hammett family had improved their lot significantly since his visit, buying back the family store, letting the apartment above to another family in need, and even making a point of donating whatever food the store could spare to help out folks in the neighborhood who needed it. Also, his mom's house was looking better than it had in years. Watching them had made Faolan proud of his little neighborhood and the people in it. All this was on the down-low, of course. If Killian or Rothstein learned about his sentimental streak, they'd use it to make trouble for him.

He had enough of that already.

"Unbelievable!" said Rod.

"What's the rumpus?" asked Enzo.

Rod turned back to the table, slumping a little in his seat. "They just announced Hitler's terms from the meeting at Bad Godesberg. it's a flat-out ultimatum for an invasion of Czechoslovakia unless they get the Sudetenland by the twenty-eighth. And Chamberlain has accepted it! He's taking it to the Czechs."

"What a punk!" snorted Paulie.

Enzo said, "I thought they was gonna give it to him a little bit at a time."

"That was the proposal, which he rejected," Rod explained, "despite having proposed the exact same terms only last week at Berchtesgaden! My God, can't anyone see what this man is doing?"

"He's playing world leaders like suckers at a three card Monte table and succeeding," Frank said from his dark corner. "We could take a lesson."

Rod was indignant. "How could you even say such a thing, Frank? He's picking up right where the Kaiser left off!"

"I don't think that's totally true," said Saberhagen. It was rare for him to voice an opinion on anything outside of the war with Boston, boxing, and music—about which he and Faolan had already had a number of lively conversations. "Remember there's a lot of Germans in that Sudetenland who want to be part of Germany again. I think this Hitler's full of hot air, trying to play at being a tough guy. He's just trying to bring some pride back to Germany and the Czechs are an easy scapegoat. He'll play hard until the last minute and then let himself get talked into a compromise and look like a hero."

Faolan was both surprised and impressed by the big fighter's assessment. "Yeah, exactly. Anyway, Rod, what's this got you so hot under the collar for? It don't concern us none."

Stephanie leaned forward, blowing smoke from the side of her mouth. "I agree with Rod. I think America should do something. He's nothing but a bully if you ask me and the only way to stop a bully is to stand up to him. It's nuts just sitting around, plotting and scheming for the future, while he does whatever he wants now."

A few of the guys chuckled while Paulie and Bennett looked uncomfortable to have a woman offering an opinion at all. They knew better than to say anything about it while Faolan was around, though. That bit about the plotting was her way of digging at him, but Faolan refused to look at her and acknowledge it. She'd been on this kick for the last few months that he should just tell everybody about Killian's crazy plans and his own desire to replace Killian, but he was getting sick of hearing about it. Frank was right. Though most of his guys were solid, there was no reason to chance it.

"Thank you, ma'am," Rod said to Stephanie, who told him he was welcome with another pointed glance in Faolan's direction.

"All right, enough of this malarkey. Any of youse got anything else to report?" Faolan asked the assembled Vampyrs. The official excuse for these little weekly poker games was so that his guys—his Bailiffs, to use the official term—could report in on how their various areas were doing. "Any other fallout from the hurricane? Enzo?"

Enzo, who Faolan had put in charge of the city's various transportation systems, had been reading some cartoon magazine called *Action Comics* with a joker in blue tights and a red cape on the cover. Enzo lowered the comic at the sound of his name. "Uh, sorry. Nah, almost all the roads and tracks have been cleared. Since almost all of the damage was on Long Island, it was pretty easy to put some funds and emergency crews to it and straighten things out."

"Okay, good," Faolan said. "Rothstein's been busting my balls about the storm damage and I want to be able to tell him and Killian that everything's back to normal." Two nights before, the entire Northeast had been hit by the worst hurricane in either decades or a century depending on who you asked, but it had definitely been bad. The fucking Empire State Building itself had swayed! It was the first and only time he'd seen Killian consider a full evacuation of the building, but they had stayed firm and everything had been okay. Power had gone out all over the city and, most unbelievable of all, Faolan had even heard about a movie theater on Eastern Long Island that was scooped up by the storm and thrown two miles out into the Atlantic with everyone inside.

Faolan took out a cigarette and lit it. He glanced around the large corner booth they occupied, and could see that Bennett, Erwin "Fingers" Martin, and Paulie King were starting to get a little antsy. Like Stebbins, these three weren't Bailiffs: they were Squires who all reported to Frank, Bailiff in charge of all criminal business. But the rackets were a big area, and Faolan still liked to get certain information first hand. "All right, then. Good job, everybody. Youse three can shove off. Nah, Stebbins, you stick around for a few ticks."

While the Three Stooges, as Faolan sometimes thought of the trio of Squires, said their goodbyes, he gathered his poker winnings into a neat stack and handed it to Stephanie. "I know how much is in there," he quipped, giving her a wink.

Stephanie sighed and shook her head, hiding her smile. As Frank's boys headed to get their coats and depart, Faolan called over to Rod: "Hey, Rod, you want to shut off the radio?"

Rod slid out of the booth and walked over to the big standing console unit that was set up for the VIP Lounge. There were similar units out in the lobby and up on stage where Faolan had arranged it so that the radio could be played over the club speakers for those rare nights when the Wolf didn't have a live band or there was some kind of important news bulletin.

Frank sat forward for the first time in almost an hour. "I don't think she should be here, either."

"Excuse me?" Stephanie asked. Faolan groaned inwardly.

Frank turned his cold gaze onto Stephanie. "You're excused. Your presence is no longer appropriate at this time, so why don't you just go home now?"

And, just like that, everybody was uncomfortable. "Wait a sec, Frank," Faolan began, "there's no—"

But Stephanie was steamed. "Why don't you go and fuck yourself, Frank?"

"Just hang on," Faolan told her.

Frank looked at Faolan again. "I realize she's your girl, but she's a Dhampir and a blood donor who has no need to be part of this conversation."

"Frank, look," Faolan said, "there's no reason to make this an issue. It's gonna affect her and there's things she might be able to help with—"

"For example?" asked Frank.

Faolan sighed and Stephanie jumped in again. "Maybe it's something you don't need to know about, Frank—after all, Faolan's the one in charge here, not you."

"Pipe down!" Faolan shouted, cutting off Frank's response, and turned to look at Stephanie. "The both of you." He took a drag off his Camel and blew it out slowly, making sure he had everyone's attention. "Stephanie stays, Frank. If you still think there's a problem when we're done, then you can stick around after the meeting and we'll talk. Now, the reason I wanted the rest of youse to stick around is because I just got the okay from Killian to make a full scale strike on the Northeast."

Nobody gasped or anything, but there was a little readjusting of posture and glancing around that told Faolan the gang was not quite fired up about the idea. As usual, Rod was the one brave enough to speak up first. "How do we make this one more successful than last year?"

Hitting the nail right on the head. Faolan nodded, giving them all a smile. "Good question. The reason we fucked up last time was we got ahead of ourselves, we let ourselves get, uh, what do you call …"

"Over-extended," supplied Frank.

"Right. Over-extended." Boy, had they ever! Last year around March, Faolan and Saberhagen had taken the enforcers and a bunch of newly-Created tough guys for a strike directly at Boston that Faolan had been sure would end Moore and the war. Instead, they had been harassed and were picked off a few men at a time from the night they had arrived. The Boston Vampyrs had chased them from location to location, made feeding difficult, and ground them down for two months until Faolan had thrown in the towel and limped home with three guys out of the original fifteen he'd left with.

Naturally, Killian had been furious and Faolan had feared losing his position or worse, but in an ironic bit of luck, Boston tried to press their advantage and attack them. His and Frank's defensive strategies proved as effective as ever and the Boston strike team was wiped out to a man. Faolan remained Marshal, but Killian's confidence in him had been badly shaken and was proving difficult to rebuild. Since then, Rothstein had had plenty of opportunity to minimize Faolan's efforts and inflate his own now that the basic weapon of the war had changed from ground forces to economics. Faolan figured he needed a high profile victory quick or he was gonna go the way of Byrne.

And then the hurricane hit.

"This time," Faolan explained, "we won't make that mistake because we won't worry about trying to crack Boston. We use this hurricane and all the damage it's done to soften things up for us and we hit Springfield, Providence, Hartford, Manchester—maybe one of them cities in Vermont if there's time—but, the point is, we flip them like we did Philly and isolate Boston."

Saberhagen set his big, thick hands down on the table. The big, blond German Jew was the type Faolan would never have pegged for a Mary if he didn't know otherwise. When that little tidbit had hit the rumor mill, Killian had suggested Faolan get rid of Saberhagen, but Faolan defended his value and earned the wrestler's undivided loyalty. The guy looked like he could have knocked out Max Schmeling *and* Joe Louis, but his smile was warm and boyish. "I don't know 'bout anybody else, boss, but I been itching to take another shot at them pikers up north."

"Yeah, and that storm really knocked them for a loop," Enzo added. "Especially Providence. I heard they're under thirteen feet of water in some places and something like three-hundred people were killed."

"Exactly," Faolan said. "So, I figure if the area got hit that hard, they had to have lost a vamp or two and the ones left gotta have their hands full."

"What about when Boston sends reinforcements?" Rod asked.

"We're counting on it," Frank answered.

Faolan picked up the thread smoothly: "See, Moore won't be able to ignore what we're doing, but he'll also suspect a trap—probably figure we want to lead his guys out and then hit Boston again, but we don't. We just keep taking cities away from him and chopping down whatever palookas they send as they come. Now, this is the important part: I want all of youse to come with me this time."

That surprised them. "Sorry, what?" asked Stebbins, more or less speaking for the rest.

"We're bringing recruits from Jersey, Philly, Buffalo, and a few other places—Killian's good for scaring our 'allies' into giving up some spare men, at least—but those are the guys we're gonna have to leave behind to hold onto the cities we take. I ain't making the mistake I did last time. I want experienced guys with me. Guys I know I can trust at my back—which, of course, means that Stebbins ain't coming."

Everyone chuckled, Enzo giving the other blond Irishman a poke in the ribs with his elbow. Then Faolan said, "Actually, I'm serious about Stebbins staying behind, but it ain't because of trust."

"What about the home front?" asked Rod. "If you take all of us for—how long?—we won't be around to keep things running properly."

Faolan nodded. "That's why Stebbins is staying—same with Stephanie. Youse should all pick your best guys to keep an eye on things while you're gone, but we'll keep Stebbins and Stephanie here to keep an eye on things for us."

"But, not that—" Stebbins began before Stephanie cut in.

"How long are you planning to be gone for?" she asked. She tried to make the question sound casual, but he could see the worry in the way her eyes wouldn't meet his, the way she sat forward, and the way her hands wouldn't stop fidgeting with her cigarette.

He shrugged, playing it cool. "Hard to say. Figure a month per city, give or take, and then we gotta figure on sticking around long enough to train the new people and get them set up so they don't just blow over with the first strong breeze. I'd like for us to sneak back for Christmas, but there's no telling how things will go until we see how things stand up there." Of course, there were also other elements he wasn't mentioning, but he'd get to that later when the others were gone.

He turned back to the boys and continued: "Rod, you're gonna be the key to getting us up there. Figure us sneaking in with the Coast Guard and relief forces is the way to go, at least for Providence."

Rod considered for a moment and nodded. "I can certainly get a few of us spread out over several boats, but I wouldn't put all of our eggs into one basket, so to speak. I think Enzo should bring at least half of the total group up overland."

"Well," Enzo began, shifting a bit. "I think Rod's got a good point about splitting up. That many of us coming into Providence all at once—hell, the whole state of Rhode Island couldn't feed that many of us for long, especially with some already there. So, I think you and most of the experienced guys should go in and get the lay of the land, estimate their forces, and set up a base. Meanwhile, I'll smuggle the new guys and whatever they send us from the other cities up to Hartford. They took some flooding from the Connecticut River overflowing and—with so few vamps up there and likely not expecting an invasion it'll be a good way to test the new fish and get them some fighting experience." He was going fine in his excitement until he noticed everyone looking at him, then he seemed to shrink up.

Faolan sat back and stared at the kid for a second while he took a final drag from his cigarette and blew it out. Slow. "That's gotta be the stupidest idea I ever heard."

Enzo's face went red and he dropped his eyes to his lap. Stephanie and Saberhagen looked at Faolan in shock, but Rod and Stebbins caught the glint in his eyes. The former shook his head in mock reproach while the latter hid his smile behind a sip of water. Finally, Faolan couldn't contain himself any more and started snorting laughter. "I'm just razzing you, genius! Christ, look at this kid, he's like to start bawling!"

Stephanie socked him on the shoulder while Enzo got even redder and Rod poked his ribs with an elbow until Enzo swatted back, and the pair play fought right in the booth. Frank just sat there, glancing around at the hilarity with those dead eyes of his.

"All right, all right, kids, knock it off," Faolan said, and Rod and Enzo broke up their mock fight. "No, really, that's a good plan, kid, and it's the way to go. You and Rod start making the arrangements you need, figure out the details. Hans, you get the boys in shape. I'll be sending the guys from the other cities to you as they start showing up. Go on home for now, all of youse, and we'll talk more tomorrow night."

The three nodded, slid out of the booth, and said their goodbyes while Stephanie got up to visit the ladies' room and refresh her drink. By the time she got back, everyone was gone except Faolan, Frank, and Stebbins.

She sat down with her drink. "So, now what's the real reason you want me and Stebbins here?"

Faolan smiled, leaning forward. "Well, with me gone along with Frank and everybody else, who's Rothstein gonna push as a scab?"

"Charnas," answered Stebbins. "So, you want us to keep an eye on him and what he does while you're gone? Keep you informed."

"More than that," Faolan said. "I want you to sell out to him. I want you to pass along rumors about how bad things are going for us in the Northeast. I want you to point out a few openings me and Frank are gonna leave in our system and steer him toward some of those guys like Paulie, Bennett, and Martin who might be happy to see the last of me and Frank."

"Wait, you think they're all crooked?" he asked.

Frank set his hand down on the table surface. "We aren't sure. So, we want you to help Charnas test as many of the Squires as you can. We want to know who changes sides while we're gone and who stays true."

"If you pull it off," Faolan finished, "I wipe everything you owe me."

Stebbins nodded, his expression thoughtful. Stephanie sipped her drink. "So what do I do?" she asked coolly.

Faolan took a sip of water and swallowed. This was tougher than he had thought it would be. He'd pictured talking to her about this by themselves with lots of playful bantering, but not like this with her looking so serious. "I need you to, uh, drop me like a bad habit."

She raised an eyebrow.

"Make out like you're sore at me for leaving and whatever we had is done." Jesus, the more he said, the more it was starting to sound like she wouldn't have to do any acting! "Um, you know, be seen with other guys and run me down to anybody who asks. I was gonna suggest cozying up to Charnas, but that would be too obvious. But, you know, if one of his guys takes an interest, then ..."

"I get the picture," she said, giving nothing away. She took another sip of her drink. Faolan was about to say more to try to lighten things up when he heard the doors open. At first, distracted as he was, he figured it was Rod or Enzo coming back for something, but then he remembered that the doors were locked and only he and Stephanie had keys to the place. Sliding to the floor, he crawled out from under the table, drew his pistol, and rose to see five goons in long overcoats walking out into the dance floor and spreading out, all toting shotguns. They were a mixed race group, which was very unusual. Behind them walked a lone Negro in similar attire, also carrying a street sweeper, but wearing a chocolate derby where the other men wore black fedoras. By the time Faolan finished registering this, he heard the emergency fire exits on either side of the VIP Lounge swing open and picked out two more sets of three gunmen moving into position by the booth and on the other side as well.

Frank stood, pushing the table out a bit, and Stebbins had drawn his pistol while Stephanie—bless her—had dropped below the table where she couldn't be seen from any of the gunmen's vantage points.

Keeping the Browning at his side behind the half wall that separated the bar and dance floor from the lounge, Faolan addressed himself to the Negro. "What can I do you for, pal?"

The Negro in the derby—whose pallor and gaunt face marked him as a Vampyr—met Faolan's gaze, cold and humorless, and adjusted his grip on his shotgun. "I'm not your pal, O'Connor. As a matter of fact, I'm here tonight with orders to kill you."

Chapter Twenty-Three

Faolan's finger twitched on the trigger of his Browning Hi-Power as his eyes shifted back and forth, taking in the entirety of The Wolf. Three gunmen to his right, on the other side of the VIP Lounge, three more at the bottom of stairs to the Lounge, right in front of him, and six more including the Negro Vampyr out on the center of the dance floor. All carried shotguns, whose spray gave them a better chance of hitting somebody than not regardless of how talented the shooters were. They were the perfect weapon for the situation, especially against Vampyrs, since inflicting massive damage and pain would be the surest and quickest way to drop your targets.

Stebbins was a decent shot, but he lacked the courage for a gunfight—he'd probably drop to the carpet and surrender as soon as any shooting started and he'd likely have the right idea. Frank was tough and slightly suicidal as Faolan had learned back at Coney Island, so he'd charge, grab one of the nearest gunmen to use as shields, and try to make it out of the fire exit into the alley. That was the smart play, but it would mean leaving Stephanie and Stebbins behind at the Negro's mercy. Not to mention that there could be more gunmen waiting in the alley. Faolan knew he was fast on the trigger—hell, Devlin was the only man or vampire he'd ever met who could beat him—but he knew he couldn't take down enough to make Frank's exit strategy even possible before they were cut to pieces by the rest. They were too spread out. Even with Faolan and Frank blasting at full, the numbers just wouldn't let it happen.

They'd be drawing dead.

Yet, in the tick of a watch it took for him to figure all this through, he also registered the relaxed grips some of the gunners had on their weapons, the way the Negro had said "orders to kill you" rather than "here to kill you", and the fact that he'd bothered to answer at all. If they had come in blasting, it would have been over by now. If he moved, everyone else would follow and the shooting would start. So, very slowly, he thumbed the safety back on and raised his pistol into view, and then set it down on the half wall. He wasn't about to toss it on the ground like in the movies, not on your life, but he did take a step back from it.

The Negro Vampyr watched all this without expression, but the irritation Faolan sensed rather than heard as he exhaled suggested that he'd been hoping Faolan and the others would opt for violence. Beneath the stranger's fur-collared camel hair coat, Faolan caught sight of a canary yellow shirt with a white collar and an emerald green silk tie. He wore two-toned brown and white wing-tips. Quite the snappy dresser, though he was a big man who moved like a boxer.

"Like I said, those were our orders," he said. His voice was gruff and deep, but with a certain melodic quality to it. His enunciation was clear. "But my partner has other ideas."

Faolan was glad to see that Frank hadn't moved, nor had Stebbins. As the sound of heavy footsteps came to his highly sensitive ears, he felt reasonably prepared for almost anybody who might come through the large double doors into the main club area. Still, he found he wasn't quite as immune to surprise as he thought when he recognized the tall, stocky, cherub-faced female Vampyr he'd once deposited safely in Newark back on his unforgettable first night.

Faolan dropped his hands as Miranda Matheson strode onto the dance floor, her men moving aside without hesitation to let her through. She still dressed like a dock worker, he noticed, but her black pea coat and wool cap were newer than the ones he'd seen her in last, as were her boots. Her boots had a good grip, too, as they moved across the waxed dance floor, and Faolan figured they must be rubber soles. She walked calmly, arms at her sides, but was unable to keep a smirk off her face as she locked gazes with him. Reaching up absently, she pulled the cap from her head, stuffing it into her coat pocket, and Faolan saw she'd cut off her long copper locks. She now sported a mannish army cut that contrasted sharply with her pale cherub face.

"Seems you're not quite running the city yet, Faolan O'Connor," she said.

"I'm working on it."

"And would you agree you'd be a dead man if I were so inclined?"

Faolan smiled. "Looks that way."

"Then would you consider the debt I owe you for sparing me life repaid in full?"

"If you continue not killing me and my friends, then yeah, I'd say so."

Miranda smiled and unbuttoned her pea coat, revealing a thick black padded vest that covered most of her chest. One of those so-called bulletproof vests, he figured, and wondered if all their men were wearing them under the overcoats. "Good," she said, shucking off the coat and beginning to unbuckle the vest. "I fucking hate being in folks' debt."

Faolan glanced around. Miranda's thugs had relaxed a bit, but were still holding a small arsenal and the well-dressed Negro hadn't taken his attention from him throughout their whole exchange. He only moved to unbutton his own coat, revealing a double breasted chocolate pinstripe and the absence of any kind of protective vest.

"You mind me asking whose orders you're not carrying out?" Faolan asked.

"Moore."

"Yeah, I kind of figured. Well, c'mon up, then," Faolan said, grabbing his gun off the ledge and ignoring the few gunmen who brought their shotguns to bear on him. He slid the Browning back in its holster. "Let's catch up. Tell your goons to help themselves to drinks from the bar and take a seat."

Miranda smiled again as she finished getting her vest off, revealing her standard denim beneath. "Don't tell me they're making you nervous?"

Faolan gestured for Frank and Stebbins to return to their seats. Stephanie seemed to have already twigged to the change in tone and sat in her previous spot, sipping her drink. "Only that one of them's gonna sneeze and accidentally blow a hole in my club."

"Go on ahead and have a seat, boys," Miranda instructed her gang as she approached the VIP Longue. She invited the Negro to come along with a wave. When she arrived, she shook Faolan's hand and indicated her partner. "This gentleman here is Abraham 'The Sandman' Huston."

"Sandman, huh?" he asked as the man hung his coat on the back of a chair and removed his derby, revealing close cropped hair. Faolan reached out to shake his hand while Miranda shook hands with Stebbins, Frank and Stephanie, but Huston made him wait while he brushed lint from his derby and set it down on a nearby table before taking Faolan's hand in his own and giving it a firm squeeze. "I done something to offend you, Sandman?"

Huston met his gaze evenly, being roughly Faolan's height (but much broader in the shoulders), and Faolan was uncomfortable to discover that he'd become accustomed to a certain subtle deference from those around him that was entirely absent from the Negro's demeanor. "I'd prefer if you would address me as Mister Huston, Mister O'Connor.

The Sandman is from my days in the ring, long passed, and only used by a select few. And, to answer your question: you're responsible for the deaths of several friends of mine in Philadelphia, so please forgive my coolness toward you."

He would have taken Huston's speech as a high-hat except that he could tell that the formality was natural rather than some kind of put-on or mockery. Huston had clearly been an educated man either before or after his time in the ring. The mention of Philadelphia also clicked in Faolan's memory, as there had been one or two Vampyrs on the rolls that were never accounted for and were assumed to have run off or been killed. Huston was one of them.

"Well," he said with a slight shrug, gesturing the pair to the unoccupied side of the booth. "I'm sorry about your friends, for what it's worth."

Huston nodded. "It's an inescapable by-product of war, but I thank you for your apology."

Huston took the inside seat, which put him at right angles to Frank, then Stebbins, and then Stephanie—who rose, grabbing her little clutch purse. "It was nice meeting you both, but I think I'm going to go home and get some sleep."

Faolan put his hand on her arm and tried to sound light. "You sure? This is probably gonna be the interesting part."

She eased past him, "I'm sure it is, but I've had enough for the night."

He kept pace with her as she walked to the three steps down to the dance floor. He pitched his voice low, though he knew Miranda and Huston could still hear them if they wanted. "Hey, what gives? You still sore at me?"

Stephanie stopped and looked at him with weariness. "It isn't that, okay? I'm not sore at you so much as I am the situation. I know you gotta play this smart, but I don't like that you gotta sound so much like Frank because of it."

That surprised him. "Hey, Frank's got a pretty good read on things. He gives me good advice."

"Sure he does," she said, her words almost a hiss, "but he also happens to be a certified loon that doesn't give a shit about you, me, or anybody else on God's green earth. What happened to making things better?"

She reached forward on that last line and gently took hold of his suit lapels. He reached up and grabbed her wrist, throwing a quick glance back to the table where everyone else was indeed watching their every move. "What have we been doing for the last two years, huh?" he whispered. "I told you a million times, I only get one shot at this and I gotta make it count! I can't go around telling everybody my plans 'cause that makes it more dangerous for everybody. The only way to keep a secret is to keep it to yourself."

"That's Frank talking."

"Well, he's right about that." He leaned forward, whispering in her ear. "Look, babe, I told you things are gonna be tough until we can finally get rid of Killian, but the fewer people who know the whole plan, the fewer chances there are for somebody to screw it up."

She scowled, pulling back. "Gee, thanks."

"Hey, don't do that," he said, getting steamed. "You know that I trust you. Didn't I just stick my neck out for you not half an hour ago? I'm talking about guys like Rod and Enzo. They're great guys, but they're too damn honest. I tell them what I got planned and who can say what their conscience might make them do? I promise you, once it's done, we can start doing things different."

She sighed, her eyes threatening tears. "But how can you ever do things differently when you've never done anything but this your whole life?"

Damn, that sounded just like Colleen there at the end, when the booze had given her the courage to make demands of him. Never a word of protest or complaint from Colleen unless she was loaded—no, she'd been raised strict in the "a good wife keeps her complaints to herself" tradition. In that same fine tradition, she drank to escape the parts of their life (and him) that horrified her, eventually clinging to the bottle because her loving husband wasn't home often enough to get her arms around. Maybe things would have been different if he'd done his duty as a good Irish Catholic and knocked her up with a litter of kids to fill her lonely days, but it just never happened. Finally, when she'd realized that the whisky wasn't enough to kill the pain of being a widow in everything but fact, she'd committed her first and only cardinal sin. She'd swung for the fences, though, Colleen had: pleasantly tipsy, she'd climbed into a hot bath in her wedding dress and cut a cross into her left wrist.

Though she hadn't left a note—which led to the investigating detective making some pointed remarks about his possible involvement during the interrogation—the wedding dress had been all Faolan needed to understand her purpose. It wasn't an indictment of him, as many suspected. No, good Catholic that Colleen was, she felt that she had failed to redeem the soul of the man she'd loved since childhood. So, if they could not have eternity together in heaven, then she would accommodate him one last time by awaiting his arrival in hell, where he could be hers for all eternity…

He stared at Stephanie, but before he could figure out how he should respond, she wiped her eyes and said: "Go have your meeting. You only got another hour or two before sunrise. I'm gonna start acting like we're finished tonight, so…" Then, without finishing her sentence—that sentence that he definitely wanted to hear how she finished—she turned and walked like a shot across the floor and out to the lobby.

Faolan watched her leave, waiting for her to stop, to turn, to say something more, but then he heard the front doors open and close. He took a breath and pushed his fingers through his sweaty blond hair. He straightened his tie, took a breath, and turned back to the waiting table of Vampyrs. *Fuck it,* he told himself. *She'll see what I'm talking about soon enough. Forget about it and get back to business.*

Faolan sat down across from Miranda. Huston leaned forward to fold his hands on the large triangular table. "Miss Matheson believes that we can be of assistance to each other and, while I remain skeptical, I'm willing to consider the possibility."

"Are you willing to help us kill Moore?" Frank asked, getting right to brass tacks.

Miranda and Huston glanced at each other as they considered and then Miranda spoke: "No, but we'd surely be fucking overjoyed to help you take out Darcy Killian."

Faolan smiled, taking out another cigarette. "Okay, fair enough. We'll start with Killian. The unfortunate truth is that Killian ain't gonna happen right away, even with your help."

"Why not?" This from Huston.

"Because there's no realistic way to get him," Frank answered. "We've run countless scenarios and they all fail—well, except for one. Are either of you willing to hide a bomb on your person and sacrifice yourself to get rid of Killian?"

"Fuck no!" said Miranda. Huston likewise replied in the negative.

Frank shrugged. "Well, then that option is out. Unless—"

Faolan cut him off. "I told you already, Frank, we are *not* hypnotizing one of the boys into blowing himself up!"

"And you'll not be using any of our men, neither," added Miranda before Frank could even finish looking her way. "But why not just blow up his car?"

Faolan shrugged. "He never leaves the building."

"Never?" asked Huston.

"Not since Coney Island," Faolan answered. "Guy's got a whole fucking little private kingdom up there, so he never goes anywhere outside of those six floors. And, just so nobody brings it up later, blowing up the whole building or floors of it is out, too. That fucking building is solid and, even if we could get enough dynamite without tipping our hand, there's just no way to do it without killing thousands of regular folks."

Huston studied him. "And why is that a problem?"

Faolan met his gaze evenly, blowing out smoke from his cigarette. "Because I say it's a problem." *See?* he told Stephanie in his head. *Don't tell me I sound like Frank!*

Huston nodded, his expression giving no clue as to his thoughts, but he sat back in a way that suggested he wasn't going to argue the point.

"Fire alarm?" Miranda proposed.

Frank shook his head. "Killian trusts the building. He won't evacuate just because of an alarm. And the sprinkler system can handle any fire we could set."

Miranda began to squirm. "But you can fucking get us up there, right?"

"Give them the low down, Frank," he said, taking a long, slow drag of his Camel.

Frank didn't move, he just started spitting out words like a radio that had been turned on. "The only way up to the Vampyr floors is the hidden elevator which could only hold ten people at a tight squeeze, and less if they're all carrying weapons. Assuming you force the guard on three to call up a false report, the elevator opens onto a long, narrow hallway with no alcoves or pillars for cover, so when the guards see more people than reported and open fire, as they've been trained to do, the only option is a full charge into the guns. Only Vampyrs could hope to survive such a charge, which lets your gang of Dhampirs out. Ten Vampyrs charging machine guns down a narrow hall, I calculate about half making it to the guards. By then, the rest of the floor has been alerted and more guards will be on their way along with any vamps who are curious and looking for a fight."

"Nah, fuck that," Miranda interrupted. "Do you think us daft, man? You two could get me and Sandman here up there through some dissembling, I've no doubt—sure I've seen the way you silver tongue your way through the world, O'Connor. Call us captured prisoners if need be, but once we're in private—"

"You'd be killed anyway," Frank said, cutting her off. "About a year and a half ago, while Faolan was away leading a strike force in Boston, some new recruit named Yarbro—one of Charnas' people—asked to speak to Killian in private and, once there, pulled a pistol and tried to gun the boss down. Naturally, Devlin and Rothstein and others rushed in immediately. By the time they arrived, Killian had already beaten Yarbro to a bloody pulp and was in the process of draining him dry to help heal the six bullet wounds in his chest."

Faolan watched the pair take in that scene before speaking. "Yeah, Killian is about as tough as they come and, thanks to that bit of stupidity, Devlin stays with Killian at all times and everybody gets checked for weapons before they see him. Even if it was all four of us, I wouldn't give us odds against Killian and Devlin bare-handed."

"Who's this Devlin fellow?" Huston asked.

Stebbins chuckled. "Oh, he's quite the charmer."

"Johnny Devlin is the most dangerous gunman I have ever met or even heard of," Faolan admitted with a touch of reluctance. "Myself included."

"And, make no mistake," Stebbins added. "Mister O'Connor is nearly without peer as comes to speed and accuracy with a firearm." True, but whenever he and Devlin had engaged in some shooting competitions over the years, Devlin had left him in the dust. Worse, he had taken Faolan's boardwalk demonstration to heart and now carried a pair of Browning Hi-Powers in his hip holsters, so he had twenty six very heavy shots before reloading. Not to mention a new double-action Colt revolver as a back-up piece at the small of his back that most didn't know about.

"Can this man Devlin be bought?" Miranda asked.

Faolan sat back, finishing his cigarette. "I tried to put the question to him just as a, you know, a hypothetical—just two guys bullshitting. He stopped me before I even got half the question out and explained to me in no uncertain terms how a man like him exists on his reputation, so if anybody ever even hinted at such an offer to him, he'd be obliged to blow their knees and shoulders apart and drag them to Killian for further questioning." He stabbed his Camel out in the ashtray for emphasis. He didn't even mention the rumors that Killian and Devlin both regularly drank the blood of newly-Created Vampyrs to increase their physical prowess, which if true would certainly explain Devlin's ability and devotion. Not to mention the fact that Killian's presence was the only thing protecting Devlin from the many enemies his abrasive manner had earned him.

Stebbins gave one of his nervous laughs. "Yes and Mister Devlin's always had a particular fondness for Mister O'Connor on account of their being cut from a similar cloth, as it were. I do believe anyone else putting such a question to him would have been answered with bullets."

Faolan nodded. "So, it's just us at this table that can know the whole deal. Everybody else is either too unpredictable to bring in or too likely to rat us out to Killian or Rothstein. Now, are you two satisfied yet that if we could take out Killian with force, we'd have done it already?"

Miranda and Huston considered for a moment before Huston said: "What about striking in the daylight? We have with us a well-trained and dedicated group of Dhampirs who are certainly a match for any of Killian's thugs."

"I had the same thought," Frank answered. "Three years ago. I paid several different members of the cleaning crew to describe Killian's private rooms to me and his sleeping arrangements. First of all, he has blood-fed attack dogs roaming his suite during the day which, I realize, might not pose a significant problem to a well-armed and trained group, but will cause noise and attract unwanted attention to any operation. Secondly, based on clues provided by each of the cleaners, I don't believe that Killian actually sleeps in his rooms. Based on studying the building plans, there are numerous possible places for him to have constructed hidden chambers within the walls, secret rooms, or even a small elevator that takes him to a different floor altogether."

"So, they fucking search, don't they?" said Miranda.

"Yeah," Faolan said, "but remember once you shoot the dogs—even if you get it done quick—then you still got Killian's Dhampir guards on their way. How good a search can somebody do in the middle of a gunfight? Plus, really, your guys couldn't get that far, anyhow, on account of not having an appointment to come up."

"Which means anyone getting off the elevator on that floor would be met with an armed response," Frank finished.

Miranda sighed and cracked her neck, then her knuckles. "All right, all right, then. So, what's your plan?"

Faolan leaned forward. "We figure the only way to get Killian to relax enough to give us an opening is for him to win the war." They glanced at each other again and Faolan said: "C'mon, don't look so surprised, it's practically happened already except this fucking guy Moore don't know when to fold his hand. I'm taking a bunch of the guys into the Northeast to snuff out the last few cities what are supporting Boston. Now, you two being here works out perfect, since there's this putz that's gonna try to take over my job while I'm gone named Ed Charnas." He leaned back and took another Camel out of his cigarette holder and lit it. "I wasn't sure how to do this before, but if me and Frank can give you the inside scoop on some of the city's defenses and Charnas' people, it would help us by making him look bad with Killian while also making you look more effective with your boss."

"He ain't our boss," Miranda said. "We've been retained on a mercenary basis."

Meaning Moore could deny knowing anything about any of their activities or being held responsible for them. Of course, these two looked like they knew that already. "Either way," Faolan continued, "It's a situation that benefits everybody. Stebbins here will be our point of contact and can get messages back and forth between us. He's gonna cozy up to Charnas while I'm gone and give him some tips. That should help him keep an eye on what Charnas is up to, so that he can tell youse two. Now, if you can manage to kill Charnas and some of his goons, that'd be greatly appreciated, but don't do nothing that would get you or any of your people caught. We're taking a big risk working together like this and I don't want it should come back to bite us."

"Very funny," Huston said. "So what else do you need from us?"

Faolan sat back with a smile. "I need you to get me a meeting with Mister Edward Moore of Boston."

Chapter Twenty-Four

The *Black Duck* sliced through the dark flood waters, dodging the floating debris of shattered houses and buildings under the sure hand of Danny Walsh. The darkness around them was almost absolute, the moon hidden behind gray thunderheads. There were no electric lights for miles, but their Vampyr night vision made it possible to negotiate the flooded streets of Providence. Still, even for vamps, it was dark and Walsh's skill at the wheel of his sleek little rum runner was impressive. At the back, Rod Chambers assisted Walsh by turning and tilting the small outboard motor whose chugging and whirring was the only sound Faolan could make out no matter how he strained to hear their opponents.

The other boat had come at them a few minutes before and Faolan had caught the weird cat-like eye shine that some vamps developed and told Walsh to haul ass. The other craft had given chase, but wasn't as fast as Walsh's

Black Duck and had fallen behind. According to Walsh, who knew the area better than anyone, they had already eliminated or converted all the native Providence vamps, which meant that the reinforcements from Boston had arrived.

Providence, along with most of coastal Rhode Island, was in worse shape than Faolan had imagined possible, even with the news reports. The flood water was still ten feet high in certain areas, down a few feet from the thirteen Providence had received from the hurricane. Whole blocks of houses were shattered to nothing and the stores that remained intact had been robbed by mobs of swimming looters in broad daylight. To hear Walsh tell it, the cops just rowed by, outnumbered and powerless to stop them. The cops were still busy pulling bodies out of cars where people had drowned trying to drive out of town and from basements where folks had mistakenly gathered for shelter.

With so much chaos and all their normal operations shut down, it had been a cinch the vamps would be out hunting among the after-dark looters, the rescue volunteers, and the poor folks trapped on the second floors of their flooded houses. The first night, they'd found one son of a bitch in particular with a whole family of five tied up to their beds like his own private food pantry. Despite Frank's objections, Faolan and Walsh gave the family some blood to help them recover, along with a little mental whammy action to make them forget about what they'd been through, then loaded them into the boat and dropped them off at one of the Red Cross stations. As for the vamp, Faolan had him bound hand and foot, weighed down, and dumped out where Walsh assured him the tide would carry the bastard out to sea. Good riddance.

"There's a small side street up ahead," Danny Walsh said, pointing at an area between two large brick buildings that Faolan could just barely make out. "Make a fine place to wait in ambush if you was of a mind to."

Before the words had finished making it to Faolan's ears, he caught the sound of another motor roaring to life, coming right from the direction their guide had just indicated. From the darkness of the flooded corridor, the enemy boat flew toward their nose like a torpedo. For Faolan, Walsh's warning made the difference between being caught completely by surprise and being able to bring up his pistol and snap off a shot that caught the enemy pilot in the shoulder. Walsh and Rod performed a maneuver to avoid the other boat as the pilot's shoulder wound caused him to steer the boat off course for a moment—both efforts combined to allow Walsh's *Black Duck* to shoot past the other in the opposite direction.

As the two boats passed, a figure made a running leap from the enemy boat to slam into Faolan—he had half a second to recognize the skeletal, hairless, half-naked Vampyr he'd privately christened Bony during their encounter on Steeplechase Pier. The Browning fell from his hand and he tumbled overboard with Bony clutching onto him tight.

The black murky water was salty and frigid. Faolan felt it soak through to his skin and freeze him. He struggled, squirmed, and stretched, but Bony had his arms pinned to his sides and held him tight, grinning that predatory, wide-eyed grin of his. Everything was silent and black except for the pounding of his heart in his ear drums and the bulging, cat-eyed glare of his attacker. The arm Faolan had taken on Coney Island had grown back and the emaciated maniac was putting it to good use, squeezing and squeezing tighter still. Not only couldn't Faolan move his arms, but the breath he'd taken was being squeezed out his lungs little by little.

He tried to use his head to push the other vamp back, but Bony took that as an invitation to introduce Faolan's neck to his teeth. Twisting and thrashing as hard as he could, he couldn't seem to get away from Bony's snake-like head and felt the sharpened canines stab into the side of his neck, followed by the pressure of the full bite. He twisted again, bucking and thrashing, as Bony swung his head away, taking flesh with him as the blackness warmed with his blood.

Goddamn it, this can't be how it ends for me! he thought, panicked and furious. *After all I done, everything else I survived—I get drowned by Lon fucking Chaney here in fucking Providence?? It ain't right—it ain't fair!*

Distantly, he was aware of his back striking the bottom, which had until recently been a street. He could feel the strength draining out of him as Bony pressed his lips to the wound at his neck and tried to drink. It would have seemed crazy, but Faolan knew that the extra energy he could steal would not only win him the fight, but might make the crucial difference when it came time for Bony to swim back to the surface. He couldn't see anything, but he couldn't tell anymore if that was his eyesight going dark or just the terrible darkness of the freezing black water. The pressure in his lungs was an intense fire, almost more than he could bear, but there was no air left in him now and he refused to suck in water. Part of him imagined that the pressure inside him might build up enough to make him explode, taking Bony with him in death, at least.

If I'm gonna die, it should be in New York, he thought. He knew nobody was coming to help him. Not only did they have a boat full of enemy vamps to fight, but trying to find anyone in this inky water was just nuts. He could feel his life flowing out of him and down Bony's throat and it pissed him off. Dying out here in the boonies was bad enough, dying underwater was worse, but the idea that his blood should go to this fucking wild-eyed stick figure was what really tore it for him. Feeling his canines slide down, Faolan shook his head and found the junction of Bony's shoulder and neck and bit down as hard as he could manage.

Fuck you, you fucking piece of shit! Think you're gonna fucking drink me, you lousy fuck? WELL, FUCK YOU! I'LL FUCKING RIP YOU APART, MOTHER-FUCKER!

The other Vampyr's flesh had an almost rubbery feel at first, but he bore down with all his anger and outrage and frustration and felt his teeth sinking deeper and deeper and Bony trying to pull away but Faolan could almost feel that big muscle that connected the shoulder to the neck like a thick twisted up rope in his jaws. He bit down hard, shaking his head in his rage like a wolf and sensing the blood in the water and wanting to suck it all down even as the feel of flesh and tendon between his teeth became intoxicating, like chewing on the finest aged steak in his mortal life—a primal urge to rend muscle and break bone and drink that sweet nectar down to the dregs—

The arms released him and he felt Bony's long, thin fingers grip both sides of his head and squeeze as the thumbs slid up his cheeks and into his eyeballs and began to press and press. The last of Faolan's strength gave way as his head snapped back with a rubbery chunk of Bony's skin still in his jaws. A foot shoved his body back down to the street as Bony pushed off of him and disappeared into the darkness.

His limbs felt like lead and darkness closed in, the burning in his chest and neck so excruciating now he figured he'd pass out, but wouldn't it be nice to just take a long, deep breath first?

Something grabbed him, a vague shape he could barely make out, and pulled at him. He tried to struggle but his body wouldn't obey him at all. Then he was moving, floating upward with something pressed against his chest.

The next thing he knew, his eyes could see something other than blackness and his body sucked in giant lungfuls of air before he even knew what was happening. He thrashed and coughed, his vision blurry with salt and the sudden "brightness" of the surrounding night.

"Hang on, I got you," he heard Rod say and realized that, once again, the former Marine had dived in to save him. *This is getting to be a habit*, he thought between coughing fits while Rod called out to Walsh, who hauled him up out of the water and back onto the deck of the boat.

"Did you swallow any water, boyo?" Walsh asked. "Get any in your lungs?"

He coughed again and managed to shake his head. Walsh took him by the chin and examined his neck as Rod finished climbing in. "Why that fella took quite a nasty chunk out of you, didn't he?"

Faolan realized that he'd spit out Bony's skin at some point during his ride to the surface, but smiled anyway. "You oughtta see the other guy."

*****

"So, as promised, sir, you are now the proud owner of the greater Providence area," Faolan said, raising his glass of blood whisky in toast. It wasn't quite the same bottled as drinking fresh from a pickled person, and while it didn't have quite the same effect as drinking booze had when he was mortal, it was refreshing after the night's events.

"Thank you, sir," said Mister Walsh, also raising a glass. They had returned to Walsh's little hideaway in Pawtuxet Village, a little outside of Providence, which had also been severely damaged and flooded by the storm. Luckily, Walsh had a place up on a hill, one of his old speaks from Prohibition. It looked like a nice big house on the outside, but the basement was still hidden and fitted out from its Prohibition days. It made a great headquarters.

As soon as Faolan and his gang had arrived in Providence, they had gone to find Danny Walsh. Walsh had been a business acquaintance of Faolan's through Big Bill Dwyer in New York and was one of the biggest bootleggers in Southern New England until somebody disappeared him in 1933. Well, as Faolan came to find out during his last adventure in New England, Walsh had actually gone the Vampyr route on behalf of the Reeve of Providence. Never one to overlook an opportunity, Faolan had passed along a few coded messages to Walsh through their human counterparts and discovered that Danny was still the same personable fella and, furthermore, that he felt distinctly unappreciated under the current regime. That had begun Walsh passing information to Faolan about the goings-on in the Northeast in exchange for Walsh's Providence mob being given assistance from the *paisans* in New York.

"I don't feature us being of much practical use to you in the near future, though, boyo," Walsh continued. Though born and raised right in the Warwick area of Rhode Island, the flamboyant Irishman liked to affect an Old World way, using expressions and phrasing that would have sounded more appropriate if connected to an Irish brogue rather than his flat, nasal New England tone. Here in his home environment, Walsh let his natural personality reign and was dressed in a blue checkered three-piece and a red bow tie. A large man with twinkling amber eyes and wavy caramel hair, Vampyrism gave him a taut and fit look that suited him and emphasized his naturally attractive features.

"Don't worry about it, Danny," Faolan said, setting his glass down. "Just having you here right near Boston should keep Moore looking over his shoulder and creates a bigger buffer that his people have to sneak through to get to New York."

They had assembled more or less everybody, except for Enzo and his crew who were still in Hartford. They sat around the large parlor/library that had a dozen wing-back leather chairs and sofas scattered around among built-in bookcases. Then there were the paintings and statues of horses. Horses everywhere you looked. Danny Walsh had a thing for horses that went well beyond a casual interest in races.

"Well," Walsh said, swirling the bloody remains of his drink in a brandy snifter with a gentle motion of his hand. "I've got a few good lads on whom I can build a foundation and—what with Boston's retaliation now in a shambles—I suppose the real work lies ahead." He drained the last of his drink in a quick swallow. "Where are you fellas off to next?"

As soon as he finished his drink, his young female Dhampir—who he'd introduced as Mae and who seemed more like a wife—came in with a freshly warmed tea pot full of the alcoholic blood. Walsh took a refill, thanking her kindly, and she then proceeded around the room filling glasses.

Frank, notably the only guy not holding a drink and wearing his full suit all buttoned up, looked over at Faolan.

"Springfield makes the most sense. We can leave tomorrow night."

Faolan took a refill from Mae and thanked her. He studied the warm red blood in his whisky glass while he considered. It would be easy to say that coming so close to death tonight had made him reconsider a few things, but that would also be a whitewash. He'd been chewing over the things that Stephanie had said for a while now, along with plenty of his own observations. His feelings about certain things had been changing. He just wasn't sure how to say most of it without the other guys taking him for a sap. The last thing he needed was his gang thinking he'd gone soft.

Then he looked up and noticed that everyone in the room was looking at him, waiting for his response. He spotted Rod giving him a faint, warm smile and made up his mind. He sat back in his chair and took a sip of the blood. "I think we're gonna stick around here for a while longer, if that's all right with you, Danny. Like you said, there's a lot of work still to do here and I figure you could probably use the help."

Walsh's face brightened in surprise, a smile spreading across his face. "Well, I could indeed, thank you! I'm sure I can fix up some better accommodations for you, as well."

Frank's expression darkened in a way that Faolan had come to recognize as Frank disagreeing with him, but not wanting to do so in public. "What about Springfield?"

"You're gonna take a few of the boys and join up with Enzo in Hartford, see if he needs any help finishing up there. Then, you guys sneak into Springfield and take it." He already knew who he'd send with Frank: the more hot-headed and hard boiled of his eggs. That would leave him with guys who would be more agreeable to lending a helping hand. "First of all, I ain't totally convinced that Boston is played out when it comes to Providence—being as how it's so close—and I don't want to see our friends here bumped off and all our hard work here wasted because we pulled up stakes too soon."

Saberhagen and a few of the rougher mugs nodded their heads, satisfied with a reason that made sense to them, and Faolan decided to plunge ahead. "And, second, as much as I realize that we ain't no charity organization—and, believe me, I understand that better than anybody—there's still sense to the idea that when normal folks are suffering on a large scale like what we got here…well, we wind up suffering right along with them after a while. So, it just makes good sense to me that the faster we help folks get back on their feet, the faster we'll be able to get back to running things normal."

"Absolutely," seconded Rod, raising his glass with a smile.

Danny Walsh nodded thoughtfully, pulling his pocket-watch from his vest and swinging it around on its chain. "You do make a point there, boyo. There's nothing like rebuilding to let you know where everything lies and gratitude's a fine foundation to build relationships on—so long as there's the threat of violent reprisal for once the gratitude's run out."

That got a chuckle from everyone and pretty much sealed it. Faolan smiled and lifted his glass in salute to both Rod and Walsh before downing it. The vamps of The Order took plenty of advantage of their relationship with the humans of the world and, the way he was beginning to see it, would it be such a bad thing if the vampires were to return the favor once in a while?

Chapter Twenty-Five

Enzo had done very well in Hartford, having gotten the place wrapped up under a tough broad by the name of Katherine Elrod by the time Frank arrived. Frank objected to putting a woman in charge of even a minor city like Hartford, but Enzo stuck to his guns, telling him: "Faolan told me to find the best man for the job and it just fell out that the best man for the job was a woman." Faolan had been forced to come down to mediate the situation and, after talking with Elrod for a bit, decided that Enzo had made the right choice. After that, Frank and Enzo had gone to Springfield and that proved to be a disaster. Both Frank and Enzo had very different ideas about how to take control of Springfield and neither wanted to give way to the other, so once again Faolan had been called away from the rebuilding of Providence to settle the problem. This time, he decided to take Enzo back to Providence with him and let Frank handle things his way. It was unfortunate for the vamps of Springfield, but the other option would have been to let Frank and the other goons stomp all over the humanitarian things they were trying to do in Providence.

Then on Halloween—just as things seemed to be settling down—Providence was attacked again by a bunch of new vamps from Boston. This time they set Danny Walsh's house on fire. With all the shooting and running around, Faolan was sure they were going to have the National Guard on their asses, but in an ironic twist, they were saved from too much public notice by the unexpected flood of calls the cops received asking about Martians because of Mercury Theater's *War of the Worlds* broadcast. After that victory, Faolan was sure they'd hear from Moore, but October became November, then December. He'd tried to get permission to bring the fellas back for Christmas, but Killian demanded they attack Boston itself, which Faolan knew would be suicide. After spending a lonely Christmas and New Year's out in Providence, he got a letter from Miranda telling him that Moore had agreed to a meeting. Of course, several more weeks had passed while they fought over dates and places before they settled on this boat-to-boat meeting at Martha's Vineyard as a "neutral" location.

Not a word from Stephanie. Not even a Christmas card.

"There's the great bitch now, just where she ought to be," declared Walsh.

The Black Duck had a big brother, which Walsh called *The Black Goose.* It was a nicely appointed, fifty foot motor yacht that he kept anchored in Warwick Cove. It had carried Faolan, Frank, and a few of Walsh's gorillas through the frigid choppy waters from Warwick to Cape Roger Bay, off the coast of Martha's Vineyard, for their secret meeting. Faolan was no boat expert, but it was the biggest and nicest ship he'd ever been on.

Moore's yacht, the *Thetis*, dwarfed it.

He'd assumed they would arrive in more or less equal style, starting the meeting off on an even keel as the boating folks said. Instead, he felt like they were pulling up to a cruise ship in a tugboat. *Thetis* wasn't quite a cruise ship, but it was close and, judging from Walsh's reaction, it was impressive by any standard. It stood three decks high, all white and stained wood, with tall sails at the front and back and a sleek shape that stretched at least a hundred and fifty feet from end to end.

"Christ," Faolan muttered, "he could have dozens of mugs on board that thing."

"Don't you worry, though," Walsh said as he maneuvered *The Black Goose* alongside the larger yacht. "If you don't come back upon the appointed hour, I'll sink that tub even if I have to ram her."

Faolan smiled, but Frank just gave Walsh a blank stare. "We'd still be dead."

As he and Frank climbed the ladder up to the main deck of Moore's yacht, he tried to make himself focus on the task at hand. They needed a way to get in touch with Governor Burlington and they had to bring this damn war to a successful end. The obvious answer to both was Edward Moore, Reeve of Boston. As Frank pointed out, it also wouldn't hurt Faolan's bid for Reeve of New York to have either a partnership or amiable relations with a major city like Boston. When he got to the top, he saw uniformed crewmen performing various tasks as well as a uniformed Captain standing on the deck. He was a short man on the far side of middle age with gray hair that had a few touches of brown left in it and a weathered face.

"Good evening, gentlemen," he said with no trace of any accent. "I'm Captain Woolrich. Welcome aboard the *Thetis*. If you'll please follow me, His Honor is prepared to receive you in the dining room."

He turned and led them through a doorway into a narrow hallway and Faolan thought: *This is where they'll make their play, while they got us bottle-necked.* He slid his hand onto the butt of his trusted Browning and strained his senses for the first hint of ambush. His conditions for meeting on Moore's ship had been that both he and Frank be allowed to retain their weapons and that Moore have only one other Vampyr on board with him. Woolrich led them into a fancy, old-fashioned dining room without incident. Faolan had no doubt that Moore had guys hidden away, either on the boat or on another just out of sight just like he'd brought reinforcements on Walsh's boat, but he hoped they didn't get called.

The room was lit by oil lanterns that hung in each of the room's four corners and decorated in a nautical theme. There were bookcases built into the walls that held books, shells, old time sailing paraphernalia, sea charts in frames on the walls, and similar things that Faolan couldn't name. When Woolrich invited them in, however, the main thing that caught Faolan's attention was the sight of their hosts. The elegant, aristocratic figure at the table was

Edward Moore. Faolan's first impression was that he resembled George Washington—or, at least, the way Washington looked in the paintings. Moore wore his silver-white hair pulled back and gathered at the base of his neck with a small ribbon, his forehead was large and his features sleek and sharp with deep, hooded eyes. He had maintained carefully groomed sideburns that descended to just below his ears in order to disguise the fact that his ears were large and stuck out a bit. He nodded at them as they entered, but didn't rise from his seat at the head of the table.

The Vampyr behind him was Bony.

Granted, it took Faolan a second to recognize his former playmate. The skeletal monster was dressed to impress tonight in white-tie and tails with a black bowler that should have been a top hat. But, somehow, the derby looked more appropriate on the grinning loon than the correct formal wear would have. The penguin suit also made the fucker look even skinnier and more like Lon Chaney's Phantom of the Opera than anybody had a right to look.

"What the fuck's the idea of bringing him?" Faolan demanded, pointing at Bony.

Moore's cheek twitched at the profanity, but he remained otherwise still and spoke in a calm tone. "Mister Strieber is my Marshal and, as such, he has every right to be party to these negotiations in accordance with the terms set forth between us, Mister O'Connor." His accent was pure Queen's English, which Faolan only recognized from the British Navy officers in Errol Flynn pictures he'd seen with Stephanie.

Bony, or Strieber, lifted his bowler and bowed, still giving his rictus grin. The light flashed off his eyes as he did, making them shine in the dim light.

Faolan held himself back from putting a bullet between his eyes, but it was a close thing.

Moore lifted one of his hands from the table-top and indicated the pair of chairs set at their side of the table. "Now, with that settled, you may both have a seat and we shall begin." The table was wider than normal, but the two chairs were still a tight fit. Another little power-play.

Smiling, Faolan took off his overcoat while Frank dutifully moved away one of the chairs, took Faolan's coat from him, and held his seat for him. They had discussed this and Frank had insisted that the only way for him to gain any respect from men like Moore would be to put on the airs of a Reeve. Frank took up position behind Faolan's right shoulder and also left his hat on in imitation of Strieber.

"Thank you for inviting us onto your boat, Your Honor," Faolan said, settling back in the chair. "It's very impressive."

Edward Moore, Reeve of the city of Boston, smiled and his unnaturally smooth face brightened. The smile was warm and gentle, which surprised Faolan. His whole manner became more animated as he talked. "Why, thank you, Mister O'Connor. *Thetis* is my newest yacht, one of the new so-called J Class built for racing. Do you follow yacht racing? No, I shouldn't think you would, as you have so many other pressing concerns, yes? Well, you see, yachts were not originally pleasure craft, not at all. The term comes from the Dutch *jacht*, meaning hunt, and were first built to pursue pirates and act as customs vessels. However, I'm quite pleased with her: so far she's made a good showing in the last few America's Cups, though she hasn't taken one yet. Of course, she races under a pseudonym and false registry."

He paused, gazing out one of the room's windows to the darkness beyond, maybe dreaming of this year's race. Faolan just waited, figuring the best thing he could do for the negotiations was to let Moore make himself as comfortable as possible. Meanwhile, Strieber stared across the table at Frank who stared back, unblinking. *Great*, Faolan thought, *two ghouls having a creep-out contest.*

The Boston Reeve slid his chair back and rose without changing expression, drifting over to the window. Faolan noted that Moore's dark gray three piece suit had the loose cut of the mid-teens, complete with the starched white shirt with detachable wing collar and Navy blue silk four-in-hand tie. For his part, Faolan had worn his best olive three-piece with an ivory shirt and emerald tie with a gold pattern and matching cufflinks, treading the line between high style and conservative. He'd even oiled and combed his hair for the occasion.

"The sea is in my blood, Mister O'Connor," he said. "My family was among the finest ship builders in England for centuries. They designed and built for merchants, explorers, and the Royal Navy. We founded the Massachusetts Bay Colony and signed the Cambridge Agreement. We drove out the red savages from these lands. We built ships, sir, ships that transformed a small harbor colony into a powerful city of Godly leaders. When my only son was lost at sea—having produced no offspring—I became the last of my line. Since my Creation, I have held Boston's most distinguished families as dear to me as my own. I have led its evolution from a small coastal town to the finest city in these United States. I have been privileged to be an intimate to our Hegemon and was once offered nomination for Governor of the East Coast of America. However, I refused because I knew there were others more worthy of the post than I, but also because such duties would have meant focusing less of my attention upon my home city of Boston. For, you see, as much as the sea is in my blood, the city of Boston claims my soul."

Faolan sat back in his chair, impressed despite himself. Unlike Killian's grandiose bombast, Moore's eloquent recital inspired him with its quiet depth of feeling and pride. *Maybe just loving your city and wanting to make it succeed ain't too simple a goal, after all*, he thought. *Stephanie's right again. Dammit, I shouldn't have left things between us like I did.*

"I can respect that, Your Honor," Faolan said. "I feel the same way about New York. I think that's why you and me could work together for the benefit of both."

Moore turned from the window and regarded him with a bemused expression. "Straight to the point, then, shall we?" He walked back to his chair and sat, aided by the skeletal Strieber. "Very well. Darcy Killian and every Vampyr who cleaves to his cause, yourself and your man here included, are under sentence of death for the murders of Reeve Johann Vandergriff and the legitimate hierarchy of New York, unlawful warfare against the North American Domain, incitement of rebellion in multiple Northeast cities, and treason against the sovereign authority of the Governor of the East Coast United States Territory and the Hegemon of North America from whom his power derives. As a duly consecrated Reeve of the East Coast United States Territory, I am not only within my rights, but frankly obligated, to execute this sentence upon you and your man right where you sit."

Faolan did nothing, refusing to rise to the bait.

"However, you have come here as my invited guest for a civil meeting and I would not besmirch my hospitality thus." Moore sat erect in his chair like a king on a throne. "But you mistake both my position and your own if you believe that you may offer an alliance to me as if to an equal. I do not know you, Mister O'Connor, and mean no offense to you as an individual, but I can say with some authority that the Irish as a race are parasites of the most unseemly sort. Thieves, ruffians, and drunkards, they have descended upon Boston like locusts to scavenge what they can. I would not have an Irishman in my service under any circumstances; however, what I have heard of you would tend to set you as an exception to your fellows."

Again, Faolan kept his pleasant expression on his face and held back any reaction. He knew already that it would make no difference in Moore's opinion if he informed him that the last members of the O'Connor family to hail from Ireland had been his maternal grandparents. Likewise, he'd certainly find Rothstein's notion of Vampyrs all being basically the same blood offensive to his Old World sensibilities.

Moore brought his hands together, forming a steeple with his fingers. "This is my offer: that you provide me with detailed knowledge of all of your activities in the Northeast, that you destroy or imprison the renegade Darcy Killian and as many of his followers as you deem necessary to end his rebellion, and that you then formally surrender the city of New York to me. These actions having been performed, I will vouchsafe for you and no more than five other Vampyrs of your selection to receive formal pardon for your crimes. In consideration of your efforts and ability, I will even see to it that you retain your current rank as Marshal of New York City once you have sworn loyalty to the Vampyr chosen as Reeve."

Sure, until he decides to have me bumped off once things have settled down, right? Thanks, but this Irish didn't just fall off the fucking potato truck. Faolan watched Moore's face and body the whole time, but the Reeve of Boston was an excellent poker player. Faolan smiled and shook his head. "C'mon, now, let's be realistic here. I can get rid of Killian for you and I can end this war, but there's only one guy fit to run New York City and that's me. I want you to introduce me to Governor Burlington and support me as Reeve. I want Burlington's signature on the deal so there ain't no unfortunate misunderstandings like happened after Coney Island."

Moore's upper lip twitched in contempt and his eyes blazed, but otherwise he remained still. "I had expected better of you, Mister O'Connor. This is not a negotiation: it is the last chance you will have to survive this war and my offer becomes void once we conclude."

Faolan glanced up at Frank, who shrugged and went back to giving Bony Strieber the hairy eyeball. He crossed his legs, reached into his pocket for a quarter, and began rolling it back and forth across his knuckles. He was done playing it Moore's way. "Look, we don't gotta be best pals here, but I didn't come all the way out here to be insulted. That's what that offer of yours is: an insult. Two years ago, maybe you could've gotten away with making an offer like that and I might've considered it, but now we got you up against the fucking wall—"

"*Mister* O'Connor, I will not tolerate your obscenities!"

"Don't change the subject," Faolan snapped. "I got the entire Northeast now and you got Boston. This war is over and you lost, so don't sit there and try to act like you're doing me a favor. I'm giving you the chance to end things now, while you can still walk away from this with some dignity."

"Dignity, you say?" Moore's voice was tight, his hands gripping the arms of his chair. Behind him, Strieber's eyes widened in anticipation. "What would you know of dignity? Less than what you know of The Order, which is nothing. You mistake me greatly if you think that I have any desire for peace! I have resources unimaginable to a vulgar street ruffian such as you. Johann Vandergriff was a friend to me and as fine a gentleman as any to ever grace The Order's ranks. So, for you to sit before me imagining that I would ever let a cockroach like you or your simian countryman desecrate his office..." he paused to take a breath, trembling ever so slightly with the effort. "Mark my words, Faolan O'Connor: every victory which you think won, I shall shortly undo. This meeting is ended. Now, get off of my ship before I forget myself and allow Mister Strieber free reign."

"Go ahead," Frank said before Faolan could respond. "I'd love nothing more than shoving that over-dressed skeleton up your ass!"

Shock and fury competed for Moore's expression as he bolted upright, toppling his chair. Strieber's lips stretched impossibly wide over brown teeth as his bony hand drew his enormous knife from his belt sheath.

Faolan kept himself from laughing, but couldn't stop smiling. He grabbed his coat from Frank and pushed the big Vampyr toward the door. "Temper, temper, gentlemen! Let's not forget them all important rules of hospitaliosity." For some reason, the situation made him think of one of those Merrie Melody cartoons where that screwball duck—a Black Duck, no less—would plant a big, wet kiss on Porky Pig. "Woo-hoo! Woo-hoo!" he shouted in imitation of the daffy duck as he and Frank hurried up onto the deck. Faolan expected to find shooters waiting, but there were none.

"Well," said Danny Walsh as he helped them aboard *The Black Goose*. "You both seem in a jolly spirit. I trust the negotiations went well?"

Faolan looked at Frank, who looked right back at him, and they both burst out laughing.

PART FIVE

JACKS OVER ACES:
February, 1939

You ain't been blue, no, no, no
You ain't been blue
Till you've had that mood indigo
That feelin' goes stealin' down to my shoes
While I sit and sigh, "Go long blues"
- Duke Ellington, "Mood Indigo"

Chapter Twenty-Six

"Killian wants me to rub you two out and be quick about it," Faolan told Miranda and Huston as they sat down at the large corner booth in the Wolf, much as they had nearly five months ago. Frank was also present, of course, as was Stebbins, but no Stephanie. In fact, Faolan hadn't seen her since returning last night and the thought of her was like a missing tooth he couldn't stop returning to despite the discomfort. According to Stebbins' apologetic explanation, she'd cleared out her room at the Doll House and left when word had spread of Faolan's imminent return.

"Was that all he said?" Miranda asked, pouring herself a coffee cup full of hot blood from the kettle on the table. She was dressed in a blue double-breasted suit which, when combined with the wide-brimmed gray fedora and overcoat she'd just hung up, did a pretty good job of making her look like a heavyset man unless you got close.

Faolan grabbed the kettle after she was done and poured another. the problem with the bottled blood was that once you heated it up, that was it. The minute you let that shit cool down again, it congealed into a disgusting mess, so you had to drink it up once you made some. "Well, he also told me to get a haircut and make sure my men did likewise," he said. "Sonofabitch barely managed to congratulate me on winning the fucking war for him before he starts in about what a fuck-up Charnas has been and how—" here he paused to do his best imitation of Killian: "'Nothing can be allowed to put the slightest hitch in this week's plans, follow? My triumph is near at hand and I'll not have any of Moore's sabotage giving that cocksucker Burlington excuse to withdraw!'"

He took a sip of the rich blood, enjoying the warmth after the bitter cold of the night outside. He'd even grown to enjoy the slight tang of the vinegar that helped keep the blood from clotting. Some vamps couldn't stand the bottled stuff and only drank fresh, but for Faolan it was like the difference between fresh fruit and preserves: he enjoyed both for different reasons.

Seemed Moore had been bluffing at that meeting since, one month and one last desperate attack on Providence later, Governor Burlington had sent an emissary to New York with a letter declaring that all hostilities between all the cities of the Northeast were to cease. Further, he was prepared to oversee an agreement to that effect in New York City, after which Killian would be officially consecrated as Reeve of New York. After being stuck out in Rhode Island for both Christmas and New Year's, Faolan had been able to bring his weary crew home. Unfortunately, if he'd been expecting a hero's welcome, he was sorely disappointed: Killian's attitude was that Faolan's victory had taken too long and been too costly, jeopardizing the successful opening of his precious World's Fair.

That was a disappointment he could swallow, however. He was planning his own welcome home party for the boys at The Wolf tomorrow night. What stuck going down was the idea of Stephanie running out on him. He never should have asked her to play double-agent for him, he knew that now. He'd figured on her being happy to help and that it would keep her from being a target if everyone thought they were quits, but she didn't see it that way. He'd taken her for granted. She was well red at him, but he still wished she'd come and tell him off face-to-face. Let him apologize, at least. He owed her that much.

"Faolan?" Miranda asked, looking across the table at him.

Fuck, he'd drifted into la-la land for a second. What the hell was wrong with him tonight? He needed to focus. He was so close now, so close!

He smiled and reached into his jacket for his cigarette case. "So, fill me in," he said, lighting a Camel. "How did things go while we was on holiday in Providence?"

Miranda and Huston glanced at each other, and then Huston folded his large hands on the table. "Your man Stebbins here has been very informative."

Stebbins smiled and went back to fiddling with the deck of cards in his hands. Maybe he was working on some new card trick.

"We knocked over a few establishments that were owned by Rothstein, Killian, and Charnas—though nothing critical—and were able to pick off five of Charnas' men as well. Unfortunately, Mister Charnas has proven more cautious than we gave him credit for and has kept his movements erratic after we almost punched his card a few weeks ago." Huston was in fine form tonight, giving his speech like he was reciting lines in a stage play. Tonight's suit was a bold, bright blue double-breasted with a dove-gray shirt—a match for his coat and derby—and a canary-yellow tie with blue diamonds for contrast. You couldn't mistake him for anything but a Harlem gangster, but that image would keep the regular Joes from getting too close.

Something smelled fishy. Faolan didn't know how he knew, he just knew.

While Huston continued giving him the details of their successes and failures, Faolan studied his movements and his eyes. Was the Philly vamp a little too rehearsed tonight? Was this all bullshit they were feeding him? What about Miranda? The burly Scot was much easier to read. Her eyes were steady, watching him and trying to read his reactions to Huston's news. Her hands kept shifting like she didn't know what to do with them. Or maybe she was anticipating some action in the near future? She grew more uneasy the longer he looked at her.

Something definitely wasn't kosher here.

He turned his attention to Stebbins, normally so animated and eager. He continued fumbling with his cards until he caught Faolan staring. He set the cards down and sat very still. His eyes darted around, meeting Faolan's for a moment before shifting to Frank then Miranda then Huston. Was his squirrelliness a sign of betrayal or some secret knowledge? Were they all against him now? Had they cut a deal with Rothstein while he was gone?

The hairs on the back of Faolan's neck twitched.

"You got them letters, Stebbins?" he asked when Huston finished speaking.

Stebbins' lips twitched in a weak impression of a smile as he pulled an envelope out of his inside pocket. His normally impeccable brown pinstripe was wrinkled, his tie loose, and his shirt collar unbuttoned. His hands trembled ever so slightly as he handed over the envelope and his hazel eyes held a look of panic as they met Faolan's. He was crooked, all right, but not willingly. As good a con man as Stebbins was, he could have hidden all his anxiety beneath a casual mask if he wanted to.

This was a set up.

The first of the forged letters was from Moore to Huston, in which Huston was directed to coordinate his sabotage efforts with one Ed Charnas of New York City and strike at targets he would provide. This would, when presented to Killian, justify or trigger the execution of Charnas and his closest followers and leave Rothstein without muscle and Faolan in charge of Killian's security. The second letter, dated tonight, was from Killian to Bill

Davidson in Philadelphia with instructions to send a group of his best shooters to New York the night before the meeting with Burlington with instructions to follow Killian's orders and no one else's. This one was trickier, but the implication was clear: Killian planning an assassination of Governor Burlington and the others either before or after the signing of the peace treaty.

"I still don't understand the Philadelphia letter," Miranda said. "Why would Governor Burlington believe that Killian would want to kill him when he's about to knight Killian? It makes no fucking sense!"

"Burlington doesn't have to believe it's genuine," Frank said, while Faolan continued to study the documents. "It's an excuse. Burlington doesn't want Killian, he never has. When Faolan tells him that Killian is planning a double-cross and gives him the letter, it starts the conversation and gives him a way to eliminate Killian and save face. Between having peace with Faolan and war with the entire Northeast, we're sure he'll see reason."

"So, Stebbins, who's got their hook in you?" Faolan asked. He didn't look at Stebbins, he watched Miranda and Huston. Frank tensed up, catching Faolan's cue.

"S-sorry?" Stebbins asked, the cigarette he'd started nearly falling from his lips.

Miranda and Huston both looked confused, but Huston's look turned to malice quickly as he sized up the grifter. Faolan had to know now if these two were on the up-and-up: if they had bent Stebbins, then they'd make a move. If not, then they all might have bigger problems. He set down the letters to free his hands. This is when it would happen.

"Don't fuck around," Faolan said, his voice hard and cold. "I can see you're practically crawling out of your own skin, so spill before I let Frank start asking the questions."

Miranda lifted up a bit off her seat and Faolan prepared to snatch his Browning from beneath his jacket, but she placed her hands on the table and leaned into Stebbins. Huston sat back, his expression hard but otherwise unreadable. Faolan was confident he could slip from the booth and plug them both before they could act.

Stebbins, seated between Faolan and Frank, went pale. "No, I-I wouldn't—" he began denying automatically before his sense caught up to him and he broke. His eyes welled up, his head dropped, and his chest heaved in a single sob, then he swallowed and whispered: "Charnas."

Faolan felt a mixture of relief and disgust. Despite his common sense, he'd come to like Stebbins over the years. Clenching his jaw, he put his hands back on the table and braced himself for the worst.

Stebbins continued: "Two nights ago, I went to get the letters where I'd stashed them—I was doing good, I thought, Charnas trusted me just like you said he would—but he must have tumbled to me somehow. I don't know when or how, but he just knew. They grabbed me. Charnas, he..." The grifter glanced up at Faolan, begging with his eyes, but Faolan refused to look at him. "They broke my fingers—Charnas and Paulie King—h-he went over to

Charnas as soon as you left—and then they burned me...I told them everything: the letters, the sabotage...I spilled. I'm sorry, boss, I—"

"This place ain't fucking safe," Miranda muttered.

"What's Killian know?" Frank demanded, grabbing Stebbins' neck with his large, thick hand.

"I-I don't know!" Stebbins cried. "I heard Charnas on the phone with Rothstein saying they should go to Killian, but Rothstein told him they needed something more solid than just my say so—"

"So they fixed you up so you could give me the letters," Faolan said, sliding out of the booth so he could pace. He grabbed the smoldering cigarette from the ashtray and took a deep drag. Was Stephanie dead? Why hadn't he heard from her?

Stebbins nodded, looking miserable. "They're waiting outside. They tailed me here so they can take you and Miranda and Sandman and the letters back to Killian and Rothstein to prove he was right. I'm supposed to open the door for them, so they can surprise you. I wasn't going to go through with it, you understand, don't you, Faolan? I just needed to figure out how to clue you in."

So, Miranda and Huston were clean. That was one small comfort. The pair slid out from the booth and grabbed their coats.

"How many guys?" Frank asked Stebbins, bringing out the sawed-down Browning Automatic Rifle he'd taken to carrying under his coat. He didn't quite point it at Stebbins, but it was close at hand.

"Probably around ten, but some are in the alley watching the fire exits," Stebbins said.

"Is there another way out of here?" Huston asked. He drew a pair of gleaming, nickel-finished Colts. "Something not visible from the street?"

Faolan blew a cloud of smoke and shook his head. "Not yet. I had an idea after your last visit: there was a door used to go from the basement here to next door back when this was the Hotsy Totsy—"

"Um, actually," Stebbins interjected, smiling. "While you were gone, Stephanie arranged for that passage door to be opened back up. She felt it was a useful idea."

Faolan caught himself smiling back, but the reminder of Stephanie sobered him. "Where is she?"

Stebbins stopped smiling as well and sighed. "I don't know, I swear."

Faolan would have known better than to let someone like Stebbins go without some kind of leverage, but Charnas was a bully at heart and bullies figured once they made you say uncle, you were theirs. Guys like Stebbins bent easy as pie, but never really broke. Faolan read his eyes and nodded. "Let him go, Frank." Stebbins smiled and opened his mouth to thank him, but Faolan silenced him with a look. "Okey-dokey, kids," he said, addressing everyone. "Here's the plan: we go out through—"

"I always said you can't trust the fucking Irish for nothing," proclaimed Crowbar Charnas as he entered from the lobby, shotgun in hand. Behind him, five more of his goons in coats and fedoras ran onto the dance floor with BARs and Thompsons ready.

Faolan pulled his Hi-Power from its holster and drew a bead on Charnas' head in a quarter of a second. "I need better fucking locks on this place," he said. "Any old mug can just wander in off the street."

Miranda and Huston, meanwhile, ducked behind the half-wall that ran the length of the VIP platform while Frank and Stebbins up-ended the triangular table they'd been seated around and readied their own hardware.

Charnas showed no fear of Faolan's pistol, his casual hold on his shotgun reinforced the contemptuous sneer on his blocky face. "Locks don't matter when youse got a key."

That's when Stephanie stumbled through the doors with Paulie King gripping her shoulder and holding a .38 snub-nose to the back of her head.

Shit, Faolan thought. *Well, at least now I know where she is.*

Chapter Twenty-Seven

"What's the matter, you couldn't find any railroad tracks to tie her to, you fucking hump?" Faolan asked, keeping a strong front while his insides squirmed. That damn heated blood he'd drunk earlier had run right through him, as usual, and now he had to piss. Perfect fucking timing. The last thing he needed would be to piss his pants, as that might be misinterpreted under the circumstances, but he also couldn't see asking Charnas if they would excuse him for a minute while he visited the little boys' room.

Charnas stretched back thin lips to display his jagged yellow teeth. This attempt at a smile made his already square features even more unappealing. "She practically volunteered! Just when I'm starting to loose my patience with that little pimp behind you, she walks up pretty as you please and unlocks the door for me!" He shrugged. "Now, all of youse drop the gats and get out from behind there. I ain't here to kill nobody I don't gotta."

No, he'd let Killian do that later after many hours of torture. Faolan watched Charnas' men spread out and saw they weren't as well-trained or experienced as Miranda's Dhampirs: one joker got up onto the main stage to give himself a better view, but it also made him an easy target. The others just spread out a little and stood around holding their guns, trusting in their firepower and the bulletproof vests he imagined were under those coats to keep them safe. From the corner of his eye, he saw Huston and Miranda crawl down to the other end of the wall across from the main stage, giving them good coverage of the dance floor and access to the fire door if necessary. The shelves for the bar also backed up against that wall, which made it pretty solid. The VIP booths were up on a U-shaped platform that surrounded the bar area to keep the dance floor clear. it was only three steps high, but it was enough to give Faolan's group a tactical advantage when combined with their cover. Only Paulie King stuck close to the lobby doors, making him a straight shot for Faolan, but he was using his small size to hide behind Stephanie. *Glad we taught him so good*, he thought.

Stephanie looked good, made up and dressed for the weather in a fur coat Faolan had bought her last Christmas. She was pretty calm considering the situation, and he was proud of her for that. If anything, she looked embarrassed to have wound up a hostage after working so hard to avoid it.

He bore down on his bladder again as it continued to demand his attention and kept his pistol aimed at Charnas. "You picked the wrong hostage, Ed. Me and her are quits—but, even if we weren't, do you really think I'd fold a winning hand over some broad? What about the others? They don't give a shit about her, either. You really didn't think this through too good, did you?"

Charnas' expression betrayed his growing doubt and, as he glanced over at the nervous Paulie and stricken Stephanie, Faolan knew he'd struck a nerve. Keeping up the pressure, he said: "Rothstein doesn't need you around once I'm gone. You're too ambitious to be the boss and he knows it. If I go, you'll be the one Rothstein pins Killian's murder on." Charnas was a lousy poker player. "You didn't think anybody knew about that? Frank helped A.R. design that plan with me in mind, but you'll fit the frame just as easy, Ed. I'll give you one chance: you put those guns down, kill that little fucking weasel Paulie, and do what I tell you. Once Killian and Rothstein are gone, I'll let you run the rackets for me."

Charnas considered for a moment and glanced at Paulie King again. Paulie, wide-eyed and slick with sweat, looked to Charnas for his reaction. Faolan caught Stephanie's eyes and winked, sliding into his killing groove…

Even as Charnas turns back, Faolan can read the rejection in the tensing of Charnas' muscles and the subtle readying of his grip on the shotgun. It doesn't matter, however, because during the exchange his men have relaxed and are watching their leader, Paulie included, so when Stephanie drops limp to the floorboards, it takes Paulie a second to register what's happened.

It's a second too long.

With the slightest shift, Faolan moves his aim and fires, punching a hole through Paulie King's left eye that sprays blood all over the wall behind him. In one smooth motion, he slides the barrel back to Charnas, who is leveling his shotgun.

Faolan's bullet enters Charnas' left cheek and tears apart that side of his face in an exploding shower of blood and bone. Charnas screams and slaps a hand to the side of his face as he collapses backward.

Behind him, Frank fires a burst into the chest of the thug to next to Charnas, knocking him down and causing his Thompson burst to go wild, shattering bottles and mirrors behind the bar. The next goon lets go on full auto and his cut-down BAR jumps up and down in his arms as he tries to simultaneously blanket the VIP area in bullets while looking around for someplace to take cover. Faolan stands still as the bullets strike around him—knowing his chances of being hit by such panic fire are minimal—and fires, hitting the trigger happy goon in the ear. He fires again, misses, and squeezes a third shot that punches through the goon's teeth and out his spine, dropping him. Ignored by everyone, Stephanie crawls into the small alcove where the lobby doors are located. It's a good spot, being out of either group's line of fire. After a moment of hesitation, she ventures back out to snatch Paulie's snub-nosed revolver off the floor before scuttling back against the wall. *Good girl.*

Sudden movement draws his attention to the main stage where the goon there drops to one knee and aims his Thompson at Faolan, pressing the stock into his shoulder.

This one knows what he's about. Faolan jumps backward and ducks around the corner of the coat closet as a barrage of bullets chews up the paneling a heartbeat behind him.

Huston raises his eyes and arms over the half-wall, keeping as much cover as possible, and fires a succession of shots from his gleaming nickel Colts. Spotlights shatter above the stage and the goon with the Thompson gets tagged in the shoulder, then the leg, and once in the chest as he topples. He's not out, but his gun is silenced for a few moments.

Miranda follows her partner's example, firing a matte-black .45 Colt long barrel revolver in a two-handed grip. Her steady aim pays off when the last vamp, busy ripping apart the bar shelves with his BAR, gains a third eye while losing the back of his head in an eruption of gore. He drops face first onto the gleaming hardwood.

Faolan can hear the thugs out in the alley hammering at the metal fire door. He notices bloodstains spreading on Miranda's back where a few of those slugs made it through the wall. He peeks around his corner in time to see Charnas firing from a crouch, half his face hanging in bloody strips that have already stopped bleeding. Faolan pulls back as the shotgun booms, spraying buckshot in a wide arc. The shotgun is a good choice against Vampyrs, since the wide-spread damage of a buckshot wound will disable more of the body and take longer to heal. Pistols are really only good for head shots if you can manage the accuracy. Behind him, Stebbins fires at Charnas while Frank reloads, but his shots strike the large man's vest area.

Beside Charnas, the goon that Frank knocked down gets to his knees and sprays full auto at Miranda and Huston, forcing them back down. Their cover is disappearing rapidly, Faolan sees, and both are taking wounds.

The goon on the stage opens fire again, laying flat to make for a difficult target. Bullets rip through the wall beside Faolan and he ducks as a bullet scorches his right ear. Frank and Stebbins push the large wooden table forward like a shield as they fire, moving up to where Faolan crouches. Frank assesses Faolan's condition for a moment while Stebbins reloads, then leaps over the railing beside him to land beside the bar stools. Recognizing Frank's play, Faolan moves into the vacant spot behind the table and he and Stebbins provide aggressive cover fire—Stebbins' normally pleasant expression replaced by a mask of rage as he spews a litany of choice curses at his torturer.

A few of their bullets hit Charnas and the goon beside him, making Charnas' efforts to pump his shotgun difficult, and the goon's Thompson runs dry. Frank seizes the opportunity, emptying his own BAR into the goon and tearing through the vest like it isn't even there. The guy on stage hits Frank with a burst and Frank drops to his knees. Faolan takes aim at the stage goon, but the goon fires again and the high caliber bullets punch through the tabletop to stab Faolan and Stebbins with lead.

Stebbins falls, clutching his belly and grimacing, while Faolan's wound is a minor graze to his right shoulder. He drops again because Charnas has chambered a new round. With a deafening boom, Faolan feels a dozen pellets hit like bee stings all over his body as the wooden table top disintegrates. In his killing groove, though, it's a distant annoyance, like the pressure of his bladder.

In a sudden giddy impulse, Faolan shouts: "That all you got, Charnas? No wonder my pals ran circles around you!"

Another blast, this one from the fire door, followed by a kick, brings two more of Charnas' men in from the alley. Miranda and Huston prove ready and ventilate the pair before they are able to do anything. Shifting his gaze, Faolan sees the goon on stage reloading. He stands, extends his arm to take aim—the Browning an extension of his hand—and fires a single shot right through the center of the goon's head. *We're in trouble*, he concludes. *Ten guys, Stebbins said. We got Charnas here, two more just came in, so there's three more coming around to the lobby. Frank's down, Stebbins is down, Miranda and Huston are hurt, and I'm almost empty.*

The sound of a shell ejecting brings his attention to Charnas taking aim at him, shotgun braced against his shoulder. As Charnas is about to fire, Frank rushes him. Charnas jerks the barrel over at the last second and fires—

Frank's legs fly out from beneath him as if jerked by a rope and he collapses in a heap.

Faolan brings his pistol to bear at Charnas' head and pulls the trigger.

Click.

Correction: I am empty, he thinks as Charnas pumps his shotgun again with a savage grin. From the lobby, Faolan hears the front doors being flung open and the wind howling from outside. As Charnas levels the shotgun, however, a small caliber pistol barks and blood explodes from the side of Charnas' right leg! *Stephanie, your timing is wonderful!*

Charnas staggers back a few steps, dropping the shotgun, and clutches his wounded leg. Faolan pops out his empty clip, pulls a replacement from his pocket, and slides it into place. Stephanie calls, "Faolan?"

Thinking she might try to come to him and pass the open doorway, he shouts: "Stay put!" He comes down the steps and spots a goon in the lobby aiming a shotgun—he rears back just in time to avoid the blast that flies through the open doorway. To his relief, however, he sees that Stephanie hasn't moved from her position beside the doorway. She's invisible to the goons in the lobby there and should be safe.

Pulling back the slide on his Browning, he fires a few shots into the lobby just to keep those guys from getting too bold. Glancing over to Charnas, he sees a bloody streak leading to the service hall door in back. *Fucking rat-bastard just won't die!*

Huston appears at his side stripped down to his shirt and vest with a shotgun in his hands. Behind him, Miranda totes a new Thompson with a grim anticipation. "Go on after him," Huston says and indicates the lobby with a lift of his chin, "We got this."

"Thanks, Huston."

The Negro smiles, his pointed canines down. "Call me Sandman."

Faolan smiles back, noticing Frank crawling toward one of the downed gunmen to feed, and sprints across the open doorway—ignoring the expected burst of gunfire that greets his appearance—toward the service door. The back service hallway runs from the lobby back to a small lounge behind the main stage with bathrooms, the coat room, and stairs to the basement in between. Most likely, he's headed to the lobby where he can join up with his goons and, if Charnas gets back to Killian before Faolan can, then he and Frank can kiss their plan goodbye.

Faolan pushes open the swinging wooden door with his left, holding the Browning in front of him with the right, and sees the blood trail smearing left toward the lobby as he figured. Stepping into the hallway, the sound of Miranda and Sandman firing at the goons in the lobby draws his attention—

And the cold steel of Charnas' namesake crowbar slams down upon his wrist, shattering the bones as the Browning slips from his numb fingers. Faolan cries out as Charnas steps from behind the door and swings again, cracking ribs with a blow to his midsection. Eyes blurring with tears, Faolan stumbles against the wall as the blurred figure limps after him, raising his arm for another blow. "Been waiting a long time for this!" Charnas growls from between clenched teeth. "You ain't nothing without that gun!"

Calling to mind all those training sessions with Rod, Faolan moves into Charnas' space to make it more difficult to complete his swing and sweeps the bigger vamp's wounded leg. Charnas grunts, dropping to one knee, and Faolan grabs his collar—since his buzz cut doesn't afford a grip—and slams his knee into Charnas' face. As he pulls back for a second strike, however, Charnas slams him on the shoulder with the crowbar—the shoulder that just started to heal—and a burst of pain causes Faolan to stagger away.

One of the greatest advantages Vampyrs have over humans in a fight, aside from their accelerated healing, is the numbing effect that occurs as their bodies heal, which makes Faolan's pain brief. Unfortunately, the same holds true for Charnas, so as Faolan steps away from the wall—his useless right arm still trembling—Crowbar Charnas is also rising back to his feet, still favoring his right leg. He sheds his ruined overcoat with a shrug, revealing the shredded remains of his bulletproof vest. His thick, massive fist holds the small steel crowbar, the left side of his face is a mass of red scar tissue, and his sharpened canines extended as he grinds his teeth. Before he was a Vampyr, Ed Charnas built a career as a strike breaker for whoever was willing to pay him. How many striking workers had their heads bashed in by that crowbar just so some factory owner could keep paying slave wages? *Just another fucking bully—just like Killian.*

"I'm still more without a gun than you'll ever be," he tells Charnas and forces his legs to move. Slowly at first, but then he's bouncing back and forth in rhythm, dancing and grinning. Out on the dance floor, the shooting stops. "Hear that? You're done, Charnas." He summons up the Edward G. Robinson impression that his friends have all begged him to stop attempting: "Yeah, it's coi-tans for you, Eddie! Coi—"

Like a bull faced with a waving red flag, Charnas roars and charges forward with his crowbar held high and Faolan jumps off with his left and kicks high with the right—just like Rod showed him. The tip of his ox-blood wingtip connects just under Charnas' chin and the big brute flips backward, nearly somersaulting in the air, before crashing to the linoleum floor. His balance being off, Faolan stumbles into the wall when he's done, but Charnas is stunned. Cradling his broken wrist, Faolan jogs over and kicks Charnas in the head football-style. "That's for Stephanie!" Then another kick. "And Stebbins!" Then he stomps him, bringing his heel down hard again and again. "And that's for Frank and for my fucking club, you big, dumb fucking gorilla!"

He came out of his killing groove and looked down at the bashed in mess that was Charnas' head. He couldn't tell if Charnas was still breathing or not, but he was out of breath, so he staggered over to where the crowbar had fallen and managed to pick it up with his left hand. "Fucking ruined my shoes, too, you miserable fuck," he muttered as he stabbed the flat end of the crowbar into Charnas' skull as hard as he could manage and left it there, listening until the breathing stopped. He slumped back against the wall. He decided he wasn't going to drink

Charnas. He didn't want any part of that asshole inside him. *Christ, I still gotta piss like a racehorse!*

Luckily, the men's room was only a few steps away.

Chapter Twenty-Eight

"I saved you one," Frank said, pointing to the stage, when Faolan came back into the room. he sat on the steps of the VIP Lounge with one of the drained goons at his feet. "Hurry up, before he gets cold."

"Thanks," he said.

Stebbins sat at a booth with another body, smoking a cigarette, while Miranda and Sandman removed wallets and other identifying material from the bodies. He'd never given it much thought before, being such a common occurrence during the war, but it occurred to him now how creepy it was seeing everyone chowing down on their former comrades like ... well, like animals. *I'm putting a stop to this cannibal shit after tonight*, Faolan decided, aware of the irony that it was this very practice of cannibalism after each battle which had given them the resilience to overcome Charnas and his crew.

When he saw her, his biggest worries vanished. Stephanie stood by a stool at the bar. She finished her cigarette and waited while Faolan made the long walk across the empty dance floor. He stopped a foot away from her unsure of whether he should get closer. Her expression was unreadable.

"Well, uh," he said, glancing around, "I suppose this place is gonna need redecorating again."

She didn't answer, just touched her hair and looked around. She couldn't meet his eyes. "I meant to come and warn you," she said, hesitant, and then the dam broke and the words poured out: "I'm sorry, I-I tried to do, um, what you said, but—and I couldn't think of anything to write while you were away that didn't sound like some 'letter from the girl back home' cliché out of a damn war movie, but I hated the way we left things and I was just so worried you—"

He stepped closer, pulled her to him, and kissed her. Her body relaxed and she closed her eyes and kissed him back, full of fire, and everything stopped being crazy for a little while and just felt right. It was like his killing groove, only stronger, like when he was dancing and losing himself completely in the music and the movement and the rhythm.

He wanted to stay here, like this, forever.

"Hey, Faolan," said a cold, insistent voice. Faolan felt dragged out of heaven. He opened his eyes and could see his frustration reflected in Stephanie's eyes. He looked at Frank, staring at them from a few paces away, and wanted to put a bullet in him.

"The cops will be here soon," Frank warned, looking slightly ridiculous in his shredded suit that showed too much of his legs. "We need to go soon."

"Frank, we own the cops," Faolan said. "They know to take their sweet time when it's The Wolf. Hell, you know that!"

Frank blinked once and continued staring for a few more seconds. "You need to feed," he said, pointing up at the body of the goon still on the stage.

He turned back to Stephanie to apologize, but she slapped him hard across the mouth. Frank took a step forward like he was going to attack, but Faolan waved him away and raised his eyebrows at Stephanie.

"That's for calling me a broad before," she said and broke into a wicked grin.

Faolan smiled, rubbing his cheek. "Oh, you just wait till I get you home."

She laughed. "Go drink your…whatever. You need to get your strength back."

Faolan noticed that Frank continued to watch them. "Go put some pants on, Frankenstein. I think Charnas is near your size." Frank nodded and headed for the service hallway.

"That fella's got a few screws loose," Stephanie observed.

"You should see his house," Faolan said. She gave him a questioning look and he added: "Never mind."

He headed over to the stage to get his drink. It was awkward and this vamp tasted vile. He couldn't remember drinking blood that was this nasty. Still, he choked down as much as he could to replenish what his body burned while healing his injuries. When he finished, everyone stood gathered around the ravaged bar, so he joined them. "Stebbins, what's the story on the rest of the gang? Any other turncoats in the ranks?"

The Irish grifter crushed out his cigarette and shook his head. "Bennett and Martin wouldn't commit. Martin didn't want to be involved at all and Bennett was holding out until he saw how things went in Rhode Island. He'll probably inform on me now that you're back."

"It's the smart move," Faolan said and Frank nodded his agreement. "So, we're in better shape that I thought. Miranda, if you and Sandman can get your Dhampirs over here and pack up these bodies? Stick some Boston licenses in their wallets?"

"I've already called," Sandman said. "They'll be here shortly."

"Great. We might need to show them to Killian to prove our story." He looked at Stebbins. "Is he likely to recognize any of these mugs?"

"Nah," Stebbins said. "Most of these are new boys Charnas Created while you were away."

Faolan nodded. Stephanie touched his arm. "You still think it's smart to go back? Rothstein knows everything Stebbins told Charnas."

"That's why I gotta go," he said. "With Charnas gone, Rothstein's drawing dead. I need to sell Killian my story before Rothstein figures a way to sell him a different one. Right now, his only move is coming onto my team and, much as I don't like the prick, he's got his uses. When all is said and done, I'm gonna need all the help I can get."

"Does that include us, then?" Miranda did her best to hide her anxiety, keeping her hands in her pockets and looking at him with a frank, steady gaze. "After all, we'd not yet come to terms before we were rudely interrupted."

Faolan glanced over at Frank, who shook his head ever so slightly, being of the opinion that Miranda and Sandman shouldn't be included in their long-term plans. "Well," he said, "my first thought was that you two might want positions back in Philly, Sandman being from there originally." The pair exchanged looks: Miranda disappointed, Sandman resigned. They'd expected as much, but it wasn't what they had hoped for.

"On the other hand," he continued, "after seeing you two in action tonight, I can't help but think Miranda would make one hell of a Marshal and you, Mister Huston, might be just the guy to run the rackets for me when Frank moves up to Steward."

That surprised everybody. "You mean ... of New York?" Miranda asked.

Faolan smiled. "Unless you'd prefer Newark."

Miranda smiled her sweet cherub smile and blushed, but Sandman looked as uncertain as Faolan had ever seen him. "Do you really believe that you can make your people take orders from a Negro?"

"No, I don't," Faolan told him, "but I think you can."

Frank said: "Faolan, you know a move like that could lead to a revolt. Put him in charge of Harlem."

"Frank," Faolan said, "what the fuck's the point of all this if we don't shake things up a little? Killian wouldn't have him. Rothstein might give him Harlem. I'm gonna run things my way and any who don't like it can take a hike. So, what do you say, Sandman?"

Sandman grinned and shook Faolan's hand. "I say it would be my honor to accept your offer." Stephanie also shook his hand and congratulated him and Miranda, while Stebbins toasted them with his flask.

"Okay, Stebbins," Faolan said, "give a call over to Rod and Enzo, tell them to bring Saberhagen and meet youse guys over at the Savoy Ballroom in Harlem. Me and Frank will meet you there once we're done with Killian. It's about time we let them know what's going on and why."

"What if Rod and the others don't like what they hear?" Stebbins asked.

Frank shrugged. "We kill them."

Faolan sighed. "No, Frank, we do not kill them." He turned back to the others. "I doubt it'll happen, but if somebody doesn't want to be part of this, then I'll need

Sandman and his Dhampirs to sit on them until it's over. Afterwards, I'll give them the choice to stay or go. See, the whole idea here is to get rid of Killian with as little violence as possible. This city's suffered enough on account of all us vampires and it needs a rest. Which reminds me of something else." He paused, unsure of how to say the next part without giving them the wrong idea. He got out a Camel and lit it to buy some time. After a long, slow, satisfying drag, he exhaled a cloud of purple-gray smoke and said: "Look, we all know this is dangerous, so there's a chance this could go sideways somehow. If that should happen—if Killian or Rothstein kills me for whatever reason—then I'm putting Rod Chambers in charge."

Surprise all around. Frank opened his mouth to object, as did Stephanie, but Faolan put up his hand and continued: "No offense to anybody here, but Rod's got the most heart I've ever seen in a vampire. Plus, he's got plain old-fashioned decency, which this place could use a lot more of. If the plan can be salvaged, then take Killian out and put Rod in. He's old enough and proper enough to make the old-timers comfortable. With all of youse to give him advice and support, he's the best person I can think of to run this city. If that ain't possible, then tell him to cut a deal with Rothstein—"

"What if Rothstein's the one who kills you?" interjected Stephanie.

Faolan nodded. "Even if he blows my brains out himself. Between him and Killian, there ain't no choice, you understand me? Rothstein's a greedy prick, but he ain't a monster like Killian and youse could eventually overthrow him if you had to. He won't have Devlin, so you'll own him." He stopped to take another drag as the rest of them considered.

"But, relax," he said. "Everything's gonna be fine. I ain't going nowhere." Stephanie threw her arms around him in a rare display and laid her head on his shoulder.

"If you were dead, I would be, too," Frank said. "Since I'm going wherever you go."

As usual, there was no emotion in that voice, but Faolan was touched by the sentiment. He smiled at Frank. "Just like a pair of wolf spiders, huh?"

Frank's expression remained blank. "No, like two Vampyrs in a partnership. Spiders don't make very accurate analogies for Vampyrs, Faolan. I gave them up years ago."

"Oh," he said, a little embarrassed that he'd never asked. "What about the bats?"

Frank shrugged. "There's still some hope for the bats."

"Good. Then what's say we go put the bite on Rothstein?"

*****

Rothstein wasn't home. Faolan and Frank were informed that the Steward was in conference with the soon-to-be Reeve and Adjutor Everett in that airplane hanger Killian called his office, so up they went to the 63rd Floor.

Hell's Waiting Room, as Faolan thought of it, was chugging along with its usual efficiency, the night receptionist listening intently to the phone while jotting down a message. The first thing Faolan intended to change when he took over was this ridiculously red room. A little bit of over-kill could be fun and playful, but this was Killian's idea of swank décor and, like everything the would-be Reeve did, it had all the subtlety of a baseball bat to the head.

Shad Newman and Greg Hendee waited on either side the office door: Newman short, dark haired, wiry, and handsome while Hendee stood just over six feet and had fair skin and hair, a thick build, and a face like a roof-top gargoyle. Newman was one of Enzo's vehicle patrol guys, good with a car and sharp, while Hendee was one of Saberhagen's less imaginative street enforcers. Killian made a point of pulling different guys for guard duty each night—and always guys who didn't work together—to make it tougher to arrange something against him.

"Hey, boss," said Newman, looking him over with concern. "You okay?"

Faolan smiled and shook his head, getting in practice. "Found out the hard way that Charnas was the rat."

"No shit? Charnas?" Newman's eyes narrowed in thought. "I can't decide whether I'm more surprised that he was stupid enough to do it or that he found the brains to pull it off so long."

Faolan chuckled along with him, getting out a cigarette and letting Newman light it. Frank turned his head to the reception desk and said: "Hey Blondie, tell His Honor that Mister O'Connor and Mister Giordano are here."

The receptionist had just hung up the phone, but she was used to dealing with Frank. "Yes, sir, Mister Giordano. His Honor gave instructions that you both join him when you arrived."

That caught Faolan's attention, since Killian already having something on his mind could be a good thing or a bad thing as concerned his plan. Hendee stepped toward them, saying, "Mister O'Connor, Mister Giordano, you know the drill."

Faolan handed over his Browning to the big vamp, who thanked him, and Frank handed him the empty BAR. Newman performed quick but professional pat-downs and, finding nothing, gave them a wink and opened the door.

The enormous office looked exactly as it had when Faolan had first been brought here, nearly four years ago: the blood red carpet streaking over an ocean of dark wood and the etched glass panels on either side directing your attention down to the grand cherry desk. The only difference being that Killian wore a severe black three-piece suit with a tie in royal purple, was clean-shaven, and sat behind the desk while Rothstein and Devlin hovered on either side. All watched silently as Faolan and Frank made the long fifty foot walk to the chairs.

He'd hoped to be able to flip Rothstein to his side before dealing with Killian, since this was going to be a much more difficult bluff to sell with Rothstein watching and poking holes in his story. He was all-in, as they said at the poker table, and not just him, but Frank, too. If this play failed, he was done. His only comfort was knowing that he'd given his friends a chance to either finish the job or make a break for it and start fresh in some other city. *Fucking irony*, he thought as they got closer. His whole purpose in taking up this vampire life had been to do things right this time, to stop playing the chump in the name of friendship, to get his due for once, and what did he do? He let himself get sentimental over a city and marched into the lion's den with nothing but a piece of paper and a bluff while his friends sat safe on the sidelines.

Chump.

Killian waited until they reached the back of the guest chairs to speak. "O'Connor, you and your man look like you've seen some action." The old Killian would have been delighted by the prospect of one of Faolan's exploits, but this new, formal Killian studied him with cold disapproval. Rothstein, at Killian's left, gave nothing away. Gray herringbone was tonight's suit, single-breasted with a matching vest and a red bow tie.

Faolan gave them all a big smile and sat down without invitation. "You got that right, boss. I'm sorry for how we look, but I figured you'd want to hear the news immediately." He paused to take a drag off his cigarette as if savoring the moment. He had to play this to the limit if there was any hope of selling it to Killian. As for Rothstein, well, he just had to hope that A.R. realized the spot he was in with Charnas dead and had sense enough to play along.

"So, what's this news?" Killian pressed.

"Well, I went out to round up Charnas and his crew, so I could find out first hand everything what's been happening since I been gone and these sabotages and such," he began, watching Killian for cues without being obvious about watching. "And me and Frank are all over town looking for the sonofabitch, but he ain't in any of his usual haunts, so we go find Stebbins since he always knows what's going on."

He caught Rothstein perk up at the mention of Stebbins, just as he figured. He had to assume that Rothstein had told Killian about Stebbins' confession to Charnas, so the story had to jive with all the facts. Still, Killian seemed to be growing impatient. "So, anyways, Stebbins is twitchy and nervous, but says he don't know nothing. So me and Frank put the question to him again," he said, cracking his knuckles to make the implication obvious, "and he breaks completely. Tells me Charnas put the screws to him over the last few nights, teaching him some bullshit about me working with Boston and a bunch of other malarkey. That ain't the point, though, 'cause he gives up where Charnas is meeting with *his* fucking moles from Boston—right in my own fucking club!" He laughed, getting into the story, with a mixture of amusement and incredulity. "Can you believe the fucking nerve? Still, last place I would've looked, I gotta admit. So, we get a couple of our guys to meet us there and high-tail it over to The Wolf and catch the fuckers all nice and cozy. Being the prick that he is, Charnas makes a fight of it and we make pencils out of the lot of 'em."

He couldn't tell whether Killian was buying it or not, but Faolan was reminded of his triumphant return from Philadelphia. Maybe this was more of Killian's new "act like a Reeve" bullshit and he wanted to hear everything before committing to any kind of reaction. Another possibility was that he was weighing this new version of the story against Rothstein's and trying to decide which to believe.

"So, what I'm trying to tell you is that I found our fucking traitor, Boston's agents are dead, and it also explains how they knew just where to hit." Faolan sat back and took another drag of his Camel.

Killian nodded, sat back in his big leather chair, and glanced at Rothstein. Rothstein betrayed a hint of anxiety that raised Faolan's spirits. "So Ed Charnas was working with Boston and now he's dead and so are Boston's agents? That's what you're telling me?" Killian asked, clasping his hands together and resting them on his belly.

"Show him the letter," Frank prompted.

"Letter?" Killian asked. Again, Faolan got the sense Killian was playing one of his little power games with them. Maybe he was annoyed because he didn't think Faolan was showing him the proper respect and maybe Faolan should have bowed and scraped a little more, but that didn't feel right, either. If he'd started playing toady, wouldn't that have tipped his hand?

"Yeah," Faolan said, reaching into his pocket for the forged letter and pretending not to notice when Devlin tensed ever so slightly. He set the letter on the empty desk surface and slid it toward Killian. "Found this on one the Boston crew when we searched the bodies afterwards."

Did Killian see him as a threat now? Like Byrne before him, had Faolan become a little too successful? A little too popular with the rank-and-file?

Killian picked up the letter, skimmed its contents, and handed it to Rothstein without looking at him. "Where are the bodies?"

Something was definitely wrong. Killian was putting on a show, his gut said, going through the motions. "Still at The Wolf, probably," Faolan told him, playing along. "I called some of my guys to get down there to clean up, but I can have them brought over here if you want."

Killian wouldn't kill them here and risk damaging his beautiful throne room, Faolan knew. But sometime between now and Burlington's visit, Killian would call him to a meeting downstairs in the basement cells, or up in the map room, or somewhere else private enough for an ambush. That's why Rothstein wasn't challenging his story: it didn't matter. He needed to talk to Rothstein before he left, see if he'd help him turn the ambush around on Killian. If they worked together, they could sell Burlington on whatever story suited them best.

"Well, Arnold, what do you have to say about all this?" Killian asked.

Rothstein read the forged letter very carefully before folding it back up and meeting Faolan's eyes. He smiled the same smug, triumphant smile that Faolan had only seen at the poker table when the gambler busted an opponent.

"I would say that Mister Stebbins is a very talented forger, but that Mister O'Connor has over-played a very weak hand."

Faolan's heart pounded, and the sound of his blood rushing through his head was almost deafening. He sighed, maintaining his cool. "Of course Rothstein's gonna say it's fake. Hell, you know he's been keen to get rid of me since you brought me in."

Killian didn't respond for a few moments, but then he nodded. "True enough," he said, smiling. "You say it's genuine, Rothstein says it's fake, and no way to know for sure…" He trailed off and sat back again. Then, almost like an afterthought, he said: "Johnny."

Fuck!

Faolan caught the movement of Devlin's arms and stood, instinctively reaching for the Browning that wasn't there, as the first bullet punched through his gut. The impact was like a strong punch at first, knocking his wind out, but then came the pain like a red hot poker and he fell back into the chair. Beside him, Frank's chest popped open once, twice, three times as the big man staggered two steps toward Rothstein. A fourth shot blew Frank's right knee apart and sent him crashing to the floor.

His belly screaming, Faolan struggled to rise, but another bullet shattered his ribs and collapsed his right lung and sent him tumbling to the carpet as well. The world dimmed, collapsing into a field of red surrounded by creeping darkness. He flopped like a fish on a boat deck as his body tried to remember how to breathe.

A rough kick to his shoulder rolled him onto his back. The field of red was replaced by the sight of Killian looming above him, eyes alight and teeth bared in a savage grin. Then the heel of Darcy Killian's shoe sent him spiraling into oblivion.

Chapter Twenty-Nine

Faolan's muscles all tightened up at once, clenching, as the electricity traveled up and down his body. His every nerve lit up to make itself known. Then the pain: burning at the base of his spine that reached out to pinch and sting everything at once. His teeth locked together as he thrashed and twitched. He couldn't control his body at all, but he could feel every inch of it. Echoing from the walls, he heard a rough, high-pitched whine and it took a few seconds to realize that it was coming from him. He was sure his thumbs were about to tear right off and he couldn't tell whether the idea made him horrified or hopeful.

Then the electricity stopped.

The pain didn't subside immediately, of course, but the twitching, aches, and fading burn were worlds better. His naked body trembled and he couldn't tell if he wept or if his eyes watered from the pain. His thumbs—tied with heavy piano wire and supporting his entire body's weight—throbbed in agony that spread to the rest of his hands. He thought he smelled blood and wouldn't have been surprised to realize that his thrashing had either cut his thumbs down to the bone or dislocated them entirely.

"You've lied to me quite enough, don't you think, O'Connor?" asked Killian. He leaned against the battered desk that was the basement cell's only furnishing. Faolan wasn't certain whether this was the same cell he'd awoken in on his first night here, but if not, it was identical. He'd woken tonight naked and hanging by his thumbs, just far enough off the ground that he had to stretch his feet to touch the concrete floor with his big toe. He'd thought the several hours' wait had been agonizing, but that was before Devlin had started in with the cattle prod after he'd claimed ignorance of any deception.

Killian had decided that royal purple suited him and had chosen it again to accent his dark gray chalk-stripe suit. From the inside pocket of the suit, he withdrew the letter Faolan had given him. "As testament to his goodwill, Reeve Edward Moore of Boston had a courier hand-deliver a letter to the building last night. Along with his congratulations on my impending Reeveship, he included a description of how a certain Faolan O'Connor and Frank Giordano of New York came to meet with him last month and offered to assassinate me in return for his support in taking control of the city. He says he refused, of course, which I don't believe for a second, but his description of you and Giordano are dead fucking accurate. Not to mention that his letter even had a wax seal on it with his personal goddamn crest, something that your little forgery here lacks!" He flung the letter at Faolan, but it only reached halfway before spinning to the ground.

That fucking asshole, Faolan thought. It never occurred to him that Moore would rat him out to Killian, or that Killian would believe him if he did, which was just plain sloppy on his part. He should have seen that possibility. Hell, he and Frank should have killed Moore and his skeleton bodyguard right there on that fucking boat. They might have been able to shoot out the windows, dive into the ocean, and swim the mile to shore without being gunned down ... sure, piece of cake.

Hearing about Moore's betrayal made him angry and angry was good. He could hold onto anger, use it drive out the fear and the pain, and pour it into defiance. Growing up in his neighborhood, there had always been plenty to be angry about and plenty of ways to use that anger as fuel.

"He's a fucking liar," Faolan wheezed. Hanging as he was put an awful strain on his shoulders and chest: he found he couldn't draw more than a shallow breath. That pissed him off more. "He lost the war..." he had to keep stopping for breath, "but he's trying to get you to...take out all your best guys for him...so's he can take you out later."

Killian raised his eyebrows and folded his arms. "That so? Then, why, pray-tell, did all your Bailiffs and Squires that you been friendly with suddenly take a powder?"

Maybe he could sell this bluff, after all. He forced a strained smile and made a show of being relieved. "Jesus, they're just panicking! We was supposed to meet up to plan the welcome home party...then they hear about you shooting me and Frank..." He struggled to take the deepest breath he could, wincing at the sharp stabbing pain in his guts where the bullet wound had closed but not fully healed. "Well, you gotta understand how they might be worried."

Killian sat on the edge of the desk and studied him for a moment, then chuckled and Faolan felt a bright spark of hope. "Hit him in the balls, Johnny," Killian ordered.

"*No!*" Faolan shouted, kicking on instinct, but Devlin stuck the cattle prod between his legs from behind. Faolan felt the metal prongs touch the back of his sack a split second before blinding agony surged through him. It only lasted a few seconds, but those seconds felt like hours as he kicked and shook and squealed.

His mind fuzzy with pain, eyes blurred with tears, he saw Killian move closer and felt the fist slam into his jaw, but it was a distant sensation. As sounds returned, he heard Killian shouting. The large Vampyr's face was inches from his own, the eyes wide and furious. The carefully built veneer of gentility had been dropped to let the savage within roar for a bit.

"...always such a smooth fucking talker, you were! You always thought me a fool for your little games, always playing the loyal man and throwing suspicion on everyone near and sundry while you played Judas for Boston!" Two more punches crashed into his ribs and Faolan felt at least one crack or break completely. Killian wrapped his large hands around his neck and began to squeeze, his thumbs pressing Faolan's windpipe closed while locking eyes.

"You think yourself so cunning," Killian hissed between his clenched teeth. "But Moore also revealed that his primary agents in New York were none other than that dyke Miranda that you claimed disposal of and some Philadelphia nigger by the name of Huston! So I'm of a mind that you've been a turncoat from the first!"

Faolan's vision dimmed and his thoughts became sluggish. There were so many agonies for his body to choose from they began to blend into a single, all-consuming pain.

"Admit it, you traitorous fuck!" Killian shouted, his voice echoing down a tunnel. "Spill!"

"Uh, boss," the deep twang of Devlin's voice seemed to come from another world. "He can't rightly answer while you're choking him out."

Faolan felt the pressure at his neck release and, very gradually, the darkness receded and the world returned.

"Well?" Killian demanded.

Faolan tried to speak and triggered a coughing fit instead. Even coughing was a fucking root canal in his current shape. When it subsided, he swallowed and whispered under his breath, the words so soft that Killian had to lean in close to hear.

So Faolan lunged forward and bit Killian's ear, clenching it between his teeth for dear life and wrenching his head from side to side as far as his circumstances would allow. Killian howled, grabbing at his head, while Devlin yanked Faolan's head back by the hair and pried at his jaw with the other hand. Faolan felt Killian's thumbs searching for his eyes and bit down harder, but the pressure of Devlin's hands proved too strong and his jaw inched open enough for Killian to pull his bloody ear free.

Clutching the mangled ear with one hand, Killian disappeared behind Faolan for a moment before reappearing with the cattle prod. "Open his fucking jaws!" he shouted. Faolan fought, but Devlin's grip was too strong, and Killian jammed the cattle prod into his mouth. Devlin pulled his hands away just in time as Faolan's world exploded in pain.

*****

"O'Connor's out of the game," said Arnold Rothstein as soon as he closed the door, "but Killian just took Devlin downstairs to question him. We have to assume he's gonna blab."

Seated behind his orderly, modest desk, Killian's Dhampir Adjutor Nathaniel Everett leaned back in his chair and grabbed an orange from the bowl of them on his desk. "Does Mister O'Connor know anything that could compromise our plan?"

Arnold ignored the guest chair and walked to the window behind Everett where he could look down upon Dhampir. It was part of the game they played whenever they met in secret: Everett flaunting his insubordination and Arnold forced to overlook it while attempting to subtly re-establish dominance. It would have been intolerable if Everett wasn't careful to play his proper role in public.

"O'Connor knows about my old plan with Frank," he said. "But he's imaginative and seems to be capable of selling ice to Eskimos, as you well know. I'm not worried about what he knows. I'm worried about what he can make up! I'm worried what Killian might be fool enough to believe." He looked down at Everett as the bearded man peeled his orange with the rough sailor's hands that belied his tailored blue suit. The Dhampir appeared unconcerned, as always, so Arnold looked out the window as he waited.

Unfortunately, he needed Everett far more than the Dhampir needed him.

He could kill Everett, of course, but that was his only move and even that might backfire. When Arnold had first confronted the Dhampir last year about the discreet meetings Everett had been having with an unidentified individual, he felt certain that he had Everett by the balls. Instead, the Dhampir had revealed his own knowledge of Rothstein's schemes and ambitions and made him a counter-offer: he would provide Arnold with a channel to Governor Burlington himself and broker a deal to make Arnold the Reeve of New York City.

Of course, Arnold could have immediately reported Everett's offer to Killian along with the proof he'd found of the Dhampir's secret meetings and walked away clean. Killian would have had Everett tortured, learned the extent of his betrayal, and then killed him. But that would have meant continuing his gamble that the unpredictable O'Connor would do his part, and then successfully maneuvering through all the fallout of both Killian and O'Connor's deaths. He'd let that bet ride too long already, however, and gotten very little payout to show for it. Everett, on the other hand, had seemed a good horse to back: he was the one who'd provided most of Arnold's information on The Order, the one who'd found and made arrangements for his blood chef, and the only one who seemed exempt from Killian's periodic suspicions, despite being a hold-over from Vandergriff's regime. Clearly, he knew what he was doing.

So Arnold had accepted Everett's offer and they'd become partners.

Since then, he'd realized how lopsided a partnership it really was. Everett had all the connections and only gave Arnold the information that he thought necessary, an arrangement which Arnold despised but was powerless to change. Worse still was the knowledge that, once he'd achieved his position, he could count on Everett's subtle hand guiding his decisions. With Charnas and his men dead, Arnold no longer had a strong arm to protect him from whoever Everett represented in the event that he tried to eliminate the Dhampir.

During the first month of their partnership, Arnold asked Everett flat-out why he'd made him the offer. Why not just stick with Killian or back someone more popular, like O'Connor? Everett's answer: "You're a sensible fellow, Arnold: practical, orderly, and not overly-ambitious. For all his efforts at conformity, Killian's stirred up too much bad blood, so to speak, and O'Connor's too brash."

In other words, they figure they can control me. Whoever they are, Arnold thought, but kept that to himself.

Everett popped a slice of orange into his mouth, then sucked the juice from his fingers. "Killian already suspects you, but he has no proof," the Dhampir said with a wistful smile. "Nothing O'Connor can say will change that. He has to choose a new Marshal from among a group of strangers who may very well still be loyal to Faolan O'Connor. He'll need your advice for that appointment. Then he has to prepare for his meeting with the Governor and Reeve Moore, which also requires your assistance. He needs you too much to even think about killing you until after he's Reeve."

Arnold frowned. "And Burlington's given his word about that?"

Everett popped another orange slice into his mouth. "Once the peace accord is signed and Killian officially surrenders New York back to the Governor, he'll be placed under arrest. You just need to step forward as a witness to Killian's cannibalism when the Governor asks. Also, make sure that whatever men Killian brings with him know to follow your lead. Anyone who tries to aid Killian will be executed along with him."

"We can only hope that Devlin tries something."

Everett shook his head. "Devlin's been paid to guard Killian, not to die for him. He won't be a problem."

Arnold turned away from the window and glanced around the modest office—well, modest by the standards of the building—the office would be worthy of any corporate executive, though the decoration leaned heavily toward the nautical. Old sea charts in frames, ships in bottles, and charcoal sketches of animals and ports from all over the world advertised Everett's time as a sea-farer. Again, it occurred to him to ask the man whether he'd been in the Navy or a civilian sailor, but Arnold honestly didn't care. He pulled his handkerchief from his pocket and dabbed at the sweat on his forehead and neck.

"We'll both die if this fails, you know," he muttered. "And your cavalier attitude is not reassuring me."

Nathaniel Everett shrugged, swallowing another orange slice. "I'm not cavalier, Arnold, I'm just jaded. I've lived under the threat of torture and death for decades now. I suppose I've grown accustomed to it."

Arnold sighed. "Well, I'd better get back to interviewing O'Connor's men so I've got some recommendations to make when Killian asks for them."

Everett nodded. "Good man."

There's got to be somebody in that crowd I can buy now that O'Connor's gone, he thought as he left the Adjutor's office. *And then it will be time for you to have a little accident, partner.* He passed the new receptionist without a glance, a satisfied smile creeping onto his face. *Once I'm officially the Reeve, the money and the blood are all mine to distribute. That's all these goons care about.* No more Killian belittling him, no more O'Connor smarting off to him: it would be just like it had been back when he'd been mortal. No, it would be better. The rest of The Order would know that it had been his brains behind the World's Fair. They would see what he had to offer and welcome it. They would change it, for sure, and they would make it serve their purposes, but that didn't matter. He wasn't an egotist like Killian, high on his own grand fantasies. Arnold knew you had to go along to get along.

All he wanted was the respect he was due.

Chapter Thirty

He slept, he woke, Killian barked questions at him, and then he suffered. More questions. As agonizing as it was to keep silent, however, Faolan had decided that silence was his only hope. Thinking about the pain to come was the worst, so he did his best to avoid it. When Killian questioned him, he concentrated on counting the seconds to himself: *one-hippopotamus, two-hippopotamus, three-hippopotamus…*

The first advantage he had was that, being a Vampyr, the agony didn't last the way it would have if he'd been human. After a few minutes would come the numbing stage of the healing process. Killian knew it too, though, so as soon as Faolan started to feel the relief kick in, Killian would put the screws to him again. Having grown bored with the cattle prod, Killian tried out some of the classics: he had Devlin rip out his finger- and toe-nails with pliers, break his fingers and toes, and burn him with cigars.

His second advantage was that Killian was a lousy interrogator. He had a plenty strong stomach for torture, to be sure, but he had no patience. If something didn't work the first or second time, he got fed up and moved onto something new. Honestly, if he'd kept up with the cattle prod he probably would have broken Faolan, but he lost his temper too easily. After a few rounds of questions, he'd blow his stack and beat Faolan with whatever was handy until he either knocked Faolan out or exhausted himself or both. Killian's paranoia was getting the better of him, Faolan could tell by the questions and the desperation behind them. Had Faolan met with Burlington? Was the peace meeting a trap? What had Faolan told Moore? What had he told Burlington? Was Rothstein in on his scheme?

Faolan smiled whenever he could manage, because that really steamed Killian, but he kept his lips sealed. He was no fucking rat.

Faolan's last bit of luck stemmed from the fact that Killian didn't turn his torture over to Devlin. From the few times that Faolan had watched Devlin work on captured enemy agents, Faolan knew that the cowboy was a ruthless and methodical monster. Whether from some kind of pride or a remnant of his inexplicable fondness for Faolan, Devlin also didn't offer to take over, for which Faolan was grateful.

The hours blurred into each other and Faolan kept his mouth shut. Far too tempting to keep talking once he started, so he made himself forget that he could talk at all. Whatever Killian asked and no matter how bad the pain got, Faolan thought of Stephanie and Rod and Enzo and the others who were counting on him. Killian tried to lie once and claim that he'd caught his friends and was questioning them as well, but Faolan hadn't been fooled. When Killian told him that he'd broken Frank and gotten the full story from him, Faolan laughed in his face. It was a rough, hideous cackle, but still enough to make Killian smash his teeth in with a hammer.

If Killian had been smart, he would have just let him hang there with a bowl of blood on the table. The damage was adding up and Faolan could feel his body eating itself for energy, which produced a hunger the likes of which he had never known. The numbness didn't touch the hunger, which burned like a lump of red hot coal in his belly and reached out into every vein in his body. His throat was raw with thirst, his tongue sandpaper, and it would only get worse as he dehydrated. Time would do Killian's work for him, if he let it. All Faolan could do was hope he could goad Killian into killing him before he reached his breaking point.

He knew his friends weren't coming to save him.

He didn't expect them to try, didn't want them to try: it would just get them killed. If they played it smart, they could still get rid of Killian. New York would continue on more or less as it always had. It wasn't everything he wanted, but it was enough.

A hard slap across his face pulled him back to the here and now, whether he wanted to be there or not. He felt nothing but a dull tingling in most of his body now, which told him that some time had passed since Killian had burned his armpits with a gasoline blow torch. It was still the third night, which Faolan could tell by the clothes Killian wore: tonight was a dark green pinstripe and yellow tie. The jacket had been removed hours ago and laid carefully on the desktop, so Killian faced him in his rolled up shirtsleeves and vest. "You're a stubborn little prick, O'Connor, I won't deny you that. You and Giordano both. After all I done for you these years—raised you up from nothing like you was my very own son, gave you good employ and a place of honor among my hierarchy—after all that, that you can betray me so cravenly puzzles me in the extreme! Why, Faolan? Tell me that much, at least."

Go sell that shit to somebody who might buy it, Faolan thought. *Everything you gave me, I earned ten times over! You'd never understand even if I could explain it. New York deserves better than you. The fellas in the gang deserve better.* Faolan had known plenty of lowlifes in his time, but even the worst had been human. They wanted money, respect, excitement, control of their lives, comfort, or pleasure: maybe not noble goals, but goals he could understand. Killian scared him because the more he saw of him, the less he understood. Darcy Killian just wanted *more*: more power, more money, more control, and more obedience, like a giant beast with an endless appetite.

Faolan tried to swallow, but he was bone dry, so he breathed in as much air as he could, stretched his cracked lips, and forced out the words: *"Fuck! You!"*

Killian's upper lip twitched and his eyes narrowed, but he contained his explosion this time. "You got balls, for sure," he growled. He turned back to the table and picked up the blow torch. The flame was low, but still visible, and Killian turned the valve to increase the spray until the gout of orange flame extended almost a foot from the nozzle.

"Since neither you nor The Ghoul feel like making confession and it seems your pals have scurried off, I've had to change my plan. You'll be happy to know that I'll be making use of your invitation to Davidson in Philadelphia. His men will be put to good use when Moore's forces attack our peace meeting." He turned back to Faolan and approached with the blow torch aimed at groin level. Faolan tried to kick, but his legs were lead and the heat increased.

"Sadly," Killian continued, "the Governor and Moore himself won't survive, but I'll be sure to tell the rest of The Order how bravely they fought to defend Governor Burlington from Moore's treachery. You, however, will barely rate mention as Moore's accomplice."

Faolan smelled the singeing of his pubic hair as a wave of pain roared up from between his legs. He shrieked, twisting and wrenching, but unable to escape. Killian moved the torch away, smiling his gruesome grin, and waited for Faolan's screams to become sobs and pants before speaking. "I want you to die knowing that you've accomplished nothing. That nothing you've done here will ever matter to anybody. You'll go to your death unrecognizable as a man, and it'll be a slow death fit for a traitor."

The fire returned and everything disappeared in wave of red hot agony.

*****

Three nights O'Connor had lasted! Three nights!

Arnold shook his head as the elevator descended. He'd been very careful not to appear too interested in O'Connor's interrogation, but it had been easy to see that Killian hadn't gotten the answers he wanted yet. Arnold hadn't been able to speak to Killian directly since this started and things were beginning to get uncomfortable. The men were starting to ask questions and Arnold didn't have answers for them. Sure, he knew what he thought should be done, but giving those orders without consulting Killian was a sure way to enrage the volatile Vampyr. Let the men question Killian's priorities and wonder what was going on, he figured: the more confusion this week, the better. Meanwhile, Arnold made his arrangements behind the scenes.

To his surprise, Giovanni "Joe" Bennett had solved his dilemma of who to suggest for Marshal. The calculating Sicilian was a proven earner who he'd known largely by reputation, but both Frank and Charnas had spoken well of him. When Arnold had met with the Squire to put the feelers out, it was clear that he had no loyalty to O'Connor. *"Mister Rothstein,"* he'd said, *"I ain't a complicated guy. I got no interest in getting killed in some fucking power play now that I finally got a shot at living forever. That's percisely why I strung that jerk-off Charnas along like I did, may he rest in peace. On the other hand, if you was to make me an honest offer for promotion, then I can tell you that I'd take my new responsibilities to heart and without regard for any prior loyalties."*

The rest of the conversation had proven equally satisfactory. Bennett was clever without being a smart-aleck, respectful without being a suck-up. He knew how to conduct business, and had enough seniority in the organization for his appointment not to raise many eyebrows. Arnold had found his man.

The elevator doors opened and Arnold stepped out into the basement corridor where the faint sound of screams led him to the electrical closet that hid O'Connor's cell. He'd been hearing rumors that members of the building's maintenance staff believed the basement to be haunted because of the strange noises heard over the years whose source couldn't be found.

Arnold was not amused.

He thought these basement cells were ludicrous, truth be told, and planned to have them eliminated when he took over. Too risky to keep something so potentially explosive in the same building where they slept every day. If it were to be discovered by someone they didn't control? Oh, the publicity! He planned to eliminate the barracks floors as well, but that had more to do with the value of New York real estate. Why waste two prime floors that could be generating revenue just to house muscle when a rooming house would do?

Once inside the electrical closet, he closed the door. The light was already on. At five o'clock in the morning, there was too much chance of someone coming down here to risk leaving the door open. Not to mention that O'Connor's screams would carry much further. The false panel with the wiring had also been left open to reveal the cell door. In the telephone closet next door, an identical setup held Frank Giordano. Frank had been even less responsive to Killian's questions than O'Connor, so Killian had given up on him for now. Arnold had an idea about what would break Giordano's silence, but since he didn't want either man talking, he kept his suspicions to himself.

He slid open the prison-style viewing slot and saw Killian burning O'Connor's privates with a blow torch while O'Connor writhed and shrieked. He snapped shut the slide and tried unsuccessfully to drive the image from his mind as he shivered in revulsion. As disagreeable as he found O'Connor, he couldn't honestly say that anyone deserved that kind of suffering. Arnold had always been a practical man and felt no qualms about having an enemy eliminated, but Killian's gleeful sadism was a sickness, plain and simple.

A moment later, the screaming stopped and Arnold overcame his reluctance and opened the slide again. If O'Connor was ever gonna talk, then this would be the time.

"Looks like he's passed clean out," said Devlin as Killian turned off the blow torch and set it down. Killian said nothing as he unrolled his shirt sleeves and attached his emerald cufflinks—a Christmas gift from Arnold along with the matching tie pin. "It's getting pretty close to sun-up," Devlin added, wincing at the sight of O'Connor's charred genitals. The stench of burned flesh made Arnold gag, but didn't seem to bother either of these two. "Figure we best head back upstairs."

At that, Killian turned, his entire manner signaling his fury. "Oh, you figure, do you?"

Devlin didn't respond but met Killian's glare evenly. Arnold wished that one of their tempers would give, but it was just too much to hope that they'd kill each other. Finally, Devlin said: "Just making an observation."

Killian wasn't in a mood to let it be, however. "Well, you keep your fucking observations to yourself until I ask for them, follow?"

"I follow," Devlin replied in a tone so devoid of inflection, it stood the hairs up on the back of Arnold's neck.

"I fucking hope so," Killian warned, putting on his jacket. "Now, go take this sack of shit to my office and set him up with a view. Make sure you ain't seen."

Devlin got to work cutting O'Connor down as Killian looked toward the door. "That you, Arnold?"

Arnold took a deep breath through his mouth and opened the unlocked door. "Yes, Your Honor. I came to let you know that the Democracity inside the Perisphere has been set up and is fully operational. The whole theme center area has been cleared of snow and decorated up through Constitution Mall to the Court of Peace. The building interiors aren't finished yet, of course, but the exteriors are done. I've pushed to get the New York City Building finished inside and out, however, so we could take the Governor through there if he wants."

Killian nodded while Devlin slung O'Connor's body over his shoulder and carried him out into the corridor after checking both directions. "We had any further word from Burlington?"

Arnold nodded. "The Governor's party will arrive at Grand Central on Friday night at eight o'clock. We're to meet him with no more than five Vampyrs, ourselves included, all unarmed. I understand that Governor Burlington has a passion for architecture and he's mentioned that he's very excited to see the fairgrounds, so you may want to suggest going out to Flushing first thing."

Killian considered and smiled. "I believe we shall give them all the tour first."

"What do you mean 'all'?"

"You see to it that Moore and his entourage arrive at Grand Central by eight. You're gonna meet them and bring them 'round to meet me and the Governor."

This was not the plan they had taken pains to arrange, and Arnold's suspicions rose. "But, Your Honor, we specifically arranged to bring Moore in later so you'd have private time with Burlington before the peace talks." *What the hell is he planning?*

"Well, I'm changing the fucking plan, then, ain't I?" Killian barked. "Tell them we're taking a tour of the fairgrounds first, so we want everyone together."

"All right, I'll handle it," Arnold promised. "Are we still taking them on the train to show off the new station?"

"No, we'll take limousines up."

Arnold sighed. "Fine. I'll have to get a parking area cleared—"

"No, I'll have it seen to," Killian interrupted. "You just handle the arrangements for the reception and leave the tour to me."

That tore it. "What? I've been handling the Fair since we started! I gathered the investors, arranged the corporate sponsors, even found the location! Why—"

Killian grabbed his throat with one of those thick, rough hands and leaned into him. "You getting uppity on me, too, you goddamned little Christ-killer? *Why* is because I fucking well told you so! Don't ever go thinking yourself the master here, you conniving shit, and don't go thinking yourself indispensable, neither! That Fair is *my* vision made solid! My work, my passion, and *my future! Is that fucking understood?*"

Arnold's vision faded, he tried to nod, but couldn't move his head. "Yes," he hissed, "I'm...sorry..."

Killian shoved him away and leveled a warning finger at him. "You'd better be. I've had my fill of men who don't know their proper place. So what's yours?"

Leaning against the cell wall, Arnold rubbed his throat and swallowed. Hating the taste of the words in his mouth, he also knew they were only words: "Behind you."

"Good." Straightening, Darcy Killian adjusted his cuffs and walked out of the cell, calling back: "Make sure and lock up when you leave."

Arnold Rothstein glared at the empty doorway as he caught his breath. Being a pragmatist and a practical man, he didn't waste his energy on hating his enemies. However, he couldn't deny that he would take great satisfaction from watching Killian die.

Killian suspected him. That much was clear. His paranoia had grown to epic proportions and now he had something up his sleeve for the meeting. Arnold hoped Killian would confide something to Everett so they could be prepared, but first he decided to see if Killian had let something slip in Frank's presence. Arnold stepped back into the electrical closet, closed up the false panel, and exited into the corridor. As he locked the door with his key, a colored maintenance man came around the corner and Arnold straightened. *I was down here looking for some wood polish if he asks—front desk gave me the key.* Should that story not hold, he would have to try mesmerizing the man to forget he was ever here…but perhaps it would be simpler just to slip him a five dollar bill.

The maintenance man passed him by with only a cursory nod, however, and continued to the next intersection where he turned. Arnold let go of the breath he'd been holding and moved to the telephone closet, unlocked it, stepped inside, and closed the door behind him before switching on the light. It was set up just like next door except with telephone wires and cabling, but the sliding panel was in the same place and he soon had the viewing slide open.

Frank Giordano dangled naked from the ceiling by thumbs cut to the bone by heavy piano wire, but had no other visible injuries.

"Frank!" Rothstein called. Frank's head twitched at the sound, but he didn't answer. "Frank, what sorts of questions has Killian been asking you? What's he planning? Please, Frank, I can maybe get you out of here if you give me something useful! I'll work something out and blame it on Boston—"

"F-Faolan..." Frank huffed, his voice dry and rough.

Arnold had figured as much. O'Connor was The Ghoul's weakness now. "Sure, Frank, I'll get Faolan out, too, but you've got to give me—"

The knob to the telephone closet turned. *Shit!* Arnold threw the slide panel back in place and turned to find himself eyeing the barrel of a Colt automatic. Taking a step back, he recognized the colored maintenance man from before.

"What's the big idea?" he demanded. After his encounter with Killian, it would take more than some punk with a gun to scare him.

"Step back inside the closet, please," the Negro said with an articulation and confidence that belied his uniform. Now, from his understanding of Vampyr healing, he didn't think that a single gunshot would kill him. However, Arnold had only been shot once in his life and that experience had been painful enough to make him wary of repeating it, regardless of whether or not he'd survive. He stepped sideways into the depths of the closet and the Negro followed, never taking his eyes off of him.

When Stebbins appeared in the doorway behind the Negro, however, what little fear inside Arnold transformed into irritation. "Stebbins," he said, "I thought you had been smart enough to skip town."

Stebbins opened his mouth to respond when his attention was caught by something in the corridor. The diminutive grifter pulled a badge from his coat pocket and seemed to increase in size as he flashed it. "Police business," he growled in a surprisingly good Bronx dialect totally unlike his normal voice. "Get lost."

He remained in the corridor while the Irish woman Matheson—dressed like a man in a double breasted suit and wide-brimmed fedora with cropped hair to complete the effect—stepped inside behind the Negro that Arnold assumed was "Sandman" Huston.

Matheson slid open the false panel and peered inside the slot. "Frank, it's Miranda!"

Huston held out his unarmed hand. "The key, if you please sir?"

Arnold sighed. "I don't have it." He held up his hand to forestall the inevitable threats. "Ask yourself: would I stand out here shouting through a view slot if I could just walk in there? Killian doesn't trust anyone but himself with the cell key."

Huston considered for a moment and glanced back at his female partner. Matheson walked back out and motioned Stebbins inside. Stebbins tossed her the badge and stepped inside, pulling a set of lock-picks from his pocket.

"Where can we find Mister O'Connor?" Huston asked.

Despite the circumstances, Arnold couldn't help a bitter smile at the irony. "You know, Mister Huston, your timing is the pits. Killian took O'Connor up to his office for some sun bathing not ten minutes ago. If you'd only arrived a little sooner, you could have saved us all a lot of bother."

Stebbins opened the cell door and he and Matheson went into the cell. Huston thumbed back the hammer on his nickel-plated Colt. "Now, you do not want to lie about something like that, Mister Rothstein."

Arnold met his eyes, bold and confident as he sensed an opportunity. "He's gone. Killian tore him apart for three nights, but I'll say this for him: he didn't squeal." He pulled the key-ring from his pocket and held up the closet key for Huston's inspection. "Next door over, it's the same setup. The cell's empty, but you can still smell the stench from where Killian burned him up." He watched his words strike home as Huston flinched, but kept the key up for effect. "I'm prepared to match whatever offer O'Connor made you. You two are talented and I'd be happy to have you in my organization."

A wail from inside the cell stopped Huston from responding, but Arnold could see the other man considering his options. Matheson and Stebbins appeared carrying Frank between them. "You hear what he said?" Huston asked.

Matheson nodded. Frank raised his head with effort. Dehydration and blood loss had taken their toll and Frank's face looked like Karloff from that Mummy picture. He stared daggers at Arnold. "Faolan's...not dead...yet," he croaked. "Takes hours...get his key."

"What do you mean, Frank?" asked Stebbins, pulling out his hip flask and pouring some water into Frank's mouth.

"...elevator..." Frank muttered, his head dropping again.

"My elevator key?" Arnold asked, unable to believe what he was hearing. "It's practically dawn! You'll all be unconscious for the day before you could hope to get out of the building, but that doesn't even matter because you'd never make it off the floor! Ask Stebbins if you don't believe me. Huston, I'm making you the best offer you're going to get going forward. I'll even grant amnesty for any of O'Connor's people who want to come back, so long as they'll follow me."

Stebbins glanced at his friends. "Perhaps we should consider it...at least bring it to Rod. I mean, Faolan himself told—"

"No!" Frank shouted, jerking around while Matheson and Stebbins struggled to hold him. "Kill him! We don't need him! Just get the key!"

"Wait!" Matheson said. "I've got an idea, now just hush, Frank! Get the key."

Huston nodded, held out his hand again, and Arnold pulled the executive elevator key from his vest pocket. He still felt confident that he'd be hearing from them or Rod Chambers later tonight, once the reality of O'Connor's death had time to sink in. He handed the key to Huston. "I'll have to ask you to step into the cell now."

Arnold Rothstein sighed and walked into the cell while they dragged Frank into the corridor where Stebbins drew a pair of pajama bottoms and handcuffs from his coat. *They'll march Giordano right out the front door in handcuffs and no one will be the wiser.* He let himself be consoled by thoughts of his eventual success as the cell door slammed shut on him. The surface of the cell's desk was cleaner than any part of the floor, so he sat down there and leaned against the wall to await the rest that sunrise would bring. He might as well tell Killian the truth about what occurred, since there was no other explanation that would serve his purposes. He just hoped his absence was noticed quickly tonight.

*****

Faolan was aware of moving, his head and arms hanging down and swaying as someone carried him. He smelled old leather with a strong tobacco smell that had seeped into it. He heard mechanical sounds that might have been an elevator. His entire body tingled with pins and needles and the hunger continued to burn. The smell of his own burned flesh clogged his nostrils.

He lost consciousness again as a wave of dizziness took him under.

When he woke again he was seated and the first sight to greet him was of his own ruined crotch: red and black, cracked and weeping blood. His gut lurched and he would have vomited if he'd been capable. His head jerked back, away from the sight, and that brought on another wave of dizziness. He held himself still for a few seconds until it passed. *One-hippopotamus, two-hippopotamus, three-hippopotamus...*

He felt pressure on his arms and legs, heard movement, and opened his eyes again. A blurry black figure secured his ankle to the leg of his chair. his wrists and other ankle had already been tied. *Devlin.*

Ahead of him lay the beautiful, unobstructed view he recognized from Killian's office. It was still night, but on the very edge of the horizon, he could see the sky lighten to dark blue. "This is where you die, O'Connor," said Killian, somewhere behind him. "An object lesson for the rest. Take a nice, long look at everything you'll never have. C'mon, Devlin, let's leave this schemer to his thoughts."

Devlin rose to one knee and considered him with those cold green eyes and a rueful smile. The gunman pressed something into Faolan's palm, and as he closed his hand around it, Faolan recognized his St. Patrick's medallion. "Sorry, son," Devlin said, speaking just loud enough for Faolan to hear. "I was half rooting for you, myself."

"Devlin!" came Killian's shout from his suite next door.

Devlin stood and walked away. The door to Killian's suite closed and locked. Faolan held it as long as he could, but after a few moments, his body began to tremble and shake and that hurt worse than letting it out.

Faolan laughed.

It was little more than a weak chuckle and would have sounded more like sobbing or hiccups to anyone else, but it was as much as his mutilated body could manage. *That fucking moron*, he thought as tears spilled down his cheeks. *Thinks he's punishing me, but he couldn't have given me a nicer going away present!*

He forced himself to stay awake as the sky lightened and the sun slowly made its appearance behind the Manhattan skyline. He clutched the medallion his Ma had given him tight. His city was beautiful from up here and seeing it in all its morning glory was worth the stinging pain. Faolan O'Connor sat, watching the sunrise and weeping, until the sight burned from his eyes and darkness overwhelmed him.

Chapter Thirty-One

"Faolan? Are you awake, honey?"

He tried to open his eyes, but the brightness was too much and he turned his head to the side. He noticed that it smelled different than the cell or Killian's office: a musty, damp odor, mildew, old sour sweat, blood, bleach, and urine. He heard movement as the floor creaked under the footsteps of several people.

Hang on, I ought to be dead...

"Faolan, can you hear me?" That was Frank's voice.

More movement and several voices he recognized: "Is he up?" "What's happening?" "Did he open his eyes?" "Keep back, would you? Let him breathe." That last was Stephanie.

He cracked open his eyelids again and could make out shapes after a few seconds. He blinked a few times and eased them open a little more until he could see Stephanie's face only a few inches from his own. He smiled and tried to greet her, but his mouth was a desert.

She beamed at him, a tear spilling down her cheek, and took a glass of water from the bedside table. He reached out to take it from her and couldn't believe how shaky his hands were as he cradled the cool glass, bringing it gingerly to his lips to sip from it. After a couple of painful swallows, he handed it back to her and tried again. "Where?" he rasped.

"We're in Brooklyn," Stephanie said. "A rooming house Stebbins owns. We brought all the girls from the Doll House, just in case, and we've been giving you blood transfusions to help you heal. How do you feel?"

He took stock of himself: he was a little sore and stiff, but he felt okay. He had to piss. Then he remembered the blow torch. "I feel all right, I suppose. How, uh, bad off am I?"

Stephanie pressed her lips together, turning away with tears in her eyes again, and leaned in to kiss him on the forehead. Frank moved closer to the bed and said: "Killian torched your pecker pretty bad. Third and second degree burns all around your groin, but we all gave you our blood at night and the girls and Sandman's Dhampirs gave during the day. All the visible damage has been repaired, but—"

"Frank, you're scaring him," said Rod, moving into Faolan's view. The handsome Vampyr sat on the edge of the bed and put his hand on Faolan's just like the movie doctor he resembled. "You're gonna be fine, Faolan. Between all the blood and rest, you'll be back up to a hundred percent in another night or two. You've had some pretty great nurses. Frank here hasn't left your bedside since we brought you here, despite his own injuries."

Faolan's head was swimming with thoughts, fears, questions, and memories and he couldn't figure what he should ask next. First things first, he decided. "I gotta take a leak," he said, sliding up to sit against the headboard, and a ripple of laughter went through the assembled vampires. Apart from Rod and Frank, he saw Stebbins, Saberhagen, Miranda, Sandman, and Enzo all standing around the foot of the bed. The room was plain and sparsely-furnished with cracked plaster walls and a worn-out area rug lying on worn-out wood floors.

Stephanie grabbed an empty milk bottle from the bedside table and handed it to him. A little bashful, he slid the bottle under the covers and eased his dick into the opening. Touching it made the skin tingle in a way that was uncomfortable, but not too painful and, aside from a sharp jab when the flow started, the plumbing seemed to work.

"So, how the hell did you guys get me out?" he asked.

Rod smiled and looked back over his shoulder. "That was Miranda's doing."

Miranda played with her hat and couldn't lift her gaze from the floor for long. "'Tweren't nothing, really. Was the Dhampirs and your girl Stephanie what really pulled it off. We got the elevator key from Rothstein and—"

"Rothstein?" he asked. He finished with the milk bottle and handed it to Frank, who took it away to the bathroom. Stephanie took the opportunity to climb onto the bed with him and he put his arm around her.

Miranda explained them finding Rothstein at Frank's cell door, his offer, and how they got Frank out. "So, I calls Stephanie and asks if 'twas possible for a small team to get onto the office floor after sunrise and she said 'twas."

Faolan glared at Stephanie. "Were you outta your mind?"

She smiled despite his anger. "Not really. The new day girl at reception used to work in the Doll House. I'm the one who recommended her for the position, in fact. I dialed her up and she was happy to help. She let the guards know that some business men were coming up for a meeting with Mister Everett and also informed me what time the cleaners would come up to clean Everett and Killian's offices."

"Aye," Miranda said. "Stebbins got a few of our Dhampirs, dressed as cleaners, up there while Stephanie and Enzo's gal Angie chatted up the guards. They went into fucking Killian's office and got you loose and covered up so we were ready to go when the 'business men' showed up with the guns in their briefcases. They got the drop on the guards and popped them in a closet while the others rushed you downstairs, then they followed. It went better than I could've hoped, surely. No one was hurt."

"What about the receptionist? They'll figure her part out easy enough," Faolan said.

"She left with me and Angie," Stephanie said, toying with his hair. "She's living downstairs with some of the other girls and expects a big raise when you give her the job back."

Faolan smiled. It was hard to believe they had pulled the caper off, especially with the timing it had required. "So, lemme get this straight: the reception desk and guard booth were empty and nobody saw this? The guards didn't bust that closet door open in ten seconds?"

"They might've," Miranda allowed, "but Stebbins suggested the finishing touch. Just while your rescue is taking place upstairs, three fucking ambulances pull to the building entrances with sirens blaring. More of our people come rushing in with stretchers and get to the third floor. Remember that all them grifters what man your fake investment company work for Stebbins and, after a word from him on the phone, they were happy to lend their support. You got wheeled out on a fucking stretcher along with two other grifters—all covered and all into different ambulances—while the rest of the team separated and slipped out various building exits. Between all the lookylous and distraction Stebbins' people manufactured, there was no chance for any of Killian's daytime cunts to stop anybody without bringing all kinds of attention to themselves."

"Christ," Faolan said, "it sounds like I was rescued by the Marx Brothers!"

Everyone laughed. Stebbins shrugged, grinning. "Well, it's one thing to mount a successful attack on Killian, but a small-scale rescue with help from inside is a whole 'nother kettle of fish. Our biggest worry was getting it done in time."

Sandman said, "Exposure to the sun kills your average Vampyr in about four to five hours, but we didn't know what kind of shape you'd be in, so we had to plan for the worst."

Stebbins' grin faded and he looked at Faolan apologetically. "I know what you said, but ...I mean, we had to get you out, man. If there was a chance you were still alive..." The smile returned. "Really, Frank would have killed us all if we didn't try."

That produced more laughter, but Frank glanced at them and turned back to Faolan, straight-faced. "He's right."

Faolan laughed with them and was surprised to find that he was glad to still be alive. As much as he might have made his peace with his fate up there in Killian's office, it didn't stop him from being thrilled to get another chance. Maybe he should have scolded them for risking themselves, but he couldn't bring himself to do it. These folks cared about him in a way that went beyond business use or practical need. They were true friends. Family, even.

Reaching up, he toyed with the St. Patrick's medal that was back around his neck. Maybe it really was lucky.

"Anyway," Rod said, rising, "as much as I appreciate the faith you've shown in me, I've made as many leadership decisions as I care to while you've been convalescing. This gang only has one leader, so I'm handing the mantle back now."

A few of the gang clapped and Faolan began to tear up before he realized what was happening. Stephanie hugged him closer, and he gave her a kiss before wiping his eyes. "All right, that's enough of all that, you saps! Rod, did you contact Rothstein at all? Make any kind of deal or set up a meeting?"

"No, sir. After we got you back, I wasn't sure how that would change the playing field, so I felt it would be best to wait for your decision."

Faolan nodded. He would have liked to know what Rothstein was thinking now that he was a factor again, but he supposed Rod's silence could work to his advantage. "Frank, how do you figure Rothstein's position now—what day is it, anyhow?"

Nobody wanted to meet his eyes and he got a sinking feeling in his gut as Frank stepped closer. "Tonight's Friday, Faolan. It's happening tonight." He'd been out for days? Jesus! The news knocked the air out of him and Frank continued. "We've come up with a couple of options, though. We figure we might be able to get a message to Burlington through Davidson from Philly. They invited him, probably as a witness. On the other hand, we could wait for the anointing ceremony itself to strike: according to Rothstein, there's a chance for anyone to challenge the Reeve at the ceremony and, as long as you have some kind of valid claim, Killian would have to accept. Of course, we could also wait and see what Rothstein's got planned and take him out after he gets rid of Killian for us. We've contacted Elrod in Hartford and Walsh in Providence and they're both willing to take us in and back us up if it gets too hot to stay here."

"Wait, no," Faolan said as memories of his last moments in the cell came back to him: *Davidson? Davidson from Philly? Killian said he'd put my letter to use, which means he's having Davidson bring his guys up! Moore's treachery—dammit, he might make it work!* "I gotta get up! Get me some clothes, grab the weapons. We gotta get to Flushing!"

Stephanie stood, looking uncertain, but she went to the closet and grabbed a suit hanging there while everyone else threw questions at him.

"Everybody quiet down!" Rod shouted, while Faolan yanked on the trousers without bothering with underwear and grabbed the shirt. "Faolan, are you sure? We're a good bunch, but I don't think we can take Killian's guards, Moore's people, and the Governor's marines."

Faolan buttoned his shirt with record speed. "We ain't going there to fight if I can help it, Rod, but we gotta stop Killian. He's gonna massacre the Governor, Moore, and everybody else right there and blame it on us!"

PART SIX

THE SHOWDOWN:
February 28, 1939

Somewhere, over the rainbow, skies are blue
And the dreams that you dare to dream really do come true
- Judy Garland, "Over the Rainbow"

Chapter Thirty-Two

The 1939 New York World's Fair site spread out over twelve hundred acres of what had been a garbage dump in Flushing Meadows, Queens. While still under construction, it had already appeared in the Doc Savage story *The Giggling Ghosts*. The Giants, Dodgers, and Yankees had all worn patches advertising the fair for the last year. They'd even gotten Howard Hughes to fly a promotional flight around the world. Now it was here, nearly done and ready to be unveiled to the world at large. Arnold had put blood, sweat, and tears into this project for the last four years. Now he, Killian, and the Dhampir Everett had brought Governor Burlington and his four marines, Reeve Edward Moore and his four bodyguards, and Reeve Davidson of Philadelphia—whose bodyguards had been left at the entrance for security—here to revel in their success.

Arnold Rothstein felt that something wasn't kosher.

As the Vampyrs approached from the Avenue of Patriots, the Perisphere and Trylon at the theme center of the fair grounds dominated the landscape. Though most of the major buildings were erected, none had the grandeur to match the 200 foot globe: pure white to contrast the colors that would eventually define the various zones of the fair, it rested upon mirrored columns that were supposed to be hidden behind the fountains. The fountains, however, struggled to operate in the cold even with the benefit of the water heating units Arnold had ordered installed just for that purpose. The effect was to make it appear that the enormous globe was being held aloft by the jets of water in the center of a pool and, come April when the fair was scheduled to open, he would see to it that it was flawless.

If the water feature was less than stunning, however, the light display made up for it. Hidden projectors bathed the white globe in alternating blue, yellow and red, and gave it the illusion of movement. Governor Burlington seemed especially impressed by this last element, pronouncing the over-all effect "bold and fantastical." Beside the Perisphere, the 750 foot Trylon pointed boldly into the sky like a white bayonet for contrast and scale, though Reeve Moore made a point of remarking that the white of the buildings against the white of the theme center made their scale less awe-inspiring than it might have been otherwise.

Killian pretended not to hear him.

"Back behind the Perisphere there is the New York City Building and down Constitution Mall there you can see the Lagoon of Nations, the Court of Peace, and the United States Building," Killian said, playing tour guide. "To commemorate the one-hundred-and-fiftieth anniversary of George Washington's inauguration here in New York, we've got a sixty-five foot portrait statue down there by, uh, James Earle Fraser. On the Science and Education building we got Johnny Appleseed, Paul Bunyan, and Strap Buckner all done in large-scale sculptures and on the Consumers Building is a..."

"*The Labors of Man*, a trilogy by George H. Snowden," Arnold supplied. Burlington nodded in appreciation. Arnold sensed something very wrong going on here. This was Killian's big grandiose display and yet he seemed distracted. Arnold could swear he was searching the surrounding buildings for something. What was even more ominous was that his shadow Devlin was nowhere to be seen. Killian had given Arnold a line about Devlin not being fit company for the dignitaries which, while true enough on the surface, struck Arnold as bullshit.

"Thank you, Mister Killian, Mister Rothstein," said Governor Burlington. "I am quite impressed by the grandeur of all that I've seen so far." The Governor of the East Coast of the United States stood somewhere around 5'6", a few inches shorter than Rothstein and almost a head below Killian. He was not an especially attractive man, as Arnold understood such things, having close-set brown eyes in a long, angular face beneath auburn hair streaked with white, with a tear-drop shaped nose, and full lips. The over-all effect was feminine, reinforced by his flamboyance. Despite being in white-tie like everyone else, Burlington's silk top hat, tailcoat, and trousers were burgundy and his cuff-links were fashioned from rubies. His ox-blood shoes had spats, which had gone out of style over a decade ago. While everyone else wore variations of wool overcoats, he sported a glossy black coat of pure sable and strolled with an ornate cherry wood walking stick.

His guards were also attention-getting in their military dress uniforms. From the way they moved and handled their weapons, Arnold had no doubt that, while these Vampyrs might have once worn different uniforms, they were all armed service veterans. They all carried carbines of a type Arnold had never seen before. For their arrival at the station, the guns had been concealed in cases, but he was glad that they'd used limousines rather than bring the group by way of the fair's newly-constructed subway or LIRR tracks.

"Part of our rules for the designers was that, aside from a few of the state buildings you see, no imitation of any existing building or historical style is allowed," Killian explained with pride. "So all what you see here is brand new innovation."

Where was Devlin? Hidden somewhere watching for trouble? What about O'Connor and his people? How would it look if they showed up to queer things? Arnold hated being kept in the dark and Killian hadn't shared a thing with him since letting him out of that cell.

"I recognize the work of Walter Dorwin Teague and Stephen Voorhees in some of these structures, unless I am much mistaken," Burlington mused.

"They're both on the board of directors, sir," Everett said, "along with Richmond H. Shreve and William Adams Delano. The Futurama exhibit in the General Motors building is designed by Norman Bel Geddes."

"A veritable pantheon of modern design. I would like to meet some of them if it can be arranged." Burlington smiled at the Dhampir and Arnold wondered again just what the connection might be between the two. As he understood it, most older Vampyrs regarded Dhampirs as servants or even slaves and treated them accordingly. "But I am curious how you come to be so taken with innovation and progress, Mister Killian."

Killian led them to the fifty foot enclosed escalator at the base of the Trylon—the world's longest, as far as Arnold knew—that would bring them up into the Perisphere where a moving platform would take them around the exhibit. Once through, they would cross the bridge into the Trylon and then down the Helicline: a 950 foot ramp that gradually curved around the Perisphere and offered a great view of the grounds. Standing backwards to face them, Killian appeared to be ascending into the darkness ahead as he spoke. "It's efficiency that inspires me most, Governor," Killian explained. "Even back when I was a humble furniture maker, I heard tales of industrial wonders taking place all over the world. Revolution was coming and there'd be no place to hide from it, so I decided right there that I was gonna find a way to master such things as I needed to make the revolution carry me along on its shoulders rather than be one of them poor sorry bastards that gets buried by it."

And when that didn't work, you grabbed onto anyone you thought could help and forced us to carry you, Arnold added in his mind. Now that his victory was so close, he found it hard to hear Killian's vainglorious boasting and suspected that the Governor felt likewise. He knew Everett's messages to Burlington mentioned that he was the true architect of this fair. Everett had already told him that Burlington would not approve Killian's plan to take control of companies based in other cities around the country.

Arnold didn't care. He'd never really bought into Killian's social revolution nonsense, and truth be told, it seemed more effort than it was worth. Arnold would control the companies based in New York, skim a little of the profits from the fair—he and his boys had already skimmed some of the inflated construction and permit costs—and he would make a ton of money. Then he would invest that money to make more. After all, the fair was a model of modern advertising and cross-promotion: it was a seductive fantasy-land designed to make the average Joe feel good about spending his hard-earned cash. Hadn't they put the world's largest cash register at the entrance to ring in attendance?

The escalator struggled a little in the cold February night, but had been turned on by someone earlier and allowed to warm up, so the ride was smooth. As Killian reached the top, one of the guards whispered something to Burlington, who spoke up: "Mister Killian, my men must enter the structure first as a security precaution. No insult is intended."

Killian smiled, but his eyes held a dangerous gleam. "Of course, Your Honor." He stepped aside to let the four soldiers enter the Perisphere before turning back. "By the way, Reeve Moore, I wanted to thank you for that letter you were kind enough to send me."

Moore shifted, clearly uncomfortable at being singled out for conversation, but nodded. "Think nothing of it. I pray only that it was timely enough to render assistance."

Killian kept smiling that vicious smile. "Oh, it was very helpful, sir."

Meanwhile, Arnold moved himself up behind Davidson and whispered: "What the hell is going on?"

Davidson glanced back at him for a brief second, and the look of miserable panic that flashed across his features shocked Arnold to his core. He almost didn't notice when Killian addressed him.

"Unfortunately, though, the traitor O'Connor contrived to escape with some outside help. Isn't that right, Arnold?" Killian stared down at him, eyebrows raised.

Arnold found everyone looking at him now, except Reeve Davidson who refused to meet his eyes. "Um, yes—sorry, Your Honor. That's correct."

"And you said it was two of Boston's agents that sprung him, was it not?" Killian pressed.

Before Arnold could correct him, Reeve Moore drew himself to his full height and his skeletal bodyguard tensed. "I'm sure that I have no idea to whom you are referring, sir, but I take great exception to your implication."

"*Mister* Killian," Burlington said with enough force to cause silence, "are you leveling a specific charge against Reeve Moore?"

Killian spread his hands and did his best impression of innocence. "Just making conversation, Your Honor."

"Then let us have a change of topics," Burlington said, slipping from American Standard pronunciation to crisp Queen's English in his annoyance. "There will be a time to speak of grievances and settlements, but this is neither the proper venue nor time... Now, what say we get out of the cold and observe this bold vision of the future we've been promised, hmm?"

Killian bowed with a touch of mockery and gestured for everyone to enter. Arnold touched Everett's arm unnoticed and shot the Dhampir a questioning look, but Everett just shrugged. Having found nothing amiss in the Perisphere, Burlington's guards exited to the bridge where they would have a view of the grounds to wait.

"Get ready for the magic carpet ride!" Killian said, giddy with anticipation, as he activated the exhibit. The "carpets" were booth-like seats on giant rotating rings that carried visitors around the inner wall of the Perisphere with the Democracity diorama in the center below. Seen as if from a distance of two miles in the early morning glow of the lights, the city of the future was a breathtaking vision of order, cooperation, and efficiency. The music began: stately, strident, and bold with a chorus of a thousand voices. Images of figures marched across the curved walls of the building in ten columns: businessmen, factory workers, miners, farmers, bureaucrats, bankers, retailers, police, firefighters, and most important of all, consumers—all the types necessary to the functioning of this future city.

There was narration planned to go with this spectacle, but they hadn't agreed on the final wording yet, so for now Killian explained some of the features, shouting to be heard over the music. Centerton with its skyscrapers would be the center of government, business, and commerce. "Most folks won't live there," he added as an aside, "except maybe some niggers and chinks who do the shit work, but eventually automation will take care of all that." If he'd meant that to be a bit of winking camaraderie, Arnold saw that it missed the mark with Burlington: the Governor interrupted his enraptured absorption with the diorama to shoot a disgusted glance at Killian that the latter missed. In concentric rings around Centerton stood the Pleasantvilles—residential apartments and suburban developments—the Millvilles which were the industry towns and factories, and finally the farms on the furthest ring that all worked in harmony to support each other.

The music built to a crescendo as day transitioned into night and the six-minute trip around Democracity came to an end. As the lights came up, Killian turned to them with eager expectation and Arnold found himself equally excited to hear Burlington's assessment.

"Well," said the Governor, conscious of all eyes upon him. "Let me first congratulate you and Mister Rothstein for having initiated and brought to fruition such a marvelous display of wonders. Truly, I found this diorama brilliantly conceived and most handsomely executed. As a conception of utopian efficiency and cooperative effort, it is inspiring. I see so much great potential in some of the ideas this display presents…but I fear that they are not the same ideas that you would have us see, Mister Killian."

Arnold held his breath and watched Killian, whose icy composure hid his true reaction. Burlington took a breath, perhaps anticipating an explosion from Killian like at their first meeting four years ago when Killian had called Burlington a "pompous, jumped-up, dickless little limey cocksucker" among other choice insults before storming out of the room. "We in The Order strive for harmony and cooperation with each other and, while we may sometimes fall short of that ideal, the one thing that we of the North American Domain prize above all is our individuality. It seems to me that you would seek to eliminate that divine fire in your drive for efficiency and, speaking as one of those who helped our Hegemon craft this Domain and nation we stand in, I cannot embrace that goal. I also will not permit your plan, as I understand it, to take control of companies that are based in cities other than New York as this would cause unnecessary conflict between Territories and runs contrary to the policies of The Order in this Domain. Do I make myself clearly understood, Mister Killian?"

To Arnold's surprise, Killian smiled. It was a tight smile and anyone who cared to look could see the fury behind Killian's eyes, but he held himself in check and nodded. "Yes, Your Honor, I understand completely," he said in a quiet, toneless voice that made Arnold shiver.

Arnold might have been tempted to claim credit for having civilized the beast, but this still felt wrong. He prayed that Killian's façade would break, that he would curse and scream and cause a scene that would create a pretext for the Governor to have him seized, and then Arnold could step forward and bring the admittedly-weak cannibalism charges against Killian. Under those circumstances, and with whatever influence Everett represented on his side, Arnold would be a perfect candidate.

Governor Burlington chose to overlook the fury in Killian's eyes and take him at his word, nodding. "Very good. Still, let me say again, a most exceptional effort."

"Thank you, Governor," Killian said. "Why don't you and the others go and enjoy the view from the Helicline for a moment while I shut down the machinery?"

Arnold began to object, more uneasy with each passing moment, but Killian silenced him with a glare that could have melted iron. Then, before Burlington could respond, one of his men shouted from outside: "Governor! Someone's approaching!"

Burlington turned and exited the Perisphere, followed by Moore's bodyguards and Moore himself, and then Everett. Arnold glanced back in time to see Killian give Davidson an expectant look. The Reeve of Philadelphia pointed at the First Aid cabinet on the wall by the exit. Then Killian looked at Arnold with murder in his eyes, so he left and joined the others on the wide concrete bridge that connected the Perisphere and Trylon fifty feet above the fair grounds.

What's the smart play here? Arnold wondered. *If I try to warn the Governor and nothing happens, I'll look like a fool! What the hell is Killian planning, anyway? Something involving Davidson...a rub-out? He owns Davidson because of those photos O'Connor took, but even Killian couldn't be that crazy! It would never work! No, stick to the plan. Another hour and we'll be back at the building and we'll spring the trap. If Killian does pull anything stupid, then just play the cards as they come and wait to see who wins.*

"One figure that we can see, sir," one of the guards was explaining to the Governor, pointing back toward the other side of the Perisphere where the Helicline ended. The other three guards all had their carbines aimed at the approaching figure. "Appears to be male, unsure if he's human or Vampyr. We thought it could be one of the men that was stationed with the cars, but then I noticed he seems to be waving a white handkerchief. Would you like us to warn him off with a shot, Your Honor?"

Arnold followed their gazes and couldn't credit what he was seeing. Faolan O'Connor, alive and apparently whole, walking toward the base of the Helicline, because wasn't it just like that *schmuck* to do everything backwards? "O'Connor," he sighed.

"Is it?" Burlington asked him, looking amused. "And waving a white handkerchief, you say? Well, this should prove of interest, then!"

"Your Honor, I advise great caution," Moore stated with a hint of urgency. His bodyguards, having no weapons, formed a shield around Moore with their bodies. "This man is quite dangerous, an outlaw, and known to be untrustworthy. He is unworthy of your company."

Burlington watched O'Connor's approach up the Helicline with expectation as his guards kept the underdressed Vampyr in their carbine sights. "I should like to judge that for myself," the Governor responded.

With everyone's attention focused on O'Connor's approach, Arnold snuck a glance back at the exit door and, sure enough, Killian stood half-hidden in the doorway and Davidson was nowhere to be seen. The wind picked up, nearly blowing Arnold's hat off. The colored spotlights shifted from blue to red, bathing the entire setting in scarlet and transforming the water beneath them into a pool of blood. Arnold made his slow and quiet way closer to the large doors leading into the Trylon. Unlike the exposed bridge on which they now stood, at least the interior of the Trylon would provide some degree of cover. Just a step, a pause, and then another step...

True to form, O'Connor was improperly attired, but tonight he really looked like a hobo: no hat, wrinkled trousers, a wrinkled shirt with no tie or jacket, and a coat hastily thrown on over it all. Stuffing the handkerchief into the coat pocket, he made a point of opening his coat and turning around to show them that he wore no weapons. The pockets of the coat were such that the bulge of a gun would have been obvious, but Arnold wasn't sure whether to be reassured or anxious about this confidence. What was O'Connor's game?

"That's far enough," one of the soldiers called out when O'Connor was about a hundred feet from the Helicline side of the Trylon, which put them all at right angles to each other.

"Well, Faolan O'Connor," called Burlington. "I've heard quite a few tales of your exploits. To what do I owe this unexpected meeting?"

O'Connor shouted: "I came to warn youse all! Killian's got sharp-shooters—"

The mechanical clatter of machine gun fire interrupted him.

Chapter Thirty-Three

So maybe it wasn't the world's greatest plan, but Faolan didn't have much time. He'd sent the gang out in small teams to check all the buildings that had a good sight line to the Theme Center, guessing that's where Killian would place his shooters. Meanwhile, he'd come straight up here with the white flag to see if he could warn the Governor and stall for time. It was simple, sensible, and straight-forward.

He didn't figure on Killian having a gun planted.

Despite not having a gun, he slips into his killing groove as he takes it in:

With all attention and gun barrels pointed at Faolan, Killian enjoys a clear field as he opens up with a cut-down Browning Automatic Rifle. The bullets explode right through Burlington's guards, causing them to jerk and twitch and drop their carbines off the bridge before falling. One of the guards manages to spin around and squeeze off a round, but it misses Killian. He does manage to shield the Governor with his body before collapsing.

Rothstein, meanwhile, dashes for the cover of the Trylon while Moore's bodyguard Streiber pushes his Reeve over the railing to the pool of water below before joining him. Killian cuts down the other three bodyguards as they attempt to rush him. Only Everett, the Dhampir, grabs Governor Burlington and shoves him toward the Trylon, then reaches down to grab the fallen soldier's carbine.

Faolan runs for the Trylon as well, knowing the Dhampir alone is no match for Killian. So far, there is no fire from any of the surrounding buildings, so he hopes that means that his friends found all the snipers in time.

"Have you gone mad?" Everett shouts, leveling the carbine at Killian, who has already exhausted his ammunition in his full-auto spray.

"Davidson, give the goddamn signal already! Devlin!" Killian screams, stalking toward Everett. "Outta my way, Nate!" Without waiting for a response, Killian throws the empty BAR directly at Everett and charges. Though Everett succeeds in dodging the projectile, Killian closes the distance before he can bring the carbine back up and the two wrestle for the weapon.

Faolan is halfway to the Trylon when out of the doorway steps Johnny Devlin, dressed for combat and drawing a Browning pistol from his coat pocket.

Fuck! Faolan skids to a stop, trying to work out a way past the gunfighter, but he draws a blank.

Killian drives a knee into Everett's gut and smashes the Dhampir across the face with the butt of the carbine, dropping him. "Kill him, Johnny!" Killian shouts as he kicks Everett off the edge of the bridge.

Faolan keeps his eyes on Devlin as he shouts back: "My pals already took care of Davidson's men, Killian! They'll all be down here in a minute! You're busted!"

Killian strides toward the Trylon, carbine in hand and madness in his eyes. "Like hell I am! I'll kill you, Moore, Burlington, and anybody else who tries to stop me 'till the rest come to heel! Well, Devlin, what the fuck you waiting for? The Resurrection? Kill him!"

As Killian disappears into the Trylon interior, Devlin regards him with those cold, calm green eyes and raises the Browning. Faolan is as good as dead and he knows it.

Frank and Rod and the others won't let Killian win, though. I made a difference.

When Devlin tosses the Browning to him, Faolan is almost too surprised to catch it. Almost. His confusion makes Devlin chuckle. "I kept hold a' that for ya. I don't reckon you're up to a real shooting contest right now, though, so maybe I'll pass back this way sometime after all this horeshit blows over." Touching the brim of his flat-crowned hat, Devlin walks past Faolan and down the Helicline.

It feels good to have his Browning in hand again. It feels right. He runs into the Trylon, hearing the echo of carbine shots from within. Rothstein runs past him as he enters and his attention is drawn up the wide, metal spiral staircase where Killian fires the carbine up at Burlington, who has reached the top of the narrow tower and the small room containing the observation window. Faolan takes aim and fires, striking Killian in the leg.

Killian howls in rage, twists around, and fires a clumsy return shot, followed by another, but the bullets ricochet off the metal railings. The echo of the shots in the high, narrow space is deafening.

Faolan fires again, hitting Killian in the chest. He shoots a few more times, but misses, and runs up a few courses to close the distance. Killian is limping now, using the carbine as a makeshift cane, but still edging closer to the room at the top. Faolan stops again and lines up a risky shot at Killian's head, but he's in the groove and fires. At the last second, however, Killian lifts the carbine high enough to interrupt the bullet because of the angle. Killian screams as the carbine is torn from his hand and clatters down three stairs before falling down the center to the floor. Faolan takes aim again. He notices that his slide has popped back.

He's empty.

Of course, I never asked Devlin if he bothered to reload it for me. With a frustrated sigh, Faolan shoves the pistol into his coat pocket and runs up the stairs as fast as he can. Hearing a commotion above, he glances up and sees Burlington club Killian on the head and shoulders with his walking stick, driving the larger Vampyr back down a step. Killian is ready for the third swing, however, and grabs the stick, wrenching it from the Governor's grasp after a brief struggle. Too furious for tools, however, he pitches the stick down the stairs and chases Burlington up into the observation room.

Faolan jumps out over the side a bit, holding the rail with one hand, but manages to catch the walking stick as it tumbles by. He rushes up the last few steps to avoid getting ambushed like Killian did, but he sees that those fears were unnecessary. Killian and Burlington are too busy struggling at the window to notice his arrival: the window is completely unobstructed and is large enough to easily fit a person through, which appears to be Killian's intent as he struggles to force the Governor out. The wind at this height buffets them with its force and frigid bite.

"Sa-wing batter, batter!" Faolan cries, swinging the stick and connecting with Killian's wounded leg. He pulls back as Killian cries out and falls to one knee and cracks the stick over Killian's head. Killian roars and slams into Faolan like a linebacker, driving him back into the wall. Gripping the broken piece of walking stick with both hands, he thinks: *What the hell, it was good enough for Dracula!* He thrusts the sheared end of the walking stick up into Killian's chest—

And feels it punch into the bullet-proof vest Killian wears beneath his coat.

Killian wraps his hands around Faolan's throat and squeezes. "You fucking ingrate!" he hisses between his teeth. "I'll end you now, by G—"

He's interrupted by Burlington punching him in the temple, which makes him lash out with a back-hand blow that Burlington dodges—the Governor is actually dancing around with his arms in old-timey fisticuffs position. Faolan takes advantage of the distraction to slam his knee up into Killian's balls and shove him away. Killian stumbles to the center of the room and swings again at the moving Governor, but the small Vampyr is nimble and side-steps, coming in again for another solid punch to Killian's face. He steps in to follow-up, but it's a mistake: Killian snaps back and delivers a vicious haymaker that sends Burlington to the boards. Even so, Killian looks winded. No longer the titan of Coney Island, the Goliath Spider has shed his skin and become vulnerable.

Faolan charges forward with one of the tricks that Rod has taught him: a strong sideways kick. It's a move Killian is unused to dealing with and hits him in the chest, knocking him back against the open window. He catches himself on the edges, but Faolan closes again, kicking his wounded leg. Killian grabs for him, but he steps away and fires off a full force kick to Killian's nuts again for payback. As Killian curls up, Faolan punches him with all his might. Killian staggers back and falls half out of the window, clutching at the frame. His knees and that one hand are all that anchor him.

Faolan thinks back to Michael, the kid in the cell, for the hundredth time but feels empowered by the memory rather than ashamed for the first time. Nothing like that is ever going to happen in his New York, he promises himself. *This one's for you, kid.*

"Wait..." Killian gasps as he struggles to pull himself back inside. Faolan punches Killian's knuckles and watches him scream all the way down to the pavement.

As he came out of his killing groove, Faolan realized that no amount of success would ever justify the things he's done. All he could do was remember them and try to make different choices in the future.

*****

Killian wasn't dead.

The fall shattered most of the bones in his body, but he still breathed. After announcing to everyone that he owed Faolan a great debt, Burlington declared Killian guilty of the murder of the four guards whose wounds had proven fatal and the attempted murder of the rest of the diplomatic party as well as violation of his obligations as host. He sentenced Killian to death by living burial and declared, "Let this place that was his intended monument, prove his tomb instead."

Rothstein mentioned a location out in the amusement zone where the foundations were still being poured and Miranda volunteered to carry out the sentence with her Dhampirs. Faolan's friends had all arrived with their captive snipers by the time he and the Governor made it down the Helicline. Rod had organized getting everyone out of the freezing water and into the blankets Enzo kept in his car trunk. Enzo and Stephanie then rushed the wounded back to the Empire State Building for blood transfusions and the rest of the shivering dignitaries were now eager to join them. Unfortunately, there was still the issue of Reeve

Davidson and his men, who knelt in a line under the watchful eyes of Saberhagen, Sandman, and Moore's skeletal Streiber.

Davidson had stayed put during the confusion, rather than try to run off, and now he knelt next to his four men: after being left by the cars, they had just moved into position, grabbed the planted rifles, and waited for Davidson to signal them by radio. Except, according to Frank and the others, Davidson never gave the signal.

"William Davidson," Burlington said, projecting for everyone to hear, "who was made Reeve of Philadelphia by my own hand, has this night conspired to violate the sacred guest right by murdering me and these other worthy gentlemen in a fashion most foul."

Faolan couldn't help but think back to the man he'd met back in Central Park, then to their many interactions in the past few years, and now as he faced certain death with dignity and class. He was a good guy and Faolan liked him.

"This being a violation not only of my word of peace that we have gathered here under, but also of the sacred oath that you swore to me as your Governor," Burlington continued, "it is a crime that demands swift and severe punishment. Before I pronounce sentence, I will listen to any statement or plea you wish to make."

Davidson looked up at Burlington, sad but resigned, and Faolan figured he'd mention the blackmail Killian had over him. Faolan wouldn't blame him. He'd been the one who put the bite on Davidson in the first place, but it wasn't like they hadn't all done the same. It wasn't what you did, though, it was what you got caught doing. "I really am sorry for helping Killian, Your Honor. Please believe that. I really like you." Davidson spoke with the plain and honest integrity that Faolan had come to trust and he could see that Burlington liked the guy, too. "I'd just like to ask that you spare the lives of my men," he said. "They were only doing what I told them and I doubt they would have fired on you even if I'd given the order."

"I see. A very honorable request." Burlington nodded, folding his arms over his chest as his expressive features revealed his conflicting feelings. Faolan could see that his nature was to be merciful, but that he needed to make an example or hard asses like Moore would think he was weak.

So, what was that before about making different decisions?

"Hey, Governor," Faolan said before he had time to think of all the smart reasons not to say anything. "I wanna cash in that debt you owe me for a full pardon for Davidson and his men."

Burlington stared at him in absolute shock, while Rothstein and Everett questioned aloud whether such was even possible. Moore threw off his blanket and stood shivering in indignation. "That's outrageous! It would be an insult to us all! Especially those brave soldiers who gave their lives tonight!"

"Faolan," Frank whispered, moving closer to him. "Fuck Davidson! You can use that debt to get the city with no strings!"

Faolan smiled at him. "Frank, you still don't get it? Friends beat favors any day."

Burlington waved his hands for silence. "Mister O'Connor, this is a very serious request you have made, even considering the debt which we all owe to you. I had understood that you wished to be named Reeve of this city?"

"Yeah, that's right, Your Honor," Faolan said with a confident smile. "But I wanna win that one fair and square."

Burlington tried to look stern, but Faolan saw a smile tugging at the corners of his mouth. "Very well, then," the Governor pronounced. "In discharge of the debt for your timely warning and assistance, I hereby grant full pardon and absolution for the actions of Reeve William Davidson and these Agents of Philadelphia. Let no more word of this incident be spoken of by any Vampyr or Dhampir from this time forward. Rise and be free, gentlemen."

Bill and his men rose, almost unable to believe what had happened, while Rothstein spoke to a scowling Moore and Streiber placed the blanket back on his Reeve's shoulders. Rod, Stebbins, and Saberhagen each shook Bill's hand and congratulated him before he made his way over to Faolan and extended his hand. "I appreciate that, O'Connor. Thanks."

Faolan shook his hand. "Don't mention it. When we get back home, I'll see to it you get all them pictures and such. Start things off fresh."

Bill smiled. "That'd be great."

Over Bill's shoulder, Faolan watched Rothstein approach Burlington. "Your Honor? If you recall, we had come to an arrangement prior to all of this...?"

"Yes," Burlington replied without enthusiasm. "Though you had given me to understand that Mister O'Connor was dead."

"Governor Burlington," Moore called, striding to center stage. "The great city of Boston supports the claim of Mister Arnold Rothstein for Reeve of New York. He would have my friendship as well as that of the cities who do me patronage."

Burlington arched an eyebrow. "Really, Edward? You would lend your support to a Jew? This is most unlike you."

Edward Moore glared at Faolan, looking like an angry dollar bill. "Against another Irish street mongrel, yes I would. The Jew is known to be a Vampyr of some culture, at least."

"Oh, for God's sake, can we please move this indoors?" Everett cried, hugging his blanket to himself and trembling.

"Yes, yes," Burlington agreed. "Let us remove ourselves to our accommodations to refresh ourselves and decide this issue of Reeve. I will see this done tonight and the peace between Boston and New York signed before I depart. So, Misters Rothstein and O'Connor, I leave it to you to agree upon the nature of your contest, but be quick about it!"

Faolan looked over at Rothstein, who met his gaze with confidence. Rothstein nodded as everyone else headed for the cars.

There was no doubt about the nature of their contest.

Chapter Thirty-Four

The stage was set for their match in the Indigo Lounge. Literally.

One of the poker tables had been brought up onto the stage to give everyone a good view and confound any help from the crowd. Burlington was delighted by their choice of contest, claiming to be an avid card player, and offered himself as dealer. Since neither Faolan nor Rothstein wanted to refuse him, they agreed and chose no limit seven-card stud as their game. Faolan had cleaned up and changed into his best evening clothes along with everyone else, and the air was as thick with anticipation as it was cigar smoke as they commenced.

Snap, snap, snap.

Rod put his radio voice to good use announcing the game for the crowd. Both Faolan and Rothstein started with a thousand dollars in chips, which gave them some room to maneuver but not enough to make the game drag on forever. Rothstein played extremely tight for the first hour, folding almost every hand at the first raise and letting Faolan chip away at him before suckering Faolan into betting big on what looked to be a bluff but turned out to be a three-of-a-kind instead.

Snap, snap, snap...

Now, halfway into the game's second hour, Faolan sat with a pair of jacks in the hole, but a six as his door card and a little over five hundred bucks of his original stack left. Rothstein's door card was a king of diamonds, so he paid the ten dollar bring-in while Faolan made a show of considering. Glancing at his hole cards again, he sighed and tossed a ten dollar chip into the center.

"So, quite a night, huh?" Faolan pulled a Camel out of the new gold cigarette case Stephanie had surprised him with in his room—after she'd joined him in the shower to help wash behind his ears. "This must be a pretty strange way to choose a Reeve, eh Governor?" he asked as he lit up.

Snap...snap.

"A five of diamonds for Rothstein," Rod announced, "king-five suited showing. An ace of spades for O'Connor: showing an ace high."

"Your bet, Mister O'Connor," Burlington said. He was proving to be as good a dealer as he'd claimed and had so far followed the game with enthusiasm. He had also proven far more receptive to conversation than had Rothstein. "And, in fact, it has not been uncommon in our history to settle such matters with cards or chess, even checkers is not unknown. I am one of those who prefer to see such contests conducted in gentlemanly fashion rather than with duels."

Faolan rolled a chip back and forth across his knuckles and smiled. "You don't say?"

"Are you going to bet or not, O'Connor?" Rothstein asked after taking a sip of water. Burlington gave the Steward a disapproving glance, but Rothstein was watching him. Rothstein's demeanor was cold as usual, but Faolan sensed an undercurrent of anticipation. Rothstein wanted him to bet. The other Vampyr was holding something better than Faolan's ace, but was it better than jacks?

Faolan leaned back, tossed the chip in the air and caught it, then said, "I'll bet after you answer something for me: What is it with you and me, anyhow?"

"What?" Rothstein asked, his composure giving way to a flicker of irritation. "What kind of nonsense is this? Make your bet or fold."

Burlington gave him a look of bemusement and Faolan leaned forward again. "No, I'm serious. Far back as I can remember, you've had it in for me no matter what I done. I wanna know why. Honest."

Rothstein rolled his eyes. "Shenanigans like this are a contributing factor."

"C'mon," Faolan said, his voice pitched low so only those at the table would hear. He didn't know exactly why this mattered, but he did know that this might be his last chance to ever ask. He looked Rothstein in the eyes. "I ain't saying we ain't both had reasons to hate each other these past few years, but I wanna know why you warmed to Jack and Eddie Diamond, but not me. From the very first day we met, there was something about me you didn't like."

"That's important to you, isn't it?" Rothstein asked, examining him. "That people like you? Well, I don't and that's all there is to it. Now make a bet or fold."

Faolan sighed and grabbed two blue chips. "Hundred."

"Two hundred," Rothstein fired back, sliding a neat stack of four into the center.

While Rod relayed the raises, Faolan sat back and considered his options. Rothstein seemed confident, but was it for show? Did he have another king in the hole? Another three-of-a-kind? He saw the tension at the corners of Rothstein's eyes and the stillness that was supposed to look like calm, but was just a fraction too stiff and decided that Rothstein was trying to scare him out.

Faolan pushed all his chips toward the center. "Five and change."

"Five hundred and sixty," supplied Burlington.

Rothstein glanced down at the chips in the center and then back at Faolan's face, trying to read him. He took a sip of water and calculated the odds. He could fold now and be down two hundred, but if he won it would all be over. On the other hand, if he went in and lost, they would be even again. After a moment of silent debate, Rothstein nodded and pushed three hundred and fifty dollars in chips to add to the two hundred ten he already had in.

"Rothstein calls, pot total is now one thousand, one hundred and twenty dollars," Rod reported.

Faolan looked over the crowd: Stephanie, Enzo, Frank, Saberhagen, and Stebbins all sat at the closest table. Stephanie looked nervous as hell, so he gave her a wink before turning back to Rothstein. "What's your plan, A.R.? If you win, I mean."

"Get rid of you, for one," Rothstein answered.

Burlington dealt Fifth Street, a two of clubs for Rothstein and a nine of diamonds for Faolan, and Faolan leaned forward again. "You know Moore's gonna make you dance to his song if you get rid of me and my people. Why don't we bury the hatchet and work together for the good of the city? We don't gotta like each other, but I know the city'll be stronger for having both of us."

Rothstein said nothing, just watched Burlington burn the next card and deal Sixth Street: a queen of hearts for Rothstein and a jack of diamonds for Faolan, giving him three of a kind. Faolan took a drag of his cigarette and smiled, wondering what Jack Diamond would think if he could see his old friend now.

"Do either of you gentlemen mind if I deal the last cards face-up?" asked Burlington.

"Not under the circumstances," Faolan replied and Rothstein shook his head.

Burlington dealt Rothstein a seven of hearts and a three of spades to Faolan. Rothstein slumped back in his seat and Faolan knew he had him, even before he turned over his hole cards: a queen and eight of diamonds. Rothstein had been four cards into a king-high flush, but missed that last crucial diamond. Faolan flipped over his pocket jacks.

"Rothstein has a king high and O'Connor has a three-of-a-kind, jacks!" Rod announced to scattered applause from the crowd.

"Why don't we make a deal?" Faolan asked, keeping his voice low while Burlington shuffled the cards for the next hand. "If I win, I'll keep you for my Steward. If you win, you keep me on as Marshal."

Burlington nodded. "That seems a very sensible proposal."

But Rothstein smacked the arm of his chair and sat forward, his agitation getting the better of him. "No, Your Honor, with all due respect, it's nonsensical." He pointed his index finger at Faolan. "You want to know why I never liked you? It's this right here. This attitude you have like you just have to sit back and wait for the world to give you everything you want. You treat everything like it's a joke, you've got no respect for anybody, and you think you're smarter than everybody else, but in the end you're just looking for the easy way up. I worked for every dollar I have, I used my brains, and I played by the rules. But you? You think the rules don't apply to you, just like Killian." He sat back again, cold and disapproving. "So, no, I won't have you working in my organization because you've got no class, and you never will. Now, let's finish this game, so I can claim the title I've spent the last four years earning."

Faolan fell back and took a last, long drag from his cigarette, taken aback by the assessment. No class, the man said. That stung. His whole life he'd looked up to men like Arnold Rothstein as role models for that abstract quality he'd always yearned for: class. He'd struggled, killed, and tried to change his behavior this way and that all in the name of attaining class. Maybe he just didn't have it, he told himself, and maybe he never would.

But maybe that was okay.

Killian had bent over backwards trying to fit into The Order and be classy, hadn't he? Instead all he'd done was turn himself into a great big phony. *Might be I'm better off staying true to who I am.* He folded the next hand after paying the bring-in and considered everything Rothstein had said. Class or not, even Arnold Rothstein didn't always feel respected. He was still climbing, too, and still trying to prove something to himself and the world.

"Well, you're not all wrong A.R." Faolan said, stabbing out his cigarette. "Just for the record, though, I always respected you. It's just my way to poke fellas who take themselves real seriously, you know?"

Rothstein looked at him with suspicion and didn't respond.

"When I started with all this vampire business, I figured it was my ticket to finally get ahead and be somebody," Faolan said, talking more just to finally say it all out loud than to convince Rothstein of anything. "But that ain't what this is about anymore. Only reason I'm here now is because I love this city. I love the people, all the different boroughs and the way they all feel different, and I even love the feeling of just walking the streets at night. I don't wanna see New York changed into some spiffy-clean city of the future or anything else. I just want New York to keep being what it is, you understand? This place is in my blood and this is where I plan to spend the rest of my life, however long that is. That's why I'm here tonight."

Snap, snap. Snap, snap. Snap, snap.

"You're here to win, just like I am, because that's what counts," Rothstein countered as Burlington dealt the cards. Rothstein's door card was a ten of diamonds while Faolan showed a jack of clubs.

Faolan glanced over at the table where Stephanie, Frank, and the others sat. *Winning is great, but it ain't the only thing that counts.* The thought made him smile as he paid the bring-in. "I used to think that too, A.R., but being Marshal made me realize that having a position ain't just about money and power—it's about being responsible for the folks under you and looking out for 'em."

Rothstein wasn't listening. He raised to one hundred, but Burlington gave Faolan an approving nod. Checking his hole cards for the first time, Faolan was surprised to see pocket aces. Very promising, but he would have to play it carefully to avoid scaring Rothstein off. He matched Rothstein's raise and waited.

Snap, snap, snap.

Seven of clubs for Rothstein and a useless two of spades for Faolan. "Your bet, Mister O'Connor," Burlington said after Rod finished calling the cards.

He wanted to get Rothstein to commit more money, but not seem so confident that the savvy gambler read his hand and folded. "One hundred," he said.

"Call."

Faolan put Rothstein on an inside-straight draw with the ten-seven, figuring he had the eight or nine in the hole or maybe both. Dangerous if he made the hand unless Faolan could get those other two aces.

Snap, snap, snap.

Ace of diamonds for Rothstein and the jack of spades for Faolan, giving him two pairs with a pair showing. Now was the time to push before Rothstein got lucky. "I'm all-in."

"O'Connor is all-in," Rod announced. "A raise of over seven hundred dollars!"

Arnold Rothstein sat back and considered him for a few moments. Calling that raise would break him if he lost and it wasn't Rothstein's style to take a risk like that. The gambler tapped his fingers on the table, narrowed his eyes, and pushed his chips into the center.

"Rothstein calls!" cried Rod. "Two-thousand dollars and potential victory rest on this hand!"

The Indigo Lounge went quiet and Faolan sat back, trying to look as confident as possible. Technically,

Rothstein would have ten or twenty bucks left if he lost, but everyone knew that such an amount would be meaningless.

Snap, snap, snap.

The king of diamonds for Rothstein and a nine of clubs for Faolan. Rothstein's chances for that inside straight were almost gone, but he might score a flush, both of which Faolan could beat if he made a full house with a jack or the last ace. One card left.

Snap, snap, snap.

Once more Burlington dealt the river face-up: the queen of diamonds for Rothstein and the jack of hearts to complete Faolan's hand. Rothstein might have a straight or a flush with those diamonds, but Faolan had made his full house and revealed the aces in his hole.

"Faolan has a full house, jacks over aces!" Rod called. There was applause and cheering from Enzo, Davidson and his guys, and a bunch of the other fellas who had worked for Faolan.

But Arnold Rothstein smiled—a smile that was almost a sneer—and turned over the jack and ace of diamonds.

"Royal flush, diamonds," Rod said, his enthusiasm gone. "Mister Rothstein wins."

The cheers died, replaced by polite applause from Moore's table and a few vamps from the financial section. Burlington and Rothstein rose and shook hands, but Faolan didn't move.

Burlington put his hand on Faolan's shoulder. "You played very well, Mister O'Connor."

"Thank you, Your Honor," he said, smiling.

Rothstein straightened his tie and smoothed his vest. "I want you and your people out of the city tonight."

Bill Davidson approached the stage as Burlington moved forward to speak and said, "Well, Faolan, you know you're all welcome in Philadelphia."

"Thanks, Bill," Faolan said as Rod came over to offer consolation, "but I don't think we'll be going anywhere."

"What's that?" Rothstein asked and Burlington also turned to him in surprise.

However, it was Frank who stood up to answer: "If Rothstein thinks he can be the Reeve of New York, let him prove it. Faolan's not leaving and neither am I."

Enzo, Stebbins, Stephanie, and Saberhagen also stood, saying, "Me neither."

Miranda and Sandman joined them with their Dhampirs. "Aye, let's see you try to fucking move us, you cunts!"

Moore jumped to his feet. "This is treason!"

"Actually," said Frank as the rest of Saberhagen's enforcers joined the growing mob, "Killian never officially surrendered this city, so we're still in rebellion."

"Chambers, as your lawful Reeve, I order you to take that man into custody!" Rothstein cried.

Rod sighed and looked at Faolan, then at Rothstein. "I'm sorry, Mister Rothstein, but I'm with him too."

Furious, Rothstein called out: "Bennett! Get your men and get rid of these trespassers!"

But Bennett had moved to the center already, along with Fingers Martin, Shad Newman, Charlie Wilson, and all the other men from Faolan's former command. There were even a few of Rothstein's subordinates in the mix now, more than two-thirds of the vampires in the room. The rest sat at their tables, quiet and still.

Rothstein turned on Burlington: "You're the Governor, for God's sake, do something!"

"I shall." Burlington had watched the scene unfold with stoic calm and now stepped forward. "Gentlemen and ladies, The Order is not a democracy!" he proclaimed, loud enough to gain everyone's attention. "However," he continued in a warmer tone, "only a fool ignores the will of the people so clearly expressed. Therefore, by the power of my office as Governor of the East Coast of the United States of America, I hereby appoint Faolan O'Connor as Reeve of New York City conditional upon his surrender of said city back into the fold of our august Order."

As the cheers and applause started again, Rothstein went livid. "But I won! What about the rules!"

Burlington sighed and shook his head. "The rules are that I can appoint anyone I choose, Mister Rothstein. How can I give you a city that won't follow you?"

Faolan stood up and walked over to them and Frank and Stephanie made their way onto the stage. "Look, I meant what I said before, Rothstein. I need you on my team."

He put out his hand, but Rothstein looked at it like it was spoiled fish and walked off the stage. Faolan shrugged and offered it to Burlington, who clasped it with a smile. "So, New York officially surrenders."

Burlington nodded, his smile broadening. "I am quite glad to hear it, since you have proven a most tenacious opponent. I look forward to seeing what we can accomplish together in the future."

Then Stephanie grabbed him and they kissed while folks came up to congratulate him. He got Stephanie to release him from the lip-lock eventually, but she kept her arms wrapped around him and that was fine by him. He noticed that Moore and his man Streiber had also left the room and figured that was one friend he'd never have. *His loss.*

The Dhampir Everett came over and offered his congratulations, saying, "I hope you might consider keeping me on, Your Honor."

Faolan smiled. "Christ, that's gonna take some getting used to! I like you, though, Everett. You got guts and you got brains. Long as you promise to do as good a job for me as you did for Killian and Vandergriff, I don't see any problem keeping you. There's some money stuff I want to talk to you about tomorrow night when we get time. Making some changes to the fair and charities and such."

"I look forward to it." He bowed slightly and moved aside to let Frank in.

As usual, Frank just stood there. "I guess you were right about the friends. Still, we could keep the blackmail and have both."

Faolan laughed and pulled him into a hug. "Ah Frank, you never give up! But I'm glad. You're the best friend a guy could ask for."

Frank pulled back and stared at him for a second, but then he smiled—it was gone as fast as it came, but it was a genuine smile—and said, "Thanks, Faolan. I'm gonna go start making plans for—"

"Yeah, yeah," Faolan said. "I know you ain't much for parties. Go have your fun." Frank turned and left by one of the stage doors to avoid the mob of people.

"So, what now?" Stephanie asked.

Faolan hugged her closer and said, "Now, let's get some music on in this place and clear that floor! I feel like dancing!"

SHUFFLE

LATER THAT NIGHT

He came back to consciousness slowly. The back of his head throbbed with pain.

He was very cold and smelled moist soil, heard wind howling and machinery chugging. His eyes opened to the night sky, but his last memories drifted back to him of being in his suite, packing a suitcase. He was going to find a hotel for the night while he considered his options ... he didn't trust staying in the building with O'Connor in charge.

O'Connor!

Arnold Rothstein realized that his arms were numb, but tied behind his back at the wrists and, as he squirmed and glanced down, saw that his ankles were also bound. He was in a large hole in the ground. As the reality of his situation sank in, Arnold felt panic take control for a moment as his heart raced and sweat broke out all over his body.

"Hello? Hey! Anyone!"

He heard an engine and saw something come into view above him at the edge of the hole, it appeared to be some kind of pipe or chute from his awkward angle. Then someone moved into view beside the pipe and Arnold recognized the form of Frank Giordano.

"Frank! Get me outta here! What are you doing?" he shouted.

Then something began to flow from the chute: concrete plopped down below Arnold's feet and began to spread. "I'm burying you in a footing for one of the amusement stands," Frank stated. "It would be more fitting to put you in the Finance and Commerce Zone, of course, but that's already done. Besides, Miranda buried Killian a few feet over, so everything was already set up."

Arnold couldn't believe what he was hearing. This had to be some kind of gag or tactic, didn't it? When he felt the chill of the concrete touch his calves, however, it sent a shiver through his entire body. "Wait, Frank! Don't do this! I Created you! I saved your life!"

"Is that what you think?" Frank asked. The Ghoul shook his head. "If Faolan didn't need me so much, I'd lie right down in that hole with you."

"I knew I couldn't trust that lying punk!" Arnold snapped. "I should've expected a double-cross!"

Frank moved the chute so that the concrete splattered onto Arnold's legs even as the rest crept higher and higher up his back. "Actually, Faolan doesn't know about this. He'd probably keep you around even after everything you've done."

Desperation found its way into Arnold's voice: "Okay, Frank, I'll take his offer! I'll work for him, for both of you! Whatever he wants!"

"And sell us out to Moore at the first opportunity," Frank answered.

"No! I swear, I'll be square!"

Frank crouched down at the edge of the pit, looming like a grave monument. "Even if you were, you'd get your hooks into Faolan and start bending him the way you bent Killian. I think he wants your approval or something like that—whatever—but you'd convince him that he needs you and he'd start to listen to you."

Arnold began to protest, but the moon came out from behind a cloud just then and illuminated Frank's ghoulish face as he spoke. Something about the expression on that face or the eerie light reflecting in Frank's normally lightless eyes made his protests catch in his throat.

"He doesn't need anybody but me," Frank Giordano said reverently. "We're gonna shoot for greatness together."

Arnold swallowed and laid his head back, feeling the cold from the concrete seeping into his body and numbing him all over. *God, he's out of his mind! Good. Those two deserve each other!* He allowed himself a smile even as he shivered and thought about Everett, the Dhampir, and whoever he worked for. Maybe he could use that as a bargaining chip to get out of here? No, Giordano would just torture him until he was satisfied and then kill him. Let them find out the hard way.

Arnold Rothstein closed his eyes and forced himself to calm down. Another few minutes and it would all be over. No reason to kick and fuss. *Besides*, he reflected as the concrete rose all around him, *this Vampyr thing never really suited me, anyway. Nobody beats the odds forever.*

AUTHOR'S NOTES

Writing is generally a solitary undertaking, but it would be ridiculous to think that I could have written a novel like this without assistance. So, I'd like to extend a few words of gratitude here to the many individuals who helped make this novel possible.

Research is a big part of any historical novel, so I'll start by thanking my late paternal grandfather for his personal recollections; Raymond Steele for many years of period discussions, first-hand gun information, and general nit-picking; and Mark Jenkins for the spider information, the design of Killian's little kingdom within the Empire State Building, and other research.

Dave Galley and Dean McMillin both spent many nights eating chicken fried steak with me at the Iron Skillet restaurant, listening to me ramble on and on about these stories and characters over the years and for that I'm giving them a special shout-out. In addition, they also read hundreds of pages of first, second, and third drafts over the seven years it took for this novel to be written.

However, I have to give special thanks to Francine Roche Key, Glenn Schiltz, and Rodney Richards of the Mercer County Writers Critique Group who gave me the support, friendship, and honesty necessary to write the second half of this novel. Even more gratifying was their willingness to read the finished product over again and again. My editor, Georgina Merry of Unique Critique, deserves a ton of credit for helping polish my diamond in the rough into a novel worthy of publication.

Finally, gratitude to Daven Anderson and Clay Gilbert of PDMI Publishing, LLC.

ABOUT THE AUTHOR

Brian McKinley doesn't really exist. He's a constructed mortal identity used by a relatively young Vampyr in order to publish the truth about The Order. Due to the world-wide influence of The Order and its minions, these accounts must all be published as fiction; however, they are all very real and actually happened. Sometimes the names and sequence of events have been changed to protect the innocent, the guilty, and to keep from getting sued.

Brian is no longer a typical Vampyr and, for this reason, lives in hiding and writes from a secret location. The real "Brian" lives a life of danger and excitement; he loves *Star Trek, Game of Thrones,* and *Boardwalk Empire* as much as he loves Chicken Fried Steak. He's a reader, a role-player, and a dreamer who doesn't believe that "liberal" is a dirty word. He's lived many lifetimes and is eager to share as many of them as possible with his readers.

Contact him online:
https://www.facebook.com/BPMcKinley/

https://www.brianpatrickmckinley.wordpress.com

Twitter: @BPMcKinley